Painting the Light

Also by Ned Manning

Playground Duty

Plays
Us or Them
Kim
The Bridge is Down
Gods of War
Kenny's Coming Home
Close to the Bone
Women of Troy
Luck of the Draw
Alice Dreaming
Short Circuit
Shakespeare for Australian Schools (9 plays)
Last One Standing
No Nudity Weapons Naked Flames
Tsunami
Sharp Darts

Painting the Light

*

Ned Manning

Proudly published in Australia in 2022 by Broadcast Books, wwwbroadcastbooks.com.au

A catalogue record for this work is available from the National Library of Australia

ISBN: 978-0-6489053-6-3 (Paperback)
ISBN: 978-0-6454445-1-3 (Ebook)

Produced by Broadcast Books
Cover design, artwork and text design by Daniel New
Typeset in Minion Pro 11/14.3pt by Hannah Schubert and Daniel New
Author photograph by James Penlidis
Printed by IngramSpark

I would like to acknowledge the support of the descendants of the Gamilaroi and Wiradjuri Nations for their consultation and contribution to the authenticity of this book.

I pay my respects to the Elders past, present and emerging, who have allowed me to tell the true history of Country on which this story is based.

I would like to extend a particular acknowledgement to the Coonabarabran Aboriginal Land Council Board and members, as well as Chairperson, Naomi Stanton, and Monique Galvin.

Ned Manning

1.

Nell Hope leant into the canvas and carefully applied a few brushstrokes to the riverbank scene she was painting. She flicked a strand of hair off her face with the back of her hand and dabbed her brush onto the palette. Nell had always been intrigued by how, in the evening light, the dark green of the Macquarie River transformed into the colour of blood, and she felt she might finally be capturing it.

This was when Nell was happiest; when she was able to disappear into her painting. Time stood still and she was free to imagine she wasn't imprisoned on her family's 150,000 acre merino stud in central western New South Wales.

Standing patiently, her horse Ginger swished his tail to ward off the flies, while her black and tan border collie, Benny, lay panting at her side. Both animals were as happy as she was to have a break from chasing sheep in the forty degree heat and unrelenting dust. Her father gave them Saturday afternoons off from sheep work, so Nell grabbed the opportunity to work on her great passion.

She looked up as a flock of parrots, disturbed from feasting on the river red gums, took off into the brilliant sunset. Not for the first time, she wished she could fly away too. She had spent most of her life escaping. She'd escaped from home schooling with her mother, had escaped from boarding school too many times to remember, and now, was planning how to escape the adult life that had been laid out for her.

Even though Nell knew she was intelligent, the only subjects she had engaged with at school were art and sport, because when she was painting or whacking a tennis ball, no one told her to 'sit like a lady'. It wasn't that she'd hated the other subjects, she loved reading for instance, but she *had* hated how she was supposed to behave while studying them. Unfortunately, her boarding school rebellion meant she had failed to matriculate, so she was dragged home to pull on her jodhpurs and riding boots, hop on Ginger, and help out with the sheep.

One thing was certain: Nell had no intention of staying on Braemar and ending up married to one of the local grazier's sons. She had a life to live and it didn't involve sheep, pruning roses or hosting tennis parties.

There was one glimmer of hope … Her parents had booked a passage to England for the 1938 Ashes tour. If she could convince them to send her to finishing school over there, she could escape to Europe while her father was watching Bradman and her mother was shopping.

'What do you think, Benny?' Nell stood back and cast a critical eye over the emerging work. 'Would Miss MacLachlan approve?'

The dog wagged his tail. Miss MacLachlan had been her mentor and inspiration; the only teacher at Ascham who had understood Nell and encouraged her. She was also deliciously eccentric. She smoked like a chimney and got so wound up inspiring her '*gels*' that she often had two cigarettes on the go at once; one in an ashtray and the other waving around like a conductor's baton.

Nell kept painting until the call of a kookaburra heralded the fall of night and the eucalypts lining the riverbank started to appear darkly sinister.

'Time to go, Ginger,' she said. 'Don't want to be riding home in the dark.'

She fanned the painting until it was dry, as Ginger stamped his hooves and jangled his bit impatiently. Then she whistled for Benny, who barked while she collapsed her easel, rolled up her painting, gathered her paints and packed the lot into the saddle bags.

She hopped onto Ginger, pressed her knees into his flanks and galloped home while Benny, his tongue hanging out and ears pinned back, sprinted after them.

✳

That night at dinner, Nell decided to be particularly helpful. She shelled the peas her mother had harvested from her extensive vegetable garden. She set the table without being nagged. She put on her best face as her father carved the lamb and talked about the rams. She even managed to pretend to swallow her brother Jock's interminable lying about his plans for the weekend. When he had finished talking, Nell dabbed her lips with her napkin and folded it neatly on to her lap.

'Mother?'

'Yes, Helen?'

'I was thinking …' Nell paused at the sight of Jock smirking. She resisted the urge to kick him under the table. 'Why don't you take me to England with you?'

Elaine coughed up a pea that had lodged in her throat, and Jock immediately put down his knife and fork. Only her father kept eating, his eyes fixed on his plate.

'I could go to a finishing school over there. It would be exciting to see a bit of the world. I mean, it couldn't be all that different from school.' She didn't mention that she was nearly expelled twice but added as sweetly as possible, 'It might be good for me and I've heard about lots of girls going.'

'You're going to learn to curtsey and fold napkins properly?' Jock asked.

Nell took a breath and continued. 'Yes. I am. As a matter of fact.'

Her brother nearly fell off his chair laughing.

'Jock! Behave!' said Elaine before turning her attention to Nell. 'I didn't think you'd have any interest in finishing school. Both Betty's girls absolutely adored it when they went.'

'I've been thinking about it for a while,' she lied.

Elaine snorted. 'Well. There you go.' She turned to her husband. 'What do you think, Frederick?'

Fred looked up from his dinner. 'Sorry, I was miles away. I think we might have a produced a cracker-jack ram,' he said. 'What did you say?'

'Helen was thinking of going to finishing school in London,' Elaine said proudly.

'Oh? Good.' Fred placed his napkin on the table and stood. 'If you don't mind, I might check some bloodlines. If that ram is from King

George, as I expect he is …' his voice trailed off as he disappeared into the hallway.

'I'll clean up,' Nell volunteered.

'And do the washing up?' Jock asked.

Nell was incredulous. Was there anyone who could seize an opportunity more than Jock?

She smiled. 'Of course.'

He could wait.

✻

Later that night, Nell lay in bed hatching her plans. She would convince her mother to send her to Paris after she got herself kicked out of finishing school. She knew there was no chance Elaine would chaperone her in France, as her mother had often declared how much she hated everything French. Then she would finally be free.

A pair of headlights flashed through the window. Jock had snuck out and was off to play poker with the jackeroos.

Nell jumped out of bed, parted the curtains and smiled. Jock wasn't the only one who could pull the wool over their parents' eyes.

2.

Alec Murray unfolded his long legs out of the rust-bucket Hudson Terraplane ute he had just picked up in Dubbo, leant over the wobbly old gate and lifted the chain off the bolt. This was the moment he had spent his whole life waiting for: walking onto his own place. He stood back, waiting for the gate to swing open but one of its hinges had loosened and it collapsed awkwardly in the dirt. Alec didn't care. He'd fix it later. He picked it up and carried it open. Then he pushed his hat back and exhaled. This was it. His place. His own place.

He strode back to the ute and carefully unwrapped the wooden sign he had chiselled out of the piece of red cedar he'd saved for something special. He tucked it under one arm, grabbed some pliers and snipped a few ties of wire from the coil in the back. Then he returned to the gate and attached the sign to it.

'Toongowan!' he announced.

Alec had never felt so alive. As he drove onto the property he'd managed to convince his mother to help him buy, he felt ten feet tall. He whistled as he negotiated the vehicle up the track that led to the slab hut that would be his home.

Once he'd pulled up, he got out and stretched. Alec wasn't one to show his emotions but here, now, he could barely contain them. He looked up at the imposing Warrumbungles. The rocky outcrops looked like a panel of craggy-faced, high court judges staring down on him. He was stopped in his tracks by the rumbling that seemed to come from them. What secrets did they harbour? What had they witnessed on this land that was as old as time itself? Was he being cautioned?

He shook off these unsettling thoughts and looked around at the unimproved grasslands that surrounded the hut and spread as far as he could see. The tall, wispy native grasses reminded him of the wheat he intended to sow. He noted the stands of eucalypts that had avoided the sleeper cutter's axe and would provide him with timber for building a house and a shearing shed. They were part of the reason that the property had appealed to him in the first place and would be a natural resource for fence posts when he started subdividing the land into manageable paddocks. One thing he had determined was, come what may, he wasn't going to raze everything to the ground and then be forced to buy new materials like his father had done. He grabbed the kit bag he had souvenired when he left the New Guard, slung it over his shoulder, and marched towards the hut.

*

Celebrating the first day of his new life, Alec leant against a log, sipped a cup of black tea and stared into the crackling fire. He had spent the day making the rudimentary hut liveable and sketching plans for the house paddock, the piggery, the shearing shed and the garden. Tomorrow, he would begin pacing out the 3,000 acre property, marking out fence lines and dividing the place into workable paddocks. He licked his lips in anticipation and looked up at the stars. They burnt so brightly against the depths of the dark sky. Apart from the fire, there wasn't a sound. He closed his eyes and let the night envelop him.

He started early, pacing the perimeter of what would become the home paddock, as the morning sun beat down. Every now and then he stopped and marked out his planned fence line with bits of coloured rag tied to sticks. He was working off the map the local stock and station agent, Tiger Raffin, had given him when he bought the place. He felt like he was finally fulfilling his destiny. He'd been dreaming of this moment ever since his father suddenly sold their farm at Grong Grong, near Cootamundra, when Alec was just nine years old. Working in a legal firm, as his father had urged him to do, wouldn't have suited him at all. Alec hated the city. The bush was in his bones. He had taken every opportunity to spend school holidays on friends' properties ever since. He loved the solitude. It gave him room to think. To ponder what the gods had in store for him and the world.

Alec had considered going to Spain and fighting for the Nationalists against the Republicans, until he discovered the Nationalists were supported by Hitler and Mussolini. He was avowedly anti-communist, which was why he'd joined the anti-leftist New Guard. But when it proved to be a sleeper for an Australian fascist party, Alec couldn't get out quick enough. He was opposed to communism, but supporting anything that had even a whiff of fascism was a bridge too far.

He worked from daylight 'til dusk, for days on end, but it wasn't long before he realised that his youthful enthusiasm needed skills to match it. His hands were red raw from chopping and sawing with his new axe and crosscut saw. At the rate he was going, it would be a year before he built anything substantial – and he didn't have a year. He needed to get cracking and earn a quid, so he called in to Tiger's agency and asked him for advice.

'There's a bloke livin' under the bridge might give you a hand,' Tiger said, as he stitched up a bag of wheat seed.

Alec wondered if Tiger was pulling his leg. He knew everyone in Coonabarabran would regard him as a wet behind the ears blow-in.

'Bridge builder,' Tiger continued. 'He's a bit ...' he said, making a circling gesture with his finger next to his ear.

'Lost an eye on the Somme. Looks like he hasn't had a feed for years and sounds like he's swallowed a bag of nails. Don't be put off by appearances though; no one knows their way around timber like Whippet.'

With that, Tiger turned his full attention to the bag of wheat seed, leaving Alec feeling anything but confident. Nonetheless, he thanked Tiger and headed off towards the bridge.

'Whatever you do, don't pay him till he's finished!' Tiger called out after him.

*

Alec found Whippet under the bridge and offered him some work. He wasn't quite sure what to call him.

'Call me anything you like, but don't call me late for dinner.'

Whippet liked this joke so much he told it at least twice daily. Or so it seemed to Alec. He'd never met anyone like him; certainly never worked with anyone like him.

One thing was for sure though, Whippet knew his way around timber. He taught Alec how to use a broadaxe and an adze and demonstrated how to toughen his hands up by pissing on them. He also gave Alec a few life lessons. He told Alec about his experiences in the Great War, or, as Whippet sarcastically snorted, 'The War to End All Wars.'

'I was on the Western Front. That's when I lost me hearing.'

Alec would notice the man's hands shaking and not always from a night on the grog. He was sure Whippet was suffering from war trauma, or as it had been recently labelled, 'shell shock'. As Whippet displayed his craftsmanship, it occurred to Alec that the saying 'don't judge a book by its cover' had never held more meaning.

Before long, Alec was cutting logs into posts that looked as if they'd been sawn at the timber mill. After a couple of weeks, he had piled up enough posts to begin fencing. Whippet took his money from Alec and disappeared. Alec never saw him again.

3.

Nell opened the shutters to the tiny studio apartment in Montmartre and filled her lungs with the early morning air. She had saved every penny her father had given her and supplemented her savings by washing dishes in a restaurant.

She leant her elbows on the windowsill, rested her head in her hands and waited for the city to awaken. She still marvelled at the softness of the light.

'*Bonjour,* Nell.'

The croaky voice snapped her out of her reverie. She wheeled around as Gabriel rubbed his hair, picked up the newspaper lying beside him and lit a cigarette. Feeling like the sun greeting the morning, she beamed at him.

'*Ça va?*'

He turned a page with a slight nod, '*Ça va bien. Et toi?*'

'*Très bon.*'

He lowered the paper and offered a gentle correction. '*Très bien!*'

'*Très bien.*'

Gabriel smiled, but when he turned back to his newspaper, his face darkened. Nell knelt on the mattress and took a peek over his shoulder at the article he was reading. He translated for her. 'Hitler is threatening to march into Austria.' The sense of doom he was feeling filled the room; he wasn't one to hide his emotions.

Nell stroked his hair, offering what comfort she could. She watched his bare chest rise as he inhaled. She loved the litheness of his body. A thin line of wispy hair ran from his belly button to his shorts. He lowered the paper, stubbed out his cigarette and looked at her with watering eyes. She took him in her arms and kissed him softly on the lips.

Gabriel fell back on the bed, covering his face with his hands. Then just as suddenly, he was on his feet. '*Je dois y aller.*'

He pulled on his trousers and put his hand out for his shirt. She wriggled out of it and passed it to him. He dressed hurriedly in silence while she wrapped herself in the silk dressing gown he had given her.

After giving each of her cheeks a perfunctory peck, he headed for the door and then turned as he opened it. '*A ce soir?*'

She smiled and nodded. '*Mais oui.* Of course.'

'*Au café?*'

'*D'accord.*'

Nell could hear his footsteps on the wooden staircase. She jumped up, leant out the window and watched him cycle down the street. He didn't look back.

She sighed. Gabriel was quite simply the most beautiful thing she had ever laid her eyes on. Nell lingered at the window, while below her someone hosed the street, shops and stalls were opening, and the early birds were rushing off to work. She loved this city.

After dressing in a white, knee-length skirt with red buttons down the side, and an aqua coloured blouse with white trimming, Nell slipped on her natty low-heeled shoes, wrapped a red spotted silk scarf around her neck, grabbed her red beret and headed down the stairs to face the day. Humming a few bars of the music they'd danced to the night before, she skipped along the bustling side streets, waving to the characters she had come to know in her *arrondissement*: the organ grinder and his monkey, the mysterious gypsy fortune teller, the old men sipping their early morning *café crème* while dissecting the news of the day. The women she passed on her way seemed so stylish and confident. She couldn't imagine any of them settling for a life of subjugation.

At Les Halles, not far from her art class, she bought a croissant and took in the sensory explosions of sight, smell, touch, noise and taste. She still shook her head in wonder at the strings of garlic, the great wheels of cheese, the impossibly luscious strawberries and the piles of freshly baked baguettes for sale in the little shops.

Her teacher, René Martin, was a huge man with long, black, often greasy hair and a moustache that camouflaged lugubrious lips. She knew not to be late for his classes. His studio was cluttered with easels holding work in various stages of completion. He didn't stand on ceremony so, with a perfunctory nod, Nell went straight to the easel she was working on, wiped her brushes dry and got to work.

Monsieur Martin, or René, as he insisted on being called, encouraged her to discover her own expression; not to be inhibited by others. He showed her some of Picasso's still lifes, pointing out that Picasso had mastered his craft before branching out to find his own style. Nell regarded René as the natural successor to Miss McLachlan, to whom she excitedly wrote about Paris, art and her progress. When Miss McLachlan replied, she signed off by warning Nell to be wary of men like René. It was a lesson Nell heeded, especially when he invited back to his apartment for a drink after a night out with his class.

Like Miss McLachlan, René encouraged Nell to overcome the little voice that chipped away at her, telling her she wasn't good enough. '*Vous devez achever l'oeuvre puis continuer. Ne vous préoccupez pas de sa valeur. Préoccupez vous de la valeur qu'elle vous apporte en tant qu'artiste.*' At night, Nell would turn his words over in her mind, finding strength in their advice. 'You must complete the work and then move on. Do not concern yourself with its worth. Concern yourself with its value to you as an artist.'

If he saw her wavering, René would swamp her with bear hugs, cajole her to do better and tease her with the nickname, '*Mon petit kangourou.*'

Over time, Nell grew to love René almost as much as she loved Paris. He had faults, but his passion for painting and drawing was unbounded and infectious. He assumed she would become an artist; discussed her work as if she already were. When he criticised her painting, which was often, she was initially floored by his comments, but gradually grew to appreciate them. Even when he told her that her paintings were *morts*.

Then, one day, as she was on her way to class, Nell passed a newsstand with photographs of Adolf Hitler celebrating the *Anschluss*. Germany had annexed Austria.

Her heart sank. Gabriel had warned her of Hitler's intentions. She had been praying that something would stop him. In the pit of her stomach, she feared the worst.

4.

'Looks like you might need another set of hands.'

Alec was shocked when he looked up and saw a black man grinning at him. He gripped his crowbar tightly and rose to his full height of six foot four. He felt himself tensing up. By contrast, the man appeared to be totally at ease. He was of medium height, looked fit as a fiddle, had curly hair and deep brown eyes. For once in his life, Alec was tongue-tied; he had never spoken to an Aboriginal person before. He had seen a few families around Coonabarabran but they had kept their distance and so had he.

'You're making hard work of it.' The man shook his head, threw his swag on the ground and opened the palms of his hands. 'Two of us'd get it done in half the time.'

Alec was bewildered. He had no idea where this fellow had come from. Nor did he know how to talk to him. He was relieved when the stranger stuck out his hand.

'Bernie Duroux.'

Meeting his eyes squarely, Alec gripped his hand. 'Alec Murray.'

Bernie nodded and kicked at the ground. 'Hard goin.'

Alec smiled. 'Sure is. It's taking longer than I anticipated.'

That brought a laugh from Bernie. He took off his hat and ran his fingers around its rim before placing it securely back on his head. 'Mind if I give you a tip?'

'Not at all.' It surprised Alec how quickly he accepted Bernie's offer. He hoped he hadn't seemed too enthusiastic.

Bernie took the bar from him. 'I bin watchin' you. You'll kill your arms banging away like that.'

'Been watching me?' Alec repeated Bernie's words to himself. Had this man been spying on him?

'You wanna let the bar go as it hits the ground. Let the bar take the impact. Not your arms.' Bernie lifted up the bar and drove it in again, releasing it with cupped hands as a spark flew off a rock. He handed it to Alec. 'Have a go.'

Alec tried. At first, he dropped the bar too early and it wobbled hopelessly in the hole.

Bernie laughed. 'You'll get the hang of it.'

Accepting the challenge, Alec toiled away without much success. Eventually he paused and turned to Bernie. 'I'd love a hand.'

Bernie laughed again. 'I thought you'd never ask.' He took the bar and pointed to the shovel lying on the ground. 'You dig out the loosened dirt.'

Before long they had dragged a fence post into the hole and banged the dirt around it to make it secure; all achieved in less than half the time it had taken Alec.

'You're right. I do need another set of hands. If you're interested …'

The offer hung in the air while Bernie surveyed the scene. Alec followed his eyes. There was a line of sticks stretching across the paddock with bits of rag attached to them. They ran through a stand of trees and connected to the new fence in the distance.

Eventually Bernie spoke. 'You gonna clear all them trees?'

Alec hadn't given it much thought. He rubbed his chin. 'I guess so …' He wasn't sure what Bernie was thinking but wasn't game to ask.

Bernie shook his head. 'Mmm …'

'Why not?'

'Well … if you knock all them down you'll have nothin' to hold the soil together. And no shade for whatever it is you're gonna stock.'

'Sheep.' For a reason Alec couldn't fathom, that brought a smile to Bernie's face.

Bernie chuckled. 'Ground lice,' he said dismissively.

Alec managed a nervous laugh as Bernie continued his interrogation. 'Gonna grow wheat too?'

'I … I hope so.'

Bernie turned and looked at him. 'This's good, rich basalt country. Never bin disturbed.' He ran a handful of rich soil through his fingers. 'Your soil here is good. It's never been farmed like you blokes farm, so you can grow whatever you wanna grow. As long as it rains, of course. You treat this country well, it'll treat you well. You abuse it and it'll abuse you.'

Alec was surprised to find himself taking advice, especially from a man he'd only just met, but it was the first of many lessons he took on board. He came to bless his lucky stars that Bernie had walked into his life.

From that day on, Alec worked in tandem with Bernie, continuing the education he had begun under Whippet. Apart from the fact that Bernie clearly knew more about the country than anyone else, he differed in another vital way. He didn't wander off like Whippet.

Alec offered him a wage, the same as any farm worker would receive, and agreed to let Bernie and his family camp down by the river. Bernie also negotiated that he would have free run to hunt and fish on the place. Alec was more than happy to shake on the deal. He helped Bernie knock up a shelter for his wife and kids, and a partnership was born.

Even though they came from different worlds and had little time for small talk, Alec soon discovered that they had a lot in common. They sometimes opened up over a cuppa, but when they were working, their minds were on the job.

A few weeks later, after they'd finished fencing a whole paddock, Alec sang out to Bernie, 'I think it's time for a celebration!'

Bernie looked up from packing the ute.

Alec proffered the two bottles of beer he had fished out of the creek. He opened a bottle with his Swiss Army knife and handed it to Bernie. He whipped the top off his and held it out. 'Cheers.'

They clinked bottles, took a swig and found a spot to sit down. Alec leant his back against a scribbly bark, closed his eyes for a second and exhaled. Bernie sat crossed legged and stared into the distance.

Alec was the first to speak. 'I couldn't have done this without you.'

He raised his bottle in a salute while Bernie nodded 'thank you'.

They sat for while in silence, enveloped by the sounds of the bush. Alec stared up at the mountains that had haunted him since he drove onto the place. 'Why do they call them the Warrumbungles?'

Bernie surveyed them for what seemed like an eternity. Alec began to think he had transgressed in asking the question. Then Bernie pointed. 'See how crooked they look?'

Alec nodded. They did look crooked.

'*Warrumbungle* means "crooked mountain" in Gamilaroi. The Gamilaroi are my people. This is Gamilaroi Country. Or was. Before you whitefellas turned up. We bin in this country thousands of years.'

Staring up at the Warrumbungles' towering presence, Alec almost shuddered. 'There are times when I swear I can hear them groaning.'

Bernie didn't reply, but shrugged his shoulders as if to say, 'What would you expect?'

Alec was learning that the country was hurting.

∗

Over the next months, Alec and Bernie went about transforming Toongowan into a working property. With the fences built, Alec purchased some merinos after being assured by all and sundry that his was good fine wool country. He borrowed a plough and a seeder from a neighbour and turned the native grassland into wheat fields. Bernie began work on the shearing shed, which Alec decided was a higher priority than renovating his hut. There wasn't much time for sleep.

As he gained Bernie's confidence, Alec probed him a little deeper about his life. Bernie didn't give away a lot, but then surprised him one day after Alec had asked if they'd always lived in the area.

'My missus is a Wiradjuri woman. Was taken from her family when she was a baby. Made her way out here to Kamilaroi country when she ran away from the mish.'

Alec was mystified but didn't think he could pry. He knew 'the mish' was short for 'the mission' – enforced Aboriginal settlements, which seemed more harmful than helpful, if the allegations he'd heard against the Aborigines Protection Board in nearby Collarenebri were anything to go by. But he'd never been able to find out the details. It seemed that records about the Protection Board were sealed up. He wondered what they might be hiding.

✳

Bernie was an expert horseman and told Alec he had worked as a stockman in Queensland when he was a kid. He taught Alec some of his skills, such as how to break a horse in gently so that it became a friend not an enemy. They had rescued a big black gelding with a white star on his forehead from a bloke who treated him badly. Alec watched as Bernie took hold of the flighty, nervous animal that was clearly wary of humans, and settled him down and gained his trust. He called him Captain Midnight.

One day, as they were unsaddling the horses, Alec bit the bullet and asked Bernie if he could look after the place while he answered the call of the campaign for men to join the citizen's militia.

'Sure you can trust me?' Bernie asked with a grin.

'Never been surer about anything in my life,' Alec said.

After he had put his saddle away, Bernie squatted down and rolled himself a smoke while Alec finished brushing Captain Midnight.

'What do you think of this Hitler fella?'

This surprised Alec. Bernie wasn't usually one for political talk, but Alec was happy to engage him on the subject.

'Hitler? I think he's on the march.'

Then Bernie asked the obvious. 'Why don't they stop him?'

Exactly what Alec had been thinking. 'Good question.'

'He gathers up speed, he'll be hard to stop,' Bernie said.

'He will.'

Bernie got to his feet and lit his smoke. He looked into the distance before turning to Alec and asking, 'There's gonna be another war then?'

'Looks like it.'

The last thing Alec wanted was go away now that Toongowan was taking shape. He had hoped beyond hope that the British and French governments would do something to stop Hitler, but was beginning to accept that this was unlikely.

'Are we going to get involved?' Bernie asked.

'I am,' Alec snapped.

'Why?'

'If your country is at war, so are you.'

'But your country isn't at war, is it?'

'Not yet.'

As far as Alec was concerned this was the end of the conversation but Bernie persisted.

'But that Chamberlain fella has made a deal, hasn't he?'

As if reading Alec's mind, Bernie explained. 'I bin readin' them *Bulletins* you toss into the incinerator pile. The missus uses 'em to teach the kids how to read.'

Bernie put his pannikin in his bag and called back over his shoulder, 'She learnt to read at the mission school.'

That night, Alec stared up at the tiny slivers of moonlight that peeked through the holes in the tin roof and thought about his exchange with Bernie. Next morning, he gathered up an armful of *Bulletin* magazines and dropped them off at Bernie's camp.

5.

Nell sat sipping *café crème,* sunglasses perched on her nose, sketching the street life. She watched a man approach a prostitute. They seemed to whisper. The girl took his hand and they disappeared into a doorway.

Nell sketched the scene in the style of her latest muse, Toulouse-Lautrec. The prostitute: skirt fanned over her as she lay back, legs akimbo. The man: trousers to his knees, pimply bare bottom exposed to the world.

As the waiter approached, she quickly screwed her work into a ball. She thought he had sprung her, but he sashayed past as though she were invisible. She guessed she wouldn't have been the first young, faux bohemian who had sketched similar scenes in his café.

The man reappeared in the doorway, attempting to act as if he had been to the barber. Nell stared at him in disgust. He was so old and ugly.

She watched the prostitute wander out, light a cigarette and lean against the shop window. Nell was entranced. She had never been exposed to anything like this, not even when she had climbed out a window at boarding school and gone into Kings Cross. There was a routineness about the scene that was both shocking and exciting.

When she returned to her apartment, Nell tried to capture the scene in its entirety. She rolled up her sleeves and began sketching. In the background, the café; in the foreground, the negotiation. Her prostitute became more glamorous, the client fatter and uglier. She gave him a cigar and a top hat, her a less worn expression.

As she began painting, Nell chose colours that conferred a certain garishness, mixing a range of bright colours among the browns and greys. The more the painting moved away from an actual depiction to an interpretation, the more excited she became.

She leant in and, with delicate brush strokes, accentuated the prostitute's lips. They dominated the painting and pushed the whole scene towards a grotesque parody. Then Nell stood back and looked at it. Everything was larger than life. The way it should be.

The smoke curled up from the client's cigar as he whispered into the prostitute's ear. She gave him a pot belly with waistcoat buttons barely containing his girth and dabbed stains onto his trousers.

Just as she began to doubt the work, its garishness and obvious naivety, she thought of René's words about trusting herself.

As she waggled her paint brush in a jar of water it occurred to her that the only thing she missed about home, apart from Benny and Ginger, was her old friend, Peggy MacArthur. She wondered if Peggy was still in training after the British Empire Games. Maybe she could convince her to come over and visit.

There was a knock on the door. When she opened it, a boy handed her a telegram and disappeared. She stared at it for a few moments before ripping it open. She took a deep breath and read, 'Come home at once. Ticket booked. Collect from Montemarte Post Office. Faithfully yours, Father.'

6.

'Atten … tion!'

Alec stamped his right leg onto the dusty parade ground, coordinating his efforts with the other recruits' he'd joined at training camp.

'Shoulder … Arms!'

In response, he lifted his .303 with his right arm, slung it across his body and landed it on his left shoulder; a drill he'd performed countless times with The King's School cadets.

'Quick march!'

Alec marched at the front of the motley platoon of young men, many of whom seemed to regard the camp as an opportunity to get away for a few days and had little interest in soldiering. Even though he was only twenty-five, Alec had been made an Acting Lieutenant, partly because of his time in the school cadets and partly because he was one of the few recruits who was fighting fit and had any sense of discipline.

'Left, right, left, right.'

Alec was determined to live up to his assignment and lead by example. He focussed on keeping in time, secretly grateful for Sergeant Thomas's barking orders. He kept his eyes locked straight ahead and tried not to think about what he would farm on the rich floodplains that lay before them on either side of the Hunter River.

'Halt!'

Sergeant Thomas began his customary abuse of everyone and anyone, telling them that they were useless and not worthy of the uniforms they were privileged to wear. In the course of his diatribe he reminded them that he had fought in the trenches with real men, not namby-pamby, part-timers like them.

A fly crawled across Alec's sweaty face and up his nose. He used every bit of self-discipline he could muster to hold back a sneeze, let alone give in to the temptation of swatting it. He knew Sergeant Thomas would love nothing more than to give him a bollocking. He had already made it absolutely clear to Alec and the other officers that he regarded them as private school imposters who had no right to be given commissions over regular serving men like him. Alec shared his disgust at the government's penny-pinching decision to run these intermittent camps for reservists rather than committing to a decent regular army.

Alec was struggling to reconcile the two conflicting demands on his future. He wanted to join the army full time if it meant he could make a contribution to stopping the spread of fascism. But he didn't want to leave Toongowan now that he and Bernie had got it up and running. The pull of duty was strong, but it tore at his heart that he might have to leave his beloved farm behind. He hoped he'd be able to call on Bernie to keep the place going if he had to go overseas.

That night he was assigned to latrine duties, which meant overseeing the cleaning of the latrines. He urged a pimply faced young man from Wahroonga to 'put his back into it' as the poor fellow manfully battled with the stench. Alec blamed the authorities for poor planning while more and more men enlisted in the militia. He was learning that the bureaucracy was often blind to the obvious. He was also learning that, even as a part-time officer, his job was to implement orders rather than question them.

'All done?' Stephen Champion looked up as Alec pushed open the tent flap.

Alec replied with a mock salute. 'Mission accomplished.' He tossed his cap on to the makeshift table, removed his jacket and sat down to take off his boots.

'You might want to put them outside.' Stephen was holding his nose.

Alec laughed. 'Of course.'

He was relieved to share a tent with someone like Stephen. It could have been so much worse. He could have been stuck with one of those pompous, born to rule types he had endured at boarding school.

Stephen was a tallish, dapper, cultivated man with mousy brown hair and a pencil thin moustache that he was particularly proud of. His background fascinated Alec. He was raised in a musical family. His father was the conductor of the Brisbane Symphony Orchestra and Stephen was a trainee conductor. He was the first real artist Alec had ever met. Not only did Stephen educate him about classical music, but opened his eyes to a different way of thinking.

Stephen was a socialist. He argued with Alec about the Spanish Civil War and defended the Republicans' cause. He helped Alec to see that there was some virtue in the socialist ideal.

'What the Republicans are fighting for, apart from wanting to end a dictatorship, is an equal distribution of the country's wealth rather than funnelling it into the hands of a few. That's not such a bad thing, is it? Sharing the spoils with the people?'

Alec collapsed on his stretcher as Stephen lowered the newspaper he was reading and peered at him over the rim of his spectacles.

'How's Sergeant Thomas?'

Alec laughed. 'Cheerful. As usual.' He pointed to the paper. 'What's news?'

Stephen showed him the cartoon on the cover of the *Bulletin* of Hitler cavorting through Europe unhindered.

'By the looks of it, we'll be shovelling more than shit.'

Alec's mood darkened. 'If we don't pull our fingers out, he'll be marching into Trafalgar Square before we know it.'

The cheeky grin vanished from Stephen's face. 'Not if I've got any say in it.'

'Me either.'

Stephen swung his legs over the side of the stretcher and ran his hands through his hair. 'I don't understand why they're procrastinating. Peace with honour. What a lark.'

'One thing's for certain,' Alec said, 'training with equipment left over from the last war is hardly going to prepare us to take on the type of army Hitler and co. have assembled.'

He undressed and lay down. He was exhausted. They would be up at the crack of dawn ready for some more marching and then he would be on the train home. He picked up the copy of Vera Brittain's *Testament of Youth* that Stephen had given him. Stephen had told him how Brittain, an avowed pacifist, was making speeches in Germany about the Nazi's treatment of the Jews. He had also introduced Alec to writers like Orwell, Hemingway and Malraux.

The last thing Alec had expected coming into camp was to have his mind expanded, but that is exactly what had happened. The two men were instant soul mates, always asking questions about the world they lived in rather than blithely accepting the status quo.

Alec watched a mosquito zero in on his arm before he crushed it.

'Get him?' Stephen asked.

'Yep', Alec replied.

7.

Nell waited for Gabriel at their favourite haunt, La Tartine. Her father's words were on her mind. She needed to see her friend.

She checked her watch. Gabriel was late. He may not have been the most punctual person in the world, but he was never this late. Maybe he had stood her up?

Just as she was about to cut her losses and ask for the bill, he came rushing in and hurriedly kissed her on both cheeks.

'Sorry, Nell. I have to leave Paris.'

He sat and poured himself some wine from the bottle she had ordered. She hadn't seen him so agitated before. He was looking around anxiously. Nell touched his hand.

'It's all right. No one is taking any notice of us,' she said.

He looked at her wildly. 'You have not heard?'

Nell shook her head and Gabriel leant in and spoke in hushed tones. 'It has begun. Jews everywhere are on the run. Thousands of Polish Jews have been expelled from Germany and dumped on the Polish border.'

Nell looked down at the table as he continued.

'My grandfather's shop in Berlin was bombed.'

'Bombed?' She sat up and stared at him.

He took another sip of wine and lit a cigarette while she tried to process this news. It was his turn to take her hand. His eyes were locked on hers. She noticed they were bloodshot.

'I have to go home,' he said.

'What –'

'The Polish Government are so scared of the Nazis they have refused their own citizens entry to their homeland. Many are now homeless, stateless. Refugees. My grandparents among them. No one wants to know them. It's terrible. How could you turn your back on people in such need?'

Nell bit her lip. She was trying with all her might not to cry. 'I'll come with you,' she said.

'You're not Polish.'

'I know but …'

He leant over and kissed her on the lips. Her heart was breaking.

'I love you,' she said through streaming tears.

'And I love you.'

As tears pricked Gabriel's eyes, Nell thought he had never looked more beautiful, even as their world was falling apart.

He stood and took her face in both hands. She felt his kisses on her cheeks before he whispered in her ear. 'Go home. I need to be with my family. You need to be with yours.'

She knew that it was over. He was going and she was going home. He drained his glass, pulled on his cap and strode out the door.

That was it.

La Tartine was suddenly not where she wanted to be. Not now. She took the crumpled telegram out of her bag and re-read it.

'Come home at once. Ticket booked … Faithfully yours …'

She folded it, placed it back in her bag and walked out.

As Nell made her way along the rue de Rivoli, past the cafés and bars she had adopted as her own, she sensed the inevitability of tragedy. People pushed by her, some laden with shopping and food from the market, others clutching briefcases or bags. Everyone was rushing to get somewhere. Everything seemed urgent. It was as if an alarm had rung or a bomb had exploded. Until Nell realised, it was the same as any day at this time and that the crowds were like Parisians on any other night, hurrying home to the warm embrace of lovers and families.

Nell felt as though she had been cut off at the knees. Tears continued to tumble down her cheeks as she crossed the road without looking for oncoming traffic. A bell rang as a cyclist weaved his way around her. For a moment she thought it might be Gabriel and that he'd had a change of heart. It was an old man, cigarette stuck in the corner of his mouth, baguette in one hand, bag slung over his coat, shouting at her over his shoulder while he gesticulated with his free hand. She watched him cycle off. His send-off seemed to somehow capture the moment.

As she put her key in the door, she rested her head on it before pushing it slowly open. Her newest painting greeted her, strangely lit by the streetlight glow coming through the window. She had transformed a bowl of bright red tomatoes, carefully arranged and delicately placed on an embroidered tablecloth, into a ghoulish image of culinary hell. There was blood oozing from the tomatoes, spreading over the tablecloth and trickling down the legs of the little mahogany table. She let the door close behind her and dropped her keys on the side table. She had never felt so lonely. There was no alternative but to pack her bags, say her goodbyes and get on a train to Calais for the long boat trip home.

8.

'Make hay while the sun shines?' asked Bernie.

'That's about the strength of it, Bernie,' Alec replied, finishing his cup of tea.

Bernie chuckled. 'Now I know what that saying means.'

Alec was relieved they had got nearly all the wheat off and that it hadn't rained. He stood and stretched his arms towards the heavens. 'I reckon there's enough light to do a few more laps before it gets dark.'

'We should have 'er all off by tomorra,' Bernie said as he tossed the remnants of his tea on the coals.

'Pity we can't work through the night.'

'Won't rain tonight,' Bernie reassured him.

'I hope you're right,' Alex said. He climbed aboard his new combine harvester and started it up.

While he took off for another round, Bernie went back to work binding the bags of wheat that were dotted all over the paddock.

Alec knew he had struck gold with Bernie. When he'd asked him if he could look after the place if he was forced to serve overseas, Bernie had replied, with typical understatement, 'She'll be right.'

The harvester was Alec's pride and joy. It had already paid its way by stripping the crop in a quarter of the time it usually took. He had an almighty argument when his father found out he had borrowed money from the bank to buy it. While his father went on about the dangers of debt, Alec pointed out that the rest of the farming world had abandoned harvesting with bullocks long ago. It gave Alec tremendous satisfaction to have proven his father wrong. The combine harvester's speed and efficiency had given him his best yield yet and offered him a glimpse of the future.

The next day they finished harvesting the last few acres, loaded the bags onto the truck and headed off to the Coonabarabran railway siding, where they were met by Rusty White. Rusty had been working at the siding for years. Aptly named, his face round and ruddy, Rusty had a permanent sweat mark on his forehead from a hat that was only removed to wave away the most persistent flies. His arms were like fence posts and his pot belly spilt over his handwoven, leather belt; testament to his liking for beer.

Rusty looked at Alec's truckload. 'You're a lucky bastard.'

Alec smiled proudly. 'I know. Couldn't have asked for a better season … '

Just as he was about to elaborate, Rusty offered some homespun wisdom. 'It's the toaster that's made the difference.'

Before Alec could respond, he continued. 'And the bread slicer.'

Alec shot a look at Bernie while Rusty elaborated. 'Everyone wants toast. That's why the wheat price is so good.'

'I see,' said Alec, barely containing himself.

Rusty thrust his hand into a bag and grabbed a handful of husks. He rubbed his palms together and separated the husks from the grain, then carefully blew the husks away, leaving a small scattering of grains in his hand.

'Here.'

He tipped some into Alec's hand, then delicately picked up another grain between his stubby forefinger and thumb and bit it. For a second, it appeared to Alec as if Rusty were sampling a delicacy in a fine restaurant – except that he was covered in dust and sweat, and stank like he hadn't had a bath in a week. Rusty bit into the grain and chewed it before spitting it out.

'You're going to be a happy man. How much did you say you owed on your mortgage?'

'I didn't.'

Rusty did a laborious calculation of the number of bags, counting aloud on his fingers. Finally, he patted his pot belly and announced, 'I reckon the demand for bread will see you clearing about … say … three to four thousand quid.'

Alec nearly choked on the stalk he was chewing. Three to four thousand pounds? That was enough to clear the mortgage and get his father off his back.

'Good thing so many people have taken to toast,' Rusty said.

A whistle heralded the arrival of the grain train at Coonabarabran on the Gwabegar line. Steam billowed from the locomotive's chimney as it chugged into view.

'By the time they unload it at the silo in Sydney, I reckon you'll be shoutin' the bar,' Rusty said as he slapped Alec on the shoulder.

When the train pulled up, the men loaded bags the wheat on board.

'That bloody harvester's incredible,' Bernie said as they bounced along the corrugated dirt road on the way home. Alec turned to him. Neither man had said a word up 'til now.

'It is, Bernie. It is.' He smiled.

When Alec dropped Bernie off, he slipped him fifty quid.

Life couldn't be better. It seemed the prospect of war had receded after the British and French had agreed to the German occupation of Sudetenland. Maybe Alec could put thoughts of military service behind him and concentrate on farming.

9.

'It's so unfair!'

Nell slapped her hand on the railing of the *Queen Mary* as she stared into the vast emptiness of the Pacific Ocean.

'Are you all right, young lady?'

She looked over to see a couple wrapped in coats and scarves coming over to her.

'Oh, yes, I was just thinking of throwing myself overboard.'

When the couple laughed awkwardly, Nell managed a weak smile. 'I'm fine, really. Just feeling a bit seasick.'

'The fresh air might help, but don't catch cold,' said the woman.

'Good night,' the man said, doffing his hat.

'*Bon soir*,' Nell replied.

She watched them walk off. The woman rested her head on the man's shoulder, and he put his arm around her and hugged her close. Nell wondered if they were married or lovers having a fling on the high seas.

She was jealous: jealous of them, jealous of anyone who was happy. The darkness of the water reflected her mood. She had never felt sadder. The wind was whipping her face. She licked her lips and tasted the salt.

Nell hated herself for not being brave enough. For falling in line and marching up the gangplank when all her instincts told her to stay in France and take her chances. While everyone else was gearing up for a fight, what was she doing? Running home as her father had commanded.

She knew she would never see Gabriel again. Her heart ached for all the people she had left behind and for the city she had fallen in love with. She had been following the news and none of it was good. Especially if you were Jewish.

She opened the letter she had received from Peggy the day she left Paris.

Dear Nell,

So thrilled that you are having the time of your life. It sounds like you were made for Paris and Paris was made for you. I can't wait to see your paintings. I always knew you were destined for great things. I ran into Miss MacLachlan and told her all your news, except for the bit about the sexy man. What's he like? Can you send a picture? He sounds so dashing.

The papers are full of talk about war. No one really knows what it all means. Wasn't the last one meant to be 'the war to end all wars'? All the boys at home are chafing at the bit to get into uniform and go over there.

I saw Jock at Carl Thomas's. It's the best thing that ever happened to Sydney. A New York nightclub owner has set it up, named it after himself. I met him! He could charm the legs off a table and he looks like a movie star. It's got the best dance floor in Sydney, they reckon.

Jock told me he's going to be on the first boat if there's a war. I'm not sure if he has told your father!

I'm back in training now the Games are over and I've had a break. I'm training for the Olympics in 1940. It seems so far away but coming fifth has given me something to aim for. Isn't it funny, you're going to be a famous artist and I'm going to win an Olympic medal! We can tell those bloody teachers to stuff that up their jumpers! And those stuck-up princesses who looked down their noses at us. At least we got something out of school, apart from being able to curtsey and talk with a plum in our mouths.

Of course, Mother wants me to give it all away and find a 'nice man' to settle down with. I just can't see myself crossing my legs and smoothing my skirt while I wait for Mr Right to sweep me off my feet. Can you?

Apart from Carl Thomas's, there's not much to report about boring old Sydney. Nothing really changes. Everyone is happy to do what they've always done.

You don't know how lucky you are being somewhere that is so exciting.

Oh well. I better get off to training.

All my love darling,
Peg

Nell folded the letter and put it away.

She reflected on what awaited her: a few days in Sydney before a long, tedious train trip across an expanse of flat, dry country populated by sheep and kangaroos. She might as well be going to the moon. She was leaving behind a city that never slept and returning to one that never got out of bed; reverting from young artist back to apprentice jillaroo.

She really did feel like throwing herself over the side.

10.

When Alec pulled up Toongowan's gate after yet another boot camp, he was shocked to see the fat lambs he had asked Bernie to take to the abattoir gambolling in the front paddock.

'They wouldn't take 'em.'

Bernie was sawing a piece of timber for the floor of the shearing shed.

'What do you mean?' Alec asked.

'There's a strike,' Bernie said as he kept sawing.

'So, we can't sell our lambs?'

It was a rhetorical question. Alec knew he wasn't going to get any change out of Bernie on the subject of politics.

'We'll see about that.' Alec was determined to get to the bottom of why the unions had closed the abattoirs, and to do what he could to restore order to the lucrative lamb export business.

*

Alec walked into the Coonabarabran Town Hall for the local chapter meeting of the Graziers' Association of New South Wales and stood among the local gentry. He'd decided this was one way he could get involved and work with other farmers.

A small, wiry man with silver hair came up to him. 'Good afternoon. My name is Fred Hope. Come and have a seat next to me.'

Alec proffered his hand. 'Alec Murray.'

Fred looked him squarely in the eye. 'I know.'

The chance to meet one of the most successful merino breeders in Australia was a boon for Alec. Not only was Hope a successful grazier but he had a well-earnt reputation for being one of the power brokers behind the scenes in Country Party politics. As a keen student of politics, Alec had heard the rumours that Fred was involved in the ill-fated move to create a breakaway rural state in western New South Wales. Alec had also heard that, although he shunned the limelight, Fred was never far from the action when it came to conservative politics in Australia.

'This is a pretty rum business. These coves are hellbent on bringing us to our knees. Before we know it, the jackeroos will be demanding better rations!' Fred delivered this last line with a wink, as though Alec was in on the joke.

'I haven't got any jackeroos on my place ...'

Fred chuckled.

'A turn of phrase dear boy, a turn of phrase.'

Alec nodded and then glanced around. The hall was full of men who appeared confident: men who looked like they had spent their lives in a pretty good paddock and had no intention of sharing their spoils.

As the meeting progressed, various speakers took to the floor to pour scorn on the workers who, they argued, were about to threaten their profits. In Alec's opinion, there was a lot of grumbling but not a lot of rational argument.

A man with a handlebar moustache and a stocky build, waved his walking stick above his head. 'Bloody commos the lot of them.'

'Hear! Hear!' the outraged gathering chorused.

'We ought to send in the army,' the man thundered.

Heads nodded gravely in agreement.

'We need a man like Franco to teach them a lesson,' another grazier shouted. Like many in the room, he was wearing the uniform of moleskins, light blue cotton shirt and wool tie.

The congregation of tweedy landowners leapt to their feet and roared their approval. Alec was tempted to point out that Franco was supported by Nazis and Fascists but decided to keep his powder dry.

Fred leant over to him. 'This is getting us nowhere,' he said.

Almost before he knew what he was doing Alec shot his hand up.

'Order! Order!' The chairman yelled, banging his homemade gavel on the table.

The men, still shaking their fists and exhorting each other to action, reluctantly returned to their seats. The chairman pointed to Alec.

'The young man has the floor.'

'Is he a member?' asked another landowner.

Alec raised himself to his full height.

'Mr Chairman, I am a member. My name is Alec Murray and I own a place fourteen miles from Coonabarabran on the Mendooran Road. I have been farming in the area for three years. Like you, I haven't been able to sell my fat lambs and I want to get to the bottom of it.'

'I'll tell you why,' a particularly angry grazier, called out. 'These buggers are getting above their station. We need to show them who's boss.'

Alec spoke. 'That kind of thinking will get us nowhere. The whole community is affected by these strikes. They are not only costing us, but the strikers too. What I would like to know is, what can we do to end this strike and stop them from happening in the future?'

His sober words and imposing presence seemed to have a calming effect on most of the crowd. He was greeted by a ripple of applause and some nods of agreement.

'We have all seen how these kinds of arguments can spiral out of control with catastrophic consequences,' he said. 'You only have to look to Spain. We don't want that kind of ideological warfare here. We need to nip this in the bud.'

He glanced at Fred Hope, who nodded in approval, so he continued. 'I have been working fifteen hours a day to turn my property into a going concern. I'll be damned if I am going to let all my hard work go down the drain because we can't find a way out of this stalemate. There has to be a solution and we have to find it.'

There was more nodding and clapping. Alec felt he was winning them over. Even though he had won public speaking competitions at school and been a champion debater, this was the first time he had ever addressed a room full of grown men on real terms. He paused for theatrical effect, then said, 'I believe fervently in the right of each and every one of us to sell our goods at the marketplace without the interference of those who want to regulate our profits for their own ends. I also believe in every man's right to earn a fair wage. There is no point in going to war with the very people who we need to keep the wheels turning.'

Then, after further pause he added, 'The fact is, we need to sell our fat lambs while they are in prime condition. We can't wait until they turn to mutton.'

Alec felt a rush of adrenaline course through his veins as the men leapt to their feet, clapping and cheering. He had never known such approval. He took it all in while composing himself and resuming his seat.

Fred Hope leant over and shook his hand. 'Well done, young man. You had them in the palm of your hands. I'm glad someone in this room can string more than two sentences together.'

After the applause had finally died down, the chairman stood. 'Is anyone going to move a motion?' he asked.

Around Alec, the men shuffled their feet and wriggled in their seats. He raised his hand.

'Yes …' The chairman trailed off as he searched for a name before Alec helped him out. 'Alec.'

'Yes, Alec,' the chairman said, re-asserting his authority.

Alec cleared his throat and spoke. 'I move that this meeting of the Coonabarabran branch of the Graziers' Association of New South Wales deplore the illegal and immoral actions of the Meat Workers Union and call on them to suspend all action immediately until a compromise is reached.'

'Compromise?' someone mumbled.

'There is no point in crossing swords when we can make peace,' Alec said.

'Hear, hear,' the rest of the members agreed.

'All those in favour of the motion?' the chairman asked.

A sea of hands waved their approval.

'Against?' the chairman asked perfunctorily.

Not a hand was raised.

'I declare the motion carried,' he announced.

Although Alec was thrilled to have the first motion he had ever put up carried unanimously, he wouldn't allow himself to show any emotion. He didn't want to appear full of himself.

'Our final business for the evening is the election of local delegates to attend the Graziers' Federal Council meeting in Sydney. I call for nominations.'

Someone up the back called out, 'Frank Moses.'

Alec knew Frank Moses by reputation. He was a well-known veteran of the landholders' war against unions and a doyen of the Graziers' Association. He had made his name in the Shearers' Strike of 1891 by refusing to employ unionised shearers.

Frank dragged himself to his feet and spoke. 'I'm afraid I have to decline the nomination. I don't think I'm up to a trip to the big smoke.'

Alec gripped his knees as he watched the octogenarian crumple into his seat. The chairman called out hopefully, 'Any other nominations?'

There was silence. Alec sat stiff in his seat as everyone seemed to pretend they were somewhere else, sitting on their hands and looking anywhere but up at the chair. Then the most influential grazier in the hall raised his hand. The room fell silent and Alec wondered if Frederick Hope was finally going to take centre stage.

'I'm sure you'll all agree with me in thanking Frank for his yeoman service to the Association,' Fred began.

The crowd applauded politely before a voice called from the back of the hall, 'Who are we going to send then?'

Alec felt Fred's gaze.

'This young fellow's got plenty to say,' Fred continued, 'Why don't we send him?' he said, winking at Alec.

Alec couldn't believe his ears.

'Are there any other nominations?' The chairman seemed impatient. There weren't.

'I declare Alec Murray elected unopposed.'

At twenty-five, Alec had been elected as Coonabarabran's delegate to the Graziers' Federal Council of Australia. He was the youngest delegate elected in the Council's history.

As Fred led him out of the hall, Alec shook the hands of men he'd never met, happily accepting their endorsement and pretending to enjoy their hearty back slapping. The two made their way through the approving crowd and escaped down the street.

Briefly pausing to regain his breath, Alec stopped and pointed to his pickup that had seen better days. 'I'm parked across the street ...'

'Come and meet my daughter. She's just back from Paris,' Fred said. He placed his hand gently but firmly on Alec's back and steered him towards his shiny black Ford.

Alec caught sight of a young woman, her brown hair tied in a bow, leaning on the bonnet. She was dressed in jodhpurs, riding boots and a blue cotton shirt with a few buttons undone. She seemed to be miles away.

Fred called out to her. 'Helen. Meet our new delegate.'

Alec felt his face reddening. He might have been on solid ground inside the hall but out on the street he felt suddenly on shifting sands. The young woman straightened herself up and stifled a yawn. She seemed miles away as he introduced himself.

'Alec Murray.' Alec removed his hat and offered his hand.

Nell took it and smiled. 'How do you do?' she asked politely.

'Very well, thank you,' he said as matter-of-factly as he could manage.

'Alec is going to put an end to these jolly strikes,' Fred announced.

'Crushing the workers are you?' she said, still smiling and throwing Alec completely off balance.

'I wouldn't put it quite like that.'

'Don't they have rights?' She tilted her head slightly.

'I ... I um ...'

Fred came to the rescue. 'Helen has returned full of righteous indignation. A few days mustering will knock it out of her, don't you think?'

Alec didn't quite know where to look as she glared at her father, opened the car door, climbed in the front and slammed it shut.

'Don't worry. She's been green around the gills since she came home,' Fred explained as he shook Alec's hand. 'Welcome aboard, lad. Let me know how you get on in Sydney.'

With that, Fred hopped into the Ford and drove off, leaving Alec wondering what the hell had just happened. He had gone to the meeting to see how things worked and come out a delegate. Not only that, but he had met the most beautiful woman he had ever laid eyes on.

11.

'Why is Jock allowed to do as he pleases?'

Nell was furious. It wasn't the first time she and her mother had locked horns about her appearance in the few weeks she had been home.

'All I did was ask you to dress for lunch,' Elaine said.

'I am dressed.'

Nell was wearing one of Jock's shirts with its tail hanging out, a pair of old moleskins held up by one of his handwoven leather belts, and woollen socks.

'Like a man.'

How little my mother knows about me, thought Nell, savouring the memory of Gabriel's shirt on her back. Hands on hips, she wasn't about to back down.

'I'm comfortable.'

Elaine pointed disapprovingly at the unbuttoned shirt. 'Do your buttons up at least. You look like a …'

'A what?'

'You know.'

'No. Tell me.'

'One of those … town girls.'

'Town girls?'

'You know what I mean.'

'A prostitute?'

'Helen, please! Just go and put something … decent … on for lunch.'

'You don't tell Jock what to wear.'

'I don't have to.'

'It's not fair.'

'Fairness has nothing to do with it, Helen.'

'Nell.'

'Don't be so ridiculous.'

Nell was sick to the back teeth of her mother's patronising comments and she wasn't going to take it anymore. 'I'm eighteen. I'm old enough to call myself what I want to.'

Elaine had no response to this, so she busied herself with peeling the potatoes. After a moment, she said, 'Your father will be in for lunch soon. Why don't you get changed and bring in the washing?'

'Jock stole money from your purse and you didn't even punish him.'

'The washing?'

'Damn the washing!'

'Helen! Don't you dare use that language in this house.'

'What are you going to do? Rinse my mouth out with soap?'

'I don't know what's got into you.'

'I'll tell you, Mother! I'm a grown woman. I've been living in Paris by myself for six months … I'd still be there …'

She trailed off, determined not to lose it. She gathered her thoughts and continued. 'Jock is allowed to go off playing cards with the jackeroos, stumble home as drunk as a skunk and pinch money from your purse to pay his debts. Imagine if I behaved like that!' Nell fumed as she watched her mother avoid the subject by filling a white, enamel pot with water.

She nearly exploded when Elaine turned the tap off and remarked casually, 'At least he paid them.'

'You are ridiculous!'

Nell stormed out to the verandah, picked up the reins from the saddle shed and marched down to the horse paddock. She whistled for Ginger, who was munching away happily. He had been her salvation throughout her teens, and she knew she could turn to him now. At least he wouldn't tell her what to wear. She approached him gently, somehow containing her rage, and threw her arms around his big strong neck.

'What would I do without you?'

Nell tossed the reins over his neck and lead him to the shed, where she saddled him up. Soon they were cantering across the house paddock.

Once she was beyond sight of the homestead, she crouched forward like a jockey, loosened the reins and let Ginger have his head. He moved effortlessly from a canter to a gallop, while she shifted her weight to her legs so that she barely touched the saddle. They moved in perfect symmetry. The river gums along the banks of the Macquarie River flashed by, and Nell noticed a bunch of emus, disturbed by the sound of pounding hooves, sprinting across the paddock.

By the time she returned from her gallop, having vented her frustration, Elaine was mashing the potatoes. The unmistakeable aroma of a mutton stew in the Aga drew Nell into the kitchen. She may have fallen for French cuisine but her mother's country cooking still had a hold on her. Elaine added some butter to the mashed potatoes, checked the beans that were bubbling away on the stove, took out the stew and stoked the Aga.

Nell decided to make peace. 'Sorry, Mother.'

Elaine smiled thinly.

Nell washed up for lunch, modestly buttoned up her shirt and tucked it in. It didn't hurt her to make her mother happy. After all, she wasn't going to be here for long and it was worth it to try to keep the peace.

When she walked into the dining room, Fred had taken his place at the head of the table. For the first time, she noticed that Jock was prematurely balding. He was waiting for his lunch with his elbows on the table. Nell resisted the urge to comment, choosing instead to inquire about their morning's work. 'How is the classing going?'

Nell had little interest in the process of culling sheep to strengthen the flock, but she pretended she did. It worked. Elaine looked up from serving and smiled approvingly. Nell was glad she had tidied herself up. Elaine handed her a plate of stewed mutton.

'They are pretty good. Only have to cull a few,' Fred replied.

'That's good,' Nell said enthusiastically. She wondered if she was laying it on a bit thick when Jock, sitting opposite, rolled his eyes.

They ate wordlessly. After a few minutes, Elaine did her best to start a conversation. 'The lime tree is doing very well.'

Everyone nodded. When he had finished his lunch, Fred wiped his mouth with his napkin and proclaimed, 'I think we might have found a future Country Party leader.'

Elaine looked at Nell and raised an eyebrow. Nell knew that politics was her mother's least favourite subject.

Fred pointed his fork at Jock. 'You might know him.'

'What's his name?'

Fred ignored his son's question and continued. 'We could certainly do with some new blood. Some of those fellows are space fillers.'

Jock tried again. 'Da?'

'Alec something. Tall chap.' Fred turned to Elaine for assistance. 'Looks a bit like that fellow in that picture we saw …'

Elaine perked up. 'The one about the about the ambulance driver and the nurse?'

'I don't know what it was about, love.'

'No. You fell asleep,' Elaine said pointedly.

'What was the film?' Nell asked.

Elaine sighed. '*A Farewell to Arms.* We saw it in London. It was so sad at the end.'

'Whatever his name is. This Alec fellow looks like him,' Fred said.

Nell piped up, 'Gary Cooper? The man you introduced me to?'

Fred laughed. 'His name isn't Gary Cooper.'

Jock slapped the table as though he had won a hand of poker. 'Alec … Alec … Alec Murray?'

Fred nodded. 'Yes, that's it.'

The men began a private conversation, as they often did, as though Nell and her mother were invisible.

'He was a few years ahead of me at school.'

'He's interesting,' Fred said. 'Not afraid to state his case.'

'I didn't have much to do with him. He didn't play cricket, wasn't much good at rugby. He was a rower I think.'

'Yes, well, he can certainly mount an argument. He might be just the chap to take Page's seat.'

'Don't know much about him. He's one of those brainy types, you know?' said Jock.

Elaine leant over to Nell and whispered, 'Any brainy type who looks like Gary Cooper is welcome to eat at my table anytime!'

While her mother enjoyed her own joke, Nell surprised herself by reflecting that the tall, slightly awkward man she had met was a bit of a good sort.

44

12.

Alec was excited about the opportunity to represent his district at the Graziers' Council meeting in Sydney. He was taking his first steps in a new direction: a direction he had been mulling over for a long time. It was proof he could be a farmer and make other contributions to society as well.

He decided he needed to do some research so, after he had booked into his hotel, he made a phone call.

'*The Land*. Stewart McKie speaking …' answered a raspy voice.

'Hello. My name is Alec Murray and I am down from Coonabarabran for the Graziers' Federal Council meeting.'

'So I heard. Youngest ever delegate.'

This comment took Alec by surprise.

Stewart got straight to the point. 'What can I do for you?'

'I didn't want to turn up to the meeting unprepared …'

'Never worried Frank!' Stewart roared, before continuing. 'Frank Moses made the most of the pleasures city life had to offer when he was the delegate.'

Deciding to let that one go, Alec pressed on. 'I don't know much about this business, so I thought …'

There was a pause before Stewart replied, 'Not sure if I'll be much use to you. I'm a newspaper editor, not a farmer, but drop in and we'll have a yarn.'

*

The next day Alec walked into the sandstone building that housed the paper and looked up at the directory. He straightened his tie and climbed the musty smelling steps to the office on the top floor, rehearsing his questions as he went. He didn't want to make a fool of himself. He had never met a newspaperman and imagined a hard-nosed, chain-smoking, middle-aged man in shirtsleeves and braces, treating him like the neophyte he was. Alec knocked on the door and stepped back.

A slightly built young man, with slicked back hair, a moustache and inquiring eyes, opened the door. He wore a spotted bow tie, a well-fitting dark suit and fashionable brogues. A white handkerchief, neatly tucked into the top pocket, set it off.

He offered his hand. 'Alec?'

'Yes.'

'Stewart McKie. Glad to meet you. Come into our little den of iniquity.'

Alec shook his hand firmly, being sure to look him straight in the eye.

The journo rearranged piles of manila folders so his visitor could fit into his tiny office. 'Shifting deckchairs on the *Titanic*!' he said.

Alec laughed. 'Don't go to any trouble ...'

'I won't.' Stewart moved a pile of papers from his crowded desk and plonked them on the floor. 'Filing system.'

Alec looked at the bookcase leaning precariously against the wall. It was jammed with reference books and past issues of *The Land*. A small window let in some light and allowed a glimpse of the cityscape. Alec took a quick peek. Trams rattled up and down Broadway, people scurried across the road, avoiding cars and the few remaining horses and carts that still delivered goods around the city.

'Long way from home?'

'I went to university up the road,' said Alec.

'Oh? A man of many parts!'

Stewart then ushered him into a wobbly looking chair and sat down behind his desk. 'What can I do for you?'

Alec leant forward. 'These strikes at the abattoirs, they're creating a lot of trouble in the bush. We can't get our stock away. It's costing us money, let alone the inconvenience of transporting them to-and-fro while these fellows refuse to get to work.'

'The cockies aren't very happy about it?'

Alec was taken aback by the editor of a countryman's newspaper using this derogatory term to describe the respectable gentlemen who had elected him as their representative.

'I'm not happy about it. We run a pretty tight operation. We fatten our lambs and feed up the cattle in the expectation that they will be sold, whatever the vagaries of the market, and that we will buy more to replace them. It's cyclical. We are prepared to cope with the variables we can't control, like the weather. It's the ones we should be able to control, like these strikes, that make it impossible to survive. It's hard enough as it is.'

The newspaper man was silent and Alec hoped he hadn't gone too far. Eventually Stewart picked up a packet of cigarettes, offered one to Alec and lit one for himself.

'Especially when you are being manipulated by the industry itself,' Stewart said.

Alec froze and said finally, 'What was that?'

'Here.' Stewart scribbled a name on a piece of paper. 'Have a yarn to this bloke. He'll set you right.'

Alec looked at the name. 'The secretary of the Meat Workers Union? I'm a "cockie", to use your term. He'll skin me alive.'

'He'll tell you what you want to know.'

'I'm the enemy. He's not going to confide in me.'

'Trust me.'

Alec searched Stewart's face. He didn't seem the type who would have him on. He took the bit of paper, folded it carefully and put it in his pocket.

'Let's go have a drink.'

Before Alec could answer, Stewart had grabbed his coat and was holding the door for him.

A few blocks down the street, Stewart led Alec up to the third floor of Federation House and opened the door.

'Welcome to the Journalists' Club.'

Alec looked around the crowded bar while Stewart signed him in.

The place was alive. Everyone seemed to be talking at once. They were shouting and arguing and drinking like there was no tomorrow. Stewart led him to the bar, bought him a beer and filled him in.

'The Club's just been opened. It's the best thing since sliced bread.' He waved his cigarette around the packed bar. 'It's a meeting place for journalists, trade unionists and writers; men and women who have been at the coal face, some of them literally. Most of them are pretty tough buggers.'

Alec had never been anywhere like this. He worried he'd look like a fish out of water.

Stewart took a sip of his whisky and said, 'I've seen a few terrific fights in here. They argue till they're blue in the face and then someone insults someone's birthright and it's on. No damage done, of course. They're all too plastered to land a decent punch. All piss and wind, most of them.'

Alec's head was spinning. The energy in the room was intoxicating.

Stewart grinned. 'Question time for pissed journos.'

He grabbed Alec's arm. 'See that bloke over there?' He pointed at a well-groomed man with red hair, holding court at a corner table. 'Ken Slessor.'

Alec couldn't believe his eyes. 'The poet?'

'He's also a journo. Writes for *Smith's Weekly*.'

'"Five Bells" is one of my favourite poems,' said Alec.

'You've read it?' Stewart asked.

Bristling at the implication, Alec replied, 'Of course.' Then, in case there was any doubt, he set Stewart straight. 'I love poetry.'

Stewart drained his scotch and raised his eyebrows. 'Renaissance man?'

Taking this as a challenge, Alec downed his beer and banged the glass a little too forcefully on the bar. 'Not every cocky's a philistine, you know.'

Slapping him on the shoulder, Stewart laughed. 'I can see that.'

He held two fingers up to the barmaid. Alec whipped out his wallet and slapped some money on the bar. He wasn't going to be anybody's fool. The barmaid handed him a beer and a scotch. He passed the scotch to Stewart. They took a sip of their drinks before Stewart changed the subject.

'You're interested in politics?'

The question took Alec by surprise. Stewart shrugged apologetically and explained, 'I'm a journo.'

They both laughed. Alec drank his beer then said, 'I guess it's in the blood. My great uncle was in Parliament. For a time, he was the whip in the Bruce–Page government.'

'Really? Stanley Bruce was no friend of the worker.'

'He had big plans for developing the bush though,' Alec said.

Stewart grunted. 'He was a bastion of the Empire, like Menzies is.'

Alec wasn't going to be intimidated, he turned the tables on Stewart. 'What about you?'

'Me?' Stewart seemed surprised.

'Yes. You don't exactly fit the mould of the editor of a cockie's rag.'

Stewart swirled the liquid in the glass and peered into it as if reading tea-leaves. 'I'm a writer. I need a job.'

Alec was intrigued. 'What do you write?'

'Books.'

'Oh …'

'And stories about sheep.'

They laughed.

✳

An hour later, emboldened by Dutch courage, Alec walked into the foyer of Trades Hall. He felt like he was entering enemy territory. John Ferrier, a well-dressed man in his forties, showed him into his office. Around the walls were pictures of workers protesting and one of Lenin above the desk. Alec sat, a little uncomfortably.

'You want to know about the strikes?' the union man asked.

'Well … yes. They are causing a lot of –'

John cut him off. 'I know.'

Alec glanced up at a photo of protesters storming the barricades. He wondered why Stewart had sent him here.

John moved forward in his seat and leant his elbows on the desk. 'Listen … I'm not calling them, mate.'

Alec didn't know what he meant. Maybe the Secretary of the Meat

Workers Union was leading him up the garden path.

'Strikes aren't good for workers,' John said. 'They cost us hard earned …' He rubbed his thumb and forefinger together. 'We only call strikes to protect workers' rights. We're not interested in disrupting your business. If you're closed down, my members go without a feed.' He paused and then added, 'They're being called for me.'

Alex was stunned. 'I beg your pardon?'

John laid his cards on the table. 'They're being called by the meat processors. They're putting on the strikes so they can depress the price of meat, buy it up at a reduced price and on sell it with a big profit.'

Alec couldn't believe what he was hearing.

John continued. 'It's a racket. It's how capitalism works. The rich get richer and the poor get poorer.'

'You're telling me your union isn't involved?'

'The union's involved because they're striking, but I didn't order the strike. Someone stitched it up and the members voted me down. I didn't have the numbers. The person who organised them is being slipped a few quid to put them on.'

✻

That afternoon, while walking around the city, Alec mulled over John Ferrier's words. The straight-talking union official was not the monster Alec had expected. Instead, Alec had met a reasonable and considered man whose talk had made a lot of sense.

Alec rang Stewart from a public phone booth. 'Do you know anything about these rackets?'

'I've been waiting for you to call. Not everyone is as pure as the driven snow as you are, my friend. A lot of people will do anything to line their pockets. If that means slipping a few spivs a quid to pull a strike, they'll do it. Everyone's got a price.'

'You mean –'

Stewart cut him off. 'I mean that the rich make money by exploiting workers. Always have. Always will. They believe in the survival of the fittest and most of the time, they're the fittest. The bottom line is profits not people.'

Alec was stunned. He'd never imagined that something like this could happen; that the people who bought the meat from the abattoirs would organise a strike for their own profit. He thought about men like Whippet who had served their country and been left on the scrap heap when they returned. He thought about the poor struggling farmers he'd come across as a kid in Cootamundra, who couldn't afford a horse and mustered their small flocks on rickety push bikes. He thought about the wages paid to workers in the abattoirs and the hours they put in.

He wasn't going to take this lying down.

The next day, in an impassioned, thirty-minute speech to the Graziers' Council, held at the Hotel Metropole, Alec argued that there needed to be a Royal Commission into the rackets in the abattoirs. After three extensions, in which there was much shouting and finger pointing, he won the day and a resolution supporting his motion was passed.

While the Council's executive lunched at the Australian Club, Alec went for a stroll through the Royal Botanic Gardens. He felt like he was walking on air. He wished he could tell Stephen about his win. He knew his army friend from Brisbane would be impressed.

When the meeting reconvened after lunch, a bitter argument broke out over the abattoir resolution. People who had supported his resolution before lunch were now arguing against it. Members of the executive held sway and, before Alec knew it, his motion was rescinded.

Furious at the apparent backdown, he stormed out of the meeting.

'Young man!' A solidly built, serious-looking fellow in horn-rimmed spectacles chased after Alec. 'You did very well in there,' he said.

'Clearly,' Alec answered curtly.

'Joe Baldry. I'm the President of the Council.' He offered Alec his hand. His grip was firm, his gaze direct.

'I know,' Alec said, returning his gaze.

'And I know why you walked out.' Joe paused before continuing. 'Look, I'm not one to beat around the bush. I'll tell you straight. Your motion was rescinded because there was pressure applied.'

Alec was horrified. 'And you folded.'

'We have to serve our members.'

'You mean to say that someone from the Graziers' Federal Council is funding the strikes.'

Joe tapped his beetroot-red nose. 'There are some things beyond our control.'

'Are you saying that someone pressured the Executive to rescind the motion?'

Joe raised a finger to his mouth. 'My lips are sealed.'

Alec fought back the urge to punch him. Disgusted, he tried to walk away but Joe grabbed his arm.

'I've wasted my time!' It was all Alec could do to contain his rage.

'No, you haven't. You are the best bit of new blood we've had in the Council for years.

'Here.' He stuffed a piece of paper into Alec's coat pocket. 'I've got to go back in but give me a bell some time. I think we might be able to find a spot for you in the Country Party. You would make an excellent candidate.'

Too shocked by this development to do otherwise, Alec accepted the offer of a handshake and watched as Joe turned and headed back into the meeting.

Had he just been offered a safe seat in Parliament?

13.

When nearly every man in the district under forty, including Jock, rushed to enlist, Nell was forced to take on more responsibilities at Braemar. She had always wanted to do the work the men did, so she was delighted when her father sent her out to muster with head stockman, Jimmy Matthews.

At first, she was intimidated by him. He had been working for Fred since he was a boy, and was as much a part of the landscape on Braemar as the scribbly barks and red gums that held its soil together.

They were moving a big mob of 10,000 merinos when he cantered up to her. 'Race ahead and open the gate will ya, Miss Helen?'

Nell looked at him doubtfully. It was a big responsibility. She knew the dangers of sheep squashing themselves as they rushed headlong through a gate into greener pastures.

Jimmy noticed her hesitation. 'You'll be right, Miss Helen. You couldn't be worse than him.' He pointed to one of the burnt-out old men who had been recycled to fill the void created by the impending announcement of war. 'At least you're not dead in the saddle.'

Emboldened by the confidence shown in her, Nell dug her heels into Ginger and cantered around to the front of the mob. She loved that Jimmy didn't care who he worked with as long as they got the job done. She opened the gate and waved the battered Akubra he had given her to moderate the flow of the mob.

When they were safely through the gate she looked back. Jimmy gave her the thumbs up, leant back in his saddle, unselfconsciously scratching his balls and stretching his legs. He took his hat off and wiped his sweaty, hatband-creased brow with his shirt. The parts of his skin that had been exposed to the elements were the same reddish-brown colour as the soil. He trotted up to Nell.

'Well done. We'll get 'em into the yards before the sun goes down.'

Ginger's bit rattled in his mouth as he shook his head to rid himself of the persistent, annoying flies. Nell leant forward and threw her arms around his neck. They had proved their worth.

Jimmy sat up in his saddle and whistled. His two border collies stopped in their tracks. Ears pricked, they awaited instructions. When Jimmy whistled again with new orders, the dogs rounded the mob, one on each flank, and drove the sheep down the hill towards the yards where Old Tommy, resurrected from garden duties, opened the gate. As Nell cantered back to help Jimmy with any stragglers, she saw Fred's truck approaching.

A plume of dust billowed behind the old Ford as it motored up the dirt track.

The truck pulled up and Fred hopped out. He took off his jacket and tossed it into the cabin. He rolled up his sleeves and tucked his wool tie into his shirt.

'I've got some good news for you,' he said.

'For me?' Nell had an absurdly optimistic flash that the impending war in Europe had been averted and her father was sending her back to Paris.

'Yes,' Fred said, casting a weather eye on proceedings. 'Jock needs someone to accompany him to some sort of ball in the city.'

The first half of the sentence made her heart sink. *Jock needs…* He who could do no wrong. What does Jock need?

'He's been in camp, so I suppose, with his birthday coming up, he deserves a bit of a reward. At least your mother thinks so.'

He smiled knowingly at her. Since coming home from Paris, Nell had the impression that her father knew exactly what the score was with Jock. He'd also been prepared to cut her a bit of slack; certainly treated her differently than before. At times like this, she felt like he understood her. She smiled; the prospect of a night out on the town wasn't the worst thing she'd ever heard of.

'Where to?' she asked.

'I think it's called Carl Thomas …' Fred trailed off, casting an eye over the sheep.

Nell straightened up. The swanky nightclub Peg had told her about!

'I'll need a new dress.'

Fred reached into his pocket and handed her some pound notes. 'Thought you might. We thought you could fly to Sydney for the weekend.'

Nell nearly leapt into his arms. There was nothing she would rather do. She could catch up with Peggy MacArthur and let her hair down.

'If you think it would be a good idea,' she said, trying to keep her cool.

'Someone needs to keep an eye on him.'

As if anyone could keep an eye on Jock, she thought, while Fred outlined her itinerary. 'Mother's packed your port. Tommy will drive you down to Dubbo and put you on the plane.'

The airport at Dubbo had only been open for a couple of years. There was still something exotic about flying and it sure beat the prospect of a long, dusty drive.

'Should I … ?' Nell tossed her head towards 'home'.

Fred smiled. 'Yes. You better get a move on.'

She leant down in her saddle and gave her startled father a kiss. 'Thank you, Father.'

'Be a good girl.'

'Me? Of course.'

Nell wheeled Ginger round, gave a yell, and cantered off for home to re-pack her suitcase.

14.

Back in Sydney, at the end of a week's camp in Singleton, Alec couldn't wait to get home. After a big night out with his friends, he'd missed the early train and had to wait until the following day for the next one.

Like his friend Stephen, Alec was growing tired of the camps and endless marching. He was also feeling a bit guilty. He knew he should be back on his property relieving Bernie, rather than living it up. Perhaps that last scotch had been one too many.

Alec was dreading another night on the town. As far as he could tell, all his friends wanted to do was hit the tiles. Not that he minded a bit of a party once in a while, as long as drinking was mixed with political debate he would argue and thump the table with the best of them. In fact, he had done that very thing the night before, surprising them and even himself by defending the striking abattoir workers and arguing, to his increasingly horrified audience, that they were being exploited by rich cockies.

There was a knock at the door. He opened it.

'The three musketeers!' Johnny Buchanan announced, beaming. Alongside him, Jim Wallace and Brian Harkness grinned, ready for action. Alec's heart sank. He knew it would cause more trouble than it was worth to shut the door on them. He might as well join his old school mates for a couple before turning in.

'I'm not going to have a late one,' he said unconvincingly.

Johnny laughed and shook his head. Alec had called Johnny a 'born to rule, silver-spoon snob,' the night before and felt he might have gone too far, as well as been slightly hypocritical. None of them could escape their background.

Like Alec, Johnny Buchanan had come down from the bush for the camp. He was trying to manage the family property outside Glen Innes while establishing a medical practice in the area. He was a nuggety little man with a raucous laugh, a generous soul and prematurely thinning hair.

'Where's your penguin suit?' Jim Wallace asked, grinning like a Cheshire cat. He was raised on a huge property in the Northern Territory: cattle country. He'd boarded with Alec at King's which was when he started wearing shoes for the first time. He was as a big as a bear and just as dangerous.

Brian Harkness, a slightly built man with a quick wit and hawk-like eyes, was tapping his watch. A budding accountant, Brian had an eye for detail and loved nothing more than quoting George Washington.

Even though he was moving further and further away from them politically, Alec felt a deep loyalty to his friends. At boarding school, they had been more of a family than his own. They'd defended him when he'd challenged some of his school's more elitist attitudes and been bullied for his troubles. Together, they had bonded and fought and forgot their families and learnt to hide their feelings. Now, that same sense of loyalty bound them together in their determination to fight against Nazism.

Alec looked at them, all dressed to the nines, and wondered what they had in mind. He had on a suit and would be the only one not wearing a dinner jacket. Before he had a chance to argue that he wasn't dressed for whatever they were planning, Johnny had grabbed his arm and was leading him out the door.

'We thought a few drinks here at the club, then on to Carl Thomas's,' said Johnny.

Alec closed his eyes. He could already see another hangover on the horizon and he couldn't afford to miss the train again.

'I might call it a night after drinks,' he said.

Jim shaped up and feinted a straight jab. 'Not if we have any say in it!'

Brian tried to appeal to his curiosity. 'You've never been to Carl Thomas's. You know the *Herald* called it Sydney's "most glorious adventure and its greatest success". We've got to go.'

'I don't think it's quite my cup of tea,' Alec replied.

'How do you know – you've never been?' Brian said.

'Jock Hope is throwing a party for his twenty-first birthday. Sure to be plenty of good sorts,' Johnny added.

Alec remembered Jock Hope. He was a few years below him, they had little in common and had barely had anything to do with each other. Then he remembered that he had met Jock's sister the day he'd been elected as delegate to the Graziers' Council. The possibility of running into her piqued his interest.

'*Undertake not what you cannot perform but be careful to keep your promise,*' Brian cautioned, quoting Washington as Alec remembered the feisty young woman.

He had already changed his mind about going out.

15.

When Nell stepped out of the gleaming black hire car on the night of her brother's birthday party, she looked up at the neon sign shining above the entrance of the old wool store. *Carl Thomas's Nightclub.*

Standing under its beacon of possibility, she was alive for whatever the night offered. She hadn't felt like this since she left Paris.

Jock was up the stairs barrelling towards the door before she had a chance to adjust her lipstick. She could have predicted that he wouldn't be burdened with chaperoning his little sister for long.

'I'll find us a table,' he yelled, disappearing inside.

Nell paused and drank it all in. She looked down at the green, orange and red lights that shimmied off the harbour. A ferry jostled with a grand ocean liner, and she wondered if it too was returning from Europe. The Sydney Harbour Bridge, just seven years old, arched across the water connecting the two foreshores on either side of the city. It was new enough to sparkle in the moonlight.

Nell followed her brother towards the main entrance. The dress she had found was daringly backless and she adopted her best Parisian nonchalance as she approached the stern looking doorman, who greeted her with a polite bow.

'Welcome, Mademoiselle.'

Nell smiled politely, quashing the temptation to scream with delight. Jimmy never called her 'Mademoiselle' when he sent her to round up the sheep. For a fleeting moment, as she stepped into the ornate foyer, Nell imagined she was back in Europe. She felt the seductive strains of Duke Ellington's 'Sophisticated Lady' beckoning her towards the dance floor. This wasn't what she had expected from stuffy old Sydney.

The club's pianist, perched on the edge of his piano stool, one leg languidly folded over the other, played with all the flair of a Broadway veteran. As Nell passed by, he caught her eye and winked. Without missing a beat, Nell winked back. There was no way some Yankee showman was going to get the better of her.

She was stopped short by the club's wall murals, exulting in their colour and vibrancy. Their depictions of early settlement were idealised portrayals of order and optimism. Women in bright dresses with wide-brimmed hats jostled with men in natty suits and bowlers. The work was light and airy, bursting with hope for the future. Like the club itself, the murals felt to Nell like a breath of fresh air after her life on Braemar.

While the club's dress code was formal, Nell loved that many women had daubed tattoos on their bare shoulders and arms with burnt cork: optimistic images of love hearts pierced by Cupid's arrows.

On the dance floor, couples began moving in syncopated rhythm as Duke Ellington segued into Fats Waller. The piano player was raising the stakes, teasing his audience, tempting them, daring them to cast off their colonial rectitude.

As Nell moved between the tables, she noticed men gaping and heard their partners whispering behind gloved hands, 'Who's that?'

'Jock Hope's little sister.'

'Been in Paris.'

'She's ...'

'Very ... sure of herself.'

Nell lapped it up. She knew she could eat women like them for breakfast. How many of them could crutch sheep? It didn't worry her if they looked down their noses at her. She couldn't have cared less. She was her own woman and no stuck-up Sydney society dames were going to cause her to miss her step.

Jock was standing at a table in the corner, nursing a martini and loudly holding court. Nell didn't mind that he was a ratbag. At least he was an entertaining one. She approached the table feeling in her element.

'Nell!' Peggy MacArthur leapt to her feet and enveloped her in a generous hug. 'I didn't know you were coming to town,' she screeched in delight.

Nell was quick to apologise. 'Nor did I until yesterday. I'm sorry I didn't ring. I had to find a dress.'

Peg wheeled her around and looked her over before giving Nell her stamp of approval. 'It suits you, darling. Very risqué.' She gently touched the delicate, white headpiece pinned to Nell's hair. 'I love this!'

Nell was pleased, she'd been worried the headpiece may have been too much.

Clapping her hands with delight, Peggy gave her another hug and proclaimed, 'We've so much to catch up on!'

Nell felt a pang of guilt that she had neglected her dearest friend. 'I am so happy to see you.'

Peg kissed her. 'Me too! Have you met everyone?'

Nell did the rounds of the table, shaking hands with all the dinner-suited men and nodding pleasantly to the stylishly dressed women, a few of whom she knew from school.

Then Peggy introduced her to a tall man in a plain suit. 'Alec Murray.'

Nell paused. Standing straight-backed with his hand extended was a vision that momentarily took her breath away. Tall, elegant, with piercing blue eyes, he was different from the other men. It wasn't only that he wasn't dressed in black tie; it was the way he carried himself. He seemed more self-contained. For the briefest second, she was thrown off balance.

She recovered, smiled politely and greeted him. 'Nell. Hello.'

'Hello,' the man replied in a deep voice.

They stood staring at each other, as if momentarily starstruck. There was something familiar about him, but Nell didn't know what it was.

He was smiling softly.

'We've met before,' he told her.

'Have we?' She laughed, searching.

'In slightly different circumstances.'

Her mind was suddenly a whirl. Where had she met him? Why did she feel attracted to him? To that smile?

Before she could process any what was happening, Peggy grabbed her arm. 'Alec is ready for war,' she said.

One of the men offered Nell a cigarette. She took it and, for a brief moment was unsure where to send her gaze. Where had she met that handsome man?

Johnny Buchanan came to her rescue. 'There's a spot here.'

He pulled out a chair for her. Gracefully smoothing her frock she sat, resting her purse on the table. Johnny flicked open his cigarette lighter and offered her a light. She held her cigarette between two fingers and inhaled. Johnny had seated her opposite Alec Murray, who hadn't taken his eyes off her. She caught his gaze and he seemed to blush. She smiled. He returned the smile. *That* smile.

'Champagne?' A waiter proffered Nell a bottle wrapped in a linen napkin.

'Thank you.'

The champagne fizzed as he poured it into the shallow glass that Nell had heard, according to myth, was modelled on Marie Antoinette's breast. Nell looked around to see an older man in a dinner suit raising his glass to her.

'Compliments of Mr Thomas.'

The waiter carefully wiped the lip of the bottle and placed it in an ice bucket.

Peggy was impressed. 'That's the one I told you about in the letter. Isn't he a dish? You must have made an impression, darling, he doesn't send bottles of fizz to everyone!'

Nell sipped her champagne and looked over at Alec. While the table buzzed around them, he exuded a kind of quiet calm. She detected that he was little uncomfortable in these surroundings. Or maybe he had something on his mind.

16.

Duke Ellington's 'It Don't Mean a Thing (If It Ain't Got That Swing)' had everyone up and dancing. Swing was the thing. Couples paired off randomly and Nell found herself with Alec. There wasn't much either could do about it, not that either of them was complaining.

Alec was confident about a lot of things, but dancing wasn't one of them. Let alone the kind of uninhibited, overtly sexualised cavorting that seemed to press in around him. He felt terribly out of place. While Nell moved gracefully and seductively, he stomped around like a man flattening long grass in a paddock. He did his best not to fall over while she glided effortlessly and smiled. He tried to return her gaze but had to watch his feet to make sure he didn't stomp on her. It was excruciating, and when the music quickened, he was relieved that she took his hand and lead him off the dance floor.

'Let's have a drink. My feet are sore.'

'You know the saying about dancing with "two left feet"?' He laughed, acknowledging that she had rescued him.

He whisked her chair back for her and poured her a glass of champagne as expertly as the best waiter.

'Sit here,' she said, tapping the chair beside her. 'We won't be able to hear each other if you sit too far away.'

He pulled up a chair next to her. 'Do you remember us meeting in Coonabarabran?' he asked, feeling himself redden slightly.

'I didn't, but I do now. You made quite an impression on my father.'

He wondered how his proposal for an inquiry into the strikes had gone down with Fred Hope.

Nell unselfconsciously touched his hand. 'What brings you to town?'

'Training,' he replied, relieved to change the subject. 'I'm in the militia.'

Her puzzled expression forced him to explain. 'It's the name for the part-time army. We're getting ready for war.'

'Oh …' Suddenly, she seemed miles away. Had he opened a wound?

'Are you all right? I hope I haven't –'

She cut him off. 'I was thinking about a friend. Someone I will never see again.'

Alec watched her as she took a sip of champagne and shrugged. '*C'est la vie,*' she said and changed the subject. 'You went to school with Jock?'

'I did … I was a few years ahead …' He tried to wave it off. The last thing he wanted to talk about was school, but she insisted.

'Was he as wild at school as he is now?'

She was looking at Jock tearing up the dance floor. Alec wished he could be as uninhibited.

'He was always … a character.'

'You're being diplomatic.'

He smiled. They sipped their drinks and he offered her a cigarette. The silence between them was making him nervous.

'You want to be soldier?' she asked.

'I want to be a farmer.'

'Why are you in the army then?' she said.

'We don't always get what we want, do we?' he said, a little too forcefully.

'No …' she replied.

He really had opened a wound. He watched as she fiddled with her glass. She intrigued him; did he spy a chink in her cool nonchalance? If he was someone else, he would have changed the subject. But Alec wasn't someone else.

'You speak from experience?' he asked.

'Of not getting what I want,' she said.

Her directness had him on the back foot. 'Well, perhaps …'

She took the argument up. 'Not many women do, do they?'

'Get what they want?'

'Yes,' she said, looking at him.

He thought about his mother doing his father's bidding, being bullied by him, being afraid to stand up to him.

Nell waved towards a young woman fawning on her partner. 'One thing I'm not, is what other people want me to be.'

To underline her point, she gestured at a group of women hanging off a self-important young man's every word. 'They make me sick. Look at them.' She sipped. 'I wonder what they really think of him?'

'They might think he's funny.'

'They might. They might be bored senseless too. One thing's for certain, they know which side their bread is buttered on.'

Alec was captivated. He hadn't had a conversation with a woman like this before. Here was someone he could really talk to. He wanted to know more.

'What do you want to be?' he asked.

The question didn't seem to faze her. 'I want to be an artist.'

He was shocked. 'Really?'

'Really.'

The determination in her voice left Alec in no doubt that she meant it. It made her even more attractive. He knew there weren't many female artists in Australia. He hadn't known of any until Stephen had told him to visit an exhibition of Grace Cossington Smith's.

'You're surprised? Just because my father's a wool baron doesn't mean I have to spend the rest of my life talking about wool prices or, worse, keeping house and ensuring the garden survives the drought.'

Alec felt his pulse quicken. He had never been more attracted to anyone. She poured more champagne for them both and raised her glass.

'*Santé.*' She smiled at him. 'If there is a war, I hope it doesn't last long.'

'Me too.'

He raised his glass in another gentle toast. She clinked hers against his and looked into his eyes.

Alec had drifted into unchartered waters and he loved it.

Her leg brushed up against his, sending a spasm through his body.

She leant over and whispered in his ear, 'I'm glad I came.'

He didn't know what to do or say. Eventually he managed, 'So am I.'

She touched his hair and gently let her fingers flitter down the nape of his neck. It was all he could do to control himself. He could feel her sweet breath on his cheek and caught a whiff of her perfume. He was intoxicated.

The world had stopped spinning. Everyone was dancing in slow motion. Even though the band seemed to be still playing, Alec couldn't hear a thing.

'You two seem to be getting along well.'

Suddenly everything returned to normal. Peg towered over them, grinning from ear to ear. Alec blushed.

Nell threw her head back, laughing. 'Oh yes!'

Alec excused himself and made a beeline for the lavatory, planning to collect himself. As he hurried off, he bumped into a chair, knocking it over. He picked it up and managed a weak smile as he stumbled off to safety.

He washed his face and looked into the mirror. Every nerve in his body seemed to be tingling. He wasn't sure what had happened.

By the time he returned, Nell was standing beside the dancefloor, talking with her friends. He kept an eye on her while chatting politely and amiably with whoever was sitting nearby, but the truth was, he didn't pay much attention to what they were saying. His mind was elsewhere. Every now and then Nell glanced in his direction. She was sparkling.

When she returned to the table, she sat beside him and touched his knee. 'Are you all right? I'm sorry. I haven't seen a lot of these people for ages ...'

He was flattered. 'You don't have to apologise.' He smiled. 'I have to go soon anyway.'

He could see that she was clearly disappointed.

'Do you?'

He tapped his watch. 'I have to be on the early train. Duty calls.'

'Duty?'

'My farm. I hate being away from it. That's why I want to get this war business out of the way ...' He tailed off. The impending war was never far from his mind.

For the rest of the evening, they never left each other's side.

When it was time for him to go, he took his leave of his friends, who were in various states of inebriation.

'Where are ya going?' yelled Johnny. 'The night's just a pup!' He thumped Alec on the back.

Nell dragged him away and escorted him to the door.

He nervously offered his hand to shake. She took it, pulled him to her, and kissed him on the cheek.

'Lovely to have met you.'

He kissed her back. 'You too.'

'I look forward to seeing you again.'

He smiled awkwardly and made a beeline for the door. His heart was thumping as he walked back down the street.

Nell paused a moment before returning inside. She was surprised at how taken she was by the young man. He wasn't like the other Australian men she knew. As she floated back to her table, Peg grabbed her by the arm.

'He's quite a dish.'

Her raised eyebrows told Nell that Peggy was digging. 'You think so?' Nell knew what her friend was up to.

'You know what we used to call him at university?' Peg said as they sat down.

Nell tried to appear only vaguely interested. 'No?'

'The stained-glass window, because he was so handsome, like one of those knights in armour you'd see in a cathedral window.'

'You knew him at university?'

'I didn't know him when I first went there. I knew of him. Everybody did. He was a bit of a hero around the place,' Peg said. 'Freshers like me looked up to the fourth years. I got to know him a bit when I joined the history club. I was there for the men; he was there for the history. He seemed very serious.'

'Oh?'

'He was always reading.'

'That's hardly a crime.'

'Trying to solve the problems of the world.' Peg laughed, then rose and sashayed back to the dance floor.

Nell was happy to sit on her own for a few minutes. She looked over at Jock, who was delighting the crowd by balancing champagne glasses on top of each other as he built a champagne fountain.

She was thinking about the man she had just met. The last thing she'd had on her mind when she came to Carl Thomas's was to fall for someone. She had barely got over the pain of saying goodbye to Gabriel, and hadn't thought romantically about men since she'd returned to Australia.

But now she had met someone who really interested her.

17.

The sun was just rising when the train to Coonabarabran shunted out of Central Station. Alec opened the sliding door of the passenger car, tossed his port onto the luggage rack and settled into his seat. Except when he was nursing a painful hangover, he was at his best in the early morning. He had risen with the sun since he was a boy on his father's farm. This morning he was feeling particularly buoyant.

Alec looked out the window at the rows of red brick bungalows that ran alongside the railway track and stretched into the new suburbs. He wondered about the people inside them. What did they hope for? Were they, like he, preparing to abandon everything they had built, to fight a war across the ocean?

After leaving the city behind and chugging up the Blue Mountains, the train rolled down towards plains that seemed to stretch forever. He thought about the families having breakfast in the isolated farmhouses that dotted the landscape, a single trail of smoke curling out of their chimneys. What were their dreams? Who was looking out for them?

Something had ignited his imagination and he was having trouble concentrating on his book. His mind kept wandering back to the night before. He hadn't been able to sleep. He couldn't get Nell out of his mind. Not that he wanted to. It was just that this was a new sensation to him. He was used to being in control of his emotions. Now he found they were running away with him.

He was feeling as good as he had ever felt. He touched his cheek where she had kissed him. He laughed aloud at the thought of nearly knocking her over on the dance floor. She hadn't seemed to mind. He had always believed that passions like the ones he was feeling now were the product of the fertile imaginations of writers like Hardy and Tolstoy. He enjoyed the discovery that they really did exist.

He had never come across anyone like Nell.

Alec started plotting how he could arrange to see her again. He would write her a letter. He started drafting it in his head.

> *Dear Nell,*
> *It was wonderful …*

Too forward.

> *Dear Nell,*
> *It was delightful …*

Delightful! He had never used the word in his life.

Was he going to tell her that he hadn't stopped thinking about her since they met? Hardly. Was he going to suggest a secret assignation? He'd like to but wouldn't be game. Was he going to leave it up to the gods to determine when they'd meet next? That would be too chancy. Besides, there was the matter of an impending war. He knew he must see her before he went.

Whenever that might be.

Alec shifted a little uneasily in his seat. It wasn't that he was beginning to question his commitment to the war effort. It was just that he now had another reason to hope that they could get it over and done with as quickly as possible and get on with their lives.

18.

Nell was woken by a knock at the door. She parted the curtain and looked out the window of the flat in Edgecliff that her parents kept for Sydney visits. She peered down the harbour towards the Sydney Heads. The sun was barely up. Who could be calling at this hour? She slipped on a dressing gown and opened the door.

'Peg? Morning!'

Peg wore the tell-tale signs of a night on the town. Her hair needed a wash. Her make-up barely concealed the bags under her eyes. She was wearing the same clothes as the night before.

'I didn't want to go home while you were still here …' Her raspy voice suggested that she'd had too many cigarettes, too much booze and not enough sleep.

Nell invited Peg into the lounge room, where she kicked off her shoes and plonked herself down on the sofa.

'I'll make us a cup of tea,' Nell said, heading towards the kitchen.

'Thanks, darling,' Peg groaned.

'Of course, if we were in Paris, I'd make you a *café au lait*.'

'If only …'

While Peg lay with her arm over her eyes, Nell put on the kettle, then grabbed a face washer, ran it under cold water, squeezed it out, and gently placed it on Peg's forehead.

'You are a darling.'

'A friend in need …'

'Exactly.'

Nell returned to the kitchen to make the tea and took it back to her ailing friend.

Peg could hardly move. Nell placed a cup and saucer on the coffee table and opened the blinds. Peg groaned and sat up.

'That's better,' she said, drinking the tea.

'Beautiful day.'

'Ohhhh …'

'I love this view.'

'So do I. Usually.'

Nell watched an ocean liner disappear through the Heads, perhaps travelling to Europe, she thought. It made her reflect on the life she had left behind. Even though she'd had a ball the night before, she knew it was a fleeting moment and that soon she would be forced to return to her dreary existence.

She waved her thoughts away and turned back to her friend.

'No Bondi laps?' she teased.

Peg laughed. 'I'd drown.'

'What about the Olympics? I thought you were in training?'

'I think I'm allowed the odd day off. After all, it's not 1940 yet.'

Nell remembered how excited Peg had been when they'd listened to the 1936 Berlin Games on her parents' crystal set.

Peg drained her cup, folded her legs under her and lit a cigarette. 'So …'

Nell joined her on the sofa. 'Yes?'

'Carl Thomas wants to see you.'

'What? Why?'

'I told him about your paintings.'

'When?'

'Last night. After you had slipped away.' Peg took a drag on her cigarette for dramatic effect.

Nell was onto her like a flash. 'Yes?'

Doing her best to feign innocence, Peg brushed a few specs of ash off her skirt. 'I … he invited me back to his flat for a drink.'

Nell's eyes widened. She didn't want to probe further and didn't need to. She knew Peg hadn't been home and that she must have spent the night with the playboy club owner.

Peg shifted the subject back to Nell. 'He was telling me about his plans for the club and I told him about your art.'

'My art? You haven't seen anything ...'

'Never look a gift horse in the mouth, my dear! You were studying art in Paris and I saw your stuff at school. That's enough for me.'

Nell laughed as Peg continued. 'Besides, he wanted to know all about you. You caused quite a stir. I was getting a bit jealous there for a while.'

Nell's mind was racing.

'It's a great opportunity.' Her friend's tone was unusually serious. 'He's looking for someone to do another mural.'

'Really?'

'Cross my heart and hope to die,' Peg said, smiling. 'He wants to see you this morning.'

'But I've never painted a mural ...'

Peg fished in her handbag for an envelope and handed it to her. 'Here you go.'

Nell grabbed a butter knife off the sideboard, carefully sliced the envelope open and unfolded the letter.

Dear Miss Hope,

I would be delighted if you could join me for morning tea to discuss your painting and the possibility of your creating something for the Club.

Yours sincerely,

Carl Thomas

Nell couldn't believe her eyes; she was being offered the chance to paint a mural at the coolest club in the southern hemisphere.

Peg gave her a gilt-edged card. 'Here's his telephone number. Ring him.'

Nell looked at it and, unable to contain herself any longer, squealed and hugged Peg.

'I thought you'd be pleased,' Peg said, when Nell had calmed down. 'Of course, it doesn't mean anything definite.'

'No. But it's a start.'

With that, Peg staggered to her feet.

'Wait,' Nell said, standing too and grasping her friend's hand. 'I've just realised. I've got nothing to show him. All my work is at Braemar.'

'I don't think he's expecting to see your portfolio.'

She gave Nell a kiss on the cheek and made her way to the door. 'I need sleep. Good luck.'

'Thank you. Thank you!'

After seeing Peg out, Nell almost skipped back into the flat. She held the card tightly to her chest and closed her eyes. She could barely believe it.

Then she remembered she was booked on the midday flight to Dubbo. What if Carl Thomas wanted to take her to lunch? She had better ring her mother. What would she tell her? That she was going to lunch with a playboy club owner who was twenty years her senior? Hardly. Elaine would have a heart attack.

Nell picked up the phone and dialled. 'Trangie Post Office. What number please?' came the voice down the crackling line.

'Hi, June. It's Helen Hope.'

'Helen. How are you?' June said.

'Very well thanks.' Nell drummed her fingers on the hall table as June chatted on.

'Looks like rain.'

'Really? Actually, I'm in Sydney.' Nell was doing her best to mask her impatience.

'Lucky girl. What's the weather –'

'I'm in a bit of a pickle. Would you mind putting me through to Mother?'

'Hope nothing's up. Anything ...'

'No. I just need to talk to Mother,' Nell said firmly.

'Of course. Hang on a sec. I'll put you through. Have fun in the big smoke.'

'I will.'

There was a click as June changed lines and connected Nell to Braemar.

'Hello?'

'Mother, hello.'

Elaine panicked. 'Helen? Are you all right? Nothing's wrong I hope.'

'No. Not really.'

'Is Jock with you?'

The last thing Nell wanted, was to talk about Jock. 'I haven't seen him since last night.'

'He hasn't been home?'

'He's staying with friends in Collaroy.'

Nell had no idea where Jock was but she was happy to cover for him and get down to business.

'What's the matter?' Elaine persisted.

'Nothing. Peggy is having a luncheon at The Women's Club and I was wondering if you minded …'

'Today?'

'Yes. Her mother is throwing it for her birthday.'

'But you're meant to be on the plane …'

'I know, Mother, but I hardly ever get down to Sydney and Peg is my oldest friend. Couldn't you just call Dubbo and get me on a flight tomorrow?'

Nell stopped tapping and crossed her fingers.

'It is very inconvenient …'

'I know but …'

'I was going to pick you up and do some shopping in Dubbo.'

'Can't you do it tomorrow?'

Pause.

'Oh yes. I suppose so.'

'Thank you, Mother!'

'Make sure you are on –'

'I will.'

'Behave yourself.'

'Of course!'

Nell put the phone down and exhaled. It wasn't the first fib she'd told her mother but she knew this was too good an opportunity to turn down. Peg had told her that Carl Thomas's murals were the talk of the town and now she might be asked to paint one. The thought excited and scared her at the same time. What if she couldn't do it? What if her father wouldn't let her?

What if it all came to nothing?

Who cares? If she was in for a penny, she might as well be in for a pound.

Nell went to the window and scanned the distant mountains on the horizon. An image of Alec, travelling on the train through them, his nose buried in a book, popped into her head.

19.

Alec and Bernie were making serious inroads into developing Toongowan. They had graded the driveway, and to Alec's delight, had built a house to replace the shack. They'd even fixed the front gate so that it swung sweetly.

Alec found it deeply satisfying that they had used timber and stone from the property to build his new home. He was glad he'd ignored his father's objections and built a verandah, so he could sit and enjoy the view of the Warrumbungles. Who cared if it would be exposed to the elements in certain conditions? Wasn't that the point? He wanted to embrace the environment around him, not pretend he was living in England.

The house had a rudimentary kitchen, a bedroom, and a study. There was an outdoor pit toilet and they had even knocked up a lean-to laundry. What pleased Alec, as much as anything, was that his only costs had been fittings and labour. The early success of his wheat crop and burgeoning wool clip meant he could pay Bernie a bonus. After relying on his mother's financial support to buy the place, he was determined to pay her back as soon as he could. Nothing would give him more satisfaction. He was also in a rush because his father had appointed trustees to make sure his mother's money wasn't going down the drain. Alec butted heads with them because they seemed more worried about balancing the books than preparing for the likely war.

Returning from a trip into Coonabarabran to buy some supplies, Alec smiled at the sight of smoke rising from the chimney. Bernie's wife, Leonie, had offered to help around the house in exchange for eggs, milk and meat. The smoke meant she had lit the newly acquired Aga in readiness for his return. He enjoyed Leonie's sense of humour and admired her quiet ways and knowledge, which he hadn't begun to fathom. Like her husband, Leonie didn't give much away.

All he needed was someone to share this with.

He could see Bernie working in the yards in front of the new shearing shed and again thanked his lucky stars that he had found such a reliable manager. He heard Captain Midnight whinnying and watched him canter down to the fence to greet him. The horse had become his soul mate. Alec adored the big gelding.

As he drove his old ute up the road, the sheep in the house paddock scattered. The season could hardly have been better and the sheep were showing the benefit of it. He looked over at the piggery while the dogs barked a welcome.

Alec's mood darkened as came closer to the house and noticed his father, Henry, standing imperiously on the verandah. Most of the time Alec managed to put his father out of his mind and get on with his life, but now here he was, checking up on him.

Alec parked under the tall box gum, gave Bernie a wave and made his way towards the house. Bernie was the ace up his sleeve, although Alec was nervous about how he would break the news to Henry that an Aboriginal man was going to run the place while he was on duty overseas.

Henry was dressed in a tweed suit with waistcoat, tie and breeches, topped off with a pork-pie hat. He tapped his shooting stick impatiently against his leg. He looked as if he was auditioning for a part in the local Gilbert and Sullivan Society, thought Alec, smiling.

He climbed the steps to the verandah and breathed in the smell of the newly laid floorboards. 'Father.'

They shook hands politely.

Alec towered over his father. He decided to take the initiative. 'How's the new place?'

His father had just bought a small property out of Rylstone, a few hours away. Alec's question caught Henry off guard.

'Oh … it's good.'

'I'd love to come down and see it.' He paused for effect and smiled at his father. 'If I ever get a minute, that is.'

'You're spending too much time at those camps.'

Alec knew what was coming but refused to bite.

Henry looked away and pointed to the paddocks in front of him. 'You've got a property to run.'

'I'd better get to work then.' He walked into the house and Henry followed him. Leonie was in the kitchen.

She greeted him warmly. 'G'day, Alec.'

He whipped off his hat. 'How are you, Mrs Duroux?' Alec still wasn't comfortable addressing her by her first name.

'Making you some bread,' she replied casually.

Alec smiled. He loved her homemade bread. 'Thank you.'

'Good to have you home.'

'How are the kids?' he asked.

'Down the creek playin' on the rope,' she said.

'Good-oh.'

He turned to his father who was lurking in the shadows. 'You know my father.'

Leonie stopped kneading and bowed her head to Henry. 'Of course I do. We met earlier didn't we, sir?'

Alec smiled. He knew she was nobody's fool. He snuck her a wink while Henry shuffled uncomfortably.

A row of Fowler's Vacola jars were lined up on the wooden kitchen table. Alec inspected them. The larger ones contained preserved plums, peaches and apricots. The smaller ones, an assortment of homemade jams. He picked up a jar and handed it to Leonie.

'Make sure you take some of this jam with you when you finish.'

'Thanks, Alec. The kids love plum jam.'

He headed off to the bedroom to get changed, Henry tapping his shooting stick along behind him. Alec was sure he could hear Mrs Duroux chuckling. Henry closed the bedroom door conspiratorially. Alec knew what was coming and decided to cut his father off at the pass.

'I'm not going to argue with you, Father. If there's a war, I'm going.

And that's that.'

Henry gestured towards the kitchen with his thumb. 'Your mother made that jam.'

'Really? I thought you must have donned the apron for a change.'

'Very funny.'

'I'm sure she won't mind my sharing it with the Duroux kids.'

'The cheek of her, addressing you by your first name,' Henry said, shaking his head.

'I told her to,' Alec countered.

'No wonder she doesn't respect you.'

Alec ignored the barb. 'I'm lucky to have such a good housekeeper.'

Henry grunted and Alec could feel himself tensing up. He knew his father was getting ready to give him a lecture. He couldn't stand his father's pomposity. It was one of the reasons he had escaped to Coonabarabran in the first place. He quickly changed from his town clothes into his work shirt and trousers.

Henry took his handkerchief from his pocket and wiped his face. 'You need to be here. You can't be gallivanting all over the place.'

Alec did his best to keep his cool. 'A training camp in Maitland is hardly gallivanting.' He buttoned up his shirt, leaving the top two buttons undone.

His father persisted, 'The sheep need constant attention.'

Resisting the temptation to snap, Alec meticulously rolled up his sleeves. 'Good-oh,' he replied cheerily.

'Fly,' Henry warned. 'Very bad this time of year.'

Again, Alec kept his powder dry.

Henry pushed the point. 'I had a look. Some of those wethers of yours look badly fly blown.'

Drawing on all his reserves of patience, Alec said, 'You cleaned them up for us, then?' He grinned as his father huffed and puffed and took a pace backwards.

'It's not my place to …' Henry said.

Alec laughed.

'What?' Henry asked.

'As you said. It's not your place,' said Alec. 'Now. If you'll excuse me.'

He stepped around his father, opened the door and headed out to the back room. Henry stood beside him as Alec pulled on his riding boots. He wanted to get away from his father as quickly as possible but, true to form, Henry tried to block him.

'The trustees …'

Alec banged one of his boots on the wood box to dislodge some dried mud. 'What do you want, Father?'

'I want to remind you of your responsibilities.'

'In case you haven't noticed,' Alec said, 'we cleared most of the mortgage with the profits from the wool clip and the wheat crop. I know we borrowed a bit more to finish this …' He waved his arm to show indicate the house and outbuildings. 'But even you would have to admit –'

Henry cut him off. 'As I was saying, the trustees aren't happy about you being away so much.'

Alec fumed. 'Does Mother know you are here?'

'Of course she does.'

'Where is she?'

'At home.'

'I'm sure she could do with some help.'

With that, Alec grabbed his favourite hat off the hat stand, pushed the flyscreen door open and strode out. The door banged against the architrave a few times before settling.

Henry pushed it open and called out after him, 'She asked me to drop that jam over to you.'

Alec marched on, without changing step. 'Thank her for me, won't you?'

By the time Henry had caught up with him, Alec had checked the rain gauge and was on his way to the saddle shed.

'Running a property like this is a full-time proposition,' Henry said.

'You still here?'

His father ignored the comment, but he wasn't letting go. 'This business with the Graziers' Council …'

Alec stopped and turned to face his father. 'So. That's what this is about!' He shook his head and smiled.

'What's so funny?'

'You are, Father.'

'Alec, you don't have time to run around like some kind of white knight.'

Alec looked at his father. He saw a pathetic man who had failed at everything he touched but was supported by a long-suffering, wealthy wife. Deciding not to rub his father's nose in it, Alec instead climbed the steps to the saddle shed and grabbed a bridle off the hook. He turned to find his father blocking his path.

'Excuse me.'

'Yes … well … your call for a Royal Commission didn't get very far, did it?'

Alec lifted his hand and pointed a finger at Henry. 'If I need any advice about running a property, I'll probably ask someone who has made one work. Not someone who bailed out like you did at Grong Grong. Now please, step of my way.'

He pushed past his father, climbed through the fence and headed off to catch Captain Midnight.

'Don't forget to thank Mother for the jam,' he called.

'You'll get your comeuppance one day.'

Alec whistled for his horse. Captain Midnight cantered up as Alec glanced back to see his father fiddling with his waistcoat buttons and adjusting his collar.

Captain Midnight nuzzled Alec's back. As he led him over to the saddle shed, Alec saw his father step in a cow pat and angrily kick it off his brogues.

Some people can't take a trick, he thought.

20.

Nell took the lift up to Carl Thomas's office. She was beside herself. What if he asked for a sample of her work? What if he was too forward with her?

She had deliberated for some time about what to wear. Luckily, she was in the habit of packing as many outfits as she could squeeze into her suitcase, so she had a few options. She wanted to present herself as a woman of the world. A woman with style and confidence. She certainly didn't want to present herself as the daughter of a rural aristocrat. Or as a society belle. It was tricky. She had met men like Carl Thomas before; urbane men with an eye for a pretty face. Nell certainly didn't want to send the wrong signals, and yet she didn't want to be anything but herself.

She settled on a cotton day dress she had bought in Paris that she hoped reflected her carefree spirit and appreciation of contemporary fashion. Bright red, dotted with tiny white flowers, it was off the shoulder with a neckline that narrowly avoided being too revealing. From a slim waist, the full skirt fanned out and sat just below her knees.

Nell had toyed with wearing her favourite silk creation, also from Paris, on the grounds that wearing it made her feel so good, but she decided that could be asking for trouble. The cotton number would do the job.

She checked her lipstick in the vanity mirror she carried in her purse, opened the creaky metal doors of the lift, and walked into the reception area.

A freckle faced young woman looked up from behind the counter and smiled. 'You must be Helen?'

Nell instinctively corrected her, 'Nell.' Then immediately worried she might have sounded too forceful. She wondered how the receptionist knew who she was.

'Mr Thomas is expecting you.'

An oak-panelled door opened and Carl Thomas emerged, smiling and carrying his hat. 'I thought we'd go for lunch.'

Nell was relieved that she'd had the foresight to change her flight.

'That would be lovely,' she said, as if it were nothing out of the ordinary to be invited to lunch by the owner of the flashiest nightclub in Sydney.

'There is a new place down by the Quay. French.'

'Sounds lovely.'

'*Très bon. On y va.*'

'*Merci.*'

Mr Thomas – Nell didn't feel comfortable calling him Carl – pressed the button and opened the lift door. As she stepped in, she suddenly panicked. What if he made a pass at her? She was trapped in a lift with a known womaniser. Nell felt as though her heart was beating so loudly he would be sure to hear to it. She was sweating. Her hands felt clammy. She was breathing heavily. She prayed he didn't notice.

He was the first to speak. 'I've heard a lot about you.'

'Oh?' She was genuinely surprised.

'From Peggy,' he said. 'I saw you the other night too, of course. Did you enjoy yourself?'

'Oh yes!' Nell blurted out, a little too enthusiastically.

'Glad to hear it.'

'I'd been dying to go there. I'd heard so much about it.'

'Really? Who from?'

Was this it? Was this when the lift would stop, he would lean over, rest his arm on the wall and plant an unwanted kiss on her lips? Nell braced herself but thankfully nothing happened. The lift kept going and he kept a respectable distance.

He was looking at her.

She remembered he had asked her a question. 'Well, from Peggy. I mean, from everyone. Carl Thomas's and Princes –'

'Princes?'

'Not Princes per se …'

He seemed offended. Princes was his competition; the other nightclub to be seen at, although it was favoured by an older generation. It was more conservative if just as stylish.

Then he laughed. A big raucous laugh. For a second, she thought he was going to slap her on the back, but he didn't. The lift bounced to a halt. They'd reached the ground floor. Nell breathed what she felt sure was an audible sigh of relief. He politely opened the wire doors, ushered her out into the bright Sydney sunlight and put on his hat while she shielded her eyes.

'It's something I've never got used to,' he said, pointing down Macquarie Street to the Quay. 'The light. It's so damn bright.'

'You should come out to our place.'

She could have kicked herself. He might have thought this was some kind of invitation.

'Yeah. I've heard that. Heard it's pretty damn glary over the mountains. Not much of an explorer myself. Leave the wilderness to the cowboys.'

She laughed uncomfortably while he continued making small talk. 'No, the light struck me the moment I landed in Sydney. It's unique, burns the eyeballs. Lucky I'm a night owl.'

Nell breathed deeply as they walked towards the Quay. She loved the taste of salt in the air when the nor'easter was blowing.

'It's down here.' He pointed down a cobblestone laneway.

She could see a freshly painted sign hanging from a post, *'Le Petit Jardin'*.

'I hear you are a bit of a frog.'

She pretended to be amused.

Inside, the French waiter showed them to the table by the window, reserved for Monsieur Thomas. Once they were seated, the waiter suggested a pastis for their aperitif – apparently all the rage in the south of France, especially in Marseilles.

'I'm game,' Carl said.

'Me too.' Nell smiled at the waiter.

'So …' Carl offered her a cigarette, lit one for himself and slid back his chair. 'I am looking for someone to do a new mural at the Club.'

She nodded, trying to mask her nerves.

'I want something bright and energetic and new. Something *moderne*. I'm told you're a big fan of Toulouse-Lautrec.'

Nell wondered what else Peg had told him about her. 'Well, yes, among others.'

'If I give you some paper, do you think you could sketch something?'

'Now?'

'Why not. You only live once.'

Nell took a deep breath as Carl pulled some sheets of paper and a bundle of coloured pencils out of his bag. He gave her the three-fingered Boy Scout salute. 'Be prepared!'

He's one out of the box, she thought, as he clicked his fingers and the waiter came running.

'We'll have a bottle of Sancerre when you're ready. Oh, forgive me. White okay with you?' he asked Nell.

'Yes, thank you.'

'And we'll have the degustation. Okay with you?'

'Fine.'

A pastis, a bottle of her favourite French wine and a seven-course lunch. Could be worse, she thought, as she imagined she heard the plane to Dubbo flying overhead. Carl pushed the paper towards her. There was a price.

She threw down the pastis, metaphorically rolled up her sleeves, and looked at the sheet of paper.

She had no idea what she was going to draw. But she had been confronted with hundreds of blank canvases in René's drawing classes. She had learnt to trust her instincts, although it was still scary.

She started drawing. The outline of a figure. Her imagination was racing, taking her to shapes she hadn't dreamt she'd draw. She scrunched up the first sheet of paper, then started on another. Before long, the floor was littered with scrunched up paper. Her host was more than happy to keep the food and wine coming as she fell deeper and deeper into her work.

Nell picked at the food, sipped on the wine, puffed on cigarette after cigarette and drew till her hand ached. She was trying to capture something elusive. A market scene. A woman, balancing a big bowl of brightly coloured fruit on her shoulder, her blouse revealing strong arms and a fulsome bosom, a bunch of stallholders behind her.

'This … this is lots of colours … red, yellow, green …' She pushed the sketch towards him, pointing out the detail.

'Fruit?' he asked.

'Yes. Fruit. Brightly coloured …'

'I can see that.' He was smiling.

'It's only a sketch.'

As she reached forward to retrieve it, he put his hand on hers. 'It's fantastic …'

Nell froze.

'I haven't finished …' she said, removing her hand.

He slapped his thighs. 'No, no. Of course not. But I can see enough … life … in this. That fish. In the basket. It looks alive. As though it is wriggling …'

Nell wondered if he had drunk too much wine or if this flattery was a kind of foreplay. She was hardly conscious that she had drawn a fish amongst the fruit. Where did that come from? Wherever it came from, the fish had done the trick and fired his imagination.

'This is bursting with … potential and … life. I love it!' He had tears in his eyes. Nell didn't know where to look.

'I love people who are prepared to go out on a limb. People who rise to a challenge. I thought you'd do a couple of sketches … but you … you're unstoppable. You're an artist.'

He raised his glass to her. She smiled bashfully and returned his toast.

An artist? Someone in Australia has called her an artist. Nell could have jumped for joy. Then she realised her hand was nearly numb. She shook some life into it while he called the waiter.

'I'm afraid I have to go back to work,' he said, before shelling out some pound notes for the bill. 'Keep the change, and sorry about the …' he said to the waiter, gesturing towards the floor where the reject sketches had dropped.

'*Ah, Monsieur, c'était un plaisir. Merci beaucoup.*'

Carl Thomas stood and Nell surveyed the scene. The table was clear, apart from the cheese, a couple of glasses and the empty bottle of wine. She was amazed that the waiter had managed to clean it all up without disturbing her.

'So, Miss Hope. Will you do a mural for me?'

Would she? Nell's heart nearly jumped into her mouth.

'Yes … of course … I'd love to,' she said, standing up.

'Drop by in the morning and we'll sort out the details.'

Didn't he know she lived hundreds of miles away? Her mind was now on overdrive. What about her father? What about the sheep? What about …

'You will be paid, of course.'

He shook her hand, took his hat and coat from the waiter and disappeared up the laneway.

Nell sat back down, sipped the last of her wine and began to hatch a plan that would let her stay in Sydney.

21.

The announcement of the outbreak of war shocked no one. Least of all Alec Murray.

The night Neville Chamberlain's fateful words came over the wireless, they were in the middle of shearing.

'This morning, the British Ambassador in Berlin handed the German government a final note, stating that unless we heard from them by eleven o'clock, that they were prepared, at once, to withdraw their troops from Poland, a state of war would exist between us. I have to tell you now that no such undertaking has been received, and that consequently, this country is at war with Germany.'

Alec's parents and his sister, Claire, were staying over to help out with the shearing. The yards were full, ready for an early start. The wool clip was looking good. The quality and quantity suggested a record year. Even the wool classer was impressed. Alec had every reason to be pleased with himself. He had weathered the various storms that lash people on the land and was now reaping the rewards of his labour.

As the BBC broadcast began, Alec carefully placed his bookmark into the *Don Quixote* lying in his lap and put the book on the side table. This was what he had been waiting for. There was a job to be done and he was ready to do it. He looked up and saw his parents standing in the doorway. Even though he was grateful that his mother, Daphne, had persuaded his father to be on standby to lend a hand should he be whisked away, he was briefly surprised by their presence. He hadn't imagined sharing this moment with anybody.

'You heard?' he asked.

Daphne nodded. He could see the fear in her eyes. She had endured the loss of one son and Alec knew she was terrified she was going to lose another. He didn't want to see his mother upset. He stood up, enveloped her in his arms and hugged her tightly. She sobbed into his shoulder.

After a few seconds he released her and smiled. 'Thank you for coming to stay.'

It was all he could do to contain his own emotions, but he knew he had to. There was no place for emotion in a soldier, let alone an officer.

'I'd better pack,' he said, as gently as possible.

Daphne buried her head in her hands. Alec turned to his father who also appeared to be upset.

'Can you keep an eye on things, Father? Bernie's going to be flat out with the shearers. If you could …'

'Step into the breach?' Henry said.

'Yes …' Alec swallowed. This was harder than he expected.

'That's why we're here.'

Alec offered his hand and they shook firmly. 'I'm glad you could come.'

He turned to pick up his book and was about to leave the room when Henry grabbed his arm. 'Don't rush …' he said, tears welling.

Alec was shocked. He had never seen his father express any emotion except anger. He gripped Henry's shoulder. 'I have to go, Father.'

'I know.'

'Look after Mother.'

Alec managed a weak smile and headed off down the hall to his bedroom. As much as he appreciated his parents' concern, he knew he had to gather his thoughts and get on with it.

He started methodically packing his trunk, trying to ignore the sound of doors opening and closing and his father's deliberate pacing up and down on the verandah. He sighed when he heard a knock on the door. The last thing he needed was an interruption.

'Come in,' he said, as pleasantly as he could manage.

Alec's heart nearly broke as his little sister, Claire, walked in. A lump formed in his throat as she looked up at him sadly. Tall and wiry like her mother, Claire was in her final year at boarding school and was home for the holidays.

'I can't sleep …'

Alec felt a deep attachment to Claire after their brother, Toby, had died of TB when he was only fourteen. Toby was a few years younger than Alec and his death had devastated the family. Claire was the youngest. Alec had taken her under his wing and taught her things like how to ride astride instead of side saddle. Although they hadn't seen much of each other since he had moved to Toongowan, they had kept in touch through letters. He felt guilty that he had abandoned her, but he knew he had to make his own way in life.

Claire plonked herself on the bed and fiddled distractedly with the tassels on the bed cover.

'You don't mind if I keep packing?'

She shrugged. He folded a shirt carefully and placed it in his trunk. Then he paused, sat down next to her and gave her a reassuring pat on the back.

'I'm going to be all right. I'll be home soon. You'll hardly notice I've gone.'

'I had a look on the atlas. It is a long way away.'

'It is.'

Afraid that he would show his feelings, he returned to his packing.

'I'm going to miss you,' she said quietly.

Alec couldn't look at her. Instead, he kept packing and avoided her gaze.

'I *am.*'

He felt her looking straight at him.

'We're all going to miss you.'

'Even Father?' he joked, hoping to lighten the mood.

'Especially Father. Who's he going to pick on if you aren't around?'

They both laughed. As much as Alec was devoted to Claire, he secretly wished she would leave him to pack in peace.

'I could hear Mother sobbing. I've never heard her crying before.'

'Look after her,' he said, looking at her directly.

'Me?'

'You. This war will mean you'll have to grow up quickly, I'm afraid. We all have to do our bit.'

She looked down at his packing. 'Are you frightened?'

'No time to be frightened,' he said.

'Why do you have to go?' This was more of a plea than question.

Claire flopped back on the bed and stared up at the ceiling. 'Do you ever think about Toby?'

Alec picked up a pair of socks, rolled them into a ball and tossed them into his trunk.

'Do you?'

'Sometimes.'

'I think about him a lot. He'd be going too if …' She let this hang as he closed the trunk. 'You will write?'

'Of course I will. Now, I'll have to get some sleep if I'm to get the early train.'

'Wake me up before you go?'

'Sure.'

'Promise?'

'Promise.'

She climbed off the bed and opened her arms. He hugged her tightly and lifted her off the ground. He was deeply touched that everyone was showing him so much love. It made him feel as though the family was finally united.

The next day Alec was up before the sun to hand Bernie the reins. 'Don't take too much notice of my father. His bark is worse than his bite.'

Bernie managed a wry smile. 'I won't.'

'I've left a list of instructions on my desk. My father has the purse strings. Don't be afraid to ask if you need money for anything.'

Bernie nodded. They shook hands.

A couple of hours later, his father drove him to the station.

He was finally going to war.

22.

Nell was grateful that her father had given her a few weeks off to paint Carl Thomas's mural.

'Now war's been declared I'm going to need you more than ever,' Fred had told her. 'So, get this business out of your system and then you can come back ready for work.'

Nell was sure she was never going to get it 'out of her system' but she was relieved nonetheless.

When Peg burst into Carl Thomas's, Nell was on top of a ladder with a cigarette in one hand and a paint brush in the other. She was gradually bringing the outline she had sketched to life with an array of colours.

'I'm going to enlist.'

Nell froze.

'Seeing as we don't have a Women's Army, I'm going to England to join theirs.' Peg waved a ticket at her. 'I'm not going to sit around an accountant's office waiting to fulfil my destiny as wife and mother.'

Nell dabbed some brown paint on her brush and added a few strokes to the stallholder's basket as she absorbed this startling news.

'When are you going?' she asked.

'In a few weeks.' Her friend sounded excited.

Nell stuck the brush between her teeth and was about to climb down when Peg stopped her. 'Keep going. I like watching you work.'

'Thanks. I'm on a deadline,' Nell said, returning to the mural.

Peg laughed. 'I bet you are.'

'At least Father let me do it.'

'Could he have stopped you?'

Nell dabbed at the basket she was painting and examined it closely. 'What do you think?'

Peg took a moment before replying. 'It's so …'

'Yes?'

'Is that a fish amongst the fruit?'

'Too much?' said Nell.

'Emerging from it …' Clapping her hands together, Peg shrieked. 'It's outrageous! I love it!'

With that, Peg sat down at a table, removed her hat and gloves, kicked off her shoes, lit a cigarette and watched.

Under Peg's gaze, the mural began to take shape. Wine gushed from a jug poured by a voluptuous woman into a Falstaffian character's goblet.

'It's so … voluptuous,' came the comment from below.

Nell laughed. 'I'll take that as a compliment.'

'It is.'

Nell didn't feel any pressure to stop. Balancing on the tips of her toes, she carefully applied delicate brush strokes to the wine. Fully aware that she was being watched, she played up to Peg by lifting one leg and balancing precariously on the other while she reached for the top of the jug. Finally, she cast an eye over her creation and climbed down.

Peg stood and hugged her. 'I'm thrilled to see you so happy!'

Nell laughed. 'This is what I love doing, Peg. This is all I want to do.'

'I can tell.'

Nell gave Peg a kiss. 'I love you.'

'You too.'

Peg picked up her hat and gloves. 'Will I see you later for a drink?'

Nell hesitated as Peg pulled on her gloves.

'I'll be at The Women's Club, meeting up with another woman who's going to enlist. Drop in if you can. If not …' She gave Nell a wave and departed.

On her own, there wasn't a sound to be heard in the Club. Nell shifted the ladder and climbed up to start on the next section, doing her best to push the thought of returning to the farm out of her mind.

23.

Instead of leading to out-and-out warfare, the eight-month period after Germany's invasion of Poland became known as the Phoney War; characterised by military inactivity from both sides. Alec and the other 70,000 Australians who had enlisted marched around and around in circles in training camps across the country while they awaited orders to ship out.

Alec was frustrated that he had to spent countless hours in simulated battle conditions instead of fighting the Nazis. He hadn't left Toongowan to pretend he was fighting. He wanted to get stuck in.

On the strength of his service in the militia, he retained the rank of Acting Lieutenant in the reformed 16th Australian Infantry Brigade. He trained his men to drag artillery and ammunition across West Maitland's lucerne paddocks in the dead of night. But the only enemies they confronted were bemused herds of Friesian milking cows, whose slumber they disturbed.

Alec was grateful that he had been allocated digs with Stephen again. Their tent was an oasis of free thought in a world of regimentation. It was the one place Alec could let his guard down. He needed to be decisive when he was in charge and knew he would lose the respect of his men if he was seen to prevaricate, while when he was with Stephen he could debate, ponder and change his mind.

After another night of exercises, Alec was resting on his stretcher when Stephen pushed the tent flap back and tossed a book onto his chest. 'This came in the mail.'

Alec looked at the brown paper wrapping.

'Open it,' Stephen said. 'It might take the blinkers off.'

They had been arguing about political philosophy. Alec had told him about the meat processors' manipulation of the Meat Workers' strikes. Stephen hadn't been surprised.

Alec opened the parcel. '*The Communist Manifesto*!'

Stephen kicked off his boots and lay down on his stretcher. 'I'm buggered.'

Reading *The Communist Manifesto* was a revelation to Alec. He had been brought up to believe that communists were the devil incarnate and a threat to the whole fabric of society.

Stephen was broadening his perspective. He argued that the Christian principle of 'love thy neighbour' was better served by the communist ideal of 'equality for all' than by capitalism.

'Capitalists serve themselves. Communists serve the community,' Stephen said.

After his foray into the meat processors' imbroglio, it was an argument that Alec found hard to disagree with. Establishing Toongowan had allowed him to see the people he worked with in a different way and to appreciate Stephen's arguments more profoundly. He loved to be challenged intellectually and Stephen was an excellent sparring partner.

24.

Nell slipped into a new satin dress, dabbed on some red lipstick and waited for Peg to arrive. They planned to hit the town. It was the last night of 1939 and Nell was looking forward to celebrating the end of a tumultuous year. She had joined her parents on their annual pilgrimage to Sydney to watch the cricket and go shopping, and was intent on making the most of the escape.

When Nell and Peg walked into Carl Thomas's, Klaus Heinrich von Guttenberg, the tall, sad-faced Austrian doorman, greeted her like a celebrity. Inside, the atmosphere was electric. The first troops to be sent overseas had received their vaccinations and been granted pre-embarkation leave. They would be departing for war any day. The champagne and beer flowed freely. Cocaine was plentiful. Fights broke out over nothing and were settled as quickly as they had begun. The atmosphere was sexually charged. Everyone was living as though there was no tomorrow.

Nell was excited to discover that her star hadn't waned since the successful unveiling of her mural and that Carl Thomas still embraced her as his latest discovery. She was quickly back in the groove, chatting with old school friends and basking in the limelight as though she had never been away. Peg had told Nell that her fling with Carl Thomas had ended amicably and she was on the lookout for a younger buck.

Nell was explaining the genesis of her mural to a stockbroker and his mistress when Alec walked in with his old mates, Johnny Buchanan,

Brian Harkness and Jim Wallace. Dressed in their officer's uniforms, they looked a million dollars. Especially Alec. The sight of him made her heart skip a beat. She watched as they handed over their caps and made their way to the bar. She prayed that Alec would look in her direction. She excused herself and made her way back to sit with Peg at her table just as Alec and his friends joined the group.

'Here she is!' Jim Wallace gave her a bear hug that nearly squeezed the wind out of her. 'How's our *artiste*?'

She punched him playfully on the chest and he grabbed her well-muscled arms. 'Someone's been doing some riding.'

'I'd rather have been painting,' Nell replied.

'You remember Alec?' Jim said.

She offered her hand. 'Nice to see you again.'

'And you.' She thought he looked slightly uncomfortable, so she lingered only a moment before releasing her grip and greeting Johnny Buchanan.

'Is Jock …'

There was an awkward pause.

'Afraid Jock's in a bit of strife,' Johnny explained. 'Got himself into a blue in Maitland. He was AWOL so it didn't go down to well with the brass.'

Brian chimed in, 'Lucky not to lose his stripes.'

'He's grounded, poor bugger. On duty all weekend,' said Jim.

'Of all weekends.' Johnny shook his head.

Nell didn't know what the subtext of this was. She looked at Alec, who managed a brief smile.

'We'll be shipped out any minute,' Jim said. 'The 2nd First Field Regiment will be the first Australian regiment to see action.'

It took Nell a few seconds to digest this. 'So … Mother may not see Jock before he goes?'

The uncomfortable silence lasted until Johnny said, 'Let's have a dance,' and swept Peg off towards the music. Jim teamed up with Peg's sister, June, while Brian and another of Nell's friends, Mary Waddell, joined the revellers on the dance floor.

Nell was left with Alec. He seemed a bit hesitant. Nell rescued him from the prospect of another turn on the dance floor.

'Let's have a seat,' she suggested.

Alec pulled a chair back for her and sat down stiffly at her side. He ran his finger around his collar.

'Are you all right?' she asked.

'Yes, sorry. New uniform. Collar's a bit tight.'

'You could loosen it.'

'I could, but I don't think it would be very good form.' He smiled. A warm, generous smile. She nearly melted.

She bent forward and placed her hand on his. 'Thanks for your letter.'

'I hope it wasn't too …'

'It was lovely.'

A hint of a blush appeared on his cheeks. She squeezed his hand. 'It kept me going.'

'Really?' he seemed surprised.

'Well, the life of a jillaroo isn't exactly all that … stimulating. There isn't a lot of inspiration to be found riding around for hours on end staring at sheep bums.'

He laughed. She remembered that he was a grazier himself and was quick to cover her tracks. 'Not unless you're the manager or … owner. I spend my time following orders. Doing as I'm told.'

Afraid that she was putting her foot in her mouth, Nell changed the subject. 'Would you like to see my mural?'

'I'd love to.'

She grabbed his hand and lead him around the dance floor towards her work. Catching sight of Peg nestling into Johnny Buchanan's shoulder in the slow waltz, she pointed in their direction. 'They make a good pair.'

'They do,' he said.

As if on cue, Johnny kissed Peg. She responded with equal enthusiasm. The thought crossed Nell's mind that she wouldn't mind Alec kissing her that way.

Alec stood with his hands on hips his gazing at the mural for what Nell felt was an eternity. Finally, he spoke.

'This is quite extraordinary. When you wrote to me in your letter about painting a mural, I had no idea it would be on this scale. It's huge.'

He took a few steps backwards. 'It's so bold. The colours are so … vital.' He turned to her. 'Is that the word?'

'That'll do.' She laughed.

He really did appear to admire it.

'You've captured the energy of the marketplace. Their faces are so alive. And it's quite dramatic too. There's … drama … action … in the whole scene.'

Nell wondered if he was just being polite.

He took a few paces forward and pointed. 'I really like the way it flows. The whole … thing … not just the jug of wine. The way her skirt is billowing. I'm not just saying it. I mean it. When you first look it seems like a pretty jolly scene but on closer inspection it reveals … what do you call them?'

'Layers?'

'That's right. Layers. Like peeling an orange. You know what I mean?'

She did and she was secretly delighted that he had recognised it.

'You can almost smell the sea … and the fish. Seriously. I mean it. There is more to this than first meets the eye.' He shifted his gaze to Nell. 'Like the artist who painted it.'

Alec lent forward, wrapped her in his arms and kissed her on the lips. She raised herself onto the tips of her toes, threw her arms around his neck, and pressed her lips onto his. Their kiss was long and deep. When they finally parted, she could feel her heart beating at a million miles an hour. They held hands for a few moments and melted into each other's eyes before they kissed again.

'We'd better get this war sorted out and you back to Paris.'

She slapped his arm playfully. 'We'd better get you a drink before I start thinking you're laying it on too thick!' She planted a kiss on his cheek.

They made their way back to the table, where Nell sat Alec down, climbed onto his lap, and poured them each a glass of champagne. They entwined forearms, holding their glasses high, then, staring into each other's eyes, shared a toast. There was no one else in the room.

'Hello you two!' Clutching Johnny's hand, Peg was grinning at them. 'Having fun?'

Nell smiled. Alec looked a little sheepish.

'We're going,' Peg announced.

'Oh?' Nell said. 'I guess, while the night is still young …'

Peg grinned, grabbed her bag and dragged a compliant Johnny off into the night.

As if taking her cue, Nell whispered into Alec's ear. 'I know somewhere we can go …'

His eyes widened.

'Unless you want to dance,' she teased.

Before long she was sneaking him up the fire escape and into a room at The Women's Club, which she had convinced her mother to book for her on the pretence that she didn't want to disturb her parents at an ungodly hour.

They spent Alec's last night on leave in each other's arms, seemingly without a care in the world. They made love, talked, drank whisky until, as the sun was just peeking through the blinds, the outside world imposed itself on them.

Alec sprang out of bed. 'God. I'd better get going. I'll be late …'

He let the words trickle away as he pulled on his trousers. 'I'm supposed to set a good example.'

She watched him. 'Shower?'

'I haven't time. We're off to Ingleburn for final preparations. Train leaves at …' He looked at his watch. '0630. Crikey.'

She pulled the sheet over her and admired his lean, taut body as he hurriedly dressed. He looked in the mirror. His hair was, naturally, a mess.

'Use my brush.'

'I'm really sorry to have to run.'

'If there wasn't a war on, I mightn't believe you. Here …' She held her arms out to him.

'Happy New Year!' Had he forgotten? 'You've got time for one last kiss.'

He glanced at his watch then took her in his arms. 'I wish I could stay …'

She laughed. 'I bet you say that to all the girls.'

'I do wish I could stay. I promise.'

He kissed her deeply, buttoned his coat and straightened himself up in the mirror.

'Will you write?' Nell asked.

'Of course I will.'

With a quick kiss he was out the door.

Nell lay back, hugged his pillow and wondered when, or if, she would see him again.

25.

On 11 January 1940, thousands lined the streets of Sydney to salute the men of the 6th Australian Infantry Division as they marched towards an unknown future.

Their shoulders were square, their backs ram-rod straight, their heads held high. Every man was marching in time. Not a button undone. Not a boot unpolished. 70,000 pairs of them clattering down George Street.

The colours of the Union Jack were everywhere. Red, white and blue streamers rained down from office windows. Red, white and blue balloons festooned streetlights and hoardings and floated into the sky.

The crowds clapped enthusiastically as some fought to hold back tears, swallowing their emotions. Old soldiers, chests pinned with medals, nodded their approval, silently passing on their batons. Children, oblivious to all but the pomp and circumstance, waved Union Jacks. Some young women swooned.

'Don't they look handsome?' said Nell.

'I love a parade!' Peg screamed, above the din.

'Who doesn't love a parade?'

They had stationed themselves near the Quay end of George Street. As the 2nd First Field Regiment approached, they waved their flags, hoping to attract their champions' attention. Johnny Buchanan marched proudly at the head of his Company, having received his commission at the same time as Alec. He allowed himself a sideways glance when he heard Peg's screams of delight rising above the general hubbub.

'Johnny! Johnny!' Peg was jumping up and down like a fan at the football. 'Isn't he gorgeous?' she said.

Nell smiled. Johnny managed a wink as he marched past.

'Isn't it exciting?'

Peg could hardly contain herself. She waved while Nell craned her neck, trying to catch a glimpse of Alec.

'I wonder if they're nervous?'

'They don't look it.'

'There he is!'

Alec was marching at the front of the 2nd First Field Regiment. He had recently been promoted to Captain. Nell hoped for a sideways glance, but his eyes were fixed ahead and his jaw was clenched. He was a man on a mission.

'Alec! Alec!' Peg called, but Alec didn't blink.

Nell swallowed and held her tightened fists to her mouth. She watched him disappear around the corner towards the awaiting troop ship at Circular Quay. Peg and Nell hugged, and then Nell lifted a little girl who was standing beside her onto her shoulders, so she could wave her daddy goodbye. She shared secret smiles with other women who were also cheering on their men and ruffled the hair of excited children who had no idea what it all meant.

Then they were gone.

He was gone.

George Street was empty except for a few balloons that bounced around sadly. Men with brooms started sweeping up the streamers. Before long it was opened up again to trams and cars and the odd horse-drawn cart, and the city went back to business as usual.

Peg suggested a drink.

'Why not?'

The two women walked, arm in arm, silently up Bent Street towards The Hotel Metropole. The doorman welcomed them and they walked into the bar with its mosaic floors and stained-glass windows. As they sat waiting for their drinks, Nell's eyes drifted up to one of the windows, its colours brilliant in the sunlight. In the centre, a knighted warrior on a steed brandished his sword.

The waiter arrived with two whiskeys.

'To the men,' they cheered in unison.

'And us,' said Peg.

'Yes. Us.'

Hours later, in the privacy of her room at The Women's Club, Nell lay on her bed feeling empty. She had passed on a farewell drink at Carl Thomas's. Even Peg had decided on a rare night in. Nell stared at the flowery wallpaper. She was booked on the early train home and would soon be swapping her dress for moleskins.

26.

As he watched HMAS *Orford* slice through the deep blue waters of the Pacific Ocean, Alec thought about Nell. He'd barely had a moment to himself since their night together. The hypnotic sound of the water invited quiet reflection.

He wondered if he would see her again. While he projected confidence and certainty, if he were honest with himself, he would admit to being apprehensive about what lay ahead. Alec had watched Whippet when they worked together and saw just how damaged he was; Whippet's nerves were shot, he jumped at the slightest sound, he didn't need to talk about his experiences for Alec to see that he had suffered terribly.

Nell had changed the way Alec viewed the world. He pulled out some paper and a pen and wrote to her, telling her how much he had enjoyed being with her. He knew he was in love. It made him feel happier than he had ever been. Nell lit a fire in him that he didn't want to extinguish. But what if he didn't come back? What if she found someone else? She was beautiful and popular. Would he disappear from her memory? Alec was feeling impatient: impatient to get this over and done with and get home. Trouble was, they had only just embarked; who knew how long they would be gone? Who knew if the letter he was writing would ever reach her?

Distracted by these thoughts, he tapped his pipe on the railing, sending sparks floating into the night air.

'Shit!'

He hurriedly cupped his hand over the pipe and looked around to check if anyone had seen the sparks. Fortunately the other officers on deck were too preoccupied with their own thoughts to notice. He knew he had to be more careful. Sparks at night could be seen miles away. By anyone. He needed to set an example.

The excitement of finally going to war soon wore off and, after about a week, was followed by the monotony of sameness. A stopover in Fremantle gave the men a chance to let off steam and Alec the chance to sit in Kings Park reading Karl Marx.

Back on board, they sailed towards the Equator and eventually 'crossed the line'. Alec picked his way among the sleeping bodies on deck. He came across his batman, Jack Fulton, with a blanket wrapped around his shoulders, leaning against the bulkhead. Jack had told him that he'd enlisted to escape a life of drudgery and to have some fun on the other side of the world. Alec didn't have the heart to give him the news that it mightn't be that much fun. As a young man, Alec had experienced similar dreams of adventures across the seas.

'You all right, Jack?' Alec walked over to him.

'Yes, sir. Good as gold.'

'What are you doing up here? There's plenty of room in our cabin.'

'Too bloody hot for me, sir. Sweatin' like a pig. Reminds me of the colliery.'

'Mind if I join you for a minute?' Alec said.

'Be my guest, sir.' He began to wipe a space clean for Alec to sit on.

'It's okay, I've sat in the dirt before.' Alec sat next to him and stared up at the Northern Hemisphere constellations. He pointed. 'I think that's the Polar Star and over there, that's the Great Bear.'

'What happened to the Southern Cross?'

'We've left her behind, Jack.'

They sat together quietly marvelling at the sky as the darkened transport ship slid silently through the inky black waters.

'You worked in a colliery?' Alec asked.

'Before I enlisted. The one at Balmain. Me dad used ta work there too. He couldn't work no more 'cause of his breathin', so Mum sent me to work.'

'How old were you?'

'Fourteen. They was drilling for methane by the time I was there,' Jack said.

'Gas?' Alec was surprised.

'Yeah. Stank like blazes, I'm telling you. There was leaks everywhere. They had to keep drillin' and drillin' to find any. We ended up 2,600 feet under Sydney Harbour. Wasn't much fun.'

Jack was a master of understatement.

'I bet it wasn't.' Alec could barely conceive of it.

With the breeze blowing gently in his hair, Jack warmed to his story and continued. ''Course it was a coal mine before that. When Dad worked there. They used ta be sent down the shaft in an old rust bucket of a cage. Dad called it a "living tomb". He reckoned you could hardly breathe down there, what with the dust from the coal and the horse shit from the pit ponies that dragged the coal buckets to the shaft. It was bad enough when I was workin' there, but we only had gas to deal with. Not coal dust. Tell you what though, it was hot as hell and pitch black. You couldn't see more than a few feet in front of you. You had to keep your wits about you down there. Dad told me about the day five blokes were tossed out of the bucket when it ran into a snag in the shift wall. They fell four-hundred feet to the bottom. The bosses coulda made it safer but that woulda eaten into their profits, wouldn't it?'

Alec had never heard anything like it, and it shamed him that he had never bothered to inquire.

'What was the pay like?'

Jack's look made Alec feel like an idiot. 'Sorry, Jack. Silly question.'

'That's all right, sir. Blokes like you don't know much about the real world, do you?'

'You're right, Jack. We don't.' He didn't know anything about Jack's world. Alec swore to himself that, if he did nothing else in life, he would do everything in his power to improve the lot of people like Jack.

Jack faced him squarely. 'I tell you one thing. I won't miss the coal mines, sir. And I won't miss me mum nagging me to clean up all the bloody time.'

Later that night, lying in his bunk, Alec thought about his experience of the Depression. Henry had sold the farm at Grong Grong to buy a row of terraces in Redfern and lost the lot when he couldn't keep up the repayments after the Crash. Alec witnessed it from behind the fence of his privileged boarding school. It hardly matched what Jack went through.

*

When the convoy pulled into Colombo for fresh supplies, the men stretched their legs and blew their wages. The brothels and bars of the port did a roaring trade as the men got the dirty water off their chests and poured anything they could lay their hands on down their throats.

While many of his fellow officers sought refuge in lavish hotels in the hinterland, Alec explored the backstreets of the Ceylonese capital in a rickshaw. It was a very different Asia from the version he had read about in Kipling's *Kim.*

A young woman relieved herself in a gutter, seemingly unfazed by his intrusion. People washed themselves in water that he wouldn't give to his pigs. Three women in brightly coloured sarongs and loose-fitting blouses sat cross-legged, variously weaving a mat, mixing spices and skinning a chicken. They looked up at him and giggled. Alec turned and waved as the rickshaw driver pressed on. Their eyes briefly followed him before they returned to work.

He was shocked by the sight of an old man, wrapped in his sarong, sleeping soundly on a pile of rubbish. It was an image that he carried in his mind as they headed towards Palestine.

27.

When Fred Hope instructed Nell to go to pick up a man from Trangie train station, she was annoyed. She had been looking forward to washing Ginger and spending the rest of the day reading. The last thing she felt like doing was engaging in small talk with some brainy, scientist type from Canberra.

'He's coming to study worms.'

Nell stared at her father. A worm man?

'It's a new biological thing. We might be able to develop a new drench to keep the fly away.' Fred kicked at a tuft of the newly sown phalaris. 'CSIR are sending him.'

'How will I know it's him?'

She knew the answer. How many scientist types would be getting off the mail train at Trangie?

'I think you'll manage.' He pulled his hat over his forehead and walked away before casually calling over his shoulder, 'You can take the Pontiac.'

This changed Nell's mood. The Pontiac. Did she hear correctly?

She sprinted towards the homestead and swept past a startled Elaine as she ran into the bathroom, grabbed a towel and tore off her work clothes. She lathered herself with soap and splashed the dirty, brown, bore water all over her.

There was a knock at the door.

'Everything all right?'

'Yes, Mum. Couldn't be better!'

Before long, Nell was zooming along the dirt road towards Trangie in her father's brand-new, shiny black, four-door Pontiac: one arm draped on the steering wheel, the other resting on the wound down window. Exulting in the car's power, she gunned it around a hairpin bend before careering out of control, up a bank towards potential disaster. In the nick of time, she remembered her father telling her about keeping her foot off the brake, and somehow, guided the car back down the bank and on to the road.

She breathed heavily. That was fun, she thought. More fun than mustering sheep, that's for sure.

As she roared along the dirt road, stirring up a cloud of red dust, her mind turned to Alec. It had been nearly a month since he'd left. He hadn't written. She wondered if he had forgotten about their night together or, worse, it hadn't meant as much to him as it had to her.

Trangie station, neatly maintained with manicured garden beds, sat proudly on the outskirts of town. When Nell drove the Pontiac into the carpark, the few punters waiting for the mail train sat up and took notice. Most had probably only seen a car like it in Humphrey Bogart movies. The stationmaster, who she knew was a car enthusiast from way back, peered out the window of his office with open-mouthed admiration.

Having made the most of the opportunity to ditch her moleskins, Nell touched up her lipstick and adjusted her hair while she waited for the train. She poked her sunglasses back on to the ridge of her nose and climbed out of the car. She felt every inch the movie star as the punters stared. Nell gave them a wave as she headed towards the platform.

When she walked past a grizzled old farmer and his wiry wife, Nell overheard the farmer say, 'Fred Hope's lass.'

'She's grown up,' his wife replied.

He rubbed his stubbled chin in approval. 'Scrubs up all right, doesn't she?'

The wife spoke in stage whisper that made Nell smile. 'She looks like Vivien Leigh.'

His response nearly had her in fits. 'She's a better sort than Vivien Leigh.'

Nell peered down the tracks for signs of the train. They seemed to stretch forever. She leaned against a post, flicked open her silver cigarette case, lit up a cigarette and blew a puff of smoke into the still air. There was nothing to do but wait. One thing was clear, no one was in a hurry out there.

At last, the train's whistle announced its arrival. Steam was pouring out of its funnel as it headed straight towards her. A couple of lovers hugged on the platform; the young man looking embarrassed at this public display of affection, the young lady desperately trying to hold back tears. Nell wondered if he was going off to war. An old bloke struggled to his feet and, with the aid of a walking stick, shuffled towards the edge of the platform. She watched him, wondering what his story was. An Aboriginal family, dressed to the nines, gathered their ports and waited patiently for the train's arrival. Nell caught the mother's eye and smiled. The mother looked away shyly. Nell thought she couldn't be much older than she was and already had a brood clinging to her skirts. One of the little 'uns was giggling, playing peek-a-boo with Nell from behind her mother. The two young women shared a moment before returning their attention to the approaching train. Nell couldn't help but think about what different paths they trod.

The stationmaster flagged down the train. It was his big moment and he made the most of it. The engine pulled in, sending the galahs that had been scavenging in the nearby silos flapping into the sky.

An elderly woman hobbled off the train and was greeted warmly by the old fella. There was no need for words. Their gestures spoke of a lifetime of shared love and deeds.

The others climbed aboard as Nell searched up and down for her scientist. A carriage door flung open and a handsome young man in a jaunty, deep crimson fedora alighted. Nell looked in the other direction. Nothing. She walked anxiously up and down the station peering into the carriages. There was no sign of a boffin. The stationmaster waved his flag, the driver blew the whistle and the train disappeared down the line.

It was all over in a couple of minutes. The stationmaster packed up his flag and whistle and returned to his office. The old couple pottered off arm in arm. Nell and the young man were left at either end of the station. They had no choice but to meet halfway.

'Excuse me, you didn't happen to run into a scientist on the train, did you? I'm worried he might have got off at Nevertire,' she asked the man in the fedora.

'You're …?' He raised an eyebrow.

'I'm picking him up.' Nell optimistically searched the empty platform.

'Lucky him.'

'It's not funny. My father will skin me alive if I go home without him.'

'Looks like you struck gold then,' he said, doffing his hat.

She ran her eyes over the man again. He was dressed in a snug-fitting, double-breasted suit with a dark red tie. His shoes were polished and he was carrying a smart, monogrammed leather suitcase.

'You're not …'

'Lance Crawford.'

He stuck out his hand. She shook it. His grip was firm, his eyes direct. For the first time in a while, she was thrown.

'I'm Nell … Helen … Frederick Hope's daughter.'

'Oh.' He appeared to be impressed.

She bent down to pick up his suitcase.

He took it from her. 'I can manage.'

'I don't know why I did that,' she said.

'You're obviously well brought up.'

What a smart-arse, she thought. Well, at least he was a handsome smart-arse.

Nell led the way to the car. Out of the corner of her eye, she saw him do a double take when it became clear that the Pontiac shimmering in the sun was hers. Feigning nonchalance, she clicked open the boot, took his suitcase from him, tossed it in and slammed the boot shut. She jumped in while he remained rooted to the spot. Clearly, this was not what he was expecting in Trangie. Nell stretched over and pushed the passenger door open.

'You coming?'

'Yes … sure … sorry.'

He climbed in and they drove back to Braemar chatting about the country and the weather and the roads and the car.

Nell was curious to learn more about her father's scientist.

28.

Nell looked up from bottle feeding an orphan lamb and saw her mother's
Fiat 500 tearing down the driveway.

'Helen! A letter! A letter for you! It's from … overseas …'

It had to be Alec … or Peg?

As soon as her mother got out of the car, Nell grabbed the letter out of
her hand and ran inside. She sprinted down the hallway into her room,
slammed the door behind her and leant against it. Heart in mouth, she
turned it over and read:

Nx 149 Lieut Alec Murray
2/1 Field Reg RAA
AIF Abroad

Shaking with anticipation, she ripped it open.

Palestine
28 Feb, 1940

Dear Nell,

I hope my letter finds you well. I haven't heard from you but
the mail is notoriously unreliable. Maybe you didn't get my

earlier letters? We've been here a while. I'm sorry I haven't written sooner but I have hardly had a moment to scratch myself.

We embarked at a place called El Qantara (pronounced 'Kwantara') after sailing down the Suez Canal. It is a relief to be here at last.

On the way here I saw signs to Damascus and Jerusalem. I couldn't believe my eyes. Imagine actually being so close to such incredible history. They are just down the road!

The country is remarkably beautiful with the orange orchards, wheat fields and olive groves (yes, I've seen olive trees!) that line the waterways – in contrast to the shimmering desert. There were the remains of poppies all along the railway track.

In some ways it's like being back in biblical times with the local farmers still using wooden ploughs and carting water in wooden buckets. I even saw them digging in the orchards with their bare hands!

It's much colder than I imagined, especially at night.

We had some leave in Tel Aviv, which is bright and modern compared with the surrounding villages. The White City of Tel Aviv was designed by German Jewish migrants and has community centres with libraries, kindergartens, shops and vegetable gardens.

You won't believe it, but the Regiment organised a surf carnival on Tel Aviv beach! Quite bizarre. Not sure what the Arabs looking on made of it!

That's about all I've got to report at the moment.

Even though we have had so little time together I miss you terribly and think of you every day.

Love
Alec

Nell read and re-read it, especially the last sentence. She had begun to imagine that their night together was a fling and that he had forgotten her.

She folded the letter carefully and put it in her shirt pocket close to her heart. She patted it and breathed a sigh of relief.

*

A few days later, when she was galloping across Victor Trumper paddock, Nell saw a horse in the distance, tied to the fence. The temperature was soaring over the century mark. She slowed Ginger to a canter and made towards the horse.

There, on his hands and knees, peering at the ground was Lance Crawford. He was so preoccupied he didn't even know she was there.

'That horse needs some shade.'

No response.

'Mr Crawford?'

He looked at her irritably. 'What?'

'Dusty. You've tied her up in the sun.'

Lance returned to his digging and measuring.

'Did you hear me?' She pointed to a stand of trees a few hundred yards away. 'There's some shade over there.'

'There used to be shade here before you cleared all the plant communities.'

'Pardon?'

He got to his feet, dusted off his knees and picked up his notebook. He made a sweep of the flat, sparsely wooded, 300 acre paddock and referred to his notes.

'This used to be covered by dense timber. *Eucalyptus populifolia-Callitris glauca, Eucalyptus populifolia associes, epiphyllum* type of the *Geijera-F'lindersia associes, Casuarina-Heterodendron* and related types of *Casuarina Atalaya associes*, like the *Acacia pendula associes* and the *Eucalyptus populifolia-Geijera-Eremophila associes.*'

She didn't have a clue what he was talking about, something he obviously enjoyed. Nell thought he was nothing but a show-off.

'You probably know it as climax and sub-climax shrub woodland. Or savannah scrub.'

She would have preferred it if he were a clichéd boffin. The fact that he was young and good looking made it worse.

'Look at this.' He rubbed his fingers over a bare patch of ground. 'Scalds.' He seemed to be enjoying himself enormously. 'No vegetation at all. The frequent passage of large flocks of sheep moving to and from water holes has completely eroded all plant cover in some places. Like here.' He pointed. 'Over there you can see signs of re-vegetation.'

'Over there I can see some shade,' Nell said with some force.

'This is what has caused the problem. Locusts and grasshoppers thrive in these conditions. That's why there was a plague. All that ring-barking has resulted in the destruction of insectivorous birds' nesting sites. A bit of spring rain and the *acrididae* flourish. There's nothing for them here but over there …' He shrugged. 'You might have increased the carrying capacity, but you've also created a potential haven for pests.'

She was gobsmacked.

'Cup of tea?'

Before she could respond, he strode over to the fence, untied Dusty, threw the reins over the sweltering horse's head, grabbed the pommel and tried to lift his foot into the stirrup. He hopped about as they danced a weird, circular tango.

Nell could hardly contain herself.

'Would you like me to hold her for you?' It was her turn to enjoy his discomfort.

Dusty snorted and Nell could swear she saw the horse wink at her.

Finally, with a clumsy lunge, Lance heaved himself up into the saddle. Nell secretly hoped Dusty would bolt and toss him.

She mounted Ginger, trotted up beside him and they rode in silence towards the shade. They dismounted and he began unpacking his saddle bag.

'Here.' She held her hand out for the billy. 'I'll get the water. You make the fire.'

She walked over to the creek and filled the billy while he did his best to light the few twigs he had assembled. There was smoke but no fire. Nell put the billy down.

'Can I give you a hand?'

'It's not taking.'

She got down on all fours and puffed; it took. Before long they were enjoying billy tea. Nell added a gumleaf for flavour and Lance looked impressed.

When he finished, he lay on his back with hands behind his head.

'Are you going to enlist?'

Lance didn't reply. She swirled the tea around in her pannikin before taking a final sip then tossing the dregs on to the bare earth.

'Are you?'

'What's it to do with you?' He seemed offended.

'Nothing. I was just ... you're young ... everyone –'

He cut her off, 'Everyone?'

'You know ...'

'No.'

She wasn't going to let him off the hook.

'My brother has gone. My ... a friend ... is already in Palestine.'

He looked at her. 'A friend?'

'Yes.'

Nell stood and wiped the dirt off her hands. She was quite pleased she'd got under his skin. She pulled her hat on and untied Ginger.

Lance sat up suddenly.

'I'm a communist.'

'I beg your pardon?'

'And a pacifist. That's why I didn't sign up. I have no intention of becoming involved in an Imperialist war.' He collected his bits and pieces and walked off.

Nell's mind was racing.

A communist? A real live communist. On Braemar. What would her father think? What would everyone in the district think? He had suddenly become interesting.

Lance returned to his scratching.

She hopped on Ginger. 'Make sure you give Dusty some water,' she called as she turned to ride back to the homestead. 'And keep her out of the sun.'

29.

The Italians' entry into the war meant that, after months of cooling their heels training in the desert, the Australians would finally see some action. Alec couldn't have been happier. He was determined to prove the British generals wrong in their assessment of his division as too 'raw and undisciplined' when they first disembarked in Palestine. He had been furious that the Australian Government hadn't insisted they be sent to the front to help stop Hitler's advance. Now, after nearly a year's training, they would have the chance to test themselves.

Relieved that he was at last doing something worthwhile, Alec supervised the camouflaging of his guns in readiness for an attack from the sea on the port of Haifa. He was afraid that, as the bulk of Allied resources were engaged in the Battle of Britain, Palestine would prove to be hopelessly undermanned and under-resourced. The artillery at his disposal was antiquated and didn't have the range to fire long distances. Alec hoped that the Italians wouldn't be able to reproduce the show of strength the Germans had displayed in advancing through Europe and into France.

Alec's focus was clear. He drew on the strict discipline he'd had since childhood and went about his work with a clarity of purpose. He dismissed any thoughts of self-doubt. Going from gunner to gunner, he ordered his men to improve, clearly defining their roles and what was expected of them. He felt incredibly alive.

On the morning of 15 July, Alec's heart began beating faster than usual as he heard the sound of approaching aircraft. His unequivocal orders had everyone racing to their stations. Alec gripped his binoculars as he spotted a glimmer on the horizon. This was the real thing: bombers arrowing towards him. His calculations had to be precise. Any error could result in tragedy. The enemy were flying in two separate formations. Five planes in each. He ordered his men to aim their guns at the planes as he silently cursed his superiors for not demanding they be given more effective, long-range artillery. The planes flew high above him, forcing him to squint, as he wondered if they were circling before diving in for the kill. One thing was certain, he couldn't panic and order his men to fire too early. He had to hold his nerve. Alec had never known pressure like it.

He ignored the sweat trickling down his cheeks as he saw the Italian bombers suddenly bank away to the east.

'Where are they going?' one of his gunners asked.

As he watched them fly away, Alec was secretly disappointed that all his preparations had been for nothing. He wanted to engage the enemy. He wanted to test himself and his men.

He was also trying to figure out why they would fly east. Then it hit him.

'They're heading towards the oilfields!'

All the men watched in horror as they heard the distinctive scream of bombs falling, followed by palls of smoke billowing into the sky. Alec's immediate thought was that they had been dismissed as small fry compared with the prime target of the oil fields. His war had begun but no Australian shell had been fired.

While exasperated that he and his men were put to work in Haifa extinguishing fires and taking care of the local people instead of engaging the enemy, Alec remained keen to help out. He offered himself and his men as blood donors for the injured Palestinians.

'We're nothing but a tin-pot army. We've travelled halfway across the world without the means to mount a serious attack, let alone defend anything. Our top brass expects us to run a show like this on the smell of an oily rag,' Alec thundered to Stephen that night in their tent.

At least he had the compensation of again sharing a tent with his friend.

'Careful. The walls have ears,' Stephen said. 'You'll be court-martialled if you're not careful.'

Alec couldn't help but laugh. Stephen had a way of putting everything into perspective.

His prayers were answered when, a few weeks later, they were sent to Alexandria to learn how to use the new equipment the Royal Artillery had given them. Before long he was back at his station, ordering his men to use the guns to repel the Italians. He watched with great satisfaction as raid after raid of Italian aircraft was sent spiralling out of the sky into the Mediterranean without causing any harm to the Australians. On top of this success, the men had the added satisfaction of watching the bulk of the Italian bombs fall unspent into the water.

Alec felt that he was, at last, fulfilling his destiny. He was confident that, the way things were going, he would soon be on his way home to resume his life on Toongowan and, hopefully, his courtship of Nell.

Just when everything seemed to be going as planned, Alec suffered the embarrassment of slicing his leg open on a scrap of metal from the fallen Italian aircraft that he was inspecting.

One of the few Australian casualties in the war so far, he was sent to Cairo to recuperate. At least it gave him time to write.

Nx 149 Lieut Alec Murray
2/1 Field Reg RAA
AIF Abroad
10th Aug, 1940

Dear Nell,

I'm writing this from a hospital bed in Cairo. I'm afraid I can't report any heroics but I'm not too upset. It has given me a chance to reflect on the past few months and to catch up on some neglected correspondence. I had some time on leave in

Jerusalem a few weeks ago. I stayed at a pension in the old German colony – high up on the hill overlooking the old city. It was rather odd really – the other inhabitants were a couple of government officials, a nurse and several kids. Everyone was quiet and respectable, including myself. I spent the day visiting the Palestine Archaeological Museum and a couple of picture galleries – ending up with a Viennese art dealer, who was dressed in a silk shirt and corduroy breeches. He had long, red hair and a little Christ-like beard and spent a whole afternoon explaining to me what Surrealists, Cubists, Impressionists, Realists and a whole host of other 'ists' were. He had stacks of reproductions with which to demonstrate and showed me a painting called 'The Poet and His Muse'.

It was curiously misshapen. I must say I preferred Lippi's 'Madonna'. I hope you are well and that you are doing lots of painting. Please don't think the worse of me but I wonder if you could send me a photograph of yourself? It can get a bit lonely here and I would love something tangible to remind me of you. As you can tell I'm a bit clumsy when it comes to expressing myself but I have spent a good many hours thinking about you. I'm so glad to have had a chance to spend a little time with you before I left. I was wondering if you would agree to be my wife when we return? I wrote to Mother and suggested we invite you to Toongowan. It might be interesting for you. I'm sure my sister Claire will look after you.

Love
Alec

He folded the letter and wrote her address on the envelope. He hoped it would reach Nell before she forgot about him.

30.

'What's a communist?' Nell asked.

Lance was hunched over a wooden bench in the old meat shed. Nell was peering at him through the wire door, but he didn't look up.

'What do you mean?'

The wire door slammed shut behind her after she let herself in. 'You said you were a communist.'

'I am.' He was examining an insect under a microscope.

'How do you define being a communist?'

Lance carefully picked up the insect with some tweezers and dropped it into a beaker. He wiped his hands.

'I'm sorry. I get a bit preoccupied when I'm working.'

'Oh, that's all right,' she said.

'I'm close to finding ... but you're not really interested in that, are you?'

She laughed. 'Not really.'

'I didn't think so. Drink?' He opened the meat safe and took out a bottle of rum and two glasses.

Nell smiled. 'The sun's over the yardarm is it?'

He gestured for her to sit down and, measuring two fingers on the glass, poured her a drink. She watched him pour himself one. He was so precise. Everything about him was precise. Not a hair was out of place. His sleeves were evenly rolled. His light blue shirt was unbuttoned to reveal a tanned 'v' on his upper chest. His tanned face showed the benefit of months of working outdoors. His grey trousers even had the remains of a crease visible as he sat down on a tea chest, smoothed them out and crossed one leg over the other.

'Cheers.'

'*Santé.*'

They raised their glasses. He took a sip and shook his head slightly. 'I don't know how you can stand being stuck out here in the bush, miles from anywhere.'

She shrugged and decided she wasn't going to be drawn into that old argument. Long ago she had decided that, whatever the cost, she wasn't going to complain while there were men and women giving their lives to prevent the spread of Nazism.

'We all have to do our bit.'

He peered into his glass. 'Yes. But what a waste.'

'The war?'

'You.'

Nell felt the blood rush to her cheeks. 'Me?'

He was staring at her intently. 'I've watched you.'

She avoided his gaze.

'Don't worry. I'm a scientist. I watch things. That's what I do.'

'I'm not an insect!'

Ignoring her retort, he continued. 'No. But we're all connected. I'm trained to observe behaviour in all sorts of species. Excuse me for being so bold but, you weren't born to be a country lady.'

Nell was secretly pleased that he'd come to this conclusion. 'Sometimes we have to make sacrifices,' she said.

They sipped their drinks quietly for a few minutes, while Nell considered the bitter truth of this statement. If there wasn't a war, she wouldn't be there.

Without warning, Lance blurted out, 'The men around here. Getting anything out of them is like getting blood from a stone.'

For the first time since she had met him, Lance was letting his guard down. Nell liked what she saw. 'Depends how you talk to them I guess.'

He countered. 'Depends on what you talk to them about! I just can't imagine you being all that interested in the weather.'

'You'd be surprised what I'm interested in.'

'Would I just?' he shot back.

She lifted her glass as if to offer a little toast. She was enjoying the banter. 'What about you? A flash jack like you must be feeling a bit homesick for the bright lights.'

'Bright lights? My CSIR work is based out of Canberra!'

She laughed as he continued. 'All I need are these ...'

He pointed to the jars of specimens that were neatly lined up on a wooden butcher's block.

'I can disappear into the world of insects, but you ... You can't tell me you find myiasis interesting?'

She looked at him blankly.

'You might know it as flystrike.'

Nell took a sip of rum and looked at him squarely. 'You didn't answer my question. About communism.'

'You're interested?'

'I wouldn't have asked if I wasn't.'

'Communism is, rather ironically, the apotheosis of the egalitarian ideal. The Great Australian Dream: All men –'

'And women ...'

'Er ... yes. And women. Are equal. You know the "bush ideal"?'

'The what?'

'In the pub. The working man, the shearer, rubbing shoulders with the squattocracy.'

'I don't think my father has ever been into a pub.'

'Henry Lawson ... No. That's the point.'

He took a sip of rum, then said, 'Who makes money out of war? The poor buggers who are sacrificed for whatever cause they are conned into following? No. We all know what they are. Cannon fodder. The only people who make money out of war are the capitalists who manufacture guns and bombs. And people like your father who produce the wool for uniforms. Business doesn't stop during war. It expands. That's why there is always another war. To keep the money rolling in.'

Nell struggled to reply. 'Isn't it because Hitler is advancing through Europe?'

'That's what capitalism is. Does. It exploits the working class. They call it a free market but it's really an excuse for a few fat men to get fatter. We need to get rid of all the old structures and create a classless society. One where there is no ownership of property and no need for personal wealth; where we all work together for the common good.'

He refilled her glass. 'Take the men on this place. That old bloke ...'

'Jimmy?'

'What does he get out of working from daylight to dusk? A feed and a bed and twist of tobacco?'

'He gets paid!'

'What he's worth?'

Nell was momentarily stumped as Lance went in for the kill.

'Where does he live? In a big house with a big garden and a brand new Pontiac? Or in the workman's quarters?'

She found herself defending the way Braemar was run. 'Jimmy loves this place. It's his home.'

'He is the victim of a society that rewards the rich and punishes the poor.'

Nell took umbrage. 'I don't think Jimmy would take kindly to being referred to as a victim.'

'We're all victims ...'

'Of the capitalist system?'

'Exactly.'

He looked at her for a moment before he held his glass out to her in an act of conciliation. After a moment, she tapped hers against it. They both skulled. Before she had a chance to refuse, he took her glass from her and topped it up. She didn't object. This was fun.

'And what about you? Where exactly do you fit in?' Nell asked.

He finished topping up his own glass. 'I'm a scientist.'

She laughed. 'That excuses you?'

'It enables me to pontificate.'

At that, they both laughed. Lance might have been a bit of a know-all but he was the most interesting person she had talked to in ages. He wasn't bad looking either. She was glad he was here to relieve the boredom.

Nell finished her drink and stood up. 'See you tomorrow.'

Lance poured himself another drink. 'If you're lucky.'

*

When Nell arrived home, a letter was waiting for her.

She thought it uncanny how they would appear just as she was exploring other options – or when other options were presenting themselves. She was finding herself strangely attracted to Lance, even if he was a bit pompous. His political views excited her. He was different and what he said made a lot of sense to her. Gabriel had opened her mind to thinking about the world differently and to questioning her privilege. Lance was continuing that education.

The arrival of a letter from the other side of the world sent her into a spin. It wasn't that she had forgotten about Alec, but the last time they were together was a long time ago and Lance was becoming increasingly interesting. And he was here.

As she read the letter, Nell smiled at the thought of Alec visiting art galleries. It had never occurred to her that Alec would be exploring the world in such a way. It was what she liked about him; he wasn't like other men.

Then she came to the final sentence: *I was wondering if you would agree to be my wife when we return?*

She put the letter down and stared out the window. *Wife?* She hadn't considered being anyone's wife, let alone belonging to someone on the other side of the world who she may never see again.

Nell knew of other women who had agreed to marry men serving overseas but she wasn't 'other women' and, as much as she was prepared to sacrifice her happiness for the war effort, she wasn't going to sacrifice her whole life.

Even so, the letter stirred something in her.

31.

After twelve months in Palestine, the war was finally hotting up and Alec was posted to Cyrenaica near the Libyan–Egyptian border. Christmas 1940 brought bitterly cold winds, tins of bully beef and the prospect of engaging face to face with Benito Mussolini's Italians. It was a far cry from the hot, dry Christmases Alec had grown up with, but he wasn't complaining. He was here to do a job and he was determined to do the best he could.

Preparations for an attack on the garrison port of Bardia had everyone chafing at the bit. As Alec moved from gun to gun, meticulously checking their sites and counting the shells piled up next to them, he noticed his men had scrawled messages on some of the shells in chalk.

'Stick that up ya, Musso.'

'Greetings from Ballarat.'

His loved his men's sense of humour.

Stiffening himself against the biting, blinding sandstorm, he completed his rounds and returned to the command post. He found Stephen sitting propped up against the wall. Alec sat on the ground beside him, took out his notebook and went over his calculations one more time. There was no room for mistakes. His bombardment had to both wipe out the enemy and provide cover for the advancing Australian infantrymen and sappers. If any shells landed short, they could kill his own countrymen.

'Cold out there?' Stephen asked.

'I don't know how the men can sleep.' He admired their resilience.

'They can sleep standing up,' Stephen said. He handed Alec his tobacco pouch and folded his arms around his knees. He seemed anxious.

'Ready?' Alec was barely able to hide his concern.

Stephen and a radio operator had been chosen to get out in front of the attack in a cruiser and report back on the success of the initial shelling. Alec was worried about the task his friend had been given, right in the firing line.

Stephen shrugged. 'As ready as I'll ever be.'

They sat smoking in silence. After a while Alec peered up at the camouflage above their heads. 'I s'pose this is what they refer to as "the calm before the storm"?'

'I guess it is.' Stephen laughed, barely hiding his nerves.

Alec checked his watch. It was an hour before the dawn attack. He grimaced as he tapped his pipe into his fist and closed his eyes. He was about to have his first real taste of land warfare. It was one thing to order gunners to shoot down planes attacking in the near distance. It would be quite another to engage face to face with the enemy.

An hour later, the Command Officer walked in and nodded at Alec and the other officers. It was time to make their way to their posts. Alec took a deep breath and was about to take up his position when Stephen grabbed his arm and hugged him tightly. He didn't need to say anything.

On 3 January 1941, the order rang out across the desert. 'Stand to!'

The battalion sprang into action. The sound of shells being rammed into guns and breeches clanking closed reverberated across the desert. The straight line of Australian artillery was primed for action.

'One ready! Two ready! Three ready ...'

This continued down the line until the Command Officer raised a megaphone to his lips. 'Fire!'

Shells hummed eerily through the air before an almighty roar broke loose on the Italian defences.

'Reload! Fire!'

The desert was immediately ablaze as the outskirts of Bardia were torn apart. It looked to Alec like a hundred bushfires exploding simultaneously across the Pilliga Scrub. Searching through his binoculars he saw they had taken out a number of Italian gun posts and smashed their defences. The pile of spent cartridges mounted as the men loaded and reloaded with speed and ruthless efficiency.

When it came, the return fire from the Italians was slow and ill-directed. The Australians quickly moved in for the kill, Alec exhorting his men to maintain, even lift, their intensity as the Italians abandoned their defensive positions. He ordered them to adjust their sights and aim their guns ahead of the advancing 6th Division as they charged across the desert to clean out the enemy lines.

When the smoke cleared, Alec could see his tin-hatted men in khaki surging towards Bardia. He could just make out the twisted shape of guns and posts that had been blown to smithereens by the 6th's devastatingly accurate shelling. Scanning the desert ahead, he saw hundreds of Italians, arms raised, walking towards him. He could barely believe his eyes. As well planned and ferocious as the attack had been, he had expected much stiffer resistance from the enemy.

'Word from the front, sir.' His radio operator passed him the hand piece.

A voice crackled down the line. Alec was so relieved to hear Stephen's mellifluous voice, radioing from his observation post in front of the shelling. He had made it through.

'All artillery defences appear to be silenced. The way is clear to advance into Bardia,' Stephen announced proudly.

Alec turned to his 2IC, slapped him on the back and gripped his hand firmly. 'Well done, Corporal,' he said, allowing himself a smile.

George Russell, just twenty years old, his freckled face caked in sand and sweat, was grinning from ear to ear. 'You too, sir!'

He shook his superior's hand enthusiastically.

Alec moved along the line congratulating his men, one by one, on a job well done. There had been no casualties and there appeared no damage done to his guns. It couldn't have gone better.

When he checked his watch, Alec could barely believe his eyes. It was 0735. It had taken just two hours to rout the opposition. The only reported Australian casualty was an observation officer.

Over the course of the day, the battery crossed the two miles of desert to Bardia, virtually unhindered. Upon reaching the surrendering enemy, the troops' already buoyant mood was further lifted by the sight of thousands of Italians, hands skywards, offering themselves up as prisoners of war.

Having not only survived but triumphed in his first battle, Alec slept like a top that night. Everything had gone to plan and he dreamt of being home for Easter.

By midday the following day, the Bardia garrison surrendered, and the 2nd First Field Regiment of the 6th Division had recorded an important victory.

While the men cleaned their guns and serviced their vehicles, Alec inspected the damage they had inflicted on the enemy. Feeling very pleased with himself, he came across an Italian gun battery that had been wiped out. Endeavouring to note the number of guns that might be still workable, he dropped to his haunches for a closer look.

An arm was sticking out from beneath an upturned vehicle. With all his strength, Alec pushed the teetering vehicle over and crouched beside the victim. The man's body was contorted, his young face frozen in a terrible expression of horror. Alec could see a gaping wound to his lower torso. His legs had been blown off.

Alec started to choke. He fell forward on all fours and dry retched, his stomach heaved. His eyes watered and his mouth dribbled. He wiped his mouth with the back of his sleeve and looked to the heavens. There was nothing noble about this. Commanding a gun post from afar had allowed him to disassociate from the dreadful toll his successful hits had inflicted.

What a bastard I have become, he thought, as he slowly raised himself to his feet and surveyed the scene. 'This had better be worth it,' he said aloud.

Alec was now acutely aware of other bodies lying around him in various states of dismemberment. They reminded him of the dead beasts he had hauled out of bogs back home. While he had been counting machinery, he'd been paying scant attention to the human cost of his actions. Although he had been part of the division that inflicted the first defeat of the Axis powers on land, it had not been achieved without a human price.

32.

When the invitation to visit Toongowan arrived, it both piqued Nell's curiosity and stirred curious feelings of longing. She read and re-read Alec's letter and slept with it under her pillow. She relived their night at The Women's Club together and wanted to know more about him.

Lance offered to drive her to Coonabarabran, which seemed uncharacteristically chivalrous of him, until he confided that he would die for a break from worms and sheep. Nell's mother was relieved that she was showing some interest in someone and that he was from the 'right stock'.

When they arrived at Toongowan, Nell was immediately taken by the incredible brightness of the stars in the night sky. She immediately began sketching them in her head.

During Nell's stay, Daphne was quite welcoming for such a naturally reserved woman, while Henry was putty in her hands. Nell and Claire got on immediately. When they were out of sight of Claire's parents, Nell delighted in challenging the young woman to break loose. She showed her how to smoke, described scenes in Paris and literally showed her how to let her hair down when she challenged Claire to a race to the gate.

Leonie Duroux also caught Nell's attention. She and her family appeared integral to Toongowan, so Nell took every opportunity she could to talk to her. She had never met an Aboriginal person before, as the only Aboriginal people she had seen lived on the outskirts of Trangie. The two women hit it off.

Leonie didn't stand on ceremony and neither did Nell. She delighted in pinching a taste of whatever Leonie was cooking and Leonie delighted in playfully smacking her hand when she did. She explained to Nell that the Gamilaroi called the Milky Way the *Warumbul*, and that it was a big river until the universe was tipped head over heels.

One day, when Henry and Daphne had gone into town, Nell asked Leonie about Alec. From their conversation, it was obvious that Leonie liked and respected him. This was an insight into the man that intrigued Nell. With Leonie's encouragement, she asked Bernie to show her how to crack a whip.

While Lance read and slept in the shearing shed, Nell began imagining what it might be like to live at Toongowan. She redesigned the house in her head, opening it up to let in more light. She visualised a bigger and more extensive vegetable garden and, in her mind, planted fruit trees around the perimeter of the yard.

Driving home after her four day 'sabbatical', as Lance called it, Nell was feeling particularly ebullient. Lance, too, seemed to have recharged his batteries and was less stitched up than he had seemed before.

Nell had decided to accept Alec's offer of marriage. What else could she do? To add to the glowing reviews he had received from the Durouxs, Peg had written to her from Cairo singing his praises and painting a picture of him as quite the hero.

Back home, it didn't take long for the excitement of the visit to Toongowan to wear off. More mustering for Nell and more staring into test tubes for Lance, which meant he was, more often than not, otherwise engaged.

The loneliness that had enveloped Nell before returned. She wasn't someone who was content on her own. She thrived on company. And Lance was the only person she could call on.

One night, after dinner, Nell snuck a bottle of whisky out of the house and invited Lance to meet her at the saddle shed for a night cap. Much to her delight, he accepted.

'Here.' She handed him the whisky, closed the shed door and lit a kerosene lamp. While he looked around for somewhere to sit, she took two crystal glasses out of her pocket and, not bothering with measurements, poured them both a healthy portion.

'Cheers.'

Nell sat on the floor, resting against the timber wall and lit a cigarette. She watched Lance as he inspected the saddles and bridles and horse blankets.

'They're all so neatly arranged,' he said, running a finger over the seat of saddle.

Nell loved the way the shed smelt of horses and the bush. It was her refuge whenever she was angry with the world or with her mother in particular. She moved over so Lance could sit beside her. He sat down and peered into his glass.

She patted his knee. 'Thank you.'

He looked surprised.

'You've been a lifesaver,' Nell said. 'I don't know what I would have done without you over the past few months.'

He brushed it off modestly.

She leant into him. 'Can I confide in you?'

'Certainly.'

'This is hard ...' she paused.

His silence gave her licence to continue. 'I don't know what to do. I don't know what I'm supposed to do. I'm engaged to someone who is on the other side of the earth, who writes me letters that are like ... travelogues ... that's unfair ...' She trailed off. She was finally voicing her deepest fears. 'I barely know him.'

With that she took a healthy slug of her drink.

'I know a lot about him. But I don't ... know him.' She shook her head, her eyes welling up. 'I don't know why I said I'd marry him.'

She lit a cigarette, exhaled a big cloud of smoke and continued. 'This whole situation ... What if he's changed? What if he doesn't like me anymore? What if I don't like him? We're meant to be getting married but we haven't spent more than a few days together and he's been over there, wherever "over there" is, ever since. I don't really know what he's thinking. I don't even know what he's been doing ...'

She stopped suddenly. 'You don't mind?'

'Mind?'

'Me unloading all this on you.'

He tried to laugh it off. 'No. No ... not at all. Be my guest.'

'I haven't got anyone else I can talk to. Not now my friend Peg's somewhere doing something ... exciting.'

She kicked at the floor. For a moment she thought that Lance was going to put his arm around her. She wouldn't have minded if he did.

'You got on well with his family,' he said.

'I know how to play the game.' She smiled. 'The thing is, they are so ... reserved. I know my parents aren't exactly the life of the party, but there was something about the Murrays. I tried really hard but, Mrs Murray ... She's scary. Seriously. She's so tall. And those black dresses she wears. And the big hat!'

They both laughed, and Nell looked over at him. 'I couldn't help but think she was judging me. Seeing if I was good enough for Alec. She absolutely adores him.' She paused again.

'And his father, Henry?' Lance asked.

'Henry's like some parody of an English gentleman farmer. Those breeches! And the shooting stick. He's got the meanest eyes I have ever seen, don't you think? And that mouth. Like a chook's bum.'

After downing her whisky, she gave Lance a look that said, 'hurry up,' waited until he skulled his and poured them both another.

'Am I being too harsh?'

He opened his mouth to answer but she cut him off.

'I mean, I liked Claire. She's very sweet but, as nice as she is, we've got nothing in common. She doesn't even smoke.'

They exchanged a laugh as Nell stubbed out her cigarette and reached for another.

'I'm sorry. That's very ungenerous. She is nice. And she was lovely to me. It's just that ... temperamentally ... we're different. I'm sure we could be friends but she's a lot more ... I don't know ...'

'Conservative?'

'Something like that.'

There was silence while Nell wondered if she had gone too far. His look encouraged her to continue.

'The thing is, I don't really know what I'm doing. Did I accept his proposal because I felt sorry for him? Is it a fantasy? I had never thought about getting married, let alone living in the bush. And being a farmer's wife, well, that's the last thing I want.'

Lance seemed to be watching her intently.

'None of us really knows what we're doing, do we?' he said.

She nodded. He was right. She had no idea what she was doing.

'It's scary,' she said simply.

'It is,' he agreed.

They disappeared into their own thoughts, the silence punctuated by the sound of crickets chirping. The kerosene light flickered. After a while, Lance laughed.

'You're a very good actor.'

'Actor?'

'Yes. When we were there, you looked like you were having the time of your life.'

'Really?' This pleased her. 'You don't think they could tell?'

'No. Not at all.'

Nell was thinking aloud. 'That's good. When I wrote to Alec, I told him I had a terrific time. The last thing he needs is to think is that I was … uncomfortable. Or that I didn't like the place. Or that I didn't want to live there. Not that we have ever talked about it.'

With that she drained her glass and picked up the bottle. 'Might as well be hung for a sheep as a lamb!'

Once again, she topped up their drinks. '*Santé!*'

Lance cradled his glass in his hands, and then put it down beside him.

'Come on,' Nell said. 'Let's go for a walk down to the creek.'

She grabbed his arm and did her best to drag him to his feet. He tried to get up but succeeded only in pulling her over on top of him. They tumbled on to the floor, sending Nell into fits of laughter. Finally, she jumped to her feet, blew out the lamp and marched into the night, leaving him to catch up.

The stars shone brightly above them. With arms around each other for support, they stumbled across the paddock towards the creek. Nell parted the fence wires for Lance to climb through and he returned the favour. They almost rolled down the slope towards the creek. A moonbeam bounced off the trickling stream.

'Isn't it magical?'

'Yes. It's … very … pretty …'

Before he could finish, Nell let go of him and whirled around, arms extended, dancing in the moonlight. She looked to the heavens and wondered what they had in store for her. After a while she collapsed on to the creek bank and lay, spreadeagled, on her back.

A frog croaked.

Nell could hear Lance breathing heavily beside her. She sensed something but she wasn't sure what. It was darker. A shadow had blocked out the moonlight. The breathing got closer. And closer. And then she felt his lips on hers. She gave in to the moment. She could feel him lying across her body, his chest on hers. He wasn't exactly an experienced kisser, but she didn't mind. She put her arm around his neck and held him to her.

Then, suddenly, she remembered where she was and who she was. She was engaged. What was she doing?

She pushed him away. He fell back and lay on the ground panting like a steam train. She struggled to her feet, straightened her clothes and stumbled up the riverbank. When she got to the fence, she tried to climb through it and in the process, managed to snare her dress. She fumbled about and gave it a yank, ripping the hem. Her mind was spinning. As she steadied herself, she looked back to see Lance pummelling the ground. She staggered towards the house, his sobbing tears ringing in her ears.

33.

After wiping out the Italians at Bardia, the 2nd First Field Regiment drove them out of Libya with relative ease. In two months, they had pushed them back 400 miles, destroyed their army, taken 125,000 prisoners of war and captured more than 10,000 guns and vehicles. Surprised by the ease of their victories, Alec was confident that his war would soon be over. The only blot on the landscape was the mounting Australian casualties. On the plus side, he had picked up some useful tips about irrigation from the Italian prisoners of war he'd come to know. They had explained how the Italian farmers had transformed the local desert into arable farming land.

Apart from lack of sleep and the inch-deep sand that caked his body, Alec's biggest challenge was writing to the families of the fallen who were under his command. These letters put the praise he received from high command into perspective. The Italians might have surrendered at Benghazi but the cost was considerable and, to Alec, personal. He had grown attached to his men and losing any of them was like losing a member of the family. One night, as he searched for the right words, he grew exasperated and threw his fountain pen down. Stephen looked up from reading his book, *Goodbye to Berlin*.

'Are you all right?'

'I was prepared for a lot of things but not for this.' He held his head in his hands.

Stephen climbed out of his stretcher and walked over to the makeshift desk. He rested his hands on Alec's shoulders and squeezed.

A few days later, the order to embark for Greece came out of the blue.

'Now we've cleaned up Libya they must need us to do the same in Greece,' Stephen said as they sat down for breakfast in the mess.

Alec wasn't convinced. 'It's all very sudden.'

'I guess they want us to get it over with so we can be home for Easter!'

Alec marvelled at the way Stephen could always find something positive to say. He watched him as he shovelled a spoonful of mush into his mouth and wiped it with the back of his hand.

He added, 'What I'm hearing is that it's just a mopping-up operation.'

Before they knew it, they were on a train to El Amiriya and transferred to the SS *Pennland* for the two-day voyage to Piraeus. Looking out over the Mediterranean, Alec marvelled at the beauty before his eyes. The water was impossibly still and glassy. The sun, so golden that it was almost orange, slowly peeked over the distant horizon. It took his breath away. He turned towards their destination and was brought crashing back to earth by the tell-tale plumes of black smoke spiralling skywards in the distance. As they approached the harbour, he could see skeletons of bombed out boats of all shapes and sizes.

Because the harbour was so shallow and littered with detritus, the only way ashore was to be ferried off the transport ships by a member of the flotilla of Greek fishing boats, dinghies and row boats that came to greet them. Alec climbed into his allotted fishing boat and took his place in the bow. He slung his life jacket over his shoulder and peered down at the oil-slicked water. The fisherman negotiated his boat around the tail of a sunken Greek aircraft and handed him a basket. When he opened it, Alec was delighted to see a feed of olives, cheese and fresh bread. The fisherman grinned as he motioned for Alec to tuck in.

He looked along the coastline and was relieved to see a more familiar landscape than the one he had recently become accustomed to. Trees and splashes of green grass dotted the shoreline and surrounding rocky cliffs. It made him think of the Australian coastline. He could see hundreds of people queuing on the wharves, clutching their belongings. Children clung to their mothers' skirts and the elderly waited patiently while injured soldiers shuffled along in various states of distress. The contrast between this and his previous post couldn't have been more stark: Greece was clearly going to be a very different situation from Libya.

The road to their camp at Glyphadia was lined with people cheering them. And when they arrived, Stephen said to Alec that it looked more like a Boy Scouts' camp than the site for a military operation. The tents were in fields surrounded by trees. They had to await the arrival of their artillery so were given leave to explore Athens while they cooled their heels.

'So, this is where it all began.' Stephen glanced around before climbing the last few steps to the Acropolis. He stopped and looked down at Alec, who was sitting a few rows below him packing his pipe.

'This is what we are fighting for,' he added.

Alec stared out over the ancient seat of democracy. He tapped his pipe on a step and dislodged the spent tobacco before repacking and relighting it. He puffed away thoughtfully while his friend held court.

'We are here to honour the dead and give praise for our constitution!'

Alec turned around to see Stephen standing, arms spread wide, on the top step. He made a grand sweep with his right hand. 'Our society favours the many instead of the few. This is why it is called a democracy. We believe in equal justice for everyone. Social standing is no barrier to advancement in public life. Nor is poverty. A man is judged solely on his merit, what he can offer in service to the state. We do not judge our fellow man but rather respect his freedom to do as he pleases, as long as he respects the law.

'We celebrate artistic achievement but reject showiness and ostentatious wealth. The greatest sin we can commit is not employing all our resources to reduce poverty.

'It is the responsibility of the public and private person to serve the state by contributing to the life of the whole. This we do by open discussion and reflection. In preserving this way of life, we may be called to confront the enemies of democracy and take up arms so that the people's voices are never silenced.'

Stephen bowed theatrically. His oration had attracted a small crowd of onlookers who joined Alec in applauding before moving on to look at other antiquities. Alec climbed to the top of the steps.

'Pericles?' he asked.

'My expurgated version of the *Funeral Oration*. Apologies to Thucydides. Not only are we fighting for democracy, we are fighting to preserve this. I wouldn't put it past those barbarians to raze all this to the ground. Can you imagine?' Stephen broke off and wiped his eyes. There was no need for more words.

In the distance they could hear what they initially thought was thunder but was, in fact, German bombs. Alec was taken aback when Stephen leant his head against his shoulder.

He couldn't help but be moved. He admired the way Stephen could express his emotions. He wished he had some of his friend's emotional honesty. He wondered what had happened to his own capacity to express himself.

They spent the rest of their leave enjoying the generous Greek hospitality that was showered on them at every turn.

Eventually, a convoy of trucks, cars, motorbikes and horse-drawn carts transported them from Pireaus to a siding at Rouf, west of Athens, to await further orders. They were then herded onto cattle trucks for the train trip north to confront the advancing German army.

'I hope our guns catch up with us.' Alec was thinking aloud. Jack looked at him with a quizzical expression on his face. 'It's okay, Jack. Don't mind me.'

He could have sworn he saw Jack roll his eyes, but he was happy to let it go.

The prospect of facing up to the Germans without artillery had done little to improve Alec's mood, nor that they were constantly being forced into sidings to allow the southbound trains, carrying refugees and injured soldiers, to pass. The situation seemed so dire that, at one stopover, their Greek train drivers bailed out and joined the fleeing refugees.

Alec turned to his men. 'Anyone know how to drive a train?'

Tim Armitage, a large, no-nonsense farmer, volunteered to try his luck. 'Can't be much different to driving a tractor.'

'I'll give him a hand, sir.'

Freddy Grace, a skinny, young, carrot-top from Tenterfield was on his feet, and before long the train was chugging along the track towards the enemy. When German planes approached, the troops abandoned the train for the relative safety of ditches on either side of the track. Alec couldn't work out why the Germans didn't blow the trains up. Maybe they didn't want to waste their bombs.

They were finally reunited with their guns and vehicles at Domokos and ordered to deploy to Thermopylae to join the New Zealand forces defending the pass and the neighbouring village of Bralos.

'Ah, Leonidas.' Stephen grinned at Alec while he prepared to take up his assigned position at the top of the pass. 'I trust you will be as successful as your namesake.'

Alec smiled grimly. They both knew that the odds of repelling an advancing force far outnumbering their own were stacked against them.

Stephen made light of it. 'Murray at Thermopylae … Hold them at the pass and you will go down in history.'

While he could usually deflect the seriousness of a situation, Alec felt far less sanguine about this one. Placing the weight of history on his shoulders didn't help. 'And you?'

'I'm taking the low road while you take the high road,' said Stephen. He broke into a jig and began singing. '*Oh! Ye'll take the high road and I'll take the low road, And I'll be in Scotland afore ye.*' Grabbing a startled Alec by the arm, he whirled him around. '*But me and my true love will never meet again, On the bonnie, bonnie banks of Loch Lomond.*'

Alec looked into Stephen's eyes. They were red raw. The war was taking its toll on him. Alec gave him a consoling pat on the shoulder. He knew that Stephen had been given the onerous task of providing cover for the retreating remnants of the Greek army and accompanying refugees. No wonder he was feeling vulnerable. But Stephen, as always, did his best to hold it together. He picked up his .303, gave Alec a few knocks on his tin hat and marched off, calling out over his shoulder, 'We're either going to go down in history or go down.'

Perched on the top of the pass, Alec surveyed the German advance that stretched as far as he could see. A unit of Panzer tanks cleared the way for snaking columns of foot soldiers while the Luftwaffe strafed and bombed the fleeing Greek civilians and Allied forces on the plains below. The scale of the blitzkrieg was beyond anything Alec had ever imagined. For the first time in the war, he began to doubt whether he could survive. The devastation was terrible as the men of the 2nd First Field Regiment fought for their lives.

When a lull in the attack finally came, he almost pinched himself to make sure he was still alive. He clambered down the pass towards the hastily erected officers' tent. Part of him felt that he was dreaming. That he must be dreaming. How could he have survived such a savage assault? All he could think of was putting one foot in front of the other. When he got there, he saw a group of strangers who bore no resemblance to the confident men who had climbed aboard boats to save Greece. He felt like a wreck and he couldn't stop shaking.

The CO, looking uncharacteristically unkempt but trying hard to project control, addressed the assembled officers in as steady a voice as he could muster.

'The order for evacuation from Greece has been made. We are to make our way south as expeditiously as possible. We have orders to support retreating civilians and infantrymen as best we can. Any equipment that can't be taken with us is to be destroyed.'

Alec searched amongst the weary faces for any sign of Stephen. He couldn't see him anywhere. While he listened to the CO's orders, he kept one eye on the tent flap, expecting Stephen to bound in at any second. Then, just as the CO was wrapping up, it opened. Alec let out an audible sigh of relief. Trust Stephen to be late for orders! His smile disappeared when he saw that it wasn't his friend but an orderly. The orderly handed a scrap of paper to the CO. The tent fell silent.

The CO looked up from reading the note and paused. Alec started to worry. Something was definitely wrong. The CO spoke steadily.

'It is my solemn duty to report that Captain Stephen Champion has been killed on a hillside below Thermopylae.'

Time stood still. The tent was swimming. Alec felt like he was going to fall over. He grabbed a tent pole. He could feel eyes glancing in his direction. The only sound was the tent flapping in the breeze.

Then the CO cleared his throat and continued, 'Captain Champion is the first officer to fall in our campaign …'

Alec's stomach clenched. His hands were numb, he felt pins and needles in his feet, his mouth was dry. The CO read aloud the sketchy details of Stephen's death from an exploding bomb, but Alec wasn't ready to hear it. He was battling to keep it together.

The CO wrapped up. 'Thank you, gentlemen. You are dismissed.'

There was some mumbling and then Alec's fellow officers began to file out. He held on to the tent pole for dear life. He felt a few hands give him a sympathetic pat on the back as they passed. A few offers of condolence came but he was powerless to do anything but nod. He didn't know how long he was rooted there before the CO was standing in front of him.

'I'm sorry, Murray. He was a good man.'

Alec nodded mechanically as the CO walked out. He tried to pull himself together but was powerless to move. The news struck him with the same force as it had when his little brother died. Alec lowered his head and began to weep. Everything had caught up with him. He started to shake. For the first time in his life, he couldn't control the emotion that poured out.

'Are you okay, sir?'

Alec raised his eyes to see Jack holding the tent flap open, looking sadly at him. Alec wiped his eyes and mumbled, 'Yes, yes … I'm … thank you, Jack. I'll be out in a second.'

He clenched his jaw and stood up. There was no time to grieve.

As he walked out into the bright sunshine, he felt his numbness dissipate. Outside, it was total chaos. He pushed briskly through frenzied soldiers. Jeeps and trucks, all full to the brim, were pulling out. The air was thick with dust and organised panic. He saw the CO striding around shouting orders. Alec called out to him.

The CO stopped and turned as Alec marched up to him. 'Murray?'

Almost before he knew what he was saying, Alec volunteered, 'Sir. I … I want to stay back.'

The CO eyed him suspiciously. Alec anticipated his concerns. He gathered his thoughts and spoke deliberately to reassure his superior.

'I'm all right, sir. I know what I'm doing. You're going to need cover. Let me put together a small unit of men and we'll provide it for you. We'll retreat after you and make sure any machinery we leave behind is inoperable.'

He paused while the CO chewed this over, then continued. 'I've got just the men in mind.'

The CO didn't need much convincing. He nodded. 'Fine, Murray. Good thinking. We don't want the Hun killing us with our own guns.'

'Leave it to me, sir.'

If there was one way to honour Stephen it was by following his lead and volunteering to take on the most precarious role. His own survival was irrelevant. He saluted and marched off to collect his unit.

When he found Jack at his side he said, 'No, Jack. You go. I won't be needing a batman. I'll see you on the other side.' Jack hesitated. 'That's an order.'

Jack saluted him, swung his kitbag over his shoulder and rushed off to grab a lift to the port. Alec turned back to the small group of men awaiting orders, among them Tim Armitage and Freddy Grace.

'Right, men. Now the fun begins. I want you to destroy everything in sight. Drain the petrol tanks, use the petrol to blow up any ammo lying around and slash the tyres of any vehicles you come across.'

Tim Armitage raised his hand. ''Scuse me, sir, but we haven't got time to drain all these vehicles.' He lifted up a big sugar bag. 'I found this. We can tip sugar into the petrol tanks of any we don't have time to drain.'

Alec wasn't going to ask Tim where he 'found' the sugar.

'Good thinking, corporal. All right men. Get cracking.'

With that, the men quickly started to set fire to anything that would burn and immobilising anything else.

When they got back to the port, Alec ordered the men to push any guns and tractors that hadn't been immobilised off the cliffs into the sea below.

Using any weapons they could lay their hands on, they fought a rearguard action against the advancing Germans.

Somehow, they managed to hold them off for long enough for most of the regiment to escape to the awaiting destroyers. The rest retreated to Kalamata in hope of being rescued.

It was nine days since they had disembarked at Piraeus. Everything was happening in a hurry.

34.

News of Allied losses in Europe reached Australia. Nell was worried. She hadn't heard from Alec for weeks. She had no idea where he was or what was happening to him. The last she had heard he seemed in good spirits, although he never wrote about how the war was affecting him. The Australian press was very measured in its reportage. She received a letter from Peg who was working as a cipher decoding enemy messages for the British army in Cairo. Typically, Peg didn't seem too worried about censorship. She was careful enough not to give away anything that might be of use to the enemy, but she didn't sugarcoat her news the way the press did.

She wrote that between Johnny being transferred from the hospital in Cairo to a makeshift one in Greece, they had somehow managed to get married in a Coptic church, and that Johnny had run into Alec somewhere. Reading between the lines, Nell suspected that the long hours Johnny spent tending the injured and suffering was having a terrible effect on him. Peg hinted that he had become violent towards her.

Nell's father had heard via the King's old boys' grapevine, that Jock was recovering from a bout of malaria in a hospital in Khartoum, and being lauded for helping to drive the Italians out of Ethiopia with a band of Abyssinian tribesmen. Nell tried to comfort their mother by telling her that his letters had probably gone astray, even though she knew perfectly well that Jock would never have thought of writing.

She feared for his safety. He was reckless and taking risks was part of his makeup. Like many, Nell had imagined that the war wouldn't last long and that both Jock and Alec would return home soon after they had embarked. The reality was far more confronting. They had been away for over a year and there didn't seem to be any signs of the war ending.

Nell felt guilty about Lance. If it weren't for Alec, she mightn't have worried about the kiss; she may even have allowed it to develop. As it was, she felt like she had betrayed Alec as he was fighting on the other side of the world.

She was deeply conflicted. Try as she might, she couldn't stop thinking about the kiss; couldn't help the way she felt. Lance excited her and she was hanging on to a memory of Alec that was fast fading. She didn't know what to do.

Nell received a telegram from Daphne. Alec had been reported 'Missing in Action'. He hadn't been accounted for when the Australians had left Greece. He could be wounded or captured. He might have been killed. There was nothing definitive, all Daphne knew was that no one had any idea where her son was.

At first, Nell couldn't work out what to do. Eventually she decided to drive down to Toongowan to try to offer Daphne some comfort.

When she arrived, Nell found Alec's family in a terrible state. Henry was walking around in a daze while Daphne could barely get out of bed. She spent hours staring at a framed photograph of Alec in his army uniform. Nell joined them in some kind of limbo. Bernie worked around the clock to keep the place running, while Mrs Duroux provided quiet support to Daphne and Henry and tried to cheer Nell up by recounting her children's latest exploits. No one talked about Alec.

Nell drove Daphne into the tiny Presbyterian church in Binnaway and sat with her while she prayed. On the way back to Toongowan, Daphne admitted that she wasn't particularly religious but asked, 'What else can I do?'

It was a good point. What could they do?

Daphne gave Nell one of her precious framed photographs of Alec. It reminded Nell of how handsome he was. She felt terrible for having cheated on him. Daphne appeared to accept her unquestioningly as her future daughter-in-law. Henry was polite and even managed to smile once or twice when they talked. When she was about to leave, Mrs Duroux gave her a big, generous hug that made Nell feel she had been accepted as one of the family. As she drove down the driveway, Bernie waved his hat in his understated way. If they only knew what she had been wrestling with.

✻

Her mother was packing lunch for the picnic races when Nell arrived home.

'I've invited Lance to come with us.'

Nell was astounded. 'How could you think of going to the races at such a time?'

'We have to keep up appearances,' her mother said.

That's exactly what we do, thought Nell. Keep up appearances. Pretend. Pretend there isn't a war on and that people aren't dying. Like Alec.

Lance tried to convince her to go. 'You need to get your mind off it.'

'It?' she replied tartly. 'You mean him?'

'Come on. I'll wait for you in the car.'

Despite her own feelings, Nell decided to do her bit to help everyone forget about the war for the afternoon. She changed into her brightest summer dress, even if it was getting cool.

In the end, she did more than that; she drank so much champagne, Lance had to carry her to the car.

35.

Having provided cover for the evacuees and destroyed as much machinery as possible, Alec and the few Allied survivors took refuge in the hills. The fighting had been ferocious; like nothing Alec had dreamed of. He fought without the slightest consideration for self-preservation. He was hardly thinking, just acting on instinct. He didn't care if he lived or died, as long as he took as many of the enemy as he could with him. Vengefulness had never been part of his personality before. Now he fought with the ferocity of a man possessed.

Night after night they had slipped down to the wharf under the cover of darkness, hoping to be rescued by one of the sailors or fishermen who had been ferrying survivors out to the few remaining battleships that offered a passage off Greece.

'Where are they?' Tim asked, as they searched for rescuers.

Alec pointed to the jetty. The Germans had set up field guns on it to cut off any more escapes. The whole area had been overrun by Germans.

He whispered to Tim, 'It's too precarious for them. They'd be sitting ducks.'

Then he spotted a Bren gun carrier that was unmanned. 'See that?' he said, pointing. 'If we can dislodge the Germans from the jetty, we might be able to get away. I'll need a driver.'

Tim put his hand up and Alec smiled. Tim could drive anything.

They snuck up to the carrier and climbed aboard. Tim kicked it over and Alec aimed the gun at the jetty and started firing. A shell hit the carrier and exploded.

Alec lost consciousness.

*

When he awoke, he was lying under the upturned carrier. Tim's bloodied body was lying across him. Alec realised that Tim had shielded him. He pushed Tim's body aside, grabbed his .303 and climbed out. He was dazed and his ears were ringing. The sky was alight with exploding shells. The noise was terrifying.

Alec staggered over the bodies of the men he had been fighting with. He could barely see. He pulled back the bolt on the .303 and shot a German soldier, hitting him in the face. Fighting like a man possessed, he made his way up the hillside and out of the direct firing line.

He saw an odd shape in front of him. As he drew closer, Alec could make out the unmistakable shape of a German parachutist hanging from a tree. He loaded his .303 and fired at him. He felt no remorse, it was just like shooting a rabbit. It seemed like an eternity since the sight of a dead human being had rattled him.

Alec found a secluded spot in the forest to hide in. It was too dark and too dangerous to get away, so he tried to sleep. The next day he watched the Germans overrunning the port and mopping up any stragglers. He spent the day plotting what to do next. He decided he would try to swim for it; there was no point in trying to escape on foot. When dusk finally settled over the ancient port, he crept towards a bridge that crossed a stream of melted snow and ice. He slid into the freezing water and let it carry him downstream. When he hit the sea, he rolled onto his back and looked up at Mount Taygetos. He remembered seeing the mountain marked on one of the army maps he'd studied.

After wrenching off his boots, Alec tied them around his neck and began to swim, fully clothed, towards the safety of the cliffs. When he thought he might be out of harm's way he stopped and trod water while he regained his breath. He was glad he'd learnt to swim at school. Looking back at the lights of Kalamata, he thought of Stephen for the first time since he was killed. Alec felt as if he was leaving his soul mate behind. He vowed that if he lived, he would honour Stephen's memory. Then he started swimming. There was a gentle rip that carried him further and further down the coast. When he could swim no more, he swam ashore and staggered up the stony beach towards a cave.

'Oi. Over 'ere.'

A figure was lurking in the shadows.

'G'day, mate, cold in?' the man asked with a distinctly Australian accent. 'That water'd freeze the balls off a brass monkey!'

It was one of the things Alec had learnt to love about his countrymen. Their ability to laugh at adversity. It was something he hadn't mastered yet, but he was still trying.

The slightly tubby, balding man greeted him with a grin as wide as Sydney Heads.

'Better get you warm, sir. You're shivering like a stuck pig.'

Alec smiled at the mixed metaphor. He wasn't sure how his rescuer knew he was an officer, but it didn't matter. He was safe. For the moment.

'Me name's Archie.'

'Captain Alec Murray,' Alec said, shaking Archie's hand vigorously.

They picked their way along a goat track towards the cave Archie was hiding in. Alec stripped off his soaking clothes and was happy to warm himself by the fire. A tall, skinny man with big ears and a handlebar moustache introduced himself as Tony Philpott and handed Alec a pannikin of hot tea.

'Bloody lucky to find this cave. It's completely sheltered from view. Unless they're sailing past, and I don't think the Hun will bother searching down this far,' Tony said.

Alec nodded. He hadn't stopped shivering and was eternally grateful for the hot tea. He pointed at the skiff lying at the mouth of the cave. 'Where did you find that?'

'Hello, sir, Graham Potts,' said a man built like a front-row forward. He gave Alec some dry clothes. 'We borrowed it from a Greek fisherman.'

'Borrowed?'

Tony was grinning from ear to ear. 'Well … you know … needs must.'

Alec changed out of his wet gear, lowered himself gingerly onto the dirt floor and collapsed against the cave wall.

'So, gentlemen. What's the plan?'

'You a rower?' Toby asked, shooting him a look over his shoulder while he stoked the fire. 'These two buggers are no use. Pair of bloody cricketers. Archie here's a leg spinner and Graham's a bloody wicket-keeper. No use to anybody.'

'I took five fa' against Bradman's Saint George side before –'

'Yes, Archie. You told us. A number of times. Googlys and wrong 'uns won't be much use in a row boat I'm afraid.'

Alec lifted his hand as if asking for permission to speak. 'I did a bit of rowing at school and university.'

'Good-oh. That means we've got a pair. I rowed for Melbourne Grammar,' said Tony. 'I reckon we sit tight for a day to let you get your strength back and we'll give it a crack tomorrow night.'

Graham pulled a page out of his pocket. '*Pix* magazine.'

He showed it to Alec.

'Map of Greece.' He smiled. 'Prettiest girl *Pix* has ever published.'

Alec looked at it closely while Graham continued. 'My wife sent it to me before we left Egypt. Thought it might come in handy.'

He pointed at the map. 'Crete. See? Reckon you two blokes can row that far?'

Doing a quick mental calculation, Alec reckoned it was about 600 miles. It didn't worry him that the skiff was designed for fishing in calm waters. Details like that didn't concern him anymore; he was content to live minute to minute.

'We don't have much choice, do we?' he said.

'We're pretty sure the last of our destroyers have left for Crete. Kalamata has surrendered and our intelligence tells us we've been ordered to try and hold the Hun off in Crete.'

'Your intelligence?'

'A party of Kiwis came past yesterday. While you were having your swim.'

Alec worked out that he must have been in the water for quite a few hours. He started to feel very tired and before long, he was out like a light. He slept through the day, waking briefly to eat before dropping off again.

It was the first decent sleep he'd had since he'd landed in Greece. He dreamt of Nell. She appeared to him like one of Botticelli's angels.

She was standing on Collaroy Beach with a towel draped over her shoulder as he emerged from the surf in his army uniform. As he approached her, she beckoned him with open arms. Before long they were lying on the beach, making love.

'You right, sir?' Archie knelt over Alec with a pannikin of tea in his hand. 'You was groanin'.'

Lifting himself up with his elbows, Alec gratefully accepted a mug of tea from Archie.

'Oh … I must have slept.'

'You been sleepin' like a log, sir. We didn't wanna disturb you. You got a bit a rowin' to do.'

Alec noticed Tony and Graham working nearby, preparing for their escape.

'We're gonna be headin' off soon, sir,' Archie said quietly.

Tony finished making food parcels, stuffed them in his bag and called out to Alec. 'Now we'll see what sort of a rower you are, Murray.'

Alec smiled. 'When are we going to push off?'

'As soon as it is dark.'

'Good-oh.' Alec stretched his arms.

'We don't want the Hun blowing us out of the water,' said Graham.

Alec closed his eyes for a second then stood up; his dream had given him something to drive him on.

They pushed the little skiff out in the cloak of darkness and clambered aboard. Graham sat in the bow ready to navigate. Tony and Alec sat side by side on the middle seat and took up their oars. Archie was last on board and assumed the coxswain's position. Before long, Alec and Tony were stroking in unison and the skiff glided smoothly out through the harbour into the Mediterranean. There wasn't a destroyer in sight. They rowed in total silence, the only sound, the oars slicing through the water. They were in perfect sync, their arms rolling forwards together, lifting as they lowered the oars and then pulling them through the water.

Graham ticked off the passing islands as they slowly made their way down Greece's long heel. After about six hours of rowing Alec was flagging. His arms were feeling like jelly, his bum ached, and his legs had cramped so much that he had lost all feeling. His mouth was dry while his empty stomach rumbled like an ancient earthquake on Mount Taygetos. He was desperately fighting delirium.

'I'm starting to fade,' he admitted.

'Me too,' said Tony.

Graham placed his hands firmly on their shoulders.

'Why don't we pull into one of these islands and try our luck? Surely we'll be able to get some food at one of the villages.'

'Good thinking,' Tony agreed.

All three sets of eyes settled on Archie's crumpled figure. He was sleeping like a baby.

'He needs a feed,' said Graham.

They laughed and turned the skiff towards land.

Tony stopped rowing and pointed into the distance. 'What's that?'

Alec peered with his stinging eyes. He could make out the shape of a battleship. His spirits suddenly lifted, though he wished he had his binoculars.

'Is it one of ours?' asked Tony.

'I don't know. All I know is that I can't row any further. Might as well try our luck,' Alec said.

They held their oars aloft and the skiff bobbed about like a toy in a bathtub. Alec lowered his oar into the water, turning the skiff around. He wasn't waiting for a committee meeting. As they came closer to the ship, he recognised the ensign of the Royal British Navy. His heart leapt.

'Ahoy there!' shouted a British sailor, leaning over the railing. 'Who goes there?'

'Jeez, sir. They're Poms!' cried Archie.

Graham waved the *Pix* as though it was a flag.

'We're Australians,' Alec called out to the small crowd of sailors and officers who had gathered on deck and were staring down at them.

'How do we know you're not Jerry?' the Captain asked.

'Do we look like …' Alec didn't bother finishing the sentence. He knew it was a ridiculous thing to say.

'Jesus. How are we going to convince them?' Graham's exasperation spoke for all of them.

Unsteadily getting to his feet, Alec started to sing the opening lines of Australia's unofficial anthem, 'Waltzing Matilda'.

At the chorus, the others enthusiastically joined in. In the second verse Alec raised his off-key, baritone voice, bowing theatrically as the song came to a close.

Alec had enjoyed a lot of drinks in his life but none so much as the scotch he drank that morning in the wardroom with the ship's captain.

36.

'Lieutenant Colonel Marshall, commanding officer of the regiment at the time, discovered when he embarked, that not all his men were aboard the destroyer. The ones who had been left behind put up a magnificent fight. They drove off the German advance guard and captured two field guns. But numbers were too heavily and hopelessly against them. Some were captured. Some got away.

'Of those, Captain Alec Murray and Captain Tony Philpott somehow obtained a rowing boat and sneaked off at night. A British destroyer sighted them and asked who they were. They said they were Australians but were at once challenged to sing "Waltzing Matilda" to prove it.'

'How dashing!' Peg laughed as Nell folded the article from the *Sydney Morning Herald* and put it back in her purse.

They were having an early morning cuppa at the Hopes' Edgecliff flat. Peg had only just returned from Cairo and Nell had convinced Fred to let her go down to Sydney for a few days to welcome her home.

Nell smiled, and yet there was something about Peg's demeanour that unsettled her. She wasn't her old self, and no amount of pretending it was 'business as usual' could mask it. Nevertheless, Nell was thrilled to have her home and to know that she was safe.

Being so isolated on Braemar had made it easy for Nell to imagine the war was a mirage. Like the rest of the country, she had been shielded from the reality of what those serving overseas had been going through.

But Alec being MIA had underlined just how serious the whole situation was. It had hit Nell hard, and seeing his family so distraught had affected her too. Not only did she understand how important he was to them, but she was now sure that she really did love him and that their time together hadn't been a fantasy.

'Do you know where he is now?' Peg asked.

'He's been recuperating on a houseboat on the Nile. We got a letter a few weeks back.'

'A houseboat on the Nile? That sounds very glamorous.'

They both laughed before Nell changed the tone. 'I don't know what to make of it. I don't know what to make of any of it. Everything seems …'

Peg finished the sentence for her, 'Crazy?'

Nell couldn't think of a better description. Peg raised her cup. 'Here's to us.'

Nell toasted her friend. 'Us.'

She took Peg's hands in hers. They shared a quiet moment before Nell spoke. 'I can't tell you how good it is to see you.'

A smile creased Peg's lips. 'I can't tell you how good it is to be here. In one piece.'

Nell hugged her tightly, then brushed a strand of hair from Peg's cheek and said softly, 'I have no idea what you have been through.'

It was Peg's turn to hug Nell. 'I've missed you,' she said with tears in her eyes.

That night, Carl Thomas's was packed with men in uniform and smartly dressed women doing their best to cheer them up. The champagne was flowing, but it was drunk more in desperation than celebration. Eyes that used to sparkle with naive optimism had been dulled by bitter reality. A good deal were hollowed out, sunken and encircled by a darkness that hinted at the horrors many had witnessed but few talked about.

Doing their best to put on a brave face, some couples laughed loudly but, to Nell's ears, unconvincingly. Others appeared distant, preoccupied. Some sat silently, uncomfortably, unable and unwilling to communicate with the wives, husbands, girlfriends and boyfriends they had been away from for so long. What secrets were they hiding? Nell felt sure that many of the women she saw doting on their men had been tempted like she had. How many had been unable to resist?

She decided to find out what had been troubling Peg. 'Your letters. Something's up. I know you too well. What is it?'

Peg looked away.

'Peg. You're hiding something. Tell me.'

When Peg turned back to her, Nell saw she had been hiding tears.

Peg wiped her eyes and said, 'Johnny's not the man he was. He has terrible nightmares. Wakes up screaming blue murder, shaking like a leaf, sweat pouring off him. It wasn't just the heat in Cairo, even though that was unbearable enough. He is drinking like a fish. It's nothing for him to polish off a bottle of scotch by himself. He anaesthetises himself. Tries to put his demons out of his mind.' She moved closer to Nell. 'He's become violent.'

Nell was horrified but not surprised. Peg had intimated that all wasn't well in her letters.

'Violent?'

For one of the first times since Nell had known her, Peg looked rattled.

'Yes. Throws things. Ripped some doors off a cupboard in Cairo and threw them out the window. Nearly killed some poor man who was cycling innocently by.'

Nell knew that Johnny had a rambunctious personality, but this sounded bad. There was no point in beating around the bush. She had to offer Peg the opportunity to talk.

'Does he ...'

Peg gave her a knowing look. 'Oh yes. He's hit me a few times.'

She might have been trying to brush it off, but Nell was having none of it. 'Peg ...'

'He's been working endless shifts in a field hospital. Imagine. Unrelenting horror. Men ... boys ... blown to smithereens. Their lives shattered. Their minds turned into spaghetti. Some of the poor buggers would have been better off dead.'

'That's no excuse.' Nell spoke more forcefully than she intended.

Peg folded her hands in her lap. 'No, it isn't but ...'

She pulled away from Nell as Johnny joined them. Nell noticed that the trademark spring in his step had gone.

'Nothing like a clean bathroom!' he said.

Somehow, Peg managed to straighten herself up and smile. 'Hello, darling. I was just telling Nell about our wedding.'

Johnny was full of beans and, Nell imagined, booze. He didn't even seem to notice that Peg had been crying.

'We tried to get old Alec to come over to Cairo, but he was otherwise engaged,' he said before he spotted reinforcements at the bar. 'Look! There's Roger Brown.'

Peg waved him off. 'Go on, darling. Go and say hello.'

He was already on his way. The spring returned to Johnny's step as he strode over to the group of men backslapping each other at the bar.

Peg laid her cards on the table. 'He'd rather be with men. Unless it's a tart.'

Nell could barely hide her fury as Peg continued. 'Yes. That's something else he picked up. A taste for tarts.'

'I hope he hasn't –'

'Picked anything else up? No. Not as far as I can tell.' She took a long drink, sat back in her chair, folded one long leg over the other and deftly changed the subject.

'Anyway, enough about me. What about you, m' dear?'

Nell was boiling. She found it hard to think about herself. She took a long drink before answering.

'Me? Compared to you, I've been on clover!'

'Painting?'

'I've been too busy helping my father to paint. I'm mustering, crutching, even classing the rams. I'm too buggered to do anything but sleep on my afternoons off.'

'You've got to make time. You don't want to lose … whatever it is you arty types have.' Uncrossing her legs and sitting forward, Peg touched her on the knee. 'It must be lonely.'

Nell blinked. 'It is. A bit. We had a fellow from the CSIR doing some research …'

That sparked Peg's interest, 'How old?'

'I don't know. I never asked him …' Nell took a sip of her drink and sat back.

'Young or old?' Peg asked.

'Young … ish.'

Peg persisted. 'Good looking?'

Nell returned serve. 'He's a scientist.'

Peg raised her eyebrows. 'Mmm?'

Nell feigned mock indignation. 'Don't you know I'm engaged?'

They dissolved into giggles as they collapsed into each other's arms. Nell was happy to have the old Peg back, even just for a few minutes.

Sitting up, they both watched as the men at the bar started to laugh loudly. Nell wondered what demons were they hiding? What demons would Alec bring home with him?

37.

Alec could just make out the Melbourne lights as the transport ship cut its way through the waters of Port Philip Bay. He had mixed feelings about coming home. Like a lot of Australian soldiers, he thought they should have stayed in Europe to defend Britain. But orders were orders and, besides, he was going to get married.

He had been thinking about it ever since they embarked. The thought of seeing Nell excited him. He hoped she still liked him. He would give anything to shed his uniform and return to the life he knew. But they hadn't discussed where they were going to live or what they were going to do. The thought had crossed his mind that Nell may not want to settle down on Toongowan. She might want to pursue her painting career in Sydney. What then? He certainly wouldn't stand in her way.

It had been nearly three years since he had set foot on Australian soil. Three long years. He wondered how much he had changed in that time? Or been changed. He hadn't had much time to reflect on such things. The only thing he was certain about was that he had left Australia with secret ambitions to become a Member of Parliament representing the Country Party. Now he was returning a committed socialist.

War had taught Alec that poverty was far from the 'moral failing' he'd been brought up to believe. His whole moral compass had been re-oriented. Now he was thinking about what he could do help those less fortunate than himself. The sight of unarmed Greek peasants fleeing the might of the German juggernaut had shown him the power that industrial might held over ordinary people. He had vowed that Stephen's death would not be in vain. He would do all in his might to honour his memory and live up to his example.

Like the waters below, all these thoughts swirled around as they came closer and closer to port. How was Nell going to react to his conversion? He hadn't said anything about it in his letters, as he couldn't imagine the censors taking too kindly to the news that a serving army officer had become a socialist. He and Nell had barely discussed politics. He suspected, even prayed, that she would empathise with his new political leanings.

As for her parents, he knew where Fred would stand, just as he knew exactly how his own father would react. It wasn't a conversation he was looking forward to. At least his mother would be happy to have him home in one piece.

One thing Alec did know, was that he had been responsible for inflicting a lot of suffering on a lot of people. The fact that most of them were hellbent on killing him didn't erase the images of human destruction that haunted his dreams.

The army psychologist had told Alec to put them out of his mind. 'Man survives by his ability to forget,' the doctor had said.

Alec would never forget Stephen proclaiming that the 'spinneys', the long, thin sausages they were served up when they first landed in El Kantara, were a part of an Italian plot to turn them around. He would never forget Stephen, full stop.

Alec was disappointed that the unit he had built into an efficient, highly disciplined fighting outfit would be disbanded. It was another decision made from 'on high' that tested his fealty to his commanding officers.

He wasn't sure where he was going next, except that he had a few weeks leave, and that more than occupied his mind as they approached Melbourne.

Marriage? What would that entail? Many men had returned from service overseas or were home on leave for a few weeks and had married almost immediately. Many, like him, must hardly have known the women they were getting hitched to.

The way Alec felt, anything that didn't involve guns and death was more than welcome. The Japanese had taken control of Papua New Guinea's northern coast and, even though they had managed to avoid the Japanese Navy on the way home, Alec was certain he would be coming up against them in the future.

As he leant on the ship's railing he reflected on how different he and his men were from the enthusiastic young men who'd left Australia all those years ago. Now they were hardened soldiers with a library of experiences and memories that none of them would ever forget. Or probably, ever get over.

38.

'A socialist!' Nell had been gazing at the faded wallpaper in their cheap hotel room when Alec made the announcement.

'I had to tell you,' he said.

She let this sink in as a fly buzzed around the room and settled on the dreary curtain. She couldn't remember ever feeling better. Or more relaxed. All she wanted to do was hold Alec close to her. She turned over and held out her arms. He hesitated for a second, as if he was expecting something else, before letting her take him in her arms.

They lay in silence for some time, each totally in sync with the other.

Alec stroked her forehead gently. 'I'm sorry …'

Nell pulled back a little and stared into his eyes. He looked different. He was still incredibly handsome but some of the light had gone out of his eyes. In a funny way, he looked much older.

'Sorry? For what?' she said.

'Oh … I don't know … I didn't know …'

'What? You didn't know what?'

'How you were going to react …'

He lay back and put his hands behind his head.

Nell watched him for a second, then burst out laughing. He had spoilt the moment with his talk and she was going to punish him for it. She grabbed a pillow and pummelled him. He tried to protect himself but only succeeded in falling off the bed.

'Take that, you bloody socialist!'

He pretended to cower.

'You'd better get used to it.' She put the pillow down and caught her breath.

Alec laughed. 'We'd both better get used to it.'

She collapsed on the floor beside him.

'You've got a tough nut!' she said as she noticed the kapok from the torn pillow covering the floor. She grabbed his arm. 'I thought you were going to tell me you wanted to break off our engagement or … that … you had syphilis or something!'

He seemed relieved. 'You're not … angry …'

'Angry?' She nestled against his shoulder and traced a circle on his knee. 'Hardly.'

He stood up, lifted her to her feet and kissed her fully on the lips. It was pure bliss, but Nell knew it couldn't last. After a few delicious minutes in his arms, she took his hands and looked up at him.

'What am I going to tell Father?'

He smiled and squeezed her hand. 'I don't know. What am I going to tell mine?'

They laughed.

'Shall I tell him I've been consorting with a communist?' Nell said.

'Consorting?'

'Well, you are the enemy now.'

He corrected her. 'Actually, the communists are on our side!'

'Don't worry, you're not the first communist …'

'I'm not a communist. I'm a socialist.'

She thought of Lance and felt her cheeks burn. 'A chap who is working for father …' She felt flustered.

Alec looked at her with a curious expression. 'A communist is working for Frederick Hope?'

Nell sat on the bed. 'Of course, Father doesn't know he's a communist.' She paused. 'He's a scientist. He's also a pacifist. That's why he didn't enlist.'

'A … young … fellow?'

She searched his face. 'You're not jealous, are you?'

'Should I be?'

She shook her head and quickly reassured him. 'No …' course not.'

She patted the spot beside her. He joined her. She pushed him back on bed and straddled him. 'So, my socialist friend, tell me …'

Once again, he folded his hands behind his head and looked into her eyes before speaking.

'It's a lot of things. When we were in Libya, I started to wonder why the mechanics, who kept the whole show going, weren't better rewarded. They were magicians, keeping the machinery ticking over in the most appalling conditions. That desert sand … couldn't keep it out … yet somehow … with the most rudimentary tools, improvising madly, they managed to keep us going. We wouldn't have gone anywhere without them. And what did they get for it?'

He paused, then said, 'I learnt that the only thing that really matters in warfare is whether someone is any good when the chips are down. It doesn't matter where they come from or what school they went to. It doesn't even matter what rank they are. A couple of pips on the shoulder is no guarantee that a man is any good. The bloke you gave an earful to for stealing an extra ration might be the man who gets you out of a scrape. You might be better off turning to him than the bloke you sat next to in the officers' mess. The fact is, some of my fellow "officers", who paraded about as though they owned the place, weren't worth a cracker in a crisis.'

Nell couldn't take her eyes off him. She saw something in him that excited her. She was glad she had waited for him.

'Who makes money out of war? Not the poor bastard stuffing shells into the guns that's for bloody sure,' he said. 'When this bloody thing is over, I'm going to do something about it.'

Nell felt herself falling in love with him all over again.

'What?' she asked.

'I don't know. It's a question I've been wrestling with. Something …'

She bent down and kissed him. 'I'll help you.'

His held her tightly. 'Will you? I … this is the best news I've had for a long time. I was afraid you would be horrified.'

They spent the rest of the night in a state of rapture. Not only were they reunited but they were joined in a shared cause. Neither wanted the night to end.

*

When the sun began shine through the curtains, Nell lay with her head on his bare chest and clung to him as tightly as she could. She heard him chuckle.

'What?' she asked as she traced a circle around the fine hairs on his chest.

'Nothing. For the first time in ages, I wasn't thinking about anything when I noticed that.' He pointed first to the ceiling and then to the wall. Nell rolled over and noticed that the paint around the ceiling fan was peeling and a watermark ran down to where the skirting was lifting from the wall.

'Not the most salubrious hotel, I'm afraid.'

'Who cares?' She sat up, wrapped a sheet around herself and gently ruffled his hair. 'Besides, I wanted you all for myself. If we'd taken a room at the Club, the whole world would have known you were home.'

He waved a finger. 'And tongues would have wagged.'

She kissed his ear. 'They would have wagged all right.'

Alec rolled onto his side, drew closer to her and closed his eyes.

Her eyes wandered down his resting body. He was so long, his feet hung over the end of the bed. He looked beautifully vulnerable.

Before long he was sleeping like a baby. Nell gently stroked his hair. He was exquisite. So young but so old. After a while she slipped out of bed, careful not to disturb him.

She was staring out the window when she heard him wake up. For a fleeting second, she thought about how far she had travelled since Paris. She turned to him.

'I've got an idea.'

'Have you just?' he said, yawning.

'Let's get married!'

'We're going to, aren't we?'

Nell grinned as she explained, 'Yes, but by ourselves.'

'What do you mean?'

She laid out the plans she'd been hatching. 'We'll find a registry office and ask Peg and Johnny to be our witnesses.'

He sat up. 'Are you serious?'

She leapt on the bed. 'Yes!'

He scratched his head. 'Why?'

Nell threw herself on top of him. 'I want to have you all to myself. I don't want to wait for all the palaver. It won't be our wedding. It will be our parents'. Who knows who will be invited? It will be a society do and we'll be consigned to playing roles we detest. I want you now.'

She placed her fingers on his lips and whispered, 'We won't tell anyone.'

She searched his face as he absorbed this.

'Just Peg and Johnny?' he asked.

'That's right. Just Peg and Johnny.' She kissed him. 'Best to strike while the iron is hot, don't you think?'

'Are you serious?'

'Deadly.'

She was having the time of her life. She kissed him again before he could ask any more questions.

Two days later, they were standing before a marriage celebrant in a registry office. Alec dressed in his uniform, Nell in a simple yellow dress that hung off the shoulder and fanned out above her knees. She held a small bouquet.

'Alec Herbert Murray, do you take Helen Margot Hope to be your lawful wedded wife?'

'I do.'

The man conducting the service in his striped, brown suit turned to Nell. 'And you, Helen Margot Hope, do you take Alec Herbert Murray to be your lawful wedded husband?'

Nell almost shrieked her reply. 'I do!'

Peg, standing beside her in a bright red frock, couldn't contain her giggles. Johnny Buchanan slapped Alec heartily on the back.

'I therefore declare you to be man and wife!'

After they had signed the marriage certificate, the celebrant ushered them out the door. There were other returned servicemen rushing to tie the knot before discovering their next posting.

A few days later, Alec left for a training camp in jungle warfare at Greta in the Hunter Valley.

39.

'Pee on some wheat,' Peg said.

Nell looked at her incredulously. She had just returned from her gynaecologist who had confirmed that she was pregnant.

They were sharing the bottle of brandy Peg had smuggled into The Women's Club. Around them were women who, like Nell, were once again going to be left behind by their men. Australian soldiers were still being whisked away to countries they had barely heard of to do battle against enemies they had never imagined would be a threat. In small groups, the women were talking in hushed tones over their cups of tea.

'Yes. You see, if you pee on a wheat seed and it sprouts you are having a girl. If you pee on a barley seed and it sprouts you are having a boy. If neither sprout you aren't up the duff!'

Nell rubbed her tummy as she had been doing since she first thought she might be pregnant. 'Where did you get that one from?' she asked.

'The Ancient Egyptians.'

'I'm glad you weren't wasting your time over there.'

Peg raised her eyebrows as Nell continued. 'At least I don't need to pee on the wheat crop to find out if I'm pregnant.'

Peg nodded thoughtfully. She placed her cup on the table and took Nell's hand. 'How do you feel?'

'All right. I haven't been sick yet.'

'I don't mean physically.'

'Oh …'

Nell gently removed her hand and took a cigarette out of the silver cigarette case Alec had sent her as a present. She flicked open her lighter, lit a cigarette and blew a cloud of smoke into the air. She was nervous, and she knew that her friend had picked up on this. She ashed her cigarette in the monogrammed ashtray.

'Do you mean about being pregnant?'

Peg nodded. Nell did her best to articulate thoughts she hadn't fully formed. 'Well … I certainly didn't plan it. I don't know how I feel. It's been an incredible month since he came home. I can scarcely believe it. One minute we're together. The next we're married. Then he's gone away to some training camp. I miss my period before we go through another wedding ceremony. I was expecting him to be around for a few months but now …'

Nell shut her eyes and pinched the bridge of her nose while she tried to collect her thoughts. 'Now he's off again!'

Peg leant forward and gently touched her knee before Nell threw her hands in the air.

'How do I feel? How am I meant to feel? I suppose I'm excited. I'm meant to be … aren't I?'

Nell became aware that she had an audience of women who seemed to be offering her support. She shrugged apologetically.

One of the woman, about the same age as her mother, smiled warmly at her. 'You're right, love. We're on your side.'

Nell nearly burst into tears. She composed herself and continued. 'To tell you the truth, I'm terrified.' She briefly closed her eyes again. 'I've never really thought about being a mother. I mean, if you're not married … if you're not planning … you don't give it much thought. Or, at least, I haven't.'

Peg smiled reassuringly, and Nell felt safe with her. She knew she could tell her anything. She knew Peg would give her time. After a few minutes of shared silence, Nell tried to explain. 'I always imagined that once this … business … was over … I'd come down here and pursue my life as an artist. Or go back to Europe. If …' She raised her arms in a gesture that said, 'Who knows?'

Her tone changed. 'I'm twenty-three, Peg. I've spent the last three years biding my time. I understood that I was … well … no one knows better than you … doing my bit for the country. I was looking forward to doing my bit for me.' Nell could see that Peg was listening intently as she bared her soul. 'Is that selfish of me?'

'Of course not, darling,' said Peg.

'Alec's going to New Guinea. I don't know when he'll be back. I don't know if he'll be back. I don't … know …'

Nell started to cry. She couldn't help it even though she didn't want to lay all this on Peg. Her friend stood up and knelt beside her. Nell fell into her arms and let herself go. One of the other women came over, gave her a hanky and gently squeezed her shoulder. As she composed herself, Nell looked around the roomful of women. All different ages and shapes and sizes. All offering her unstated support. All united in solidarity.

She sniffled. 'I'm glad you brought me here,' she said, wiping her eyes. She felt bad that the whole thing had been about her. She took a sip of brandy and changed the subject. 'You're not following Johnny to New Guinea?'

Peg hooted. 'No! That would be a bridge too far! I thought of joining the Land Army and doing some farm work, but all that fresh air would drive me batty. I'm going to do a teaching degree by day and work in a factory in Mascot making bomb casings at night.'

'Teaching?'

'Yes. Why not? With all the men at war there is a shortage of teachers. I want to teach Ancient History.'

Nell grabbed Peg's hands and squeezed them tight, 'You'll be a great teacher!'

A broad smile spread across Peg's face.

'And you'll be a great mum!'

Once again, Nell rubbed her tummy. 'I hope so.'

40.

As the *Joseph Lane* negotiated its way through a coral reef that was every bit as pristine as the Great Barrier Reef they had left behind, Alec began to see why Port Moresby was a prize the Japanese were keen to grab. It was a perfect harbour from which to launch an assault on an unwitting Australia. Looking up at the mountain ranges that surrounded the island, he realised that this conflict was going to be very different from the last one he'd fought in.

The events of the past month had him feeling like he had been tossed like a salad. It was one party after another, and he'd loved every minute of it. Anything to divert his attention from the next military engagement. But now, sailing into Port Moresby, he put all that behind him. One thing the army had taught him was how to compartmentalise. It was the only way to survive at war.

Before he knew it, Alec was fighting his way through dense tropical rainforest towards the village of Ango. Giant trees towered over him and made him anxious about what they were concealing. The jungle could provide endless cover for their enemy. He managed to hold back intense nausea as he trudged through putrid, slimy water, some of it containing the rotting remains of fallen soldiers. His bare shins were sliced by sharp-leafed kunai grass that cut like a knife. And he tried to swat the ever-present, malaria-carrying mosquitoes that attacked at will.

When his men had finally hacked their way into a clearing, Alec was assaulted by the sight of the mutilated bodies of Australian soldiers hanging from trees. The Japanese had used them for bayonet practice. Dismembered body parts were scattered around the undergrowth like dog bones. The final horror was the discovery of severed heads on the ground or stuck on bamboo poles.

This was a living hell; nothing had prepared Alec for the horror. Being one of the leading officers in the Expeditionary Force, he had to draw on every bit of fortitude to carry on.

Not only were the conditions horrific, but as in Europe, Alec had the added responsibility of ordering his men to land their shells in front of the advancing Australian troops, clearing any defending Japanese out of the way, and any miscalculation on his part would mean the death of his own men. He couldn't see a foot in front of him through the foliage, so he had to rely, mostly, on intuition.

Back in Sydney, Alec had been celebrating life, now he was taking it. He had to muster all his reserves of self-discipline to stay focussed. He'd never felt intimidated like this before, but he couldn't show it. He had to lead from the front. When he broke his ankle diving for cover from a Japanese bomb, he was forced to strap himself up and carry on regardless.

41.

Four months after the whirlwind of her romance and the two weddings, Nell did her best to make the most of her predicament. She had survived the first four months of her pregnancy and was growing accustomed to the prospect of being a mother. The constant vomiting was over, and she was surprised how relaxed she'd become about the growing bump in her belly. She talked to it, stroked it and fell in love with it.

One major consolation was that her father had relieved her of farming duties and she was able to return to her painting. Much to Elaine's dismay, she rode Ginger down to the river, where she painted on the small, leftover pieces of timber she found around the place. Her paintings, she decided, were like picture postcards interpreting the Australian bush. She discovered a darkness that in some ways expressed the pain that had descended on her world. Pain she tried to hide but that expressed itself in her paintings. They owed more to Frida Kahlo, to whom Lance had introduced her, than Margaret Preston.

She hadn't heard any news from Alec since he had left for New Guinea. Thankfully, Lance had returned from Canberra to complete his research.

'Even though he's closer, he seems further away than ever,' she said.

Lance was filing samples in his makeshift laboratory in the dairy. 'I don't know how you do it,' he said admiringly.

She stuck a label on a test tube.

'I couldn't if I didn't have you to lean on.'

Lance stopped working for a second and tentatively approached her. 'Actually ...'

When he didn't finish the sentence, she knew something was up. 'What?'

He stumbled around for the right words. 'I'm ... I've got to go back. To Canberra. When I finish this ...'

Nell couldn't believe what she was hearing. She had come to rely on Lance for moral and emotional support. Their relationship had effortlessly segued into a close friendship. She confided in him about her doubts and fears while he opened up too. Far from being the stuck-up brainy box that he had first appeared , she discovered he was a man who was wrestling with many unresolved questions, not least his sexuality.

Lance had confessed to Nell that she was the only woman he had ever been attracted to in a way that was emotional rather than physical. He had kissed her as an experiment. When he told her this, she roared with laughter and admitted that she too, had been swept away by the combination of alcohol, loneliness and the magic of the evening. His admission made her somehow feel less conflicted.

'I have to go back to the CSIR to write this stuff up.'

She could see that he had been nervous about telling her. She put down the test tube and hugged him. She wasn't going to let him feel guilty.

'I know. We all have to do our bit!' she said, trying to make light of the news. 'I'll miss you terribly but ...' she trailed off, hugging him tightly.

When she finally released him, she saw that he was crying.

'You're the only person who has ever listened to me. Or wanted to listen to me. I don't know what I'm going to do without you, Nell.'

She took him in her arms again. Eventually she pulled away, wiped her eyes and laughed. 'Look at us! Pair of sooks.'

Lance joined in. 'I've always been a sook.'

'Me too.'

*

A few weeks later, Nell drove Lance to the station and waved him off. She reflected on how far they had come since she first picked him up all those months ago. On the way home, she consoled herself with the thought that he was only going to Canberra, not some place she had never heard of and from which he might never return.

Without Lance to confide in, Nell became increasingly worried about what kind of mother she would be. Her own mother's well-intentioned but constant advice was driving her crazy. She tried to imagine life with a new baby: changing nappies, not sleeping, missing Alec. Lance's departure highlighted the loneliness and trepidation she was feeling.

It took every bit of self-control she could draw on to tolerate the patronising old doctor in Dubbo who treated her like a child and advised her not to give up smoking.

'Giving up smoking turns placid, sweet tempered girls into intolerable shrews,' he announced while prodding her belly with his stubby little fingers.

'I'm neither placid nor sweet tempered,' she said, smiling.

'Feel that?' He placed her hand lower on her belly.

She nearly exploded with joy as she felt the movement.

'She's kicking!' Nell shrieked with delight.

'She?' He peered over his tortoise-shell spectacles.

Nell just laughed; nothing had prepared her for this.

And when Elaine dropped a catalogue for maternity girdles onto the kitchen table while Nell was having a cup of tea at breakfast the next day, it was all she could do not to burst into a fit of giggles.

'I picked it up for you last week when I was in Sydney,' Elaine said, nodding at the catalogue. 'Girdles will help you keep in shape.'

Nell read aloud, 'Abdominal rotundity is a handicap.'

Elaine fussed about awkwardly. 'You have to lie on your back to put it on ...'

'Why?' Nell asked, as innocently as she could.

Her mother didn't reply, but started to prepare some fruit for preserving.

Nell read on. 'Lying on your back will make your uterus collapse and therefore it won't be as obvious ...'

Elaine nearly dropped her preserving jar.

Nell lowered the catalogue and asked, 'Do I have *special radiance*?'

She knew her mother was doing her best. She appreciated the afternoon tea parties she arranged for Nell, so she could meet up with some of the other expectant mothers whose men were away at war. It was a lovely gesture, but Nell was bored witless by the endless talk about babies and nurseries.

She had to get away, and convinced Elaine that she needed her own place. Her parents offered her their flat in Edgecliff but it would still be their flat, not hers. Peg did some research for her and discovered that the prospect of a Japanese attack had many Sydneysiders taking to the hills, leaving their Northern Beaches seaside cottages empty. Nell was quick to find a house at Collaroy and Fred generously offered to pay the rent.

It didn't worry Nell that coils of barbed wire were stretched out along the beach to keep the enemy out. She was happy to have her own place and she was near Peg. She used any spare time she had to paint and organise her little house for the baby's arrival. Lance came up from Canberra as often as he could and he and Peg helped her decorate the nursery.

All she needed was for Alec to come home.

42.

Sitting on the beach with the sea breeze on her face, Nell was sketching when she heard a voice.

'Not going in?'

She wheeled around to see a handsome man in military uniform, silhouetted against the setting sun, striding towards her.

'Oh my God!' she screamed, trying unsuccessfully to spring to her feet.

She felt like her heart had leapt into her throat. She had been wrestling with the thought that Alec might never come home and now he was here. In person. Real. She burst into tears of joy.

Alec helped her up. He enveloped her in his arms and hugged her tightly. She nestled her head in his chest and felt a wave of relief and joy roll over her. She looked up at him, he was the most beautiful thing she had ever seen. They kissed. It was all she could do to contain herself.

'My knight in shining armour,' she exclaimed, wiping the tears from her cheeks.

'I think the armour might have lost some of its sheen,' he said. He pointed at her tummy. 'When?'

'Anytime soon. Very soon, I hope.'

Alec placed his hands gently on her shoulders. 'I wish … I wish I could be here for you …'

Nell's mood darkened. 'What …'

She bit her lip. For a moment she had imagined that she would have someone to hold her hand when her waters broke. Someone who would drive her to hospital. Someone who would be around to share the birth of their first child.

'We only have the weekend off,' he said apologetically, 'before we go to Townsville for more training. I've got to learn about naval warfare and air reconnaissance ...' His voice trailed off.

Nell wasn't interested in the details. She just wanted him home. She did her best to hide her disappointment as she sat back down and stared out to sea. He joined her and took her hand.

'I'm sorry.'

The sound of children playing and waves breaking on the shallows filled the silence.

Alec pointed at the rolls of barbed wire that the swimmers and playing children were careful to avoid.

'What is it?' she asked, thinking he was going to talk about the children.

'The army,' he said, shaking his head. 'As if a few rolls of barbed wire are going to keep an invading army out.'

Nell was alarmed. 'You don't think ...'

Alec put his arm around her, and she let her head drop on his shoulder.

'No. There isn't going to be an invasion. We are pushing them back. One of the reasons I'm here is to hasten proceedings. They want me to help ...'

Nell looked away. She wanted him to help *her*. Desperately.

Not seeming to notice, Alec waved at the barbed wire. 'This type of thing is for domestic consumption. It's to show that the government is doing something to protect you.'

Nell straightened up and looked over at the rolls of wire.

Back at the house, she prepared lunch. 'Father dropped off some meat when he was last in town.'

She had pulled herself together and was putting on a brave face. If she only had Alec for a few hours, she had better make the most of it.

He seemed to read her mind. He gently took the knife she was slicing the meat with from her hands, placed it on the bench, turned her around and kissed her with all his being. They made love like there was no tomorrow. She wished it could last forever.

While Nell returned to preparing lunch, Alec sat at the laminated table and opened his rucksack. Nell couldn't remember if he liked pickles or not, but took a punt on her homemade batch.

'I thought these might come in handy,' he said, placing packets of tea and sugar and some butter on the table.

'And these …' He reached into his top pocket and took out some tickets.

She wiped her hands and placed their plates of corned beef, mashed potatoes and fresh peas on the table. 'I got the veg from a market gardener up on the plateau,' she explained, reading his mind.

'Have a look,' he said as he tucked into what Nell guessed was the first fresh meal he had eaten in months.

She picked up the tickets. 'Motor Spirit Ration Tickets? 5 Gallons? How did you get these … with all the rationing?'

He smiled proudly.

'Aren't you a clever boy,' she said, though she would have happily swapped anything for having him there. They ate for a moment in silence, before he took a slurp of beer.

'It shouldn't be long. I should be home soon.'

Nell was relieved that he hadn't entirely missed the point. She looked at him closely. He looked older, more worn. Even though he wouldn't admit it, the war was clearly taking its toll.

43.

On Victoria's Mornington Peninsula attending a naval bombardment course, Alec was studying distances and angles when a fresh-faced orderly poked his head through the tent flap and handed him a wire.

'Excuse me, sir, I think this might be important.'

His cheeky grin told Alec that whatever the news was, it must be good. He unfolded the message.

Douglas Henry Murray born 1650 hours. Mother and child doing well. Regards Elaine Hope.

Alec stared at the telegram. The tent flap fluttered wildly while the orderly waited to be dismissed. Alec had momentarily forgotten he was there.

'Thank you, Smithers. You can go.'

'Yes, sir. Thank you, sir.'

Smithers pushed the flap open and was halfway out when he stopped, inadvertently letting the wind scatter everything not nailed down. He turned back and offered Alec his hand.

'Congratulations, sir.'

Alec smiled and shook his hand. 'Thank you.'

'Must be good being a dad.'

It took Alec a second to digest this.

'It is ...'

The orderly departed, once more sending everything flying.

'I think.'

Alec secured the tent flap before sitting down. He picked up the telegram. It was dated May 24, 1943. He was shocked. He reflected that he had embarked for Palestine at the beginning of 1940. Although it was only a bit over three years ago, it felt like a lifetime. Thanks to this war, he had missed what was probably the most important event in his life. He didn't question his commitment to the cause, but he had begun to question how long he could continue in active service before he handed over the baton to someone else, someone less damaged.

He could tell how upset Nell had been when he'd announced he was just dropping in. He couldn't do anything about it but still, it had stung. He swore that, whatever else he did, he would devote the rest of his life to ensuring it was all worth it: that changes would be made to prevent such horror from raining down on innocent people again. Alec knew those changes were structural. The people who made decisions had to be accountable to everyone and to represent everyone. Not just the ruling class. He might be a loyalist, but he was also committed to helping create a more equitable society. Alec didn't see those two things as incompatible.

He had come the admire the British Labour figure, Nye Bevan, after Stephen had introduced him to his writing. Like Bevan, Alec was starting to believe that they had to get rid of outdated social structures, and that this war had provided the opportunity to tear them all down and start again. Ever since he'd met Stephen, Alec had been thinking about a new society and what it might look like. The birth of a son only stiffened his resolve.

He bent down and picked up the sheets of paper that had scattered all over the tent. They needed to be rearranged into some sort of order. It gave him a small sense of control. Since he was returning to Port Moresby in a few days, there would be no chance of seeing his newborn son.

44.

Absolutely nothing prepared Nell for how she would feel about motherhood. Her little treasure was so tiny she could scarcely touch him without worrying that she would damage him in some way. She marvelled at how his little fingers gripped hers, how he raised his head to her breast when she put him on her stomach, his indescribably beautiful smell that reminded her of lanolin. His every movement filled her with wonder and she was desperate to share it with her husband.

That Alec was so close, made it even worse. He occasionally dropped in for a few days en route to somewhere or between doing something or other. Truth be told, like everyone else, she was heartily sick of the war, especially the uncertainty that came with it. When Alec was on the other side of the world, she'd had no choice but to get on with her life. Now she never knew when he was going to turn up bearing gifts and forced good cheer. Their brief time together only reinforced how lonely she was without him. He would come home and help with the baby for a day or two and then disappear, leaving her to cope as best she could. But he was missing out on what, to Nell, was nothing short of a miracle as Doug's eyes opened, he started making sounds and became a real, living, human being. It touched something in Nell that she never knew existed and she wished Alec was there to experience it with her.

She received scraps of information about his whereabouts from a few sources. Peg heard that he had been seconded as a naval bombardment liaison officer on the HMAS *Shropshire* and had sailed to Milne Bay to join US Task Force 74 at the end of October. There were rumours that there was light at the end of the tunnel, and they were preparing for a naval bombardment to cover the counterattack against the Japanese in East New Britain, Papua New Guinea. Not that Nell knew or particularly cared what all this meant.

By the time Doug was six months old Nell was feeling the isolation. The occasional visit from Peg or Lance gave her momentary respite, but once they departed she was left on her own to cope with the increasing demands of being a single mother. This was not what she had imagined when she'd discovered she was pregnant. Elaine offered advice and support but didn't seem too keen on lessening the load for her daughter.

The endless rounds of changing and washing nappies, feeding, washing bed clothes, swaddling and deliriously pacing with her crying baby in the dead of night were exhausting. Then there were times when it felt as if her own body had betrayed her: the shooting pain after feeding, cracked and sore nipples, back pain.

Nell never had a moment to herself. Her paint brushes were hardening through neglect. Realising that she would never have time to use them, she packed them away. It was all she could do not to feel resentful.

Her prayers were finally answered when Alec was granted extended leave in early January. The Japanese were on the run and Alec had ended his secondment to the American Navy. He might have missed Doug's first Christmas but at least he was finally coming home.

These few days at Collaroy with her little family were possibly the most joyous of her life, Nell thought. It had been eighteen months since they were married and Alec had spent virtually no time with her and almost none with his seven-month-old son. She wondered how he would cope.

Much to her relief, he took to fatherhood like a duck to water. She determined to make the most of having another pair of hands around, and do some of the things she had dreamt of since Douggie was born. At the beach, she had looked on with envy as fathers built sandcastles on the water's edge with their children and couples walked hand in hand along the sand. Even though she loved swimming, she had ignored the pull of the surf as there was no way she could have left Doug, to enjoy catching a few waves.

She took advantage of Alec's return by sunbaking while he played with Douggie in the shade of the brightly coloured umbrella. She pulled the straps of her bathers down to get an even tan on her back and avoid zebra stripes on her shoulders. She lay on her tummy and watched Alec hold his son aloft with big, strong arms. The little boy giggled. Alec pushed his sunglasses to the back of his head and gave him a horsey ride by bouncing him on his stomach.

'Careful!'

'He's got to learn to ride.'

Nell briefly closed her eyes. She prayed she wasn't dreaming.

'Whoa up!'

Alec lifted his delighted son into the air before gently placing him down on the sand. Douggie wobbled a little uncertainly before gaining his balance. He reached for his little red shovel. Just as the little boy was about to fall face first into the sand, Alec grabbed it for him. Nell laughed as Doug innocently flicked specks of sand into his dad's face.

While their son happily amused himself digging in the sand, Alec crawled out from under the umbrella, lay on his back beside Nell and took her hand. She entwined her fingers in his and held on for dear life. She didn't ever want to let him go. After a while his grip loosened, and he was snoring softly. Nell rested her head on his gently moving chest. She traced a heart in the sand. Would they ever be able to share the hidden secrets of the past few years? She lifted her head and looked at him closely. He looked older than his thirty-one years.

A couple of older women walking arm in arm along the beach caught her eye and smiled approvingly.

Nell lifted herself up on her hands and watched the waves swelling up to a peak before breaking for the body surfers to slide down. It was a good surf. Just as she contemplated waking Alec, she heard his deep, baritone voice, 'Long time since I've seen a good wave.'

She turned and squinted at the bright sunshine. 'You're awake?'

He was leaning on his elbows. 'Why don't you go in? I'll keep an eye on our little friend.'

This is more like it, Nell thought. Before he could change his mind, she leapt to her feet, gave him a peck on the forehead and sprinted into the water.

She dived under a wave, pulled her arms back and emerged outside the breakers. She trod water for a few minutes, searching for the next wave. She noticed the swell picking up, turned towards the shoreline and began swimming as quickly as she could. When she felt the wave take hold, she pulled her arms to her side, lifted her head and let the surf take her in. Just as she felt the wave was about to break, she tucked her head into her chest, did a tumble turn and stroked out the back to catch another.

Time stood still as she exulted in the freedom of surfing unencumbered. She loved the water and laughed at the thought of all the hours she had spent staring longingly at the surf while she played with Doug. Now Alec was home she was determined that she was going to get her life back.

After she had run out of steam, she caught one last wave in. Arriving back at the towels, she flicked the water off her hair playfully at Alec, then grabbed Doug and gave him a feed. She couldn't have been happier.

The two old women, who had smiled approvingly before, stopped and stared at Nell breastfeeding in public. She gave them the 'thumbs up' with her spare hand. They tottered off muttering under their breath. Nell restrained herself.

By the time they had walked back to the house, Doug had fallen asleep in Alec's arms.

'I'll put him down,' he said.

Nell tied her hair back, slipped into a light cotton dress, slung a tea towel over her shoulder and began preparing lunch. 'Are you hungry?'

He patted his tummy. 'Could eat a horse.'

'We might be able to stretch to something better than that.'

'Horse is okay.'

Her eyes widened. 'You didn't?'

'Who knows what we were eating half the time.'

She paused for a second before breaking off some lettuce leaves and tossing them into a bowl with slices of tomato.

'I bought these from an Italian market gardener on the plateau. Although he doesn't admit to being Italian. For obvious reasons.'

'I liked the Italians. Most of the ones we came across weren't all that keen on fighting …' Alec trailed off, disappearing into his own thoughts.

Nell placed the green salad on the table, sprinkled some chopped parsley over a potato salad and added it and a plate of corned beef to the spread. She kissed him. 'Well. You're home now.'

He took both her hands in his and smiled. 'I am.'

She put a plate in front of him, pulled up a chair and raised her glass. 'Here's to our little family.'

'Indeed.' He beamed as he helped himself to a feed, then cocked his head in Douggie's direction. 'He's sleeping well.'

'You wore him out.'

After they had eaten, they made love on the bamboo lounge and fell asleep in each other's arms.

Soon, a little voice rang out.

'Uh oh. Someone's awake!'

Before Nell could respond Alec was on his feet. 'I'll get him.'

She stretched her arms and yawned. She could get used to this. He returned with Doug, handed him to her and started cleaning up.

Later, as they sat drinking tea and Doug rolled around on the floor, Alec pulled a book from his kitbag.

'Can I read you something?'

'I'd love you to.'

'Walt Whitman. A Yank officer gave it to me as a thank you present.'

He flicked through the pages and cleared his throat.

'I dream'd in a dream I saw a city invincible to the attacks of the whole
of the rest of the earth;
I dream'd that was the new City of Friends;
Nothing was greater there than the quality of robust love – it led the rest;
It was seen every hour in the actions of the men of that city,
And in all their looks and words.
Isn't that … inspirational?'

Nell smiled. She was glad he had the old spark back.

'City of friends? I like that.'

'I'm thinking of starting an Australian chapter of The Common Wealth. A few of us have been talking about it. I learnt about it from the sailors who picked me up off Greece. It was started by Priestly and other writers.'

'Of what?'

'It's a British movement. It's not a political party in the traditional sense. It's a movement. A movement where everyone has a say in policy. The idea is to create cooperatives so workers have a share in the industries they work for. Take them away from private individuals so the profits go back to the people who get their hands dirty instead of the owners who sit in the back of Rolls Royces smoking cigars.'

Nell thought of Lance. It was the kind of thing he would say. The idea excited her. She could see that Alec had come back with new a sense of purpose. She didn't know where it would take them, but she was more than prepared to go along with it. Like Alec and Lance, she was committed to changing the status quo, even if it would cause tension at her parents' house.

Nell wrapped her arms around her legs and rested her head on her knees. 'Go on.'

Alec began to outline his manifesto. 'What I am proposing is that all land should be state owned. Once the state has control of the land it can be leased back to the current landholders. I've come to the conclusion that centralised control of farming practices is the only way to ensure we can return the land to its former glory.'

Nell laughed. 'My father's going to love that idea.'

'So is mine.' He continued. 'We have to make sacrifices. Our families might be collateral damage. They can't keep exploiting the land and its people. Let alone the people who work on it.'

'You mean jackeroos?'

'Jackeroos, jillaroos, shearers, fruit pickers. Anyone who isn't getting a fair day's wage for a fair day's work.'

Nell covered her mouth as though shocked. 'I knew you were a communist!'

He shrugged. 'That's what a lot of people will say.'

For the first time in years, Nell felt there was something she could really get stuck into. She had always been uncomfortable with the superior attitude of many of the privileged people she had grown up with, both at home and at school. It was something she shared with Peg, a desire to pull the pompous down a peg or two. As Peg had said to her once, 'They all shit like we do.'

Nell liked the idea that ownership should be shared by everyone, and that local shires and councils should take care of leaseholds. She just couldn't see her father giving up his ownership without a hell of a fight. Working as a glorified jillaroo had made her see just how low on the rung the workers really were.

A couple of days later Alec received notification that the 2nd First Field Regiment had seen enough action and were being transferred to the Army Reserve.

'I'm not going to sit around twiddling my thumbs in the Reserve. If I'm not fighting, I'm going farming.'

'When ...'

'Now.'

Nell grabbed him and hugged him tightly. This is what she had been dreaming of.

45.

When Alec pulled off the road and turned onto the track to Toongowan, Nell took a deep breath. She felt a sense of nervous anticipation as she bounced Doug on her knees while Alec opened the gate. He paused and stretched his arms.

'Daddy deserves this,' she whispered to her son.

Alec strode back to the new Dodge that Fred had given them. Nell pondered over the fact that it could well be the last present her father ever gave them. She saw Alec staring up at the mountain range.

'What is it?' she asked as he climbed back into the car.

'It's the High Court. Awaiting judgement.'

She let it ride. He obviously enjoyed his joke.

Alec negotiated the Dodge through the gate, jumped out to close it, hopped back in and kissed Nell on the cheek.

'Well, here we are!'

He leant forward on the steering wheel as though searching for something.

'What is it?'

'I can't see Captain Midnight. He usually welcomes me home.'

She could see how disappointed he was.

'Well, it has been almost five years.'

He squeezed her hand, slipped the Dodge into gear and they headed up the driveway. Signs of an early frost were still on the ground.

'This is your new home, Douggie,' Alec said.

Nell grinned and wound the window down. Doug's wispy brown hair blew in the breeze as he sucked in the crisp country air and exhaled a cloud of foggy breath. Nell bounced him happily on her knee.

But the sight of her father-in-law's car parked under the pepper tree brought her crashing back to earth. She had hoped she and Alec could have this special time together with their son. She secretly scolded herself for being so selfish, but she had been dreaming about this forever, or so it seemed.

She detected that Alec's mood had changed too. He strode a little too purposefully around to her side of the car and opened the door. She handed Douggie to him, took out her little makeup kit and applied some lipstick, ran her finger under her eyes and applied a little pancake to cover any bags.

'I wouldn't worry too much about that.'

'I'd forgotten they would be here,' Nell said, suddenly nervous. She got out and straightened her skirt. 'How do I look?'

'Beautiful. As always.'

He handed Doug back to her, took her hand and lead her towards the house. Daphne Murray stood at the garden gate dressed in a brown woollen twinset and a dark green, knee-length skirt.

'Hello, Mother.'

Nell noted how business-like his greeting was. She had only seen them together at their second wedding at Braemar, but everyone had put on a good show that day.

Daphne straightened herself up to her full six foot one. 'How was the drive?' she asked, as though they had been into town for some shopping.

She hasn't seen her son for more than eighteen months, he's come home alive, couldn't she be a bit more effusive, thought Nell.

Alec apparently picked up the tone too. 'Long. But we're here now.'

Nell was relieved that the woollen skirt she had chosen was a similar colour to Daphne's. She was desperate to start on the right foot.

When Daphne opened the gate for them, Nell noticed that one of the hinges had fallen off.

'How was Douglas on the trip?' Daphne asked.

Nell ruffled his hair. 'He was all right. Weren't you, Douggie? A bit grizzly but he slept for a lot of it.'

'Let's get you a cup of tea,' Daphne said as she turned and walked towards the house.

'That would be lovely.'

Nell hated small talk at the best of times, but this was excruciating. It was like she wasn't the mistress of her own domain, even though she appreciated her mother-in-law's offer of refreshments.

She held Doug tightly as they walked around the side of the house towards the verandah. She ran a finger over the peeling paint on the weatherboards. Alec was standing, hands on hips, in the garden, surveying the scene.

Nell could tell that something was troubling him. Alec pointed to where the piggery had once stood. All that remained was a pile of burnt ash.

Henry Murray was peering down at them from the verandah in his grey, three-piece suit, dark green tie and white shirt. She gave Alec a gentle dig in the ribs. He took the cue.

'Father ...'

There was an uneasy pause before Henry welcomed him. 'You're home.'

To Nell, Henry's greeting sounded like an accusation. There was tension in the air.

'We are,' Alec replied stiffly before adding, almost as an afterthought, 'The fruit trees have grown.'

Nell hesitated as he climbed the steps. She thought it wise to give father and son a little space.

She thought she saw Henry's face soften briefly. Surely, he must have been happy to see his son in one piece. Alec towered over him as the two men formally shook hands. Nell held Doug tightly, taking the opportunity to survey the front yard. She had already made plans for the garden and was pleased that it was pretty much as she remembered. Douggie wriggled impatiently in her arms. She called up to Alec, 'Can I put him down?'

He smiled. 'Of course! It's your house. You can do what you like.'

She placed him down on the sparsely grassed yard. 'He wants to do some exploring.'

They all watched as Doug crawled off. Henry leant over the railing. 'You better watch out for snakes.'

'In winter?'

Alec smiled and she winked at him.

Daphne called out from inside the house. 'Come on, Helen. We'll leave the men to it while I make you a cuppa.'

With Doug playing happily in the dirt, Nell sprang up the steps and gave Alec an affectionate squeeze on the elbow.

'Will you keep an eye on him, darling?'

Alec caught her arm and gave her a kiss. 'I will.'

She left them to it and found Daphne in the kitchen warming the china teapot. She had arranged a tray with neatly stacked cups and saucers as well as a bowl of sugar, a jug of milk and a plate of freshly baked biscuits.

She smiled at Nell. 'Talking about the weather, are they?'

Nell surveyed the little kitchen as Daphne filled her in.

'It's been one of the driest autumns on record.'

She tipped the hot water out and dropped in a couple of teaspoons of tea before pouring the boiling water into the pot from the cast-iron kettle. She pulled a knitted tea cosy over the pot and set it down.

'We'll let it draw.'

Watching Daphne fuss about the kitchen, Nell appreciated the trouble she had gone to for them.

'Thank you. It's nice to be here.'

For the first time since she had met her, Daphne let Nell into her thoughts. 'I've been praying for this day for five years.'

She clasped her hands in front of her and closed her eyes. When she opened them Nell could detect a tear.

'I can't tell you how happy I am to see you.' Daphne paused and added, 'All three of you.'

Nell's heart went out to her. 'It must have been terrible for you.'

'It was. And for you too.'

Nell began to feel a bond with Daphne that she hadn't felt before, realising that her stern exterior hid a warm heart.

Daphne pointed to a row of jars. 'I've left some preserved fruit for you. Alec's favourite: peaches.'

It was clear she adored her son. Nell hoped she could live up to her mother-in-law's expectations.

'We'll be off first thing in the morning,' Daphne said.

Even though Nell was relieved to hear this, she tried to cover it up. 'Don't feel you have to go …'

Daphne was quick to reassure her. 'We need to get back to our little place at Rylstone. We've had a chap looking after it for us and Henry's been to-and-froing a bit … it's not that far … but now you're home …'

Nell was grateful for Daphne's considerate words.

Daphne continued. 'The car's packed. We'll head off at the crack of dawn.'

She picked up the tray and indicated the tea pot with a nod of her head.

When they returned to the vernadah, Nell saw that Doug had covered himself in dirt. 'Look at him!' she said, as she placed the tea pot on a round table. 'Happy as Larry!'

The two men were standing at either end of the verandah, not talking. Paying no attention to them, Daphne put the tray down and poured the tea. She passed a cup to Nell. Alec hastily grabbed a weathered, wicker chair and held it out for her.

'Help yourself to milk and sugar if you need it,' Daphne said.

They all sat around the table while Douggie continued to amuse himself in the dirt. Daphne handed the plate of biscuits to Alec.

'Gingernuts. Your favourite.'

He took one and bit into it, snapping a piece off. 'Thank you, Mother.'

In the silence that followed, Nell's eyes were drawn up to the imposing mountain range that loomed over them. When she looked back at the men, she could see that something was wrong.

'Bad news?' she asked.

Alec grimaced. 'The Durouxs left.' His tone was dark.

Nell placed her cup on the saucer.

'Oh …' She had been looking forward to seeing Leonie again.

There was another awkward silence broken only by the sipping of tea and the clatter of china cups on saucers.

Nell tried to break the ice. 'We'll manage,' she said. 'Won't we, darling?'

Alec smiled thinly as Henry did his best to explain. 'We couldn't afford to keep them on.'

'Afford?' Alec glared at his father.

The tension between father and son was unmistakable. Henry waved in the direction of the creek behind the house.

'They ended up with a whole tribe down there.'

Alec ignored this. 'No wonder the place looks like it's falling apart …'

Henry took the bait. 'What do you mean?'

'From what I've seen already, it looks like there hasn't been any maintenance done since I went away.'

That was enough for Henry. 'You've got a bloody hide. Swanning in like some absentee landlord and throwing your weight around. You have no idea how hard we've worked. I've had two places to run –'

Daphne cut him off. 'He has been away at war, darling.'

Far from the homecoming Nell had dreamt of, she felt like she'd walked onto a battlefield.

While they were washing up, Daphne told Nell that Claire had moved to Queensland to work as a governess. It was obvious that Claire's decision not to go on to university was a great disappointment to her mother. Nell wondered if Daphne wanted her daughter to avoid the pitfalls of being dependent on anyone.

Their first night at Toongowan as a family was spent sleeping on the floor in the office, after Nell insisted that Alec's parents stay in the main bedroom. She started to envisage the office as a nursery, with a little wooden cot in the corner, an armchair for feeding, a toy box. Alec seemed to be miles away as he leant on the windowsill, staring out.

'Should we paint it blue?' Her question hung in the air. She tried to snap him out of it. 'Alec!'

'What?'

'Douggie's room?'

He stared at her for a few seconds before shaking his head. 'I'm sorry. Ever since Father told me, I've been trying to work out how I can track down Bernie.'

'Come to bed.'

He plonked himself down beside her and put his arm around her. 'You can paint it any colour you like.'

She smiled. 'Oh good. I was thinking … off white.'
 'Not pink?'
She dug him in the ribs. 'One pinko's enough!'
His brow furrowed. She apologised, 'Sorry. Bad joke.'
He kissed her. 'I love you.'
'I love you too.'
He went to kiss her again, but she stopped him and gestured towards Doug sleeping on a cushion on the floor.
'Not in front of the children!'
'Couldn't we put him outside?'
'He's not a dog!'
They both laughed. Nell showed him her sketch of the nursery.
'Do you think we could put in another window? And replace that little peephole with something that lets in a bit of light?'
'Your wish is my command,' he replied with a mock salute.
Nell rested her head on his chest. They lay together, lost in their own thoughts, before she gazed up at him and asked, 'You all right?'
'Me?'
It crossed her mind that it might have been a while since anyone had asked him how he was. She prodded his chest. 'Yes. You.'
'Why do you ask?'
Nell could tell that the question had made him uncomfortable. She softly stroked his cheek and whispered, 'I can't imagine what's going on in your head.'
There was a brief silence before he squeezed her and spoke softly, 'I am the luckiest man in the world. I know that. It's … just …'
She finished the sentence for him. 'There's a lot to think about?'
He smiled and kissed her gently. 'Yes. Exactly. A lot.'

46.

With the war winding down on all fronts and an Allied victory looking inevitable, Alec decided that at last he could focus his efforts on rebuilding Toongowan and bonding with his family. Fences needed to be mended, outbuildings repaired, stock supplies replenished. Alec knew he couldn't do the work on his own, and the place wasn't the same without Bernie.

'I'm going out to Burra Bee Dee to look for him,' he told Nell as she stripped paint off the walls of the office.

'Where's –'

'It's an Aboriginal mission out at Forked Mountain. North of Coona. The people there will know what happened to Bernie, if anyone does.'

'You want us to come?'

'Only if you'd like to.'

'I'd rather finish this, if you don't mind.'

Alec smiled and gave her a kiss. 'As long as you're happy.'

Nell threw her arms around him and planted a kiss on his lips. She pointed to Doug playing with some blocks on the floor. 'We're happy.'

*

Alec was feeling apprehensive as he pulled up in front of a small, blue timber house with a well-pruned rose garden out the front. He had never been to Burra Bee Dee before and he was uncertain how he'd be received, especially if his father had thrown Bernie off Toongowan. He had to get to the bottom of it, though. Alec wasn't going to mark his return home by sweeping any kind of injustice under the carpet.

He hopped out of the car and opened the white gate. Unlike his, it swung easily on its hinges. As he walked up the path, Alec admired the freshly prepared flower beds. He knocked respectfully on the door, then took a step back to wait and glanced around.

A row of neat and tidy houses stretched along one side of the dirt road, while cattle and a few sheep grazed along the other. He looked over the fence at the neighbour's neat vegetable garden boasting rows of broccoli, cabbages and brussels sprouts. Melted frost dripped off the leaves.

Hearing footsteps, he turned around. The front door opened and a smiling woman peered through the flyscreen door.

Alec raised his hat. 'Hello. Sorry to disturb you …'

The woman stepped onto the veranda, pulling a big, brown woollen coat around her. She closed both doors behind her.

'Gotta keep the heat in.'

Alec blew on his hands and smiled. 'It has been cold.'

She held out her hand. 'Dolly McCosker. How can I help you?'

Slightly put off by her forthrightness, Alec shook her hand and cut to the chase. 'I'm looking for someone; Bernie Duroux.'

Dolly drew back. 'You from the Protection Board?'

He didn't know what she meant. 'The Protection Board?'

She looked him up and down. 'You don't look like a typical gubberment man. What did you say your name was?'

Feeling ashamed of his oversight, he apologised, 'I … I didn't. I'm sorry. How rude of me.'

'Yes?'

'Alec Murray.'

'You a cocky?' She had him pegged. 'Thought you blokes had better manners.'

He was relieved when he realised she was teasing him.

She opened the fly-screen door and he held it while she opened the front door.

'To tell you the truth … I … I don't know much about the Protection Board.'

Dolly walked inside without looking back. 'Lucky you.'

He followed her in. The old verandah had been enclosed to make a sunroom and was full of neatly arranged pot plants. As he walked down the hall, he looked at a row of framed family photographs. One man was in uniform.

He wanted to know more about the Protection Board. 'Have they been … bothering you?'

Dolly opened the kitchen door and kept talking over her shoulder. 'Nah. They never come near us unless they wanna take something. We bin after them to give us some money to fix up them places.' She pointed out the back window. 'Over there.'

Alec could see a few houses that looked a bit worse for wear.

'Since they took over, the place has bin falling apart. We bin on this mish for years and done well before they stuck their bloody noses in.'

She picked up a tea towel, folded it neatly and hung it over the stove. 'We do our best to look after it but it's a losing battle. Council come out and agreed we needed some coin for maintenance, but the Protection Board even knocked them back. They don't like us being able to look after ourselves. Since they took over Burra Bee Dee they brought in all these restrictions to keep us in our place. You wanna cuppa?'

'Thanks. I'd love one.'

Alec sat at the kitchen table with its checked tablecloth and vase of wattle sprigs.

'A local Gamilaroi woman called Mary Cain set this place up in the 1890s,' Dolly said, passing him a cup of tea and a slice of cake on a floral-patterned plate. 'She and her white shearer husband had taken up the land and were developing it as a farm. The gubberment gave in to Mary's nagging and let 'em have it.'

Alec sat forward. 'To own?'

'Yep. She got herself a four-hundred acre lot in 1892, and then two more parcels of land to follow, until the lot was gazetted …' She stood up and walked over to the sideboard, opened the drawer and took out what looked to Alec like a ledger. She licked her fingers and flicked through it '… as the Burra Bee Dee Aboriginal Reserve on 21 February 1912.'

Dolly closed the ledger and put it back. 'Word is, she was a bit of a terrier, Mary Cain. They gave in to her to shut her up, people reckon.

'In them days, the Protection Board left us be. There were heaps of reserves in New South Wales that were run by blackfellas. Most of 'em were like this one. People farmed sheep and cattle, grew their own fruit and veggies as well as gatherin' bush tucker. They come here because they wanted to, not 'cause they was sent. Then the gubberment got scared that we were gettin' too big for our boots so they started takin' everything away from us, includin' our kids.'

She paused and reached for a knife. 'More cake?'

Alec self-consciously patted his stomach. 'No thanks.'

'You're as skinny as a bloody rake. You need a bit o' beef on ya.'

God, she reminds me of Mrs Duroux, he thought.

She put the cake carefully back in its tin.

'They bin whittlin' away our rights ever since.'

Alec was getting a lesson about his own country. 'I didn't know anything about this.'

Grinning broadly, Dolly tapped her finger on her head. 'Up here for thinkin', down there for dancin'.' She chuckled. 'Before the First World War there was plenty of my people farmin' like you blokes.'

'That's why I need to find the Durouxs.'

Dolly eyed him suspiciously.

He was quick to allay her fears. 'Bernie used to work on my place. Near Binnaway ... before I went away ... to the war.'

'You won't find Bernie.'

Her tone had changed. She wiped some crumbs off the table onto her hands, stood up and tossed them out the window. When she sat down again she looked him in the eye. 'You don't know, do you?'

He shook his head.

'Someone tipped Welfare off that there was a mob of kids livin' down by the crick on ... now I know it was your place ...'

Alec could feel his face reddening. He clenched his fists. 'Go on, please. I need to know.'

'Well, you know the story. A truck come down in the middle of the night, looking for 'em but Bernie and Leonie were too smart. They was hiding in the piggery.'

Alec's stomach tightened as he recalled the sight of the ash-heaped remains of the piggery upon arriving home to Toongowan. He began to fear the worst.

Dolly seemed to read his mind.

'Leonie's my cousin. She told me all about it before they took off.'

'They got away then?'

'Oh yeah. Too smart for Welfare.'

Alec lowered his head. Is this what Stephen had died for?

'They're wipin' us out.'

He slowly raised his head and looked into Dolly's eyes. He could feel himself burning with rage.

'I'm sorry, Dolly. I'm so sorry,' he said, barely able to contain himself.

She reached her hand out to him. 'It's not your fault, son. You didn't open the gate.'

✳

As he hurtled along the dirt road back to Toongowan, Alec vowed that he would get to the bottom of what had happened to Bernie. How could something like the Protection Act exist? Wasn't one of the reasons for going to war to end discrimination? He promised himself that he would become more involved in local politics. There was more to life than rubbing shoulders with the squattocracy.

Preoccupied with these thoughts, he almost didn't notice an oncoming truck, squeezing between the railings of a narrow bridge, heading towards him. He slammed on the brakes and skidded to a halt.

The truck driver poked his head out of his cabin. 'What do you think you're driving? A Messerschmitt?'

Alec gripped the steering wheel tightly as he watched the truck pass. He hadn't survived a war to kill himself in a head-on. He got out of the Dodge, climbed the fence, slid down the creek bank and washed his face in the creek's icy waters.

He didn't need any more lucky escapes.

47.

Nell had found the perfect solution to Alec's struggle to get Toongowan back in shape. The government was allowing Italian POWs, housed in nearby camps, to work on local farms. She knew Alec well enough by now to pick her moment. As he was saddling Captain Midnight, before he'd got lost in his day's work, she approached him with the idea.

'I'm happy to do the paperwork and so on …'

Alec checked the saddle was secure, lifted his foot into the stirrup and hoisted himself up. She thought what a wonderful picture he made, sitting up so straight with his hat pulled rakishly over his brow.

'Sure,' he said. 'Makes sense. See you tonight,' he called as he waved and cantered off.

Nell was delighted. She thought that perhaps working alongside the people he'd fought against would provide Alec some kind of atonement. One of the few things he had told her about the war, was that he hadn't been able to reconcile killing people who had been forced to fight someone else's battle. And she was pleased to gain another pair of hands to help transform the house.

She hired three men. One, Alberto Vedda, worked with her, while the other two worked with Alec. Alec paid all three a decent wage and provided them with adequate lodging in the shearers' quarters. They soon become part of the fabric of the local community, shopping in Coonabarabran on Saturday afternoons and attending Sunday mass at

St Michael's Catholic church in the tiny village of Purlewaugh.

Alberto was a cheerful, curly haired, olive-skinned young man, who had been captured in North Africa and sent to Australia. He built cupboards and bookshelves for Doug's room using timber from the property. He also helped Nell transform the dirt patch outside the kitchen into a vegetable garden. With spring approaching, they planted zucchinis, eggplants, red and yellow capsicums, cherry tomatoes and garlic, along with more traditional 'British' staples. To her surprise, Nell was deliriously happy building a new life for herself and her family with Alberto's help. He taught her some rudimentary Italian and played Italian music on the improvised mandolin he had crafted in the camp.

Nell watched her Australian child and the Italian prisoner of war find a common language in games. Alberto amused Doug with impromptu clowning performances that he told Nell sprang from *Commedia dell'Arte*, a form of theatre she had never heard of. Much to Nell's delight, Alberto introduced Doug to another language.

While she was digging and planting and painting and decorating, Nell gave her little boy licence to anoint himself king of the castle and free rein to explore. His only boundaries were self-imposed. She delighted in watching him clamber to his feet, toddle about, wobble over, clamber again, toddle for a few paces and wobble over again: all without a care in the world. He was a threat to no one and, it seemed, no one was a threat to him. Mr Chips, the sausage dog Alec had surprised Nell with, had taken Doug's welfare as his personal mission. His belly barely an inch off the ground, he waddled around after Doug, a dutiful protector. Watching them through the new glass doors Alberto had installed, Nell marvelled at how quickly her life had turned around.

She witnessed Alec working cheerfully with the other two men, Emmanuel and Natalino, and comforted herself with the thought that it was a winning situation for all of them. Not only did they help Alec return Toongowan to working order, they also helped him deal with some hidden demons. In return, he gave their days purpose and looked after them.

One day, when they had gone to town to get some stores, the sergeant in charge of the Coonabarabran Control Centre bailed up Emmanuel and Natalino and accused them of stealing Alec's car.

'Put that bloody thing away before you shoot yourself in the foot!' Alec demanded of the sergeant, who was waving his pistol about.

'You outta be careful letting an enemy alien drive your car. How do you know they ain't gonna make a run for it?' said the sergeant, sucking in his considerable stomach and puffing out his chest.

Alec took a few steps towards him and calmly placed his hand on his weapon, forcing him to lower it. 'If you were so keen for a scrape you could have gone over to New Guinea to take on the Japanese.'

He opened the Dodge door for Nell, put the shopping in the boot and asked the sergeant, 'Was something holding you back from enlisting?'

As they drove off, laughing, Nell chimed in, 'Imagine if we told him we left Dougie at home with Alberto?'

48.

'We'd like you to stand for Council,' announced Sam Ogilvie as he handed Alec a beer.

They were having a drink at the Imperial Hotel in the centre of Coonabarabran. Sam was a straight-shooting, quietly spoken shopkeeper with a bald patch and a gentle disposition. He was president of the Returned Services League after serving in the First World War and was active in Legacy, because, as he'd once told Alec, he believed that the men who'd made it home should look after the families of those who hadn't.

'We need a bloke like you to shake these buggers up.'

Sam had a reputation for pricking people's consciences. As Alec listened, he warmed to the idea.

'Council do bugger-all for the men and women who've sacrificed everything for their country, let alone the poor bloody widows and kids who are suddenly cut adrift without a breadwinner to support them.'

Resting his elbow on the bar, Sam pointed his middy at Alec. 'We need some new blood.'

He ordered another couple of middies and handed one to Alec. 'We'll endorse you in first position on the ballot.'

Alec was flattered by Sam's offer. Ever since he'd made the trip to Burra Bee Dee, he'd been thinking about how he could do more for the community. Here was his chance to put his money where his mouth was. There was just one hitch. 'Hang on, Sam, I'm not in any party.'

'Exactly. No baggage. As a returned serviceman you can stand for the RSL. We run candidates in council elections to serve the interests of the people that everyone else has forgotten about.'

Alec took another sip as Sam carried on with his well-rehearsed pitch. 'You've got a very good war record. You're a local lad. Now that you've been reappointed to the Graziers' Council, you'll have the cockies on side.'

'How long have I got?'

'To make up your mind?'

Alec nodded. He could see this was too good an opportunity to turn up, but he wanted to run it by Nell before he made a decision.

'Nominations close in a few days. We need to hold a meeting in Binnaway to endorse you and your running mate. There's a lot to do –'

'My running mate?'

'Well, yes. You need a running mate.'

Sam put his hand on Alec's shoulder and quoted the famous First World War recruiting slogan, '*Your district needs you.*'

Sam laid out his plans. 'We'll endorse you in first position, so you'll need to run with whoever we endorse in second.'

'Such as?'

'We're working on it. Don't worry; he'll be a Services supporter too. You'll have plenty in common.'

Alec was being handed an endorsement on a plate. How could he refuse? He held out his hand to seal the deal. 'All right. I'll do it. I'll give it a go.'

Grinning broadly, Sam shook his hand, then slapped him on the back. 'Good-oh. We'd better get cracking. You'll do us as the Binnaway candidate.' He drained his drink and was out the door before Alec could change his mind.

Alec lingered over his beer. He had just taken the first step of his political career and he wanted to savour the moment.

When he got home, he broke the news to Nell.

'You what?'

She was dressed in a loose-fitting cotton dress, gum boots and one of Alec's old woollen jumpers that reached below her knees, and was painting the windowsill.

'The meeting of the Binnaway branch of the RSL is tomorrow night. They needed an answer.'

She wiped her brush with a rag. Alec watched her nervously as she pondered his announcement. 'What do we need to do?' she asked.

That was a point. He had no idea what the next step was. 'I don't know … go along …'

He started to wonder if he had been too hasty. He should have consulted her first.

'You're standing for the RSL?'

'Yes.'

'Father can't argue with that,' she said, smiling.

Alec began having doubts. 'I haven't been endorsed yet. Even if I am, there is no guarantee we'll win the election.'

Nell stopped wiping the brush and fixed him with a determined look. 'You'll win. You've got me in your team.'

She winked, dipped the brush in paint and returned to painting the windowsill.

He was glad to have her on his side.

*

The next night, Alec stood nervously in the small Ladies Lounge out the back of the Royal Hotel in Binnaway. The lounge was half-filled with an odd collection of war veterans, recently returned soldiers and other members of the Binnaway branch of the Returned Services League. In the group he spied Walter Frater, the local butcher. Walter, a squat man with receding hair, big ears and an impressive moustache, was dressed in a three-piece suit replete with fob watch and chain. He was an incongruous sight among the farmers, shopkeepers and farm labourers dressed in their working clothes. Walter was popular and well respected in the local community. Alec knew that he had contributed significantly to the administration of the War Loans Scheme and helped raise money for widows of veterans and the needy. He was also a member of the Communist Party and a wealthy landowner to boot. He had boasted to Alec that he owned the most extensive Marxist library in New South Wales.

Alec walked over to him. 'Hello, Walter. What are you doing here?'

Walter, twenty-five years Alec's senior, shook his hand. 'I'm your running mate.'

Before Alec could recover from the shock of hearing this, Sam Ogilvie was on his feet, extolling the virtues of both men.

'We need people who will represent Binnaway and Mendooran on the Council, not just Coonabarabran. Walter needs no introduction. He's a community man through and through. We all know that Walter will put the needs of all of us before his own. As for our other nomination, this young man represents the future. Alec Murray has a remarkable war record having served in Egypt, Greece and Papua New Guinea, and was mentioned in dispatches. Alec is a local farmer and a member of the Graziers' Council. These two men represent a broad cross-section of our community and, with their different perspectives, you can be assured they will keep the Council on its toes while representing people like us.'

The small gathering clapped politely and, as there were no other nominations, Alec and Walter were unanimously endorsed.

Hugh Masterton, a fellow ex-serviceman whose family owned a property near Toongowan, took Alec aside. 'You do know you're running with a commo?'

'What can I do, Hugh? I gave them my word I'd run.'

'You'll have to pull out.'

Alec found himself defending Walter. 'We've been fighting alongside commos the whole war. If Uncle Joe hadn't come to our aid, we might have lost. Besides, you know as well as I do, that a man's word is his bond.'

'You're making yourself a cross to bear,' his neighbour warned.

Alec looked over to see Nell chatting amicably with Walter. But when Hugh stormed out, he wondered if this was the first taste of what was to come.

49.

Nell was happy that, within a few short months, they had transformed the house and garden. Alberto had crafted windows and glass doors that let in the light and Nell had chosen colours that lifted the mood of the place. While Alec was absorbed with his election campaign, she took the opportunity to fly to Sydney to buy some prints to decorate the walls and introduce old friends to her son.

She found prints of Alec's favourite works: Filippino Lippi's *Madonna and Child with Two Angels* and Sandro Botticelli's *The Birth of Venus*. She caught up with Peg and proudly showed off her growing boy. She even outlined some plans for paintings of her own.

She dropped in on Carl Thomas who was not only delighted to see her but commissioned another mural. Nell felt hopeful that her star was still rising and she might yet blossom into the artist she dreamt of becoming.

When Lance travelled from Canberra to catch up with her, she excitedly told him about Alec's latest move while she cooked him dinner at her parent's flat.

'Why doesn't he join the Communist Party?' Lance asked, as he popped the cork out of a bottle of the red he'd brought.

'I think that might be a bridge too far,' she said. 'He's running with an avowed communist, that's bad enough in the eyes of some.'

'Like your family?' Lance asked.

'I don't know if they are aware of that minor detail.' She laughed.

As the night wore on Lance opened up about the challenges of being a homosexual man in a heterosexual world.

'We're like a secret society,' he told her. 'It all has to be cloak and dagger.'

Nell was aware of the challenges Lance was facing and what the cost to him might be. She offered him all the love and support she could.

✳

Both Nell and Alec knew that the speech he was going to make to the Graziers' Federation Council would be a watershed moment in his career as a politician, not least because Fred Hope would be there. Sitting at his desk under the Botticelli, Alec spent hours crafting it while Nell gave him feedback. One of the things he promised her he was going to do, was to give women the opportunity to have a voice on the Council.

When the day came, she straightened the Australian Infantry Forces tie she had selected for him to wear, gave him a good luck kiss and, with Doug at her side, waved him off.

He approached the meeting outwardly confident but inwardly nervous. While clear about his vision for the future of the district, he worried about how the cockies would take it.

Fred Hope greeted him warmly and introduced him to the other delegates.

'Welcome back,' said a ruddy faced man Alec had previously met through Fred. 'Percy Dutton.'

Alec shook his hand, then went around the table shaking hands with all the other delegates, before Fred spoke.

'Although I may be accused of bias, I am very proud of this young man's decision to return to the commitments he initiated before he was called away to defend the Empire. I have invited Alec to this meeting to outline the plans he has for the area as a member of the Council.'

Looking around the table at the assembled tweed-wearing graziers, Alec could feel butterflies in his stomach. He knew they weren't the most progressive thinkers. They and their forefathers had been helping the country ride to prosperity on the sheep's back since the 1870s. They saw themselves as the rightful custodians of the land.

Fred continued. 'If I may be so bold, I think this may be the first step in an illustrious political career. Of course, he'll have to join the Country Party first!'

Everyone laughed. Alec stopped his leg jiggling under the table.

'Over to you, Alec.'

Alec pulled his speech from his coat pocket and began reading. 'Thank you, Mr Hope. I have written a few words to try and encapsulate everything I have been thinking about since I went away. Apart from the obvious, I learnt a lot while I was at war. I was forced to challenge my thinking and, surprisingly, my upbringing. I quickly discovered that I had to put my own interests aside to serve the greater good.

'What I saw in Egypt and Libya has opened my eyes to the future of agriculture in this country.'

He paused. A few members of council shifted uncomfortably in their seats. He knew he had to hold his nerve. He continued reading. 'We cannot fool ourselves that we can continue with farming methods that are degrading the soil and turning the country into a wasteland.'

Again, he paused, looking around the table.

'Put simply, it is time we farmers and graziers stop flogging the soil 'til it's dead.'

Percy Dutton grunted loudly, Fred Hope removed his glasses and stared. Alec continued.

'We have made little or no attempt to conserve water or stop erosion. We have cleared the native vegetation that not only holds the soil together but provides nutrients and attracts all sorts of native species. Without water, the land is turning into a dustbowl. The Italians created irrigation channels in Palestine and transformed arid land into farming land. Why can't we do something similar? We have to manage our water resources more efficiently. We have no choice but to change the way we approach farming before it is too late.'

Alec sensed he was losing the room but wasn't about to compromise. 'What we need is nationwide action.'

Percy Dutton interjected, 'What we need is a drink.'

'No, Mr Dutton, what the land needs is a drink. Clearing every tree in sight not only degrades the land and causes erosion, but removes vital shade for stock which means they are thirstier and need more water.

Mussolini might have been a fascist dictator but in some ways, he was a visionary. The Italians in Libya planted trees. Acres of them …'

Percy Dutton was having none of it. 'The I-ties? What would they know about farming?'

Refusing to be intimidated, Alec argued. 'Plenty. They turned the desert into arable land. We're turning arable land into desert. There is no point burying our heads in the sand. If we're not smart about it, *sand* is all we'll have left. We need to open our eyes to the devastation our current farming methods are causing to the environment.'

He put down his speech and looked around the table at the delegates.

'What we need to do is to take a leaf out the local people's book. We need to talk to the Elders. They have managed this land for thousands …'

That was enough for Percy Dutton. 'The blacks?'

'What would they know about farming?' another delegate said.

'Nothing,' another added.

Alec wasn't giving up. 'If we had the sense to listen to them …'

The hostility coming from the delegates was palpable.

'I understand how threatening this is to many of you …'

Fred put on his glasses, looked at his watch and picked up agenda. 'Thank you, Alec. We should move on. We have a few other items on the agenda we should address.'

Feeling like an admonished schoolboy, Alec pleaded, 'What kind of people ignore the wisdom of the ages? We are new to this country. Only a fool would turn his back on …'

The delegates avoided eye-contact, making it clear he had lost them.

'Yeah? Well, we're turning our backs on you, you bloody commo,' Percy Dutton stage whispered to the delegate beside him, loud enough for Alec to hear.

Any questions Alec had held about how his own elders would receive his vision for the future had been answered; there was no doubt. They hated what he had to say, and many, he suspected, outright hated *him*.

Alec had begun another war.

50.

'Here's Daddy!'

Nell was feeding Doug a mash of freshly picked homegrown vegetables, as she heard footsteps on the verandah. The front door opened and in walked Alec looking slightly dazed.

'How'd it go?'

He smiled, gave her a kiss and ruffled Doug's hair.

'I might have a wash,' he said. Then he drifted wordlessly through the living room and out into the kitchen.

Nell heard the screen door swing open as he tossed his hat on the hat stand. She raised a spoonful of mashed veggies to Doug's mouth. 'Here comes the aeroplane.'

She moved the spoon in a big circle before homing in on her target. 'Coming in to land.'

Doug wriggled in the chair. He wasn't having any of it and shook his head vigorously.

'Come on, darling.' Nell held the spoon in front of him. 'It's good for you.'

He refused.

'For God's sake!'

Doug pouted and turned away from her. It was all Nell could do to stop herself forcing the food into his mouth. It had never been this hard feeding a lamb a bottle.

Alec walked back in, wiping his face with a towel. She was relieved to see him. She took his towel and handed him the spoon.

'Your turn. I'm not having much luck.'

He offered a spoonful of food to Doug, who opened his mouth and ate it. Alec scooped up another spoonful.

Nell was impressed. 'The magic touch, eh?'

Alec laughed. Doug took the opportunity to knock the spoon out of his hand.

'Now look what you've done!' Nell said in mock horror.

Alec surveyed the mess on the floor while his eighteen-month-old grinned at him. Nell tossed him the towel. He got down on his hands and knees and cleaned it up.

'He's been quite a handful,' she said.

Alec sat back on his haunches, wiped his hands and climbed back into the fray.

'Don't think you're going to get away with this!' he said, waving the spoon at Doug.

He determinedly scraped another spoonful out of the bowl and pushed it towards his son. 'Eat up!'

There was something in his tone that told Doug the game was over. He reluctantly opened his mouth.

'You're going to finish it whether you like it or not.'

While Nell looked on approvingly, Alec finished feeding Doug, wiped his face with his Gumnut Twins bib, lifted him out of the highchair and set him free. Nell put her arm around Alec as they watched Doug waddle out to the kitchen. He pushed the screen door open and made for the little cubby house Alberto had built for him. Mr Chips brought up the rear.

'Well?' Nell asked.

Alec breathed deeply and sighed. 'I need a drink.'

Nell laughed. '*You* need a drink!'

'We both need one!'

She sat down in the armchair while he poured them both a generous scotch, handed her a glass and sat opposite. He took a sip and sat back in the chair.

'I don't think the graziers are going to endorse me.'

Nell smiled. 'That's hardly a surprise. They never were.'

'I guess …'

She looked at him in disbelief, 'You didn't think …'

He raised his shoulders. She chuckled and shook her head.

He stared at her. 'What?'

'I love your optimism.'

She watched him as he took another sip. She could see that he was hurt by the experience. 'You didn't say anything about the state taking over their land, did you?'

He let out a loud belly laugh. 'They would have skinned me alive!'

Nell wagged a finger at him. 'As long as you stuck to the script.'

'Oh yes,' he paused. 'Thank you.'

'It was a pleasure. We're in this together. All of us. You're going to have worse days than this. What's important is that you have laid your cards on the table,' she said. 'They might have turned on you but at least they know what you stand for. Otherwise, you may as well have stayed home.'

Alec took a moment, then said, 'I'm worried about how it's going to affect you.'

'Me?'

'Your father wasn't very happy.'

She got up, walked over to him, sat on his lap and kissed him on the lips.

'We're not doing this for my father. We're doing it for the future of the country. It's a choice. If you stick your neck out, you're always in danger of getting it chopped off.'

'You're not worried …'

'Of course I'm worried. But I'm excited too. You've got some great ideas, the community hotel idea is an absolute corker. You've just got to get out and sell it. Win them over.'

He enveloped her in his arms and kissed her deeply. 'I'm lucky to have you.'

'You are!'

51.

While electioneering, Alec was in his element. He thrived on getting out, meeting people and listening to their concerns. Many in the towns around the district told him they felt they had been abandoned and responded enthusiastically to his pledges to put them back in the picture. He built quite a following and gained confidence from the fact that people could tell he was more than a seat warmer.

While ferrying Walter, who couldn't drive, around the electorate he took advantage of absorbing some valuable lessons from the veteran of local politics. Walter taught him that every vote counted, and he should listen to everyone, no matter how outlandish their claims might be. For his part, Walter seemed to enjoy having a captive audience on the road and tried to convert him.

'I'm not going to join the Communist Party, Walter,' Alec told him when Walter tried to sell him the virtues of George Dimitrov and world communism.

'We'll all be communists one day,' Walter insisted.

Even though he didn't share Walter's ideology, Alec admired his passion. Walter was an idealist; a butcher who didn't drink and who lived in a big, beautifully kept country house with his cats and dogs. He dressed snappily and bought meat for his butchery from his political enemies who were happy to sell to him even though they didn't buy his politics. His wife had walked out on him when he joined the

Communist Party and taken their children with her. Yet Walter was prepared to sacrifice all for the cause. It was a lesson Alec took to heart.

On the day of the election, Alec picked him up as usual and drove him into Coonabarabran for the count. Alec was worried that Walter might use him as a stooge and grew concerned that they wouldn't win.

'If we happen to win, Walter, I don't want to suddenly discover we're operating under instructions from Moscow.'

'I think Joe Stalin might have a bit too much on his plate to have time to worry about the ins and outs of Coona Council,' he said, then laughed.

Alec couldn't help but smile. He loved Walter. But he still wasn't sure they would win.

All day, Alec had handed out how-to-vote tickets and checked on booths. He seemed to be polling well but, being a complete novice, he didn't know whether he was imagining it or if people were having him on. By the time they arrived at the Imperial Hotel with Nell for the count, Alec was like a cat on a hot tin roof.

The news that they had achieved a resounding victory was a huge relief. When Sam Ogilvie read out the result, Alec quietly thanked his lucky stars. There was a lot riding on it. He gripped Nell's hand tightly and accepted beers from some of the assembled well-wishers as though it was all in a day's work.

When Sam called for him to speak to the boisterous crowd, Alec stood up on a chair and gratefully took the applause and whistles with studied nonchalance. Looking down at the gathering he thought what a different mob they were from the tweedy graziers he had addressed a few weeks before. He was quickly discovering that these were his people.

After thanking Walter for showing him the way, Alec turned his attention to the people. 'This is a victory for you: the small businessmen, the workers, the shopkeepers, the farm labourers. This isn't our victory. It is yours.'

His words were greeted with enthusiastic applause.

'On behalf of Walter and myself, I pledge that we will serve the needs of the people of Binnaway on Coonabarabran Council and ensure that your voices are heard.'

There was more applause as Alec warmed to his task. 'Walter and I campaigned on a platform of change and change is what we intend to bring to the district. I didn't fight in a war to come home and settle for the old ways. The old ways gave us two world wars and a Depression. We have to find another way. A way that better represents your needs and interests.

'We are going to start by improving services in the district. We will build a school so that you don't have to send your children away to get an education. We will build a community hotel and a preschool. We will update the library.

'In short, my friends, we will devote the next few years to making Coonabarabran Shire the most progressive shire in the country.'

*

'You were brilliant!'

Nell's eyes were blazing as she gave him a kiss on the cheek.

Alec looked proudly at his wife and son, then leant down to Doug. 'Things are going to change, my boy.'

Nell laughed then said, 'They already have.'

He had been so preoccupied, it hadn't occurred to him that Nell was breaking the law by being in the bar, let alone with a child. It didn't worry Rowdy Watts, the well-proportioned publican, so it didn't worry anyone else. Alec pushed his way through the crowd and ordered Nell a shandy.

'On the house, Alec,' called out Rowdy.

Things really are looking up, Alec thought, as June, the doubtful barmaid, mixed a beer with some lemonade. He handed it to Nell.

She took a sip and screwed up her face. 'I reckon I deserve a full strength,' she said, winking and handing him back the shandy.

Alec felt like an idiot as he returned to the bar.

'Could I make that a brandy?'

Rowdy locked the doors and the celebrations continued well into the night. Nell charmed everyone, Alec outlined his plans to anyone who would listen, and Doug was entertained by Rowdy's cheerful daughter on the well-worn piano.

Alec was sure he had never felt better.

As they drove home to Toongowan, Nell started humming *L'Internationale*. Grinning broadly, Alec drummed along on the steering wheel while Nell kicked off her shoes, put her feet up on the dashboard and they sang together:

'This is the final struggle,
Let us group together,
and tomorrow
The Internationale
Will be the human race.'

Doug slept soundly in the back seat as the Dodge pulled in at the gate. Captain Midnight galloped to the fence in the house paddock, whinnying a homecoming.

52.

While Alec was busy transforming the Coonabarabran Shire into the most progressive in the country, Nell took on the role of overseeing a lot of the day-to-day work on Toongowan.

The end of the war in Europe in May 1945 saw Italian prisoners of war freed and able to return home. Nell had cooked a farewell dinner for Alberto, Emmanuel and Natalino. and mourned their absence. They had helped her transform the place and been good company for her on the long days when Alec was busy farming or electioneering. Now that he was a councillor and the Italians had gone, Nell faced even more time without adult company. And had another baby on the way.

She decided to take a quick trip to Braemar so her parents could spend time with their grandson, and to give them her news. The two-and-a-half-hour drive, on a dirt road that needed grading, gave Nell plenty of time to think. She knew she had to be on her best behaviour. Any talk of politics was definitely out of bounds. She didn't want to suffer the same fate as Alec, who was virtually disowned by Henry. His father added insult to injury by threatening to bar Daphne from seeing Doug if Alec continued his radical ways.

Nell's life hadn't exactly turned out the way she had envisaged it, but she wouldn't have traded it for anything. She was excited by the prospect of using her privileged upbringing to influence change. She knew all about the people who had no compunction in exploiting those who worked for them. Thankfully her father wasn't like that, but plenty of their neighbours were.

Although they had got there by travelling different paths, she and Alec shared a deep commitment to do all in their might to create the same opportunities for working people in the country that city people enjoyed. This meant lobbying for Council to build a kindergarten like the one Peg sent her little boy to. She reminded Alec about the health and recreation centres he had so admired in the White City of Tel Aviv. Why couldn't they build them in Coonabarabran?

Among other things, being a mother had made Nell acutely aware of how hard it was for women who were expected to raise a family, run a household and support their husbands with a couple of kids in tow. Let alone pursue their own interests, like painting, for instance. They needed assistance and she convinced Alec that it was as important to provide that assistance as it was to find work for the returned soldiers he was committed to helping.

The visit to Braemar went well. Elaine doted on Doug and spent so much time with him that Nell was able to catch up on some sleep and even do a bit of drawing. Having a child brought her closer to her mother than she had ever been.

Fred was his usual, pre-occupied self. He was driven to breed heavier, more resilient merinos that could survive in challenging conditions and produce denser fine wool. Fred and Nell danced around the question of Alec's politics. She sensed he was disappointed that Alec had jumped ship, but Fred wasn't the type to hold someone's beliefs against them, even if they held diametrically opposed views. It was one of the things Nell loved about her father. He was a hard taskmaster and set in his ways, but he was an honest man and paid his workers a 'fair day's wage for a fair day's work'; not that he would dream of using the term.

While she enjoyed visiting her parents, Nell was glad to return home after a few days being spoilt by them. She wasn't interested in standing still. She was excited by the prospect of being part of a mini revolution. The fact that many of the people she had grown up with saw Alec as a turncoat only stiffened her resolve to work with him. Also, she was relieved her parents hadn't ostracised them in the way that Henry had.

Nell thrived on being the mistress of her own domain. Turning Toongowan into a home brought her unexpected pleasure. While she wasn't painting as much as she would have liked, she was using her creativity to make something she could be proud of. Growing her own vegetables was a bonus, and she had always loved cooking. The first trimester of Nell's second pregnancy passed in the whirlwind of the election and she was now into her second with no obvious challenges. She had plenty of energy, and needed it. Two-year-old Doug was proving to be a handful. Without Alberto around to help keep an eye on him, Doug was constantly demanding her attention and it was draining, especially as she had the responsibility of running the place when Alec was away on Council business. Alec had employed a returned soldier, Donny Wingfield, to help out in the sheep yards, mend fences and grub thistles. Though he could never replace Bernie, Donny was a good worker, as long as Nell kept him on the job.

As a bonus, Donny's wife, Mary, loved kids and occasionally helped Nell out with Doug, which freed up some time for painting. Nell began sketching ideas for the Carl Thomas mural but wondered when she would find time to complete them. Lucky for her, Carl wasn't too insistent and told her to 'take her time.'

Nell looked forward to the day when Doug would have a sibling to play with, though she was tormented by a recurring nightmare of being stuck in the middle of a vast, desolate, salt lake nursing two small children. Putting such thoughts out of her mind, Nell steeled herself for the challenges that lay ahead.

53.

Alec was delighted that many in the local community were quick to embrace his and Walter's reformist agenda. Any opposition came mainly from the older townies and property owners, afraid of change and suspicious of his running mates' motives. The fact that Nell was prepared to put her relationship with her family on the line for the cause was crucial; if she was willing to make that sacrifice, so was he.

Alec outlined plans for the construction of new, modern, well-designed hostels to address the district's housing crisis and provide homes for returned servicemen and distressed women. When Walter's motion for a sixty per cent rate rise was passed, Alec was confident the community would support spending the eight-thousand pounds it would raise, on developing the district. His goal was to make the Shire's standard of living the envy of every district in the state.

Alec's boldest plan was to engage an architect with an interest in town planning, to draw up plans for the three ridings of Coonabarabran, Binnaway and Baradine. He had never forgotten what he saw in the White City of Tel Aviv and had always dreamt of implementing that kind of town planning in his local area. He was particularly excited by the Bauhaus style with its geometric shapes and focus on functionality, style and simplicity. It fit in with his own practice of using easily accessible, locally produced building materials.

It took all of Alec's considerable powers of persuasion to win over his fellow councillors, many of whom had served on Council for years. In time, Alec felt that the local communities were starting to support his ambitious vision, and he was determined to make the most of it.

✳

Alec arrived home on top of the world. The Council had just agreed to send him to Sydney to meet Eliot Gunning, a town planner with exemplary credentials. He was just the man to help Alec bring his vision to reality. His plans for the district were taking shape, he had won the backing of his fellow councillors and, apart from the tweedy graziers' usual opposition, he was on track to bring about the reforms he had spent months planning.

'We had a win!' he announced to Nell as she emerged from Doug's room.

'Is that so?' she asked curtly.

Not picking up on her mood, he carried on. 'Yes. Isn't it terrific? I thought it would be much more of a battle …'

'The only battle I give a fuck about is the one I've been having with your son. I had to virtually wrestle him to sleep.'

She walked past him. 'I'm going to bed.'

'But …'

Alec was left standing in the kitchen while Nell disappeared into the bedroom. He noticed a jumble of dishes and bowls in the sink. He poured himself a glass of water and retired to his newly built office lined with the Medici prints Nell had bought for him. He opened his briefcase, took out some folders, unscrewed the lid off his fountain pen and began writing.

Trouble was, he couldn't concentrate. He realised he'd been so caught up with his own plans that he'd ignored Nell's needs. He had underestimated how much of the load Nell was carrying but didn't know what he could do about it. He couldn't bring about the changes the Council was planning without being away for days on end. If they compromised, they might as well give up. And Alec had no intention of giving up.

The next morning, when he handed Nell a cup of tea in bed, she sat up and looked out the window. He sat on the bed next to her.

'I'm sorry.'

'Where's …'

'He's up and about. I've done the washing up.'

Her look told him that he shouldn't expect a medal.

Alec had a plane to catch in a couple of hours. He knew he had to try to support Nell but he didn't know how; he couldn't be in two places at once.

She yawned. 'Did I sleep in?'

'I thought you needed it.'

She smiled. 'I did,' she said and gave him a kiss. 'I'm sorry too.'

She took a sip of her tea. 'There are times … it's hard. I get so frustrated. I'd like to be out there. Helping you. I'd like to be part of … the movement or whatever it is. Sometimes I feel like a passenger. Other times I feel so useless I can't do anything … properly. I want to do that mural for Carl but, to be honest, with everything else, I don't have the energy. There's nothing you can do about it. And sometimes … I feel like I'm the worst mother in the world. Especially when I snap at Doug.'

Alec didn't know what to say. She looked so vulnerable. He leant in to her but she pulled away.

'I'm all right,' she said. 'I'm just being precious.'

'You're anything but precious.'

'What time is your plane?'

He looked at his watch. 'I've got to go.'

She nodded.

'Are you going to be –'

She cut him off. 'Yes. We'll be fine. As long as you keep winning.'

That brought a smile to his face. 'We're winning all right. I'll bring Douggie in to you.'

He leant down and gave her a kiss.

∗

Two days later, Alec was sitting in Eliot Gunning's office overlooking Hyde Park.

'This is ambitious,' Eliot said as he closed Alec's submission. Alec was nervous. The stakes were high. He was trying to turn a sleepy rural town in central western New South Wales into Australia's version of the White City of Tel Aviv that had so impressed him during the war.

'I like the idea of housing that prioritises community needs over developers' greed,' Eliot said, smiling. 'The thing is, developments like this cost a lot of money.'

Alec leant forward. He was prepared for this. 'We've done a survey of the housing needs of the shire and discovered that we need three hundred new houses in the three major towns. It's dire. People are living in conditions that we shouldn't tolerate in a country like ours. We need one hundred new houses immediately.'

Eliot nodded. 'Do you mind if I do a few rough calculations?' he asked and began scribbling on a piece of paper. Eventually he looked up, settled back in his swivel chair and folded his hands in his lap.

'Let me get this straight. You're proposing to build a large reservoir and a first-class airfield in addition to the housing?'

'That's right. Water is the key to developing the district. I want farmers to have access to the same kind of irrigation I saw work so well in Libya. And a modern airfield will bring the city to the country,' Alec explained.

'And all this housing is to have sewerage?'

'Of course.'

'And these?' Eliot pointed to the council submission on his desk.

'Community centres. One each for Coonabarabran, Binnaway and Baradine. We'll hold a public poll to see which one the community wants built first.'

Eliot smiled and listed each of the public facilities Alec had proposed. 'An infant welfare centre. A kindergarten. A preschool. Children's playground.'

Shaking his head, Eliot waved the report in Alec's direction. 'Did I say ambitious?'

Alec smiled. 'Once you've drawn up the plans, we'll submit them to the Minister for Local Government for approval,' he said, trying to sound as though it was a fait accompli.

'What about this?' Eliot opened the report and pointed to the paragraph headed, *Community Hotel.*

Alec was happy to explain. This was the project he and Nell had spent hours dreaming up. 'Yes. A hotel owned by the community with its profits returning to the community rather than lining the pockets of brewery owners. It will have a family lounge bar and a beer garden, as well as meeting, games and card rooms. It will house a library with a technical section. There will be a small theatre for debates and theatricals as well as a restaurant, tea rooms and, of course, accommodation for couples and singles.'

Eliot shook his head in amazement. 'This is the most … what's the word … breathtaking concept I've ever come across.'

'It is my wife's pet project. She has been arguing that we need to be more … European … in our social habits. I don't think she approves of men-only bars, or the six o'clock swill, for that matter.'

Alec watched anxiously as Eliot took it all in. He had invested lot of himself in this project. If he couldn't get it up, he would lose considerable face, especially among his critics. He nearly leapt out of the chair when Eliot walked around the desk and pumped his hand enthusiastically.

'Let's see what we can do.'

Alec picked his hat up. 'Let's. Oh –' He ran his fingers around the brim of his hat as he remembered he had forgotten something. 'And let's not forget the Memorial Swimming Pool.'

Eliot burst out laughing and slapped his thigh. 'No. Let's not. What better way to honour the memory of the fallen?'

Alec strode out of Eliot's office on cloud nine.

54.

Nell walked out of the general store in Dalgarno Street carrying an armload of groceries and dragging Doug along. She came to a group of local women and children, who seemed to snigger as she passed them. Ignoring them, she negotiated her way to the Dodge, dropped the groceries on the bonnet, opened the door and pushed Doug into the back with Mr Chips, who had been waiting for them. She closed the door, turned and walked back across the street.

Joan Betheridge, a plump, youngish woman, was gossiping with Helen Crowley, the equally well fed, flush-faced wife of the local pharmacist.

'What did you say?' Nell stood in front of them, hands on hips.

Joan spluttered an unconvincing response, her neck reddening as she tried to placate Nell. 'Um … nothing …'

'Nothing, eh? I heard you. So did my son.' She nodded in the direction of the Dodge, where Doug and Mr Chips were looking through the window.

'Why don't you call me "the wife of the commie" to my face?'

The two women scratched around, trying to cover their tracks.

'We … we … didn't mean anything …' Joan said.

'No, we didn't,' Helen added.

Joan's eldest boy was staring at Nell with his mouth open wide. Nell softened and gave him a reassuring pat on the head before addressing his mother.

'It's all right. I know you've probably heard all sorts of terrible things about my husband and his intentions.'

They looked uncomfortably at each other.

Nell decided they would be better as allies than enemies. 'He's committed to making the lives of young mothers, like us, easier.' She rubbed her pregnant tummy. 'There are some plans up at the Council. You ought to have a look for yourselves. I'm sure you will be pleasantly surprised.'

Both women seemed to breathe a little more easily as Nell swivelled on her heel before pausing theatrically. 'Did you know he's planning to create a community hotel? One where we will all be welcome, with a play area for the children.'

Nell knew this had done the trick; the women were genuinely impressed. She left them to it and walked to the car. As she was about to open the door, she looked around to see a few of the town's shopkeepers watching from their windows and doorways. Among them, Walter Frater, with his butcher's apron tied neatly over his smart grey trousers, waved cheerily.

'Morning, Nell.'

'Morning, Walter.'

'Good day for it,' he said, with a knowing smile.

Grinning from ear to ear, she winked at him.

She hopped in her car, did a U-turn in the gravel, wound the window down and called to the women. 'He's going to get Dalgarno Street sealed too!'

The birth of William Kenneth Murray in Coonabarabran hospital in October 1945 was a very different experience for Nell than Doug's birth had been. This time around, she had Alec on hand to give her support and encouragement. While the birth itself hadn't been much fun, the memory of the pain was soon overtaken by the deep bond she felt with Alec after William's arrival. He showed her a side of himself she had only briefly glimpsed before. He was clearly moved when the hospital staff allowed him into the ward to meet his second son. Watching Alec doting on their tiny baby, Nell understood how much he had missed out on when Doug was born – not that Alec ever talked about it.

One of the nurses watching Alec cuddle William said, 'Your son will be one of the first customers at our brand new baby health centre.'

Nell chimed in proudly, 'You couldn't get a better endorsement than that for Councillor Murray!'

Alec laughed as the nurse wagged a finger at him. 'Careful. This little fellow's not a lamb. Even though he looks like one! I'll leave you to it,' she said as she walked to the door.

Propped up in bed and still feeling slightly dazed from the birth, Nell made room for Alec to sit beside her. Nestling their new son in his arms, he sat on the edge of the bed.

He stroked the baby's head with his finger. 'He's so little.'

Nell smiled. She loved seeing Alec like this. All his reserve was in danger of falling away as he looked down on William.

'He's …' he faltered, searching for words.

'Yes?' She wanted him to elaborate.

Shaking his head slowly, Alec's smile was as wide as the sky. 'I really didn't expect …'

'No. Nothing can prepare you for the birth of a child. Nothing.'

Nell was deliriously happy. She and Alec felt as one. She wished she could bottle this moment.

55.

When Jim Keeping Brown stood down, Alec was elected to replace him, becoming the youngest Shire President in New South Wales. He was pleased, not least because it meant he could continue revolutionising the Coonabarabran Shire. At the same time, Ben Chifley's Labor Party was re-elected in the 1946 federal election. Alec was intrigued by Chifley's move towards centralised control of education and health and supported his successful referendum giving the federal government control over all social services including maternity allowances, sickness benefits and child endowment.

The Murrays were making headway. Alec felt he was really starting to make a difference. Nell was his unofficial policy advisor while successfully balancing the needs of their expanding family. Doug seemed pleased to have someone to play with other than Mr Chips, and to Alec's amazement, William was always happy.

Alec was working in the yards one morning when Nell joined him with the boys.

'To what do I owe this honour?' he joked as he let out some lambs he had been marking.

'William's christening,' she reminded him.

'Oh …' He closed the gate behind the lambs. 'Couldn't it have waited?'

The last thing Alec wanted was a big social christening. Truth be known, he didn't want any kind of christening. If he had questioned the existence of God before the war, his experiences only reinforced his doubts. He described himself as agnostic to his parents, but in his heart, was firmly an atheist.

Still, he felt guilty that they hadn't visited Braemar for ages. Neither did he want to be the cause of a rift between Nell and her family. His politics were one thing, but they didn't need to interfere with the boys' relationship with their grandparents.

Nell persisted. 'I'm sorry but I have to get back to Mother. You know how she likes to keep up appearances.'

Alec looked at the boys running around chasing the lambs.

'I think, under the circumstances, it would be … both polite and politically savvy,' Nell said. 'We haven't seen them for ages. Peace offering?'

Alec smiled and wiped his blood-splattered hands. 'All right. I don't suppose a few days away would do us any harm.'

'A few days together won't do *us* any harm,' Nell said pointedly.

✳

William's christening in the tiny Braemar chapel went smoothly. Alec hadn't been inside the chapel since their second wedding. As with that event, the church surrounds didn't seem to cause much harm. Alec was glad he'd bent to keep the peace.

Henry and Daphne had travelled from Rylstone. As Alec had suspected, Henry wouldn't miss an opportunity to rub shoulders with Fred Hope, nor Daphne the chance to see her grandchildren. Nell had dressed them in their finest blue sailor suits with white trim. As far as Alec was concerned, they would politely deal with the formalities, have a few celebratory drinks and head back home. They had negotiated the church service without a hitch. All they needed to do was keep up appearances back at the homestead.

Decked out in spring flowers, Braemer looked a picture. Elaine had organised a big spread, as usual, and everyone seemed to be enjoying the grand occasion. Alec looked at his watch. He was keen to go, but he could see Nell was making the most of the chance to catch up with people she hadn't seen for ages. She was charming the pants off everyone. There was no reason why he couldn't stretch it out a bit. After all, she deserved a break.

While getting himself another beer, Alec bumped into Jock. 'It's a … wonderful day,' he said, trying to make small talk. Alec was determined to keep it light. The last thing he wanted was to engage his brother-in-law in any kind of serious discussion.

'What's this nonsense about building public housing in Coonabarabran?' Jock asked. He'd had a skinful and was spoiling for a fight.

'Oh, it's … it's an opportunity … to provide for fellows like us who … you know … went away,' Alec said, looking for an escape.

'I read it's the only place outside Sydney that the Housing Commission are building them.'

'That's right,' Alec said, a little too proudly.

Jock sized him up. 'What makes you so bloody special?'

His aggression didn't necessarily shock Alec. Jock had been discharged with a busted knee, malaria and a carefully concealed case of syphilis. He had a reputation for flying off the handle. But the last thing Alec wanted was a public spat in Nell's parents' home. He could feel people watching.

'I … I'm just trying to … you know … make things a bit better.' He was floundering. This was exactly why he had been avoiding Jock all day.

Just as Jock was about to launch into a tirade, Fred Hope grabbed him by the elbow.

'Hello, my boy. Would you mind helping Mrs Carter with her car? She appears to be having trouble starting it.'

Jock muttered something and unwillingly stumbled off. Alec was relieved to see that he still obeyed his father.

'I'm sorry about that,' Fred said. 'I was worried he might forget where he was.'

Alec appreciated his father-in-law's words. It was common knowledge that Jock was a loose cannon, particularly when he was on the grog.

Fred confided in Alec. 'He's been quite a handful since he came back.'

Sympathising, Alec did his best to reassure him. 'Understandable … The Middle East, Abyssinia and one of the first officers in Kokoda … He had a hell of a war.'

Fred gave him a grateful pat on the arm and walked off. Alec detected a sadness in his father-in-law. Class doesn't prevent you from suffering, he thought. It was a lesson he learnt in the war. Bullets didn't discriminate between officers and serving men, even if some officers had kept themselves out of the firing line.

Alec and his father exchanged pleasantries about the weather and Alec assured his mother that she was welcome at Toongowan anytime, before he rounded up his team and piled them into the Dodge for the trip home.

Nell was a bit tipsy. 'That was fun!'

He was relieved that she hadn't heard Jock's accusations and had enjoyed herself. As they drove home, he thought about what Nell had given up for him and his cause. He knew she supported him and shared his beliefs, but it was impossible to escape the fact that his progressive outlook had soured her relationship with her parents.

'There was a bit of grumbling about the direction the Council is heading in,' she said, as if reading his thoughts.

'Oh?' he asked, feigning ignorance.

Nell snuggled up to him.

'Thank you for being so understanding.' He touched her lightly and looked in the rear-view mirror to see the boys sleeping like tops. It had been a good day.

It didn't take long for them to discover that there were rumblings among Alec's former allies. The Graziers' Council had organised a public meeting to discuss his 'radical agenda'. Alec decided he had better get along to see what was brewing. When Nell insisted on going with him, he had to point out it was men only.

'Then I'll listen from outside!'

The public meeting was in full swing when Alec walked into the Memorial Hall. Percy Dutton was thumping the lectern.

'We are not going to stand idly by while men like Ben Chifley destroy everything we have fought for. The war against fascism might be over but another one has begun. The war against communism.'

Alec was surprised that the debate was focussing on Canberra. He had thought the discussion would centre on local issues.

'Make no mistake about it, we are facing a far more pernicious threat than the one we have repelled. It is more pernicious because it comes from within,' Percy said, waving his finger threateningly.

'We have a communist in our midst ...' someone shouted.

A few heads turned towards Alec, standing at the back of the hall. He was confused. Were they talking about him?

'The enemy within,' another man added.

Percy continued with his address. 'And, friends, that enemy is the Prime Minister of this country. There is no doubt that Chifley is under orders from Moscow and his goal is to destroy everything we hold dear.'

Percy paused and nodded in Alec's direction. 'Coonabarabran Council is clearly singing from the same song sheet.'

This was too much for Alec. He pushed forward and raised his hand. Percy dismissed him.

'We don't want to hear from you. You are a bloody commo too,' a man shouted.

Alec tried to make his way to the front. 'I'm Shire President. After Jim stood down, I was elected unopposed. I'm entitled to speak.'

Tim Masterson, the burly grazier who was at his preselection in Binnaway, blocked Alec's path to the stage. 'No way.'

Looking around the crowd, Alec could see quite a few of his supporters. 'All right then. If you won't give me the chance to respond in here, I'll be outside if anyone wants to hear what I have to say.'

There was stunned silence as he turned and walked out of the hall.

Snowy Carmichael, a third-generation stock and station agent got to his feet. 'We may as well hear him out. After all, as he says, he is Shire President.'

With that, Snowy pulled on his hat, and with a limp he'd sustained from the First World War, he headed for the door. He was followed by most of the audience, leaving Percy Dutton and the assembled graziers to themselves.

Determined to say his piece, Alec walked into the night, placed an upturned apple box under a lighted lamp post and stood on it. He was grateful to see the bulk of the meeting filing out of the hall and surrounding him. The sight of Nell leaning on the car across the road gave him strength.

Dave Armstrong, the local copper, stood nearby, watching the crowd grow. 'Looks to me like you're conducting an illegal street meeting, Alec,' he cautioned.

Alec smiled at his friend. 'You might have to look the other way, Dave,' he said, before turning to address the crowd.

'Thank you for giving me a few minutes of your time. I'm not going to say much, but what I am going to say is … That in a democracy, every man and woman should be able to state their case. That's why I am standing here. I am your Shire President. I am not immune from criticism. I am prepared to have Council's decisions challenged. But I am not prepared to have those challenges made behind closed doors by faceless men. If you have a beef with me or my fellow councillors, come into the light and state it.'

He pointed up at the streetlamp shining above him. 'Not so many years ago, citizens of this community petitioned against the new-fangled electric light, then a water supply, and most recently, to have a parson thrown out because his style of worship didn't appeal to some of his parishioners. Now, I have nothing against petitions, in fact I support them as a means of expressing opinion in a democracy such as ours –'

Brian Redding, a small-time farmer, interjected, 'But you're a commo, aren't you?'

The comment sent a ripple through the meeting.

'No, Brian. I am not a commo. I have never been a commo. I will never be a commo. As you know, I am not a member of any political party. I was tossed out of the Country Party. Being unencumbered puts me in the unique position of not having to do the bidding of any one group. You know the Council. You know who we are. We represent a wide range of opinions and we are united by a desire to serve all of your interests.'

People nodded.

Alec continued. 'As Jim Brown says, this council is the most progressive in the shire's history. We are not just planning for tomorrow. We are planning fifty years ahead. Some people say that we are moving too fast. I say we are not moving fast enough. Let's make Coonabarabran the town everyone wants to move into, not away from.'

He had them in the palm of his hands. Nell gave him a thumbs up.

*

A few days later, Nell was shelling peas when Alec walked in waving a copy of the *Daily Telegraph*.

'Look at this!' He wrapped his arms around her waist and lifted her up, making her spill the peas into the sink.

'Careful. Look what you made me do!'

'Here.' He gave her the paper and watched closely for her reaction.

'Ahh!' she shrieked, pointing to a caricature of Alec heading up a full-page article. She read the headline. '*The Visionary, Alec Murray.*'

Alec feigned nonchalance while she continued reading the article. '*The Council has done a tremendous amount of work producing what is probably the most important piece of local social planning this country has known, and with government cooperation and financial help, that plan can quickly become a fact and put Coonabarabran district on the map for all time.*'

She put the paper down. It was her turn to wrap him in her arms. 'I'm so proud of you.'

'I couldn't have done it without you.'

'I know.'

He took her hands in his. 'I feel like we are making headway.'

'We are.' She squeezed his hands before clenching her fists and doing a little hop in a gesture of support. 'It's fun.'

56.

Walter handed Nell a beer.

'I hope it's not a shandy.'

'I'm not that brave,' he replied, placing his lemonade on a coaster.

Nell caught Joan Bethridge's eye. Joan was having a quiet drink with Helen Crowley in the Ladies Lounge while their children played with some toys in the playpen. She raised her glass and toasted Nell from across the room.

'To what do I owe this honour?' asked Nell, turning back to Walter.

'Alec's attracting plenty of attention,' he replied.

She waited for him to expand.

'That story in the *Telegraph*.' He leant in and spoke conspiratorially. 'Have you heard of Billy Scully?'

'Of course. The Member for Gwydir.'

'Yes,' Walter said. 'Labor man.'

Nell wasn't sure if Walter meant this as praise or criticism. After all, Walter was a communist.

He spoke slowly and deliberately. 'Billy showed Alec's lamp post speech to Chifley. They reckon he's on the lookout for new blood. He wants to broaden the Party's appeal, beyond the unions.'

'Hang on. Why are you telling me this? You're a union man.'

'I am. I also believe we need good people in Canberra and your husband is one of the best.'

She was suspicious. 'You want a revolution. You want to overthrow the government.'

He didn't argue. 'I'm prepared to wait for the right climate. It will come. Believe me. In the meantime, I want what's best for this district. Nothing's black and white, Nell.'

She laughed. 'No.'

'The thing is, Chifley wants to meet Alec.'

'Why? He isn't in the Labor Party.'

'Politics is a very unpredictable game.'

'So, I'm learning.'

'It's not every day the sitting PM wants to meet you,' said Walter.

'You want me to convince Alec to go?'

His look left her in no doubt that he did.

'He'll get a call. I wanted you to know first.'

'I appreciate it.' She raised her glass. 'Thanks, Walter.'

On the drive home Nell couldn't help but laugh about what had just transpired. An avowed communist had asked her, the daughter of one of the country's most influential conservatives, to get her husband to go to Canberra to meet the recently re-elected Labor Prime Minister.

'Of course you have to go,' she said, as they discussed it after dinner that night.

Alec was hanging a Henoch Raberaba painting on the lounge room wall. Peg had sent it up on the train after she bought it for them at an exhibition of the Hermannsburg School in Sydney. Nell loved the colours.

'A bit to the left. That's better. Mark it.'

He drilled a hole in the wall and hung the painting.

'Looks good. Don't you think?' he said.

She was pleased that Alec liked her new acquisition. She straightened it up and stood back with her hands on her hips.

'You've got to go,' she said firmly as he packed up the tools.

'I'm not in the Labor Party. I've got no intention …'

Nell warmed to her theme. She'd been planning her pitch for hours.

'You've got all these big plans. How are you going to pay for them? This is your chance to put your case for more federal funds for the area, postwar reconstruction, that sort of thing. You'll never get a better opportunity to lobby for the shire. I've booked our flight for the morning. Now that Doug's boarding at Tudor House, Mary will only have William to look after. Donny will run the show while we're away. It'll do us good.'

She took over packing up the hammer and nails. 'It's all settled then.'

Dumbfounded, Alec didn't argue. 'As long as we come back with something more than empty promises!' he said eventually.

She punched him playfully on the arm. 'You'd better. The district expects it! Don't forget you're putting us on the map.'

57.

Alec bounced on the balls of his feet on the steps of Parliament House, a habit he had acquired as a student while waiting for exam results. He looked out across the dusty plains to the meandering Molonglo River. He could make out a few trees and a few scraggly sheep. No wonder Canberra is called the 'bush capital', he thought.

'Alec?'

He looked up to see a big man with a shock of curly white hair and a generous smile standing at the top of the steps. He was carrying a battered old brief case in one hand and a pipe in the other. Alec was immediately struck by the apparent ordinariness of the Australian Prime Minister.

'That's right.' Alec tried to appear cool and calm.

The Prime Minister stuck his pipe in his mouth, made his way down the steps and held out his hand. 'Ben Chifley.'

As they shook hands, Chifley reminded Alec of an old shearer. He was strongly built, with a firm hand shake and a no-bullshit demeanour.

'Sir ...'

'How was the trip?'

'Oh ... good thanks.'

'It's a funny place to put a capital city. Still, might say something about us that they chose it because they couldn't agree on a site and it's halfway between Sydney and Melbourne.' He touched Alec's elbow lightly.

'I usually walk back to the hotel, helps me clear my head after all the argy-bargy in there.' He cocked his head in the direction of the classical white brick building that housed the Australian parliament.

'Why don't you join me?'

'I'd be … yes … that sounds good.' Alec was kicking himself for being so inarticulate.

'Good. It's this way. I like to walk along the river. Even if it's a bit longer.'

He led Alec on a detour along the banks of the Molonglo towards the Hotel Kurrajong.

'Being an old engine driver, I've never been too comfortable with the hire cars and all the folderol that goes with this job. I come from Bathurst …'

'Yes. I know.'

A flock of white cockatoos took off noisily across the river. As the men walked along in silence, Alec began to feel more at ease.

Finally, Chifley spoke. 'I'm very interested in your ideas.'

Alec was flattered, it wasn't what he expected to hear.

Chifley continued. 'Of course, we can't do as much about the things you're proposing as we'd like. As I'm sure you know, they fall under the state government's jurisdiction. Jack Renshaw will look after you. He's a good man.'

Alec glanced around and noticed how dry the countryside looked. He was about to mention it when Chifley surprised him with his next comment.

'You know Nehru?'

'Well … I … ah … the Indian Prime Minister, yes, I know who he is…'

Chifley continued. 'He's a fascinating man don't you think?'

Alec agreed.

'"Tryst with Destiny" – quite a closing phrase.' Chifley laughed. 'I wish I'd come up with it. Might have shut up some of the doubters and nay-sayers in caucus.' He paused, then added, 'I wish this country could "awake to life and freedom". I fear it's going to take a lot longer to shake us out of complacency.'

'I agree,' Alec said. 'Trying to drag the conservatives in my district out of the nineteenth century is proving quite a challenge.'

Chifley stopped and eyeballed Alec. 'That is exactly why I asked Billy to get you down here. There is going to be a redistribution in your region. A new seat. Lawson. Named after the poet. It'll be one of the biggest electorates in the state.'

Alec's heart was pounding. 'Billy's seat is pretty safe but that's because it includes a lot of mining towns, like Kandos. Lawson will be much tougher. The cockies aren't our greatest supporters, as I'm sure you're aware.' He smiled knowingly. Then his tone became more forceful. 'If we're going to do the things we need to do, we have to win seats like Lawson. We must have the support of rural people.'

Is he saying what I think he's saying? wondered Alec.

'We want you to stand for it.'

Alec was stunned. 'Me?'

'We need men like you. Men who are different; cut from a different cloth. I'm the past, and the trouble with people like me is: we're bitter. Look … I stopped my engine in the strike of '17, got the sack and nearly starved as a result. It took me a long time to get back and I was persecuted for years. So sure … I've got hatred. The important thing about people like *you* is, you haven't got that hatred. You can build a party for everybody. That's why we need you. That's why *I* need you.'

Chifley's words stopped Alec in his tracks. He had never imagined that his summons to Canberra would result in being asked to stand for the Labor Party in a federal election. He may have sympathised with the Labor Party and briefly considered joining the ill-fated, Common Wealth movement after the war, but these days, he was happy representing the RSL.

Before he could protest, Chifley said, 'I've heard that you're a good servant to your district and that you're not stuck up. I've got one bit of advice. The important thing about being a successful politician is humility.'

While Alec did his best to digest this, Chifley took out his matches, shielded his pipe from the breeze and lit it. He took a deep drag and exhaled before continuing. 'We'll get you a membership ticket. You need to join before the end of the year. Two tickets. One for you. One for your wife.'

'One for my wife?' Alec was flummoxed.

Chifley made it sound like it was a fait accompli that he and Nell would not only join the Labor Party but stand for Labor in a federal election.

'I'm ... sir ... Mr Chifley. I'm very flattered but things haven't been great lately. After the last season I'm pretty broke. I already had enormous debts ...' He stuck his hands in his pockets awkwardly. 'Besides. I've got two young children and a wife who has had a tough time of it. She didn't see me for eighteen months after we were married. She had to raise a baby on her own. I can't just –'

'What would have happened to your wife and one kid if you'd been killed?'

Alec didn't want to think. Chifley answered for him. 'She would have battled on. Not much point going to war if you don't fight for your beliefs when you get back.' He concluded, 'I guess she'll have to put up with it, won't she?'

There was a brutality about this comment that Alec found confronting. Then Chifley added, 'We all have to make sacrifices. We don't matter. The people do.'

With that, he resumed walking, leaving Alec to ponder. When he had recovered sufficiently, Alec caught up with Chifley. As they arrived at the entrance of the Hotel Kurrajong, Chifley stopped and made his final pitch.

'All these things you have been proposing are just the kind of initiatives we need to implement to close the gap between the rich and poor. Health and community centres controlled by government rather than capitalist individuals who are only interested in their own profits. That's why we're going to nationalise the banks.'

Nationalise the banks? Alec's jaw dropped. Had he heard correctly?

Chifley casually leant on his shoulder for support while he tapped his pipe on the heel of his shoe, dislodging the spent tobacco. He put the pipe away in his coat pocket.

'Think about it, Alec.'

He smiled warmly, shook Alec's hand and turned on his heels, doffing his hat to a woman who was heading out for the evening.

'Oh, by the way, Alec,' he called. 'I didn't tell you; my grandfather was a cocky. We've got more in common than you might think.'

Chifley had impressed Alec. He had a steely determination that Alec hadn't expected. He was clearly no pushover. Even though the PM projected an easy, avuncular demeanour, he combined it with compassion and toughness and certainly didn't beat around the bush.

Alec had some big choices to make.

58.

'What do you think?'

Lance Crawford opened the door of his new, bright red MG and hopped out. Nell gasped in mock horror and covered her mouth. Lance had offered to pick her up from her hotel while Alec was meeting the Prime Minister.

'I thought you were a communist!'

'I am.'

She pointed at the car. 'What's a communist doing driving a car like that?'

He raised his arms in supplication. 'It's red, isn't it?'

Before she could reply, he embraced her warmly. She had missed him too. He ushered her into the passenger seat with a little bow. Nell smiled as he sashayed around to the driver's side; he was grinning like a Cheshire cat.

They roared off down National Circuit.

'Geez, you're a showoff!' Nell teased, as she threw her head back and closed her eyes. The wind blew her hair and the crisp Canberra air lightly stung her face. With Lance she could let go of all the reserve she was forced to display as a wife and mother. She stood up in the passenger seat, gripping the windscreen as he negotiated the roads.

'Woo hoo!' she called out.

Admiring Lance in his natty, herringbone driving cap and flowing scarf, Nell thought how much she loved him. As they pulled into the drive of his Deakin bungalow, she smiled, pleased that she had decided to come to Canberra with Alec.

They made light work of one of Lance's bottles of red while they picked up where they had left off. Nell felt like she could open up to him, voice thoughts that she held back from everyone else, even Alec. They had forged such a bond since the fateful night on the riverbank.

'Tell me everything,' he said, as he refilled her glass.

'Everything?'

'Everything.'

Nell fiddled with a cigarette before lighting it.

'I'm all right,' she said, exhaling. 'I … I sometimes miss having time to myself. Time to be myself. So much is … expected of me.'

She took a sip of her wine. 'I love what Alec is trying to do. He encourages me to be part of it but … I'm not really. I might contribute ideas and do the odd bit but, the truth is, I'm not much more than his wife and the mother of his children. When it comes down to it, I'm just window dressing.'

'You! Window dressing?'

'He's up there making the speeches. I'm in the front row clapping along like a dutiful wife. Or, worse, waiting outside until the meeting is over.'

She paused, feeling that she may have gone too far. 'Did that sound catty?'

His raised eyebrow told her it did.

She sat forward. 'I'm worried I'm losing myself.'

Nell was finally articulating something she had been feeling for weeks, months, even years. She had felt herself gradually slipping away as she fulfilled other people's wishes. The whole reason she had escaped to Paris was to do her own thing. To be herself. To find herself. There was something inside her that she wanted to let out and, for a brief time, in Paris, she was able to find it. And begin to express it.

'I know what you mean,' said Lance.

'Why can't we be ourselves?'

Nell let this hang. One of the things she loved about her friendship with Lance was that they understood each other deeply. They enjoyed the silences between them. Eventually he broke it.

'What about your painting?'

Nell paused, fiddling with her wine glass.

'I've tried to pick it up. Carl Thomas offered me a mural … I do a bit.'

'Not enough?'

She shrugged and smiled ironically.

'We all have to make sacrifices. So I am told …'

She took another sip of her wine and cleared her throat.

'Anyway, enough about me. What about you, my friend? How are you?'

Lance told her about his double life as a gay communist and scientist. There was a move afoot in the Liberal Party and pressure from the Catholic Church to make being a member of the Communist Party a criminal offence. Homosexuality was already illegal.

'It's what I like about sleepy Canberra,' Lance explained. 'As long as I keep my head down and find a cure for wheat's weevil problem, no one bothers me.'

Nell felt terrible. She was complaining about her privileged existence while her friend was forced to deny who he was.

'It's quite exciting,' he said, before confiding, 'I'm a contact.'

Nell had no idea what he was talking about. When Lance admitted that he had been contacted by Communist Party officials to try to persuade her to influence Alec's political leanings, she was horrified.

'How did they know we were coming to Canberra? Hang on … Walter?'

Lance smiled knowingly. For a second Nell wondered if she was being used.

'We live in volatile times,' Lance said.

On the way back to the hotel, Nell thought about her friendship with Lance. She adored him and she did love seeing him so happy, but she didn't like being used by him. He had badgered her about the reason for Alec's meeting with Chifley, but she didn't know the details and assumed it was to get federal financial support for his projects. It hurt her that their relationship had become transactional.

59.

When Alec told her the real reason for their trip to the national capital, Nell nearly fainted. Federal politics was a huge leap up from local council. And they would have to move to Canberra.

She didn't know what to think. She'd already had to defend Alec's more radical proposals for the shire. Joining the Labor Party would be another league altogether. People in her circle were convinced it was a front for communists. Such a move could cause her untold damage.

Surely, she had sacrificed enough. Now Alec was asking her to sacrifice lifelong friendships and her family. She hadn't married him to join the Labor Party. She had married him because he was interesting, different and, well, very attractive.

Though Alec sought her approval before making a public pronouncement, she knew he had already made up his mind. He was obviously in awe of Chifley and she couldn't blame him. Who wouldn't be flattered by the Prime Minister making a personal plea to join his party?

Further complicating matters was that if they were going to do it, they had to do it quickly. If Alec was going to stand, he needed to be registered before the cut-off time.

'How long do I have to think about it?' Nell asked.

'Not long, I'm afraid. The deadline's next week.'

'We better get cracking then.'

Nell was under no illusions about the consequences of such a drastic step, yet a part of her was excited by it. She had always encouraged Alec's ambitions and conceded that many aligned with Labor's. She too, supported the idea of public ownership. While she enjoyed the trappings of a privileged upbringing, she could see that there was plenty to recommend sharing the cake. Her time in Coonabarabran had shown her how people really lived; something she had never encountered growing up as the daughter of a wealthy wool grower. On the rare occasions she had gone into Trangie as a child, it had been to do some shopping or pick up something or other from the stock and station agent. Going to events such as pony club meetings hadn't exposed her to the community at large. She had been brought up in a very narrow, privileged world, and she knew it. Getting to know the Coonabarabran community had allowed to her see the world very differently, as had living on the smell of an oily rag in Paris.

In the end, although it had been foisted on her, Nell chose to support Alec's conversion. Not only that, but she decided she was happy to join the party. She had no intention being left behind.

When they completed the necessary paperwork at Sydney's Trades Hall, Nell felt a sense of pride. They were signing up to change the way society was organised. The Federal Secretary of the Labor Party told her that Australia needed men like Alec who didn't carry a whole lot of revolutionary baggage. Men who had a clean slate. She was more than ready to join in the fight.

She decided to take the opportunity of being in Sydney to catch up with Peg and her little family. They caught a taxi out to Wahroonga for dinner. Johnny bounded down the steps to greet them. Nell was pleased that he seemed to have regained his old effervescence. While Johnny and Alec reminisced about old friends, Peg showed Nell around the house and introduced her to her boys. Nell was thrilled to see her great mate so obviously in her element.

Dinner was a riot, as Johnny regaled them with tall tales and true. When he was on song, he was the life and soul of any party and Nell was happy to be entertained by him. She could see that Alec was enjoying a night of hilarity too. They both needed a break.

Peg queried Nell about her painting and they exchanged notes on child rearing. Both Johnny and Peg seemed impressed by Alec's new-found notoriety as a harbinger of change.

When Nell blurted out that they had some news, Peg thought she was pregnant again.

'No …' Nell teased.

'What then?' Peg was insistent.

Nell looked at Alec who was fiddling with his glass. She decided that if she couldn't tell her best friend in the world, who could she tell?

'Alec's joined the Labor Party.'

She looked around the table. Johnny looked like he had been hit by a bus while Peg was opened mouthed.

'You've what?' Peg asked.

Alec shifted uncomfortably in his seat and tried to make light of it. 'Yes. I…ah…I've taken a ticket with the enemy.'

Johnny stiffened.

'You're joking?'

'No. I'm afraid I'm not.'

The mood had changed dramatically. Johnny was apoplectic. 'You've joined the commos!' he shouted.

'Don't be ridiculous.' Nell countered.

The combination of alcohol and politics made the situation combustible. Johnny's bonhomie had well and truly disappeared.

'You know what Stalin's been up to, don't you?' he challenged.

'Ben Chifley isn't Stalin,' Alec countered.

Nell could see he wasn't backing down.

'He isn't far off. He's going to try to nationalise the banks. What's that if not communism.'

'It's socialism.'

'Don't give me the shits.'

'Johnny!' Peg was trying to calm things down, but Nell knew that the horse had bolted.

Johnny was on a roll. 'What? He's joined the Reds. What do you want me to do?'

'Calm down,' Peg pleaded.

'I'm not having a bloody communist in the house,' Johnny thundered as he threw his napkin onto the table and stormed off.

Peg looked at Nell and shrugged apologetically. Nell closed her eyes for a moment and took Alec's hand.

'We wanted to tell you ourselves. You are our closest friends …' Nell grimaced, doing her best to cover her feelings of dismay.

The room fell into an uncomfortable silence. Peg attempted to lighten the mood.

'Chifley's plans aren't going too well out in suburbs.' she explained.

'Let alone the bush.' Nell said. 'We haven't told our parents yet.'

Peg raised her eyebrows and looked squarely at Alec.

'You're going to be seen as a traitor, Al. You realise that don't you?'

Alec nodded.

Nell leant over and took his hand. 'He's not the only one. I've joined up too.' She paused. 'One in, all in.'

For a brief second Nell feared that Peg's reaction would be like Johnny's. She was relieved when Peg stood, took Nell's head in her hands and kissed her.

'You were always going to go out on a limb, weren't you?'

Nell laughed and did her best Mae West impersonation. 'You only live once, but if you do it right, once is enough!'

They both burst into giggles bringing Johnny storming back into the room.

'I'm afraid I'm going to have to ask you to leave.'

Peg did her best to intervene.

'Darling …'

Alec pushed his chair back and stood. 'It's all right Peg. It's getting late and we've got an early flight.'

They gathered their things and made their way for the door. A cab was already waiting by the curb.

Peg took Nell in her arms. 'You be careful. This isn't going to be easy. You're going to make a lot of enemies.'

As the cab took off, Nell looked out the back window to see Johnny silhouetted in the bedroom window looking down on them. She squeezed Alec's leg and nestled into his shoulder. She suspected Johnny would never talk to Alec again.

*

While Nell was worried that this would be a harbinger of things to come, she was surprised to see Alec so sanguine. There was a glimpse of the warrior in his attitude.

Driving to the airport, she was left in little doubt about the personal challenges that lay before them when. A billboard screamed, *Labor Attack on Individual Freedom*. Back home, she soon discovered that Alec's decision to throw his hat in the ring for Labor candidacy in Lawson was tantamount to a declaration of war. While Chifley saw him as the kind of man the Labor Party needed in Canberra, their social group saw him as a Judas.

Alec told her that another old school friend, Brian Harkness, had hung up on him when he rang to ask him to lunch at the Australian Club. When Alec attempted to visit the Club, he was refused entry and banned for life, until her father told the Club's committee that if they didn't immediately reinstate Alec, he would resign as President. At least Fred Hope's word was still respected – that got the black ban lifted, but there was more to come.

Henry Murray was so disgusted that his son had joined the Labor Party, he tried to get the trustees to foreclose on their loan and toss them off Toongowan. Fortunately, Daphne wouldn't go along with it, and it was her word that counted. Although Henry reinstituted the prohibition on Daphne visiting her grandchildren, she refused to budge on foreclosing. Nell was forced to make up excuses for the boys, to explain why Granny had stopped coming to see them.

She was shocked by the extent of the backlash and its ferocity. People she'd had cordial relationships with, crossed the road to avoid her, others stopped their children playing with William at preschool.

When the Matron at Doug's boarding house sent Nell a note that he seemed very unhappy, she decided to drive to Tudor House to see what was going on.

'It's a long drive on your own,' Alec cautioned.

Nell knew full well that Moss Vale was over 300 miles away and that it would be a seven hour drive. 'If I can't get to the bottom of why my son is so upset, what kind of a mother am I? I'll leave at the crack of dawn.'

The long drive gave Nell the opportunity to think about the cards fate had dealt her. She had no regrets about the path they had taken but she did begin to question the wisdom of accepting her father's offer to pay for boarding school fees. Though she missed Doug terribly, she had been convinced that it would be better for him to be away from the hurly burly of an election campaign.

When she arrived in Moss Vale she was horrified to find that Doug had bruises on his little arms.

'What happened darling?'

He put on a brave face.

'Oh nothing …'

'These aren't nothing.'

'I … fell over.'

She took him in her arms and squeezed him tightly. 'Oh. My poor little warrior.'

Doug pulled away. 'Please don't tell anyone.'

Her heart was breaking as she looked down on his tiny, desperate face.

'Promise?'

She swallowed. 'Okay. I'll do you a deal. You tell me exactly what happened and I won't tell anyone. Apart from Matron.'

This seemed to satisfy Doug. 'They call me "commo" and punch me when they walk past.'

'But you're only six!'

'Everyone gets bullied, Mum. It's what the big boys do.'

Nell was horrified but she couldn't show Doug. She had to put on a brave face. She had made a deal and she had to keep her side of the bargain. When she suggested to Doug that he come home with her, he refused.

She didn't know what to do. He was so upset at the suggestion that she agreed to see how he went over the next few weeks.

'He's got to learn to fight his own battles,' the sympathetic Matron told her. 'It will toughen him up.'

She took Nell's hands. 'I promise you, I'll put a stop to the bullying.'

'You promise?' Nell pleaded through tears.

'I promise.'

On the way home, Nell couldn't stop crying. For the first time in her life, she felt cornered. One thing was certain, if there was another hint of bullying, she would bring Doug home, no matter how many hours he would have to spend in a bus.

*

Alec's nomination wasn't universally acclaimed by Labor either. Walter told Nell that members of the Railwaymen's Union were suspicious of his motives and needed winning over. Nell felt as if they were being attacked from all sides. While Alec seemed almost immune to it, the aggression frightened her.

As far as many of her friends were concerned, joining the Labor Party meant that Nell and Alec supported Stalin's barbarity and were hellbent on bringing the country to its knees. Nothing Nell could say could appease them. On top of that, it soon became clear that winning Lawson, in the heart of conservative, rural Australia, was going to be a challenge of epic proportions.

Sermons from pulpits around the district warned of a communist plot masterminded in Moscow. And according to Walter, the Roman Catholic Church in Melbourne had launched a campaign to tar men like Alec as communists and convince electors that government control of education, health and the banks would be the end individual freedoms.

Nell felt trapped. She had to support her husband, she wanted to, she believed in him. But she hated the idea that her children were collateral damage. She knew it would be hell for Doug to witness, firsthand, what was surely coming down the turnpike. Johnny's performance made that very clear. As she pulled into Toongowan it was pitch black save for a flickering candle in Alec's study. He was waiting up for her.

60.

Walter convinced Alec that the only way he was going to make a dint in the conservatives' stranglehold on the electorate was to embark on an extensive door-knocking campaign in towns such as Parkes and Dubbo.

'It's in the towns where you have the most hope. Get in the pubs and talk to the people. Show them you're not a Johnny-come-lately and you've got something to offer. Talk about local issues. The airport in Dubbo has brought people to the Central West. TAA is a government-owned airline. Government ownership isn't the monster the conservatives make it out to be. You need to remind them.'

Alec pointed out to Walter that Lawson was 150,000 square miles and bigger than many European countries. He was quickly realising the enormity of the task in front of him.

Walter showed Alec how to take tiny sips from his glass and to sit on it when people offered to buy him a beer. He needed to look like he was drinking but there was no point in being as blind as a bat before lunchtime when he had so much country to cover.

'And make sure you shake everyone's hand,' Walter told him.

Travelling around the region might be good for the campaign, but it meant being away from home for weeks on end, and Nell was her own once again. Alec had to hope that Toongowan would keep functioning as a working property in his absence; otherwise, Henry would have the ammunition he needed to throw them off their land. They were big sacrifices but ones Alec was prepared to make. Just like he had in the war.

When he ran into his old batman, Jack Fulton, working the points on the railways in Gilgandra, he asked him to join him as his campaign manager. He didn't take much convincing.

As he and Jack crisscrossed the electorate, Alec was relieved that people seemed to warm to him. There was plenty of opposition to Chifley's plans to nationalise the banks but, on the other side of the ledger, plenty of support for change in the towns, as Walter had predicted. The progressive ideas Alec had introduced through Coonabarabran Council held widespread appeal among working families.

Nell was playing cricket with Doug in the front yard when Alec arrived home from electioneering. He watched her encourage the little boy while William ran around pretending he was something or other. He was glad to have his family back together for a few days.

'Why don't we go to the Trangie Show?' Nell suggested after Alec had read a bedtime story to the boys. Alec grabbed a tea towel and started wiping up. The Trangie Show was on enemy territory. Nell read his mind.

'You're going to have to get out and show your face, no matter how much flak you receive. You can't hide your light under a bushel.'

She emptied the sink, wiped down and looked him the eye.

'Show them what you're made of.'

Alec took this in. He had been avoiding the squattocracy to focus on votes he could win.

'Besides, with Douggie home from school it'll be an opportunity for the boys to see their grandparents.'

And their uncle, Alec thought. He kept this to himself. Nell had already made so many sacrifices for him he knew he couldn't deny her the chance to see her family.

'Okay. Why not?' He said taking her in his arms and kissing her lightly on the cheek.

*

The Show was the biggest event on the district's social calendar. Everyone and anyone was there; selling all kinds of things – from sheep to preserved fruit – trying their luck in the boxing tent, or just shooting the breeze. As Alec walked around, with Nell on his arm and the boys in tow, they ran into his opponent, Eddie Raymond. Eddie had been the district's sitting Country Party member before the new seat of Lawson was created. He was a cheerful man with a confident manner who dressed like a farmer even though he was an accountant from Dubbo. Alec and Eddie exchanged pleasantries while Nell managed a bit of small talk with Eddie's wife, Phyllis.

When Alec saw a group of old school friends, including Hugh Masterton, he went out of his way to greet them. But the men walked straight past his outstretched hand. Their wives followed, glancing at Nell, before deliberately ignoring her. Alec could barely contain himself. It was one thing for people to cut him loose; quite another to dismiss Nell.

Trying to shake it off, he took his family over to the woodchopping where they were greeted by the railway workers trying their luck. The boys loved it. Then, they joined Fred and Elaine for a picnic lunch overlooking the showground. Elaine had made chicken sandwiches for the boys.

'The cattle look good,' said Fred.

Alec thanked him for not allowing the Australian Club to black-ball him.

'Every man is entitled to their opinion,' Fred said, closing the discussion.

While supervising lunch, Alec saw Jock bowl up to Nell. He had clearly spent the morning in the beer tent.

Alec could see that Jock was getting stuck into her. He left the boys to their sandwiches and strode over. Jock turned his back on him and, just as Alec was about to confront him, Nell grabbed him by the arm and led him away.

'What did he say to you?' Alec demanded.

'He told me you were a traitor to your class.'

Alec shook his head. 'What did you say?'

'I told him that if he had half of your integrity, he might be able to comment, but as he was a lying, cheating bully, he should keep his mouth shut.'

Alec knew how lucky he was to have Nell in his camp. She had clearly enjoyed putting her brother in his place.

*

On the drive home, Nell lit a cigarette and put her feet on the dashboard. 'At least we know what we're up against,' she said.

He laughed. 'Better the devil you know …'

He squeezed her knee. Not only was she his greatest ally, she was prepared to put everything, including her family, on the line for the cause.

61.

When Chifley sent a note to say he would be speaking at Alec's campaign launch, Nell was over the moon. In an election race where he wasn't widely known, the PM's endorsement would bolster Alec's chances. Nell was worried about how the abuse from Alec's so-called friends was affecting him. He put on a brave face but, underneath, Nell knew he must have been hurting.

She and Jack sat in the front row of the Dubbo Ex-Servicemen's Club waiting for Alec to walk on stage.

'I hope I get to shake his hand. He was my dad's hero!' Jack said.

'I'm sure you will, Jack, just try and sit still.'

The hall was packed to the rafters but strangely quiet.

'You could cut the air with a knife,' said Jack as he looked around at the crowd of shopkeepers and workers all stretching their necks for a glimpse of the PM.

Nell agreed; the atmosphere was electric.

'Look!' Jack pointed at the portly figure with curly white hair who had taken to the stage next to Alec. 'It's Ben Chifley!'

Nell thought Jack was going to pass out.

She was immediately impressed by Chifley. He had a modesty about him that was as genuine as it was appealing. He exhorted his audience to work for the betterment of all mankind. It was their duty, he told them, to reach for the 'light on the hill'. Nell felt she could follow him to the ends of the earth; she had never felt so inspired. When he talked about the country looking beyond its borders to the world at large, he sounded to Nell like the statesman Alec had described.

His praise for Alec as 'a new broom' sounded genuine, and the crowd applauded when Chifley told them that Alec was 'just what the country needed'. It was heady stuff.

He quietly nodded throughout Alec's speech, which was along the same lines as his – with a bit about his war service thrown in for good measure.

At one point during Alec's speech, Chifley winked at Nell. She was initially flattered and then thought what an old flirt he was.

By the time the speeches came to an end, Nell had decided that the launch was a triumph.

She was sharing a beer with Alec's foot soldiers in the lounge of the Royal Hotel when Chifley came over.

'You were sitting in the front row,' he said.

'I was.'

'Did you enjoy the speeches?'

'I did.'

'Are you working for Alec?'

Nell chose her words carefully. 'Sort of. I'm his wife.'

The Prime Minister rocked back on his heels and burst out laughing. Nell grinned. She had caught him out.

'Well, he's a very lucky man.'

'Yes. He is.'

He looked at her with empathy. 'I hope this politics business is not going to be too tough on you.'

She was having none of it. 'It'll be tougher on the single mothers who are thrown out on the street because they can't afford to pay the rent, or their children who can't go to school because they have to work to make a quid for their families.'

Chifley puffed thoughtfully on his pipe for a few moments.

'That's exactly why I am determined to nationalise the banks. Profits should be shared, not line the pockets of the rich,' he said.

Looking every inch like the conquering hero, Alec pushed through the crowd in the public bar to join them. 'Here you are, Prime Minister.'

Chifley corrected him. 'Ben. Yes. I wanted to thank your helpers.'

Nell interjected. 'One day they'll let us in the public bar.'

Chifley turned to her. 'You really think so?'

'I know so.'

'We might have to get you to stand,' he said.

'You might.'

Alec ushered his old batman forward. 'Prime Minister –'

'Ben.' He corrected Alec again.

'Ben. I'd like to introduce you to my campaign manager, Jack Fulton.'

As though in the presence of royalty, Jack, shaking like a leaf, removed his hat.

Chifley offered his hand. 'Welcome aboard, Jack.'

'Jack was with me in Palestine and Greece. Although I thought we'd lost him in Greece,' said Alec.

'We lost a lot in Greece,' Chifley replied, clearly upset.

Alec continued. 'Jack's been working for the Railways, in Gilgandra.'

Chifley's eyes lit up. 'Engine driver?'

Jack could barely get the words out. 'Signals.'

'Jack's one of the most organised people I know. He kept me on the straight and narrow.'

Nell thought she could see Chifley's eyes watering as he firmly patted Jack on the shoulder.

'We need good men, Jack. It's going to be a hell of a fight. Alec's going to require someone to get the troops mobilised behind him.'

Lighting up like a Christmas tree, Jack bounced on his feet. 'The Gil. branch are ready to rumble, sir.'

'Good on you, Jack.'

'I'm going to go back in the front bar and catch up with a few blokes I know,' Jack said. He winked at Alec, acknowledged the Prime Minister with the hint of a bow and strode off triumphantly.

'How do you think it went?' Alec asked Chifley.

For a brief second, it looked to Nell as if Alec were asking for parental approval. There was certainly something of a father–son relationship in the way they spoke to each other.

The PM drew on his pipe and looked him in the eye. 'How do *you* think it went?'

'I … pretty well, I think.'

'It's going to take time, Alec. You've got to win their confidence. Jack will be a big asset, being a working man. Prove yourself. There are some tough characters in these bush towns. Blokes who've had it hard and are suspicious of anyone who isn't cut from the same cloth. A lot of them don't trust me, so you can imagine how they feel about a cockie beating one of their own for pre-selection.'

Nell noticed Alec shuffle his feet. He looked anxious as Chifley said, 'If we're going to seriously challenge the Tories, we need some educated men like you, son. Old engine drivers like me are yesterday's men. You're the future.'

He tapped his pipe in the ash tray, stuck it in his pocket and doffed his hat towards Nell. 'Lovely meeting you, Mrs Murray.'

'You too, Mr Chifley. You'll have to come up to Coona. See some of the things we've got going. Like the Community Hotel.'

'I would enjoy that,' he said. Then he shook Alec's hand, drained the rest of his beer and walked out, shaking hands with all and sundry on his way.

Nell smiled to herself; she had been casually shooting the breeze with the Prime Minister of Australia over a beer in the Royal Hotel in Dubbo.

62.

Alec was invited to lunch by Walter Frater.

'Don't let anyone see you,' joked Nell, they're already calling you a commo. I wouldn't think it wise to give them more ammunition.'

Alec laughed. He'd been to Walter's place lots of times, and he told her that it was no big deal.

Nell was screen printing some campaign posters. She carefully dragged the squeegee across the mesh. 'In that case, go. He's an old hand at electioneering and rich as Croesus.'

She held up a poster with an image of Alec holding his pipe with the slogan, *Labor for Lawson* underneath. 'What do you think?'

He smiled.

*

When Alec pulled up at Walter's, his host was waiting to greet him. Inside, a man in a dark suit and red braces was waiting for them. His bushy eyebrows seemed to form a hood over two probing, dark brown eyes that met Alec head on.

'Alec. This is Harry Fox.'

Harry offered Alec his hand. Even though he had a strange feeling that he had walked into an ambush, Alec took his hand and looked him in the eye.

Walter gestured, 'Have a seat.'

Harry sat in a leather armchair while Alec pulled up a chair from the dining table.

'Scotch?'

Alec could have done with a double. 'Thanks.'

Walter measured two fingers of scotch into a glass and handed it to Alec while Harry Fox took a sip of his before meeting Alec's stare. 'You've got a big challenge in front of you.'

Where's this leading? thought Alec.

'Gonna take a pretty big swing to oust Raymond.'

'It is.'

'About ten per cent in a safe Country Party seat. Big ask.'

Walter sat in the other armchair and crossed his legs. 'Harry is the National Secretary of the Communist Party.'

Alec was more than relieved that they hadn't met in the Commercial Hotel.

'So, Alec ...' Harry paused for effect, took another sip and placed his glass on the table. 'No point beating around the bush. We'd like you to join us.'

Alec nearly fainted.

'Walter assures us your heart is in the right place.'

He glared at Walter.

'We wouldn't want to embarrass you in any way. You wouldn't even ... we wouldn't even expect you to see much of Walter.'

'But I'm ...' Alec stuttered.

'Yes. Of course. You're a member of the Labor Party. At the moment. There is more than one communist sympathiser in the Labor ranks. Just as there's more than one right wing Catholic. As you know, you're obviously being tagged as a communist because of your association with Walter. We'd arrange a separate contact and ... uh ... that would mean we'd throw our party organisation behind your campaign. We can be very effective. We have cells all over the place.' He smiled and let his offer sink in.

Alec was speechless. Had Walter sold him a dump? Was Harry Fox seriously suggesting he stand as a Labor candidate and defect to the communists once elected?

Gathering his thoughts as quickly as possible, Alec shot back, 'Yes, but you know what you are going to do if you do acquire or seize power? Take the waterside workers …'

'Once we're in power they'll realise they've got a workers' government and stop striking,' Harry argued.

'Like hell they will,' Alec said. 'Look at what the coal miners did to the government – brought the bloody state to its knees. Had to turn the army on them to get them back to work.

'I don't call that working for the common good. I call that feathering your own nest. You blokes incited the workers to strike when the only man who truly represented them was begging them to get back to work. You were doing Stalin's bidding, not your own Prime Minister's. You were prepared to go to any lengths …'

'I didn't approve of the violence,' Harry said. He sat forward and spoke in a reasoned tone, 'You've got to understand; some people have to be eliminated if we are to achieve our goals.'

Alec couldn't believe what he was hearing. 'What are you going to do with a priest who fills his church up with guns?' Harry asked.

'That's a Russian thing. No bloody priest in Australia has a church full of guns,' Alec said. He put his glass on the table and grabbed his hat.

Harry stood and offered his hand. 'Think about it. We'll get a guy to contact you.'

Alec ignored his outstretched hand.

'We're not trying to destroy Labor governments or destroy the Labor Party. We simply want them to accept certain changes to their constitution,' Harry said.

By the time he got home, Alec had cooled down. He recounted the story of the meeting to Nell.

'I thought I was in a spy novel,' he joked.

For the first time, she told him about her encounter with Lance in Canberra.

'Do you have any idea what it would do to our chances if it got out that my wife was consorting with a communist?' he said.

'Lance is a dear friend.'

'He's not the only "dear friend" we're going to lose.'

Nell gulped down her drink, turned and stormed out of the room, slamming the door behind her.

Alec stood, rooted to the spot. He thought about going after her but decided to let her calm down. It had been a hell of a day.

The one thing he was certain of was that no matter how much Walter's mates could help, he wasn't going to take a penny from them.

He wasn't going to compromise his principles for anyone.

63.

Alec discovered that it was one thing to have principles and quite another to follow them through. Electioneering was going to cost a bomb, let alone finding the funds to keep Toongowan afloat. His opponent was rolling in donations, most from wealthy landowners in the electorate.

He decided to test the waters with Chifley. After all, the communists weren't that bad.

'I could do with bit of cash. It's very expensive running a campaign like this. As far as I can tell, they're pretty harmless.'

'Don't be silly. You'll learn very soon why,' Chifley replied with what Alec now recognised as the trademark steel in his voice. 'Suffice to say, when people find out exactly what Stalin has been up to, they will understand just how dangerous the communists are. We have no truck with them. None.'

Chifley had taken Alec under his wing. It had become customary for Alec to regularly check in with his leader over the phone.

'You need to fly down to Sydney for the Labor Council meeting. Show them your colours.'

'They're not making it easy …'

'No.'

The Labor proposal to make union membership compulsory for all workers hadn't gone down well with the shopkeepers in Alec's electorate. He was finding it difficult to balance the conflicting demands of being a Labor candidate in a rural seat. Everything seemed to be shaded grey. He had communists secretly wooing him, unionists creating hurdles for him, local businesses growing suspicious, and old allies turning sworn enemies. Alec drew on all his army training to fight each battle on its merits, without worrying too much about what was over the horizon.

Flying back from Sydney after the Labor Council meeting, Alec looked out the window at the acres of flat, dry land, stretching below. He watched a car cutting its way through the wheat fields and thought how it resembled an ant on the front lawn. How infinitesimal it was. How small their lives were. He was like that ant on the lawn, just one man trying to convince all those farmers, isolated by distance and remote from the everyday struggles of the average person in the city, to change the voting habits of a lifetime.

He watched a tractor circling a paddock, ploughing up the land for next year's crop, and thought about the challenge that lay ahead. How was he going to explain to the farmer that nationalising the banks was a good idea? The farmer would be happy if profits were more equally shared but would he trust Labor? He was working twelve-hour shifts getting the paddock ploughed in time for planting. He was most likely on his own and struggling to stay afloat. He didn't have time for politics. Not only that, but the scare campaign Alec's opponents were running told the farmer that Alec was in bed with the commos and he was going to take the farmer's tractor from him.

Back on the campaign trail, Jack drove Alec to Bathurst to pick up a few tips about campaigning from Chifley. They found the PM sitting in the gutter outside the office of the *Bathurst Advocate,* shooting the breeze with the locals.

Jack admiringly rubbed his hand on the bonnet of the shiny black Pontiac parked behind them.

'That's Chif's car,' Alec said.

Jack pulled his hand away and Alec laughed. 'Don't worry, Jack.

I don't think Chif would mind you touching his car.'

Jack was in awe. 'Geez, I'd give anything to be his driver.'

'He hasn't got a driver.'

'He drove himself?'

Alec nodded.

They looked across the road to Chifley. His hat was perched back on his head, his tie loosened, his jacket slung across his knees. He was gesticulating with his pipe as he made a point, surrounded by a group of men who appeared to be in serious disagreement with him. It looked to Alec like the most normal thing in the world.

'I reckon that's what you've gotta do more of.' Jack pointed towards the animated discussion unfolding in the gutter.

'You mean get off my high horse?'

'Exactly. Show the punters you're not afraid to mix with them on their own terms.'

They crossed the road to get a better view of proceedings. The debate was raging.

'For heaven's sake, Chif, nationalise the banks? What's next, make it a crime to earn a decent quid and get ahead?' The local bank manager, a little man dressed in a natty, three-piece, double-breasted suit and horn-rimmed glasses, was poking his finger at Chifley as he spoke.

The PM tried to defend himself. 'No –'

'You're just appealing to the lowest common denominator,' the bank manager said.

Alec grabbed Jack's arm to restrain him, as Chifley patiently explained that what he wanted was for everyone to have a slice of the cake.

Alec and Jack stood to one side, taking mental notes, as Chifley quietly rebutted the attacks and modestly accepted praise. There was nothing phoney about the meeting. It was what Chifley had always done when he was campaigning. Alec felt a tug on his arm. Jack was pointing at his watch. They had a meeting to get to in Mudgee; it was at least two-and-a-half hours away.

'We'd better make tracks.'

Before they could move the PM called out, 'Alec.'

Chifley was looking up at him. 'Welcome to our community forum! Good to see you, comrades. Glad you dropped by!'

As they walked back across the street, Alec understood what Chifley had meant about humility. He was the living embodiment of it.

He hoped he could live up to his example.

64.

Nell imagined Alec triumphing against the odds and had been making plans to move to Canberra. They would be able to send their children to the local schools and get away from the people who had given them such a hard time during the campaign. She imagined that her parents would eventually come around if Alec was a Member of Parliament, perhaps even a Minister of the Crown.

All of those hopes came crashing down when the results were published. They had lost by 5,600 votes and the Country Party had gained a 7.6 per cent swing. It was a landslide. The conservative, anti-communist campaign had scared the electorate and the Liberal–Country Party coalition had romped home.

Nell was frustrated. Alec had taken the loss with his typical stoicism, pulled on his hat and riding boots and got back down to work. It wasn't so easy for her. She had burnt her bridges with family and friends and, she hated to admit, lost face. It was hard to go shopping in Coonabarabran knowing that the likes of Joan Bethridge were laughing at her behind their hands.

She dreaded the humiliation of seeing her family. Jock would be unbearably smug and she knew just what Alec's parents would be like, especially Henry.

Nell started drinking heavily. She was finding it harder and harder to get out of bed in the morning; there was nothing to look forward to.

Toongowan was beginning to look very small and her life even smaller. She couldn't imagine how she could escape the sense of abject failure she was feeling.

Alec suggested she go down to Sydney for a break. After rejecting his suggestion, she eventually agreed.

Sitting in The Women's Club with Peg, she felt the weight lift from her shoulders. She was relieved that Peg had jumped at the chance to see her, because Nell had feared that she might have lost her friend for ever. While Peg was in the bathroom, Nell stood up and read aloud a quote on a plaque hanging on the wall, which had been donated to the club by the *Sydney Stock and Station Journal* of 1908.

'The Women's Club in Sydney is the outward and visible sign of the progress of women in our country.'

This is what I've been missing, she thought.

'It is so good to see you,' Peg said, taking her hand as she sat down.

Nell let out a sigh of relief. 'And you.'

Something was clearly troubling Peg. 'I'm sorry I haven't been in contact.'

'That's all right. It wasn't your fault. I know that.'

'I feel like I've ...'

It was one of the few times Nell could remember her friend faltering.

Peg took a sip of brandy. 'I've let the side down.'

She pointed at the names on the honour board of prominent members of the Club who had been leading lights in advocating for women's rights. Nell read them out, 'Jessie Street, Louisa Macdonald, Lady Fanshawe, Linda Littlejohn and Adela Pankhurst.'

'What do you mean?' Nell asked.

'Staying with ... him. Johnny.'

Nell was alarmed. She was also surprised; she hadn't imagined counselling someone else. All her troubles seemed to fade as she listened to Peg.

'He's ... he hasn't been the same since the war. I've told you that but ...' She paused and took a breath. 'It's like I don't exist. I'm like a glorified housekeeper. I look after the children, do the cleaning and the cooking ...'

Peg shrugged. It was a sad shrug. The shrug of a defeated woman.

Nell had never, ever seen her like this, and her heart went out to her. Peg was crying.

'If I saw you or had any contact with you, he threatened to leave me and take the children with him. It wouldn't have worried me if he left but … the children.'

Nell could see that Peg was a mess. She gave her space to recover.

Peg lit a cigarette and continued. 'We all have choices … sacrifices … to make. Imagine what I would have to go through to divorce him? I'd have to prove he was unfaithful, hire a private detective … It's too terrible to contemplate.'

Nell agreed. She also thought how outrageous it was that the odds were always stacked against women. The women on the honour board may have led the way but her generation still had a long, long way to go.

'Is he still … violent?'

'No. Not physically. He gets angry and throws things but … I don't give him the chance. I keep out of his way. He goes to work early. Often stays out late. Spends his weekends on his yacht with his floozies.'

The way she said this made Nell understand that Peg had virtually surrendered to existing separately to Johnny. She found it hard to believe; Peg was the last person she could imagine settling for such a life.

They spent the rest of the afternoon swapping stories about their children and reflecting on how differently their lives were turning out from how they had imagined them. Nell explained how close to the wind they had sailed in funding Alec's campaign.

'At least we've got a bit of money in the bank from the wool boom. God knows what we'd do if the wool price hadn't been so good. Alec's father is like the Grim Reaper, pacing around with his sickle waiting to cut us down.'

Peg chortled. 'Hammer and sickle?'

They both laughed before Nell said, 'Now Alec can get back to farming and maybe, with the kids at school, I can get back to painting.'

'You must.'

Finally, it was time to leave, Peg pulled on her gloves, gave Nell and kiss on the cheek and they walked out, arm in arm, into the late afternoon light. Nell glanced at the sign above the door. She was grateful that The Women's Club provided a refuge where they could stay in touch, no matter what was swirling around in the outside world.

On the way back to Dubbo, Nell thought about Peg. She wondered how much Alec had suffered from the war. Like Johnny, he never talked about it. Nell guessed it was the same way he dealt with the election defeat, and wondered if she needed some of that stoicism.

She thought about the choices she had to make. She wasn't living with a philanderer. Alec had never even looked like raising a hand to her. He had sulked but had never been violent. Their sex life was still good, if sporadic. Poor Peg. Nell couldn't imagine being in her shoes.

There was plenty for her to get stuck into: the house, her relationship with her parents. And, she dared to imagine, her painting.

65.

Alec had no choice but to brush off his battered and bruised ego and throw himself into getting Toongowan back into shape. He thought about the campaign and how much he had enjoyed it. He'd known it was a huge mountain to climb, and the more he had campaigned the more he began to believe he had a chance.

In the cold light of a devastating loss, he saw the impact of the proposal to nationalise the banks. In the climate of the Cold War breaking out between the USSR and the USA, it was political suicide. It was easy for Menzies and his supporters to portray the idea of nationalising the banks as communism in disguise and that Labor really was the stooge for Stalin's plans for world domination.

Alec was angered by the way the press portrayed Chifley and his proposals; their villain was totally unlike the Chifley he knew. His respect for his leader had only grown during the campaign. He admired the way Chifley was prepared to stand up for what he believed in. What was the point of being in politics if you didn't believe in anything? The fact that he had encouraged blue bloods like him to join the Labor Party was evidence that he had a much broader view of the world than the press made out.

As much traction as he had gained in the country towns, Alec came to conclude that he had been fighting a war on too many fronts. Outside of the Coonabarabran district, no one knew him, he would have had to convince rusted-on Country Party supporters to change a lifetime of voting habits and, finishing him off, came the coal strike in the middle of the campaign.

Mending fences in the outlying paddocks, Alec thought long and hard about the experience and secretly swore to have another crack if the chance presented itself. He had four years to build up the necessary support and he thought about how he might do it. One thing was clear, he had to distance himself and his policies from the communists.

Alec had other fences to mend. He owed a huge debt of gratitude to Nell for what she had done for him and his cause. It was obvious that she was down and needed something to lift her spirits. Even though he had reservations about Lance's politics, Alec put them and his own ambitions aside and convinced Nell to invite Lance up to stay.

The three of them got on like a house on fire. Alec was delighted to see Nell so animated in the company of her old friend. She cooked up a storm with Lance and they spent long nights on the verandah drinking his wines and solving the problems of the world.

Alec was so grateful to Lance for helping pull Nell out of the quagmire she had been in before she went to Sydney. When he arrived home from the back paddocks of an evening, he found them in the kitchen testing sauces, discussing how much salt to add and generally having a culinary ball. A couple of times when he got home late, he found them sitting on the verandah with a bottle of whisky discussing plans or the latest developments in the art world.

He couldn't have been happier that Nell was back to her old self, even if her improved mood seemed to be fuelled by an increased consumption of alcohol.

When he talked about trying some of the rotation farming he had witnessed in Palestine, Lance suggested using some of the chemicals they were developing at the CSIR to control pests. Lance encouraged Alec to plant trees to prevent erosion and talked about maintaining soil quality.

The government's proposed Communist Dissolution Bill had Lance worried about being jailed for his beliefs. Alec assured him that Labor would never support it, but in truth, he was also worried about the bill and how it would play out. Banning membership of certain political parties was the thin edge of the wedge and smacked of the kind of authoritarianism he had gone to war to fight against. It was already causing ructions within the Labor Party.

Alec was horrified to discover that the Catholic right faction in Victoria had overruled Chifley in caucus and forced the Labor Party to support Menzies' bill. Alec was learning that politics created strange bedfellows. The Waterside Workers Union, which had caused Chifley so much grief with their intractable demands, now came to his rescue by challenging the Dissolution Bill in the High Court.

After Lance left and things returned to normal, Alec was happy to bide his time and put all his energy into adding to the 4,000 pounds he had in the bank from the wool boom to pay off the mortgage. Then they would be free of the axe that hung over their heads.

＊

Alec was cleaning mud off his boots one evening when Nell sang out, 'Phone for you.'

'Tell them I'll call back.'

'I don't think Mr Chifley …'

The screen door slammed after him as Alec bolted in. Nell winked and handed him the phone.

'Ben?'

'Sounds like you've got your hands full.'

Chifley's distinctive working-class twang brought a smile to Alec's face. He had missed his mentor.

'I won't keep you for long.'

'It's fine. I was … wasn't doing anything important …' Alec replied, trying to sound as relaxed as he could.

'How are you feeling?'

Chifley's question caught him off guard. 'I'm … I'm … we're …'

'About the election …'

There was a pause. Even though Chifley had sent him a note, they hadn't spoken since the defeat. Alec struggled to find an adequate reply. 'It's in the past now … I'm getting on with …'

'I'm sorry it's taken so long for me to call you. We've had a bit on.'

Alec noticed Nell standing in the doorway listening.

Chifley continued. 'You fought a good campaign. People like you. You've laid the groundwork for another tilt. The thing is, comrade, it's no good crying over spilt milk. All we can do is bail up another cow. Not to worry. Menzies won't be able to carry out his promises.'

Alec wondered how much Nell could hear of this as he tried to absorb Chifley's words.

'I don't believe the Australian people will support banning a political party, whatever its hue. If the High Court supports the Waterside Workers' challenge to the bill, which I reckon they will, Menzies will call an election and we'll be in the ring again.'

Chifley's tone darkened. 'We live in dangerous times, comrade. This growing sense of hysteria. People are turning on each other. Accusing each other of all sorts of things. The press has fallen in behind Menzies, tagging anyone who opposes this Communist Dissolution Bill as being part of a communist conspiracy.'

He paused. Alec could hear him take a deep puff of his pipe before speaking again.

'I'll promise you one thing. I will go to my deathbed fighting for the right of people to believe what they want, as long as they don't hurt anyone.'

Alec knew that Chifley hadn't been well and was pushing himself too hard.

'What worries me, Alec, is that this kind of campaign of fear and hysteria may result in grave injustices for individuals. The multitude can make serious mistakes. It was the multitude, by its vote, that sent Christ to be crucified.'

It had always intrigued Alec how Chifley managed to rationalise his Catholicism with his socialist beliefs. He would have given anything to discuss it with his hero over a scotch and a pipe.

'You still there?'

'Yes. Yes. Sorry, sir, Ben ... '

'Between us, the last thing I want is to fight another bout. I'm exhausted. All I want is to get back to Bathurst but ...'

He left it hanging. By now Alec was in no doubt about the reason for the call.

'I'll be ready,' he reassured Chifley, without hesitation.

'Good man. I knew I could rely on you. Give my best to Mrs Murray.' With that, he hung up.

Nell was still in the doorway.

'He sent his best …'

'I heard,' she said. Then she turned on her heels and walked out of the house.

Alec found her sitting down by the creek having a cigarette. 'There you are.'

She didn't reply.

He sat next to her and watched the water trickling through the rocks. They needed rain.

He was about to speak but she started first.

'It's all right. I just needed space to gather my thoughts. I mean, I knew you'd probably stand again … the next election isn't for nearly three years. The boys will be older. This one …' she patted her pregnant tummy, 'will be up and running.' She flicked at the grass with the stick she was holding. 'I just thought I'd have some breathing space. We'd have some breathing space.'

She tossed the stick in the creek, got to her feet and dusted herself down. 'Come on. We better get on with it!' She walked off leaving him to catch up.

✳

Even though the election was a long way from being called, Alec had learnt enough from his previous campaign to know that he had to get out early and build support if he were to have any chance of winning.

A month later, he addressed his local branch in the meeting room of the newly converted Community Hotel.

'We can't sit around and let Menzies and his supporters trample on all we believe in. He's going to piggyback on this McCarthy fellow in America, who is running around accusing hundreds of people who work in the US State Department of being commies. Menzies is a brilliant politician. If he can link what is happening in the Soviet Union and China to us, he'll put the labour movement back decades.

That's what he's aiming for with this Dissolution Bill. He'll do anything to get control of the Senate. Before we know it, he'll be banning trade unions. That is why it is essential that we voice our support for the Waterside Workers' challenge.'

A few men, dressed in blue overalls and work boots who were repairing the rail track, exchanged knowing looks. Alec might have been poison to the cockies, but he knew he was winning over the workers.

'As the great Franklin D. Roosevelt said when introducing the New Deal, "We have nothing to fear but fear itself." And that is what I am going to offer you, whenever the next election is called. A New Deal. A New Deal for all Australians, not just those with silver spoons stuck in their mouths.'

Nell led the enthusiastic applause.

66.

When Nell's waters broke Alec was, thankfully, on hand to rush her into Coonabarabran hospital. Nell held her stomach and her breath as the Dodge roared along the Binnaway Road. The last thing she wanted was to give birth on the side of a dusty country road in the middle of the night. They were both mightily relieved when the Dodge pulled up in front of the hospital.

Inside, she was ushered into the maternity ward by an older woman who introduced herself as Nurse Gordon. Before long, Nell was lying on a bed, her head propped up on pillows, while her doctor, Dr Hawthorne, pressed at her stomach with a stethoscope and smiled encouragingly.

'He's an energetic little bugger.'

'He?'

Although she would never admit it, Nell was praying for a girl to break the male hegemony that had dominated her life.

Dr Hawthorne chuckled. 'Turn of phrase. Boy. Girl. Whatever.'

It never ceased to amaze Nell, the way that men made assumptions, even supposedly educated men, like doctors.

The contractions were hitting her with increasing regularity and ferocity. At least she had an idea about what was coming, even if the knowledge didn't lessen the pain.

'Breathe in, dear, you'll be right,' said Nurse Gordon.

Far from feeling all right, Nell felt as though she was going to burst.

She had imagined that giving birth would get easier with each baby, but the signs for this one weren't promising.

On the drive in, Alec had told Nell he wanted to be there at the birth, but in the hospital he was overruled. He had argued with Nurse Gordon that he'd delivered hundreds of lambs and calves and should be allowed to support Nell when she gave birth.

'I don't care what you've done. Out you go,' Nurse Gordon said as she pushed him out the door.

When her little baby decided to come, it was in a hurry, making the contractions a distant memory. Nell was filled with relief. At age thirty-one, she hadn't really planned on this little accident. Now that the baby had arrived, all her maternal instincts kicked in. With tears streaming down her face, she held her hands out. Cradling her newborn, she felt nothing but joy and relief.

When Nell saw that she had given birth to another son, her heart sank a little. She summoned up every ounce of self-control to stop herself crying. He was gorgeous. He was perfect. But he was a boy.

Nell had dreamt of having a daughter. She had wanted a daughter. She had imagined having someone to share in all the things she loved. It didn't diminish her love for her boys, but girls were different. It wasn't a value judgement. As far as Nell was concerned it was a statement of fact.

When she was cleaned up, Nell was wheeled back to her bed in the ward. She was in torment. Try as she might, she couldn't get over the disappointment of having another boy. She would put on a brave face for Alec, but it would take an almighty effort to hide her true feelings. Nell knew she shouldn't be feeling like this; she should be overjoyed but she wasn't.

Alec tentatively opened the door and peeked inside.

Nell managed a smile. 'Come in. We won't bite …'

She looked down at the little bundle in her arms, wrapped in a cotton blanket, and gently stroked his brow with a finger. Alec closed the door quietly behind him and walked in. He smiled the smile that had won her heart all those years ago, rested an arm on the bed head and kissed her. She took his hand and squeezed it tightly. They shared a moment in silence. It was another thing she loved about Alec; he wasn't afraid of silence.

After what seemed like an eternity, she remembered she hadn't told him about the baby's sex.

'It's another boy,' she said, desperately trying to sound excited.

Alec nodded. She might have told him that the grass was growing.

'That's good,' he said, without giving anything away.

Maybe he does think it's good, she thought. He clearly wasn't fussed.

'Would you like to hold him?'

Nell handed him to her. He enveloped the tiny boy in his arms and rocked him gently. At least he is a good dad, Nell thought, whatever the baby's sex.

'What are we going to call him?' she asked.

'Not Henry,' he said laughing.

'No, not Henry.'

'Little friend of all the world.'

She blinked. 'Sorry?'

Alec looked very pleased with himself. 'Kim.'

Nell quite liked the sound of it. 'Kim?'

'Kipling,' he explained. '*Kim.*'

Of course, she thought. Kim gurgled.

Nurse Gordon appeared at the door. 'I'll take him now. He needs a rest. And so do you.'

She whipped the newborn out of his father's arms and strode off to the nursery.

Nell shut her eyes and fell back into her pillows. She heard Alec shifting from one foot to the other uncomfortably. After a moment she opened her eyes. 'I guess you had better go and wet his head,' she told him.

Alec didn't argue. 'I s'pose Walter and co. will be down the pub.'

'The birth of a third child should be a good alibi for drinking with a commo. Even in these fraught times. Have you got a cigar?' she asked.

'I do actually.'

He fished a Cuban cigar out of his coat pocket and rolled it over his fingers. He beamed at her. 'Be prepared.'

He kissed her again and she gripped his hand tightly, trying as she might to contain herself.

'We're not a bad team,' he said as he picked up his hat, gave her a little wave and walked out.

After he left, the floodgates opened. Nell couldn't stop; she sobbed uncontrollably.

A pair of headlights beamed in through the lace curtains. Alec was heading off. Nell rolled over, pulled the pillow over her head and cried herself to sleep.

67.

Alec read the letter from Chifley once more.

> *I was much encouraged by your letter and I deeply appreciate the courage you have shown in the face of a great deal of phobia in fighting against the introduction of legislation such as the Communist Dissolution Bill. I hope that a turn of the political wheel will permit you to become a member of the Commonwealth Parliament, because we do need young men like yourself who are prepared to stand up for the convictions they hold.*

He folded it and put it in the top door of his desk. The looming election meant that in the weeks and months following Kim's birth, Alec had kept one eye on Toongowan and one on Canberra.

Nell was changing Kim's nappy when he walked into the nursery.

'The High Court has upheld the Waterside Workers' challenge,' he announced.

Nell dropped the dirty nappy in a bucket and picked Kim up.

'They won?' she asked, as she tried to settle the squirming baby.

Alec was too consumed with the news to notice Nell's lack of enthusiasm. 'The Communist Dissolution Bill is invalid! Lance and Walter are free to practise what they want without fear of being tossed in the clink.' He paused for a moment, then said, 'It's on. Menzies has dissolved both Houses.'

He waited for a response from Nell, but she didn't seem to hear.

'He's called an election!' he added.

'I heard you.'

Alec checked the calendar. 'Two weeks before Christmas,' he said, 'Could be the best Christmas present we've ever received.'

He heard the nursery door slam shut as he went into his study to begin to plan his next move.

He sat down at his desk and started to write but was distracted by Nell trying to settle Kim. He got up, closed the study door and returned to work. Halls needed to be booked. A door knock schedule had to be drawn up. He racked his brain trying to think of ways to increase his visibility in the electorate.

Alec knew this was going to be the fight of his life; he had to put everything on the line if he was going to win. Unlike last time, he couldn't afford to think about anything else. There would be no visits to Braemar or attempts at conciliation with family and friends. He knew where they stood. He couldn't risk being seen with Walter. He had to make it clear as crystal that he had no truck with the communists, no matter how close they may have been to him in the past. He needed Nell to stop communicating with Lance for the duration of the campaign. Absolutely nothing could be left to chance.

The experience of the last election had taught him that he needed a significant fighting fund if he was to match his better-resourced opponents. He made the big decision to seek approval from the bank to extend his mortgage.

✳

Arthur Bell was a cheerful man. As a country bank manager, he was used to the vicissitudes of farming life and intrigued by Alec's unconventional beliefs. He rocked back in his chair, stuck his thumbs in his waistcoat and checked his fob watch.

'I don't approve of your politics, Alec, but that's your business. You've been a good farmer. You got out of trouble after the war. You got out of trouble after the last election. I can't see any reason you won't do it again.'

With that, he closed his ledger and offered Alec his hand. 'I'll sign off on the overdraft after you buy me lunch.'

Alec was so relieved.

'The Commercial?' Arthur suggested, and was on his feet in a flash.

'Thanks, Arthur.'

'Don't thank me. It's banking policy to support farmers through hard times. Whatever their personal predilections.'

He laughed as they walked out on to the timber footpath. 'At least I won't have to worry about you nationalising the banks.'

It was Alec's turn to laugh. That one had been put to bed. As they crossed Dalgarno Street, a ute full of jackeroos roared into view, cutting them off. Alec paused and raised his forefinger to greet them in time-honoured country fashion.

'Red! Red! Red!' they chanted as they drove off.

'Well, I guess we know what they think,' Arthur said. 'You have a battle on your hands.'

Alec grimaced. He needed a beer.

*

The timing of the election couldn't have been worse for Alec. There hadn't been much rain and feed was scarce. Sitting at his desk, going through the books, he decided that the money he had earmarked for drought relief would be used on the campaign. Too much was riding on this to compromise.

As well his financial concerns, Alec was worried about Chifley. The PM was in no shape to fight an acrimonious election campaign and the betrayal by the Catholic right in forcing him to support a watered-down Communist Dissolution Bill had nearly killed him. Alec knew that Chifley wanted to stand down as leader but wouldn't risk handing over to Doc Evatt. He had told Alec that Doc was too volatile and that there was no one else; it had to be him.

If Chifley was willing to risk everything, including his health, Alec made a quiet vow to give his all. After all, he reasoned, hadn't Stephen done the same?

With Nell's assistance Alec got to work planning the campaign. They agreed that he had to appeal to the townspeople. He had a story to tell; he just needed the means to tell it.

*

The next morning, while he was getting ready to head off, Alec received a phone call.

Juggling Kim in one arm and the phone in the other, he spoke into the handpiece. 'I'd love to,' he said, then hung up.

Nell was making sure he had packed everything he needed.

'Guess what?' he called. 'We've got a Sunday night slot on Radio 2DU,' he said, walking Kim to her.

'You're going to be a radio star?' she asked, taking the boy from him.

'I don't know about that, but it is a way to get into a lot of homes. We're on after *Clocktown* …'

'I love *Clocktown*. Everyone loves *Clocktown*. We'll be tuning in, won't we, Kim?'

Alec watched as Nell lifted Kim into the air. He wasn't sure if she meant it or was pulling his leg. He had taken heart from the insistence of the wise old heads of the local branch that the early election call would work in his favour.

'Getting this radio spot is proof that my recognition factor is up,' he told Nell as he picked up his briefcase. 'At least I'm not starting from scratch like I was last time.'

Alec knew he was sugar-coating the fact that he was going to be away for a while and that he was, literally, leaving Nell to hold the baby.

'We'd better hit the frog and toad,' called Jack from the front lawn. He stubbed his cigarette out with his heel and pushed his hat back on his head. They had a lot of ground to cover and Jack reckoned they should get an early start.

Alec leant down and kissed Nell.

'Look after Mummy,' he said to his little boy as he ruffled Kim's blond hair before lifting William up and giving him a hug.

'I'm relying on you two!'

He put William down, smiled at Nell and walked down the steps to the awaiting Jack.

Alec could see Nell waving Kim's arm as he looked back in the rear-view mirror. He wound down the window and waved back. He knew he was lucky to have Nell on his side.

68.

'*Menzies or Moscow?*' Alec read the headline out loud, then tossed the newspaper onto the table. He knew this was a taste of things to come. The gloves were off. There would be no holding back from a press backed by big-money interests and the Roman Catholic Church. They were going hell for leather against Chifley and, somehow, Alec had to counter their propaganda.

Chifley's failing health wasn't helping Labor's campaign. He wasn't able to electioneer as effectively as he had in the past, and didn't have the energy to counter the growing influence of the Catholic right in Melbourne.

As Alec and Jack crisscrossed the 150,000 square miles of the electorate of Lawson, from Molong to Boggabri, Merriwa to Coonamble, Wee Waa to Mudgee, they got word that Alec was building significant support in the towns. Early polling showed he was bucking the national swing against Labor.

When Chifley decided to make his only public appearance outside his own electorate at Alec's launch in Dubbo, Alec was ecstatic. He'd heard that there was a feeling in the party that he could pull off an incredible upset; Jack told him that his open approach made people warm to him. His wartime experiences had taught him how to rub shoulders with men of all persuasions and he had learnt from Chifley's example in the last election. Alec was at home in the front bar or leaning on a railing in the cattle yards. He could mix with shopkeepers and shearers. Even though he was standing for the Labor Party in an election that was ostensibly about the Cold War, Alec was able to transcend this because of his work on Toongowan and war record. Alec believed that his record with the Coonabarabran Shire Council spoke for itself. No one he met seriously believed he was a communist sympathiser. He was able to convince people that he was there for them.

News of his successful campaigning started alarm bells ringing for conservatives around the electorate and beyond. Men like Jock Hope were horrified that one of their own might win a rural seat for the enemy.

'We used to shoot deserters in the back,' Jock had said when he and Alec ran into each other in town.

Alec had politely ignored the insult and asked Jock to pass on his regards to his parents.

'You can't afford this galivanting all over the countryside,' Henry told Alec when he and Jack called in to see his parents on their farm near Rylstone. Even though he knew it was going to be uncomfortable, Alec couldn't, in all conscience, not visit his mother when he was passing by.

'I think you've said that before,' Alec said.

He was glad when his mother appeared from around the side of the house. She was wearing a big, floppy canvas hat and had dirt on her knees.

'Gardening, Mother?'

She smiled. 'Keeps me sane.'

They both laughed.

Alec called out to Jack, who was sitting on the bonnet of his Holden coupe having a smoke. He came over and Alec introduced him to his parents. Henry simply nodded.

'Mother planted those and watered each one by hand,' Alec said, proudly pointing to the long line of poplar trees lining the driveway.

'Looks like somewhere in Europe,' Jack said, smiling.

Alec jumped slightly when Daphne took his hand. His mother had never been one for physical affection.

'We haven't seen you for ages.' Her voice quivered slightly.

Alec felt for her as she self-consciously rubbed the dirt off her knees.

He knew having a son who was seen as a class traitor would have created issues among her circle.

'Let's have a cuppa,' she said, pulling herself together.

'Thanks, Mother.'

Jack stubbed his cigarette on the driveway and excused himself. 'I … I might check the tires.'

Alec turned to his father. 'Can we borrow some fuel?'

Henry's eyes narrowed. 'Borrow?'

Daphne intervened. 'Of course you can. The pump is at the back of the machinery shed.'

Jack tipped his hat politely while Daphne stepped up on to the porch, kicked off her boots and turned and smiled at Alec.

He had guessed that his mother would get a kick out of spoiling them, even if they couldn't stay long. He was dreading the inevitable confrontation with his father, but that was a price he was prepared to pay.

When the flyscreen door swung shut and Daphne disappeared down the darkened corridor to make the tea, he faced up to his father.

'I know you don't approve –'

'You know what Stalin's up to don't you?'

Alec closed his eyes and took a deep breath. 'Can't we just let bygones be bygones?'

'You've brought shame on the Murray name.'

Alec could tell Henry had been storing this up for years.

'Father …'

Henry advanced on his son, pointing his finger at him. 'I'll tell you one thing. Something's going to give. You can't keep this up. The trustees are fed up with the profligate way you are throwing your mother's money around. You should be tightening your belt and paying your debts instead of this nonsense. Quite apart from the fact that you have betrayed your family and friends by aligning yourself with the commos.'

The sound of the kettle whistling in the kitchen was Alec's cue to go inside.

Henry called out after him, 'I'm warning you. This is the last straw.'

'I'd better win then.' He left Henry fuming.

✳

Ignoring Henry's warnings, Alec spent the overdraft to complement the financial support he received from local unions. As Walter had advised him the last time around, he needed to knock on every door and shake every hand if he was to have any chance of capturing the seven per cent of voters he needed to upset Eddie Raymond.

With Jack calling the shots, Alec made speeches from the back of trucks, in town halls, standing on bar stools, at smokos. It was nothing for them to head up to Boggabri for a meeting of shearers, then jump back in the Holden and drive through the night to a meeting of meat workers in Mudgee.

They knocked on front doors and outlined plans for infant health centres and preschools and the kind of community programs that had transformed Coonabarabran. Many people were surprised and flattered that the local candidate took them seriously enough to come to their house and seek their support. Most had never even clapped eyes on a candidate before.

The meeting of shopkeepers and small business owners in the Dubbo RSL was the first real challenge for Alec to test how he was going with undecided voters. He knew if he didn't win them over, his campaign was dead in the water.

'I am no supporter of the communist cause. I spent six years of my life fighting against fascism and totalitarianism. I lost many friends in that war. I have not returned home to sully their sacrifice.

'Communism breeds on poverty and discontent. The greatest bulwark against the rise of communism isn't trying to ban it and encourage its underground, underhand expansion. The greatest weapons we have against the spread of communism are British Commonwealth conceptions of law and justice. These hang on the notion of free speech, and banning a political party, no matter what hue, is an attack on free speech. The Communist Dissolution Bill was not an attack on communism, it was an attack on free speech. We need to do everything in our power to protect every citizen's right to free speech.'

The generous applause that rang out in the RSL gave Alec the fillip he needed.

'We need to help our Asian neighbours to develop along democratic lines, rather than going over to communism. Democracy is the way to curb the spread of communist ideals, not attacks on civil liberties as carried out by this government.

'Banning a political party is just a prelude to the suppression of ideas and debate. It is the very thing many people gave their lives to prevent happening. Jailing dissidents and destroying trade unions smells to me like the agenda of the enemy we fought. The idea that a person who declares themselves to be a communist should be banned from holding public office isn't that far from banning them for their religious beliefs. That is not how a thriving democracy works. It is how fascism works.

'I didn't go to war to raise my children in a two-tiered society that banned freedom of speech.'

The nodding heads told Alec he was winning over the doubters. He went on. 'I want to help create a society where there is true equality. That is why, in Coonabarabran, we have built a kindergarten and a preschool. It is why we have built a swimming pool. It is why we built the Community Hotel with a reading room and meeting rooms; a place where everyone can congregate, where children can play in the playground instead of being left in the car while their parents have a drink.

'With your support we can turn this whole electorate into the most progressive in the country. We can lead the way. We can look out for those who have been left behind, the returned soldiers, the poor, the Aboriginals who have been shunted out to the outskirts of our towns. We can create a new Australia!'

With Jack leading the way, the crowd were on their feet clapping enthusiastically. Alec was more than satisfied, he could see that they had won over the crowd.

69.

It was a hot summer at Toongowan. The creeks were dry, offering little by way of escape from the relentless heat. When Nell finally got Kim down to sleep, she sat out on the verandah and stared up at the Warrumbungles, towering over her. After a while, they began to make her feel small and insignificant. Her solution was to turn her back on them, hitch up her skirt, stick her feet on the table and polish off a bottle of brandy.

There were mornings when she awoke to Kim's screams with a pounding head, unsure of how or when she had gone to bed. She'd struggle to her feet, feeling like a wreck, pick him up and do her best to face the day.

The heat and loneliness were wearing her down. It seemed like it would never rain. The stock were failing and, apart from the odd call from Alec, she had no one to turn to for farming advice. Even then, she didn't feel like she could burden him with her troubles. He had enough of his own with the campaign. Their finances were stretched to the limit but she couldn't run the place without help, so she kept Donny on. When she was needed in the yards or mustering, she asked Mary to help out with baby Kim while William joined her on the job.

Looking at the emaciated state of the stock, she decided to cut their losses and put them on the market before they were completely worthless.

She was keeping a close eye on Doug's situation at Tudor House but she wasn't going to risk William getting the same treatment, so she decided to try home schooling with the assistance of The Royal Flying Doctor's School of the Air.

Doug seemed to be coping but she missed him terribly and his absence only worsened the sense of isolation she endured. Nell had no one she could confide in. She couldn't go to Sydney to see Peg, or Canberra to see Lance.

In desperation, she invited Peg up to visit but knew it was unlikely she could come. Not only would Johnny make Peg's life hell if she did but the logistics of travelling so far with young children made the idea impossible.

She assumed Lance had gone to ground when he didn't reply to her letters. Nevertheless, Nell continued to write to him and ride optimistically down to the letter box in the hope of replies. When none came, she felt more and more that the world had forgotten about her.

While her relations with the likes of Joan Betheridge and Helen Crowley had thawed, they were never more than cordial. The two women had been won over by Alec's programs and were delighted to coo over Kim or discuss homemaking, but their focus was on Coonabarabran, not on the outside world. Nell socialised at fundraising cake stalls with them on Saturday mornings, but that was about all.

She approached the Country Women's Association but was quickly shown the door. There was no place for the wife of a commo at the CWA, no matter how good her baking was.

Alec seemed further and further away. She wished she could confide in him, share her pain, but she knew that the women at the Telephone Exchange could eavesdrop on every word. It would soon get out that the wife of the Labor candidate felt she had been abandoned. Nell did her best to keep up with the news of the election, but she only received titbits from Alec and media reports that were negative more often than not. As absurd as it was, hearing Alec being called a traitor to the men he went to war with weighed heavily on her. Listening to Alec chatting merrily on the radio only increased her sense of isolation. He didn't spend any time chatting merrily to her.

Searching desperately for a release, she handed William and Kim to

Mary, saddled up Toulouse, the grey mare Alec had given her, and went for a ride. Riding was the one thing that had sustained her all those years ago on Braemar and she hoped it would do the same now. The trouble was, Toongowan lacked the beauty of her family's property, especially when it was drought stricken as it was now. Cantering through dusty paddocks, past the handful of emaciated sheep that she hadn't been able to sell, didn't do much to cheer her up. Nor did the fact that the creek was dry and the light harsh – too harsh to paint, inspiring nothing but bleak images.

There were days when she didn't think she was contributing anything to the world around her. She adored Kim but needed more than being a mother, even if she didn't know what it was. William tried his best to help out, but he resisted home schooling and she had to virtually wrestle him to the dining table to do his lessons.

After once again returning empty handed from the letter box, Nell unsaddled Toulouse and made her way back to the house. She struggled up the stairs of the verandah and went inside, leaving Mr Chips wagging his tail hopefully at the door. She glanced at the silver cigarette case lying on the table next to the ash tray full of stubbed-out butts. It had the Australian Infantry Services crest monogrammed on the lid. Flicking it open, her eyes rested on the engraved words, *Alec from Nell 4.9.42.*

It was looking a little tarnished.

70.

When Nell arrived in Dubbo for the vote count, her heart was pumping. This was all or nothing. She was greeted by Jack, who escorted her into the Ladies Lounge and bought her a gin and tonic.

'It's looking good, Mrs Murray.'

He shuffled his feet awkwardly, avoiding her gaze. Nell knew that Jack was the kind of man who was never too comfortable in the presence of women.

She took a sip and smiled at him.

'The word from our scrutineers is that we're well ahead here in Dubbo.'

She suddenly perked up. 'Oh?'

'Early counting is favouring Alec ...'

For the first time in ages, Nell felt optimistic. Maybe it had all been worth it.

'Where's Alec?'

He jerked his thumb in the direction of the front bar. 'I'll tell him you're here. He's been doing a few interviews. He asked me to get you a drink.'

Nell stood and picked up her glass. 'If the mountain won't come to Muhammad, Muhammad better go to the mountain.' She was going into the public bar whether they liked it or not. 'Come on, Jack. My shout!'

Alec was holding court. Not for the first time, Nell's entrance caused heads to turn and conversations to stop dead. She moved through the throng of thirsty drinkers like Moses parting the Dead Sea.

Alec put his drink on the bar and straightened himself to his full height. 'Darling.'

He bent down, planted a kiss on her cheek and grabbed a bar stool. 'Here.'

Fully aware that all eyes were on her, Nell handed Alec her drink, climbed on to the bar stool, straightened her dress over her knees and crossed her legs, revealing a pair of well-muscled calves.

Alec picked up his glass and was about to offer a toast when she interrupted him.

'One for Jack?'

Jack looked a bit sheepish, but Nell quickly put him at ease. 'Come on, Jack, drink up.'

Everyone cheered as Jack downed his beer and Alec ordered him another.

Nell raised her glass and toasted the grinning drinkers. 'A new dawn!'

The bar chorused, 'A new dawn!'

Rory Thompson, the rosy cheeked publican, joined in the fun and announced, 'Next round's on the house!'

Everyone cheered again.

Nell noticed the old Coonabarabran Shire President, Jim Keeping, forcing his way towards them through the crowd of drinkers. She tapped Alec on the shoulder and nodded at Keeping.

'Jim's been keeping an eye on the scrutineers for us,' Alec said.

'The trend's continuing here at all the big polling stations. We reckon you've got a swing of over eight per cent,' Jim announced breathlessly.

'Eight? That's enough …' Nell gasped.

'After last time, he only needs a seven per cent swing,' Jack reminded her.

Jim grinned. 'Yep. If it keeps going like this, you'll buck the national trend.'

'It's not so good in the rest of the country,' Peter Morton, a veteran of Labor politics in Dubbo, said as he joined the group around the bar.

'No, but it's not as bad as some predicted. Australians don't like the idea of banning free speech, even if they don't agree with the speaker.

I reckon they like to let them have their head so they can heckle them!' Jim looked like he was enjoying having the floor.

'Chif will be devastated,' Alec said.

Peter Morton put in his two bobs' worth. 'They were never going to win, Alec. Not after Calwell and the tykes ratted on him. People won't vote for a party that's squabbling among themselves.' He patted Alec on the back. 'But you? The bookies have you odds-on favourite.'

Nell could feel the weight of the world slipping off her shoulders. It looked like they were going to pull off the impossible. She squeezed Alec's hand tightly. Was all they had endured going to pay off?

'They reckon you're nearly a thousand votes ahead of Raymond,' Jim added.

Alec looked shocked. 'A thousand?'

'That's the whisper.'

Jack raised his glass. 'Here's to Alec!'

Nell tipped her glass to Jack and nodded approvingly.

'Steady on.' Alec was standing tall. The bar fell quiet. 'It's not over yet. We might be doing all right in the towns, but we know it'll be won and lost in the outlying booths.'

He turned to Jack. 'When you've finished that, get out and see how we're going in the smaller booths.'

Jack downed his beer in one gulp. 'Done. I wouldn't worry, though. The scrutineers reckon we're romping in.' He grabbed his hat and walked out of the bar.

The party continued at the Dubbo Royal as the numbers kept climbing for Alec. The word was that, with most of the votes in the big towns counted, the swing was holding at between four and five per cent. Nell could barely contain herself. By this stage of the night in the last election, Alec had been dead and buried. It looked increasingly like they would be going to Canberra, after all. After weeks of feeling down she was now flying high, charming all and sundry with her vivacity.

For his part, Alec was doing his best to keep a lid on the excitement. He cautioned Nell, 'We can't celebrate until all the small booths are in.'

Peter Morton slapped him on the shoulder and said to Nell, 'Don't listen to him. He's a pessimist. All those small landholders and farm workers who are jack of being treated like dirt will have voted for Alec for sure.' He cupped his hand and whispered in her ear, 'Don't tell anyone but I had a few quid on him.'

Nell's eyes widened. 'People are betting on the result?'

Peter nodded in the direction of a man hunched over a beer at the end of the bar. 'Don over there's the SP bookie. Alec was odds on. Tightened at the close of counting but that's to be expected in a two-horse race.'

Nell laughed. It was so good to be out amongst it.

'My shout,' said Peter.

He turned and ordered a round of middies as Jack joined them.

'Any news?' Alec asked.

'Not really. Old Smiley Walker was dead to the world when I got there. Had a few too many.' He mimed drinking. 'Empty bottles all over the place.'

Nell noticed a concerned look cross Alec's face.

'Wasn't he the scrutineer?' Alec asked.

'Yep. North Dubbo. Tiny booth,' Jack said.

Alec was clearly worried.

'He shouldn't have been drinking on the job.'

Jack laughed. 'Prob'ly celebrating.'

'As long as the votes went in.'

'There weren't any boxes there so they must have,' Jack assured him.

Alec held his finger up to Rory for another beer for Jack.

Rory called, 'Last drinks!' then leant over the bar and confided in Nell, 'The coppers have given me the nod. Better call it a night. They already let us go way past closing time.'

'Fair enough, Rory. Don't want you losing your licence.' Nell giggled. She felt a bit tipsy. Rory winked at her. She wondered if he was flirting.

'They're all right. Good Labor men,' he added before collecting some empty glasses lining the bar.

Nell was so happy that at one point she had considered dancing on the bar, but decided that as the wife of the new member, it might have been a bit indiscreet. She had never experienced anything quite like the mood in the front bar. It was a night when all the rules were broken. It felt as if Alec's win against all odds was compensation for Labor's crushing defeat federally. Nell sensed that everyone saw him as the great hope of the side.

She couldn't have been prouder. All the frustration of the past few years had poured out of her. She felt as if she was finally going to break the shackles of her past and move forward towards a new life. Who cared if they had been snubbed by family and friends? She was going to be the artist wife of a Member of Parliament. They would be able to settle their debts and thumb their noses at all the people who had made their lives a misery. She couldn't wait to send the likes of her brother and Henry off down the drive with their tails between their legs.

'I'll have a couple of bottles of champagne please, Rory.' Alec pulled a few pound notes out of his wallet and waved them at Rory.

Nell sidled up to him. 'Thirsty?'

He put his arm around her and gave her a big, sloppy kiss, which she laughingly wiped off. It was not often Alec was given to such outward displays of affection.

'I'm buying one for Jack. His wife has never drunk champagne. I'd like to buy her a bottle to thank her for putting up with all Jack's absences.'

Nell climbed up on the bar stool, threw her arms around Alec and planted a kiss on his lips. The few stragglers remaining cheered wildly.

'Well, Jack. It's been a hell of a ride. Here you go.' Alec handed him the bottle. 'All the way from Palestine to Lawson!'

Grinning from ear to ear, Jack pumped Alec's hand. 'Thanks, Boss.'

Clutching the champagne like it was the holy grail, he staggered out and off into the night. Back in their room at the hotel, Nell and Alec collapsed on their bed and savoured what had been a truly remarkable evening.

71.

Alec woke early, opened the curtains and looked out on the sleepy town of Dubbo. A horse and cart clumped down the main street delivering bread and milk. Smoke curled up from the rows of chimneys, coming from the Agas that had been fired up to cook breakfast. A few early birds wandered off to work, their bags slung over their backs.

He turned and looked at Nell. She was sleeping like a baby, curled up with the sheet wrapped around her, her silk nightie hitched up over her thigh. He smiled. How lucky was he to have her in his life? How different would it have been if she hadn't supported him unequivocally? He noticed the unopened bottle of champagne sitting on the table, smiled and looked back out the window.

He wondered how Chifley was faring. It was already clear that Menzies had won, even if it was with a reduced majority. He knew how devastated his mentor would be. Maybe he should ring him with his news. Maybe that would be premature.

Later that morning, as they were getting ready for the drive home, there was a knock on the door. Nell stopped brushing her hair.

'Can you get it? The way I feel, I don't think I can face anyone this early.'

He went to the door and opened it. 'Owen?'

A mousy looking man with thinning grey hair and a pencil thin moustache was standing in the doorway. 'Morning, Alec.'

'What's up?'

'Can I come in?'

'Of course.'

Nell stood up.

'My wife, Nell.'

Owen shook Nell's hand and twiddled nervously with his hat while Alec said to her, 'Owen runs 2DU.'

'Good to meet you, Mr … Owen.' Nell smiled at him.

Owen's eyes settled on the bottle of unopened champagne. 'I wouldn't be opening that if I were you.'

He walked over to Alex and said, 'You think you've won but you haven't. You've been beaten by between two-hundred to two-hundred-and-forty votes.'

Alec's jaw dropped.

'They've got it sewn up. I won't tell you anymore. Mark my words. Drink that and you'll look silly.'

'But …'

'Trust me, Alec. I've been round long enough to smell a fix.'

'Haven't we won Dubbo?'

'Yes. Most of it.'

Owen moved to the door. 'That's all I'll say.'

With that, he opened the door and walked down the stairs.

Alec felt like his world had just come crashing down.

'Owen used to work for Jack Lang,' he explained.

'And …'

Alec could see that didn't mean anything to Nell.

'He was on Lang's staff.'

'So…' She was none the wiser.

'They were famous for … you know … fiddling the books. Fixing elections.'

'Really?' Nell sounded astounded.

'Apparently they got up to all sorts of tricks.'

Alec thought about the stories from the old days that he'd heard on the hustings. He was feeling uncomfortable.

'Go on,' Nell said.

'Switching ballot boxes. That type of thing.'

Nell persisted. 'You mean they were corrupt?'

Alec couldn't imagine such a thing could happen in Lawson. 'I'm told there were some interesting types running around the labour movement in those days,' he said, watching from the window as Owen got into his car.

The room was silent as they both considered the implications of what Owen had told them

'You don't think … That they could … what did you call it?'

Alec could see the worry in her eyes. Whatever the truth was, it wasn't fair on her.

'Fix an election in the bush? The Country Party? I don't think so. They might be out of touch, but they'd never stoop …'

He took her in his arms and hugged her tightly. She buried her head in his chest. After a few minutes she rested back in his arms.

'He did look like an extra in a James Cagney movie,' she said and laughed.

'Owen's paranoid. He doesn't know as much as he thinks he does. Too much …' He mimed drinking. As much as he was trying to reassure her, he was doing his level best to reassure himself. 'Blokes like him see a rat in every corner.'

He took her hand. 'Come on. Let's go home.'

Alec was relieved to be finally heading along the corrugated dirt road to Coonabarabran. He made a mental note to put sealing it high on his agenda. He looked at Nell, feet on the dashboard as usual, hair blowing in the breeze. He'd missed her.

He'd been thinking about what Owen had said. It seemed so far-fetched that he couldn't take it seriously. He knew his opponents. They just weren't the types to rig an election. They weren't clever enough, for a start. Those men were old-school conservatives, not the sharpest knives in the drawer, but pretty honourable in their own nineteenth-century way.

They drove into Gilgandra and Alec pulled up outside the Royal Hotel.

Nell pointed to the sign above the front door and laughed. 'How many Royal Hotels do we have in this country?'

'I don't know. One in every town?' Alec said as he got out.

'Exactly,' replied Nell. 'Couldn't they have come up with something more imaginative?'

Alec opened her door and helped her out. 'There is the Railway.'

'Don't tell me. Next to the railway line!'

They both laughed. Alec gave her a loving pat on the bottom before he strode towards the butcher shop.

She sang out to him, 'I thought we were getting a cuppa?'

Without missing a beat Alec called back, 'I want to thank Froggy Morris. He was tireless in his support.'

'Does he serve tea?'

'I'm sure we can rustle one up for you somewhere.'

The small town was virtually deserted apart from a truck rattling down the street with a load of bleating sheep.

The doorbell rang as Alec pushed the door to the butcher shop open. Froggy Morris looked up from the wooden butcher's block he was making sausages on. He wiped his hands on the apron that barely covered his portly stomach.

'Here he is. The new member!' he exclaimed.

Alec offered his hand. 'Not so fast, Froggy. Don't want to tempt the gods.'

Froggy shook his hand firmly.

'We're lay down *misères*. I've seen the figures,' he told Alec.

'We're not over the line yet. I just dropped in to thank you …'

The bell rang again as Nell tentatively pushed the door open.

'Morning, Mrs Murray.' Froggy was beaming.

'Good morning, Froggy,' Nell said, putting a hand up to her head.

'I thought you might call in. I've got a bottle on ice.'

He disappeared into the cool room.

Nell took the opportunity to grab Alec by the arm and whisper in his ear. 'Please, can't we just get home?'

Alec wasn't going to brush his supporters. 'We can't offend Froggy. He's worked like a slave for me.'

Before she could reply, Froggy emerged with a bottle of champagne and three tumblers.

'Here we go. We gotta toast our new member. He's home and hosed.'

Froggy poured the fizzing champagne into a tumbler and handed it to Nell. She smiled thinly as he filled the other two tumblers, gave one to Alec and raised his.

'Been a pleasure working for you, Al. You're just what this area … make that the whole country … needs!'

As he toasted the doorbell rang again. They turned to see Billy Grant, the local copper, standing in the doorway. He was holding his cap in his hand.

'You three are starting early!' he said.

Froggy grinned and proffered the bottle. 'G'day, Billy. Like a tipple?'

'No thanks, Froggy. Sun's barely up. Besides I'm on duty.'

Not about to let anyone rain on his parade, Froggy tapped his nose conspiratorially. 'I won't tell anyone if you don't.'

'Actually, I wouldn't mind a quick word with Alec.'

Nell looked up from considering her champagne as Alec put his tumbler down.

'Don't tell me I've parked in the wrong place.'

Billy opened the door and held it for Alec.

'Outside.' The tone of his voice suggested it wasn't a trivial matter.

Shooting Nell a quick look, Alec made his way out. Billy nodded to her and walked out after him.

'Have you got another horse you want to flog to me?' Alec joked.

Billy's mood had changed, he was deadly serious. He was about to speak when Nell joined them. He looked at Alec.

'It's okay, Billy. We're in this together.'

The policeman got straight to the point. 'Something fishy.'

He glanced up and down the street. Apart from a stray dog crossing the road, no one was around. He hitched up his trousers and lowered his voice. 'I used to work in the fraud squad.'

Alarm bells rang for Alec.

'I'm telling you this because I like you and we've had a lot of fun with the horses. I also happen to think you'd be a terrific local member.'

Alec noticed Nell grimace.

'This is off the record,' Billy said, almost whispering.

Alec took Nell's arm. Billy continued. 'A school teacher, the Chief Returning Officer in Gilgandra, rang me last night and said, "You know a bit about forgeries. I'm worried about some of these ballot papers. Will you come and have a look at them?" So I did. We spent a few hours going through them. There was a striking similarity in a whole bunch of ballot papers from some of the smaller booths. The twos were written in the most unusual fashion. Not just from one booth but from lots of them. We were convinced they were written by the same hand.'

He paused before carrying on quietly, 'So, I decided to do some digging. A few people reported they'd seen a flash looking car at different polling booths. Off the beaten track. One bloke told me he'd seen it pull into one of those properties where there was a tiny booth. They also reported seeing a couple of city-looking spivs around the place. Apparently, they were throwing money around, getting chummy with scrutineers at small booths and buying them beers.'

Alec let go of Nell's arm and ran his fingers through his hair.

Billy gripped his shoulder. 'If you can identify the hand that wrote those twos you'll know who switched the ballot papers. My tip is to get one of your scrutineers on to it quick smart.'

He raised his cap to Nell and pulled it on. 'Mrs Murray.'

Alec offered his hand. 'Thanks, Billy.'

'Might be a coincidence, but I thought you should know.' He headed off before throwing an afterthought over his shoulder, 'I'll give you a call if I come across any more good stock horses.'

Alec raised his forefinger in a gesture of thanks.

*

They drove home in silence, until Nell slapped the dashboard abruptly, startling Alec.

'What?'

'Jesus!'

He swerved to avoid a pothole.

'What was the result in that booth where Jack found that bloke passed out?' she asked.

'North Dubbo?' he said, racking his brain.

'Yes. North Dubbo.'

'I don't know, we won all of Dubbo … hang on …'

Then he remembered what Jack had told him about Smiley Walker at the North Dubbo booth and Owen's warning. He had a sinking feeling.

Nell was looking at him with doubting eyes. 'Yes?'

Alec ran through the results in his head. 'I think we lost North … yes, that's right. It was the only one …'

'Fuck,' Nell said, closing her eyes.

Alec gripped the wheel tightly while he silently added everything up. The result in North Dubbo was aberrant. It was exactly the kind of booth Billy had talked about. And Jack had found the scrutineer passed out. The votes at that booth could easily have been swapped. A feeling of foreboding crept over him.

He glanced over at Nell; she was deep in thought too. He tried to put on a brave face. 'Even if it's true, which I doubt, early polling suggested we were romping in. A few aberrant results shouldn't make any difference.'

Nell's look told him she was as worried as he was.

72.

Back home, Nell played with Kim while Alec paced the verandah. He was trying to put the pieces together. When the phone rang, Alec rushed inside to answer it.

'Yes, Jack?'

'There's a bloke here reckons he needs to talk to you.'

'Who?' Alec asked.

'He's the Assistant Returning Officer. I'll pass him on to you.'

If Alec wasn't worried before, he certainly was now.

'Murray?' The speaker sounded anxious.

'Yes.'

'I can't talk over the phone. Come alone. After midnight. And I'll tell you.'

'Where?'

'I'll leave the address with your mate.'

Jack came back on the line. Alec spoke quickly. 'Thanks, Jack. I'm on my way.' He walked back out to the verandah. 'I've got to go back to Dubbo.'

'When?' Nell asked. Her look told him she was feeling the same as he was.

'Now.'

There was no need for more words. They both knew there had been a counterattack.

He looked into her eyes. Like him, she was doing her best to put on a brave face. He wanted to reassure her, but how could he? He had no idea what was going on. He gave her a quick kiss and headed off.

✳

The front bar of the Royal was dead quiet. Jack was sitting at one end of the bar nursing a beer. Rory, tea towel slung over his shoulder, was drying and stacking glasses. Alec pulled up a stool next to Jack and stared at the untouched beer in front of him. They sat in silence, each man trying to make sense of this turn of events.

'You know what, Jack?' Alec said at last. 'You've done more than enough. You should be getting home to your wife and family.'

'I signed up for the duration.' He took a sip of his beer. 'I've got the scrutineers going through the ballot papers. Have to wait and see what they come up with. The Returning Officer told me he'd grant you a recount if there are any inconsistencies or if it was close. He reckons you're that far ahead it won't make any difference.'

'Did you ask him for a recount of postal votes?'

'I did. His exact words were, it was "a helluva bore" and that you were going to win anyway.'

'Let's see what his assistant has to say,' Alec said as he stood. Deep down he was questioning whether he should go or not, but he decided he had to face the music, whatever it was.

The Assistant Returning Officer's house was shrouded in darkness. Alec walked gingerly up the path, climbed the steps to the verandah and knocked on the door. There were footsteps.

A muffled voice spoke from behind the door. 'Murray?'

'Yes.'

'I've only got one thing to say to you.'

'Yes ...'

The door opened a couple of inches.

'Find out where the bodgy ballot papers were printed and you'll find out who rigged the election.'

With that the door closed and the footsteps receded.

✳

The next day Alec and Jack fronted up to the office of the Returning Officer in Dubbo.

'It's just not adding up,' Alec said while the Returning Officer looked down at the Electoral Roll.

'There are sixty-five votes in the Gilgandra subdivision that were filled in irregularly. There is a pattern of this emerging in many small subdivisions in the electorate,' Alec told him.

The Returning Officer looked up and wiped his glasses with a handkerchief. 'Look, Alec, you're going to win this at a canter. Even if there are a few "irregularities" as you call them, they're not going to affect the final result. Tell Mrs Murray to get ready to move to Canberra.'

He closed the Roll, shook their hands and ushered them out.

Alec was more than worried. They were running out of time before the cut-off date for recounts, and he started to suspect there were bigger forces at play. Not that he had a clue what they might be.

The next morning, he and Jack continued their inquiries. There were more rumours swirling around the district about the couple of well-dressed city fellas who had been sighted at a number of booths on polling day.

At the pub, Alec asked Rory if he'd seen them.

'Yeah, they stayed the night,' he said, putting the cloth down on the table he was cleaning. 'It was funny. They told me they were bank clerks. One reckoned he was from Albury and the other from Wagga Wagga. They told me they were doing audits or something. I didn't think anything of it 'til one of them left a very flash hair brush behind and I rang the Albury branch of the Bank of New South Wales so I could send it on. They'd never heard of him, so I rang the Wagga Wagga branch and they hadn't heard of him either.'

Jack clicked his fingers. 'I bet they're the same blokes Smiley Walker told me about.'

*

Over the next few days, Alec and Jock drove frantically all over the district, trying to get to the bottom of the rumours. There were plenty of sightings of the two mystery men. They had stood out because they were driving a sports car.

Alec called in to talk to the publican in Wellington.

'I hope to Christ you don't think I was in on this. I wasn't. I assure you I wasn't.' Finn O'Brien's face was redder than usual. He seemed agitated. 'You know I'm on your side, Alec,' he added.

Why is he telling me this, Alec wondered.

Finn was nearly weeping. 'I wouldn't do anything ...' he said, touching Alec's hand. He stopped, searching for the right word.

'What, Finn? You can tell me.'

'You know ... All the fuss that's going on.'

'What fuss?'

Finn fiddled nervously with the crucifix that swung from the gold chain around his neck. 'I wasn't in on it.'

Alec exploded. 'What? For Christ's sake ... sorry, Finn, for Pete's sake, what?'

Finn shrugged and returned to stacking the fridge.

A postal worker, dressed in Post Master General's blue overalls, looked up from his beer.

'Are you Murray?' he asked.

'Yes.'

'I bin fixing the telegraph lines out've Mudgee. I heard a bloke tell the publican that you were gonna be a bad loser.'

Alec and Jack cornered him.

'He reckoned you were starting to scream.'

Jack whispered to Alec behind his hand, 'The word's out that we asked for a recount.'

Feeling things were going from bad to worse, Alec demanded of Jack, 'Who leaked that?'

His former batman shrugged and said, 'Search me.'

The postal man cut in. He seemed to be enjoying the intrigue. 'You wanna hear this or not?'

They gave him the floor.

'Well, when he said that about you screamin' ... this other fella says, "I don't blame him. I saw two-hundred ballot papers chucked in a fire on polling night."'

Alec and Jack downed their drinks and walked outside. Jack spoke first.

'Do you believe him?'

'I don't know what to believe. But we better get back to the Returning Officer and demand a recount, quick smart.'

✳

Alec pulled into Walter Frater's driveway a few days later.

'Come in.'

Walter invited him to sit and down poured him a scotch. He sat opposite Alec and, resting his elbows on his knees, clasped his hands together.

'It's not good news, Alec.'

Taking a sip of his scotch, Alec indicated for him to continue.

'We know about ten-thousand pounds was raised to keep you out of Canberra.'

Alec was astonished.

'That's a lot of posters and fliers,' Walter added with typical under-statement.

He stood and walked over to the fireplace. 'What's happening with the recount?'

Alec shook his head. 'I don't know. They keep telling us it won't be necessary.'

'Stalling?'

The penny dropped for Alec. The longer it took for a recount the less likely there would be one. They would be past the cut-off date.

Walter stood staring into the fireplace for what seemed like an eternity before eventually speaking.

'The Catholics in Melbourne have been wanting to extend their influence outside of Victoria for years. They wanted to test the waters in New South Wales and, with the war chest they accumulated, saw this as the perfect opportunity to try it out. Those tiny booths dotted around such a huge electorate presented themselves on a plate. All they had to do was send a couple of stooges out with suitcases of cash to bend a few elbows and swap a few sugar bags of voting papers. That's why all those twos were the same. It's why you lost where you should have won. Simple really.'

Alec had been fearing the worst, but the way Walter put it, everything made sense. He kicked himself for not insisting on a recount earlier. He knew he shouldn't have been so trusting. Walter was too decent to say it, but Alec knew, then and there, that he should have enlisted his support. At the very least he should have sought his advice when the count was looking dodgy.

He was paying now for playing by the rules and believing in the institutions he had so much faith in. Even when the whispers about dirty money had become roars, Alec had maintained his faith in the system he'd gone to war to defend.

It was beyond his comprehension that he could lose in such a way. He hadn't felt like this since he was in Greece and a force way beyond his imagining had overwhelmed them.

As Walter saw him to his car, he tried to console him. 'There's nothing new about rigging elections. Both sides have been doing it for years.'

It did nothing to ease Alec's distress.

73.

Nell was giving Kim a horsey ride when she saw the Dodge's headlights swing off the road into Toongowan. She watched as the car moved through the gate and meandered up the driveway towards the house. She didn't need to be told that Alec was the harbinger of bad news. If it had been good, he would have been tearing up to the house.

'We're buggered,' he said as he wearily climbed the steps. 'The Commonwealth Electoral Officer in New South Wales told the papers that the Returning Officer in Dubbo had advised him against a recount.'

'But weren't you ahead by 381 votes?' Nell asked.

'I was. Until the distribution of preferences. That shonky Independent's preferences went against me two to one. We lost by 276 votes.'

'But he's a communist!'

'He's a crook.'

It was over. Nell knew they had run out of money to launch an appeal. She had never seen Alec so shattered. He wasn't one to admit defeat, but it was etched all over his face.

'Would you like a drink?' she asked gently.

Alec didn't seem to register. Nell hesitated. Her hand hovered over his shoulder. She didn't know whether to kiss him or not. He seemed unreachable. She decided against it and headed towards the door. She turned the handle and was about to go inside when he spoke.

'You know where the money came from?'

She froze. Alec had told her about the 10,000 pounds. It was a small fortune. She waited. He kept silently staring ahead.

At last, he said, 'Your father.'

She wasn't sure she had heard correctly.

'And your brother.'

He might have been talking about sale prices.

'They put in a few thousand each.'

Nell was floored. 'My father? You're saying my father contributed to the campaign against you?'

Alec just nodded.

'And Jock?'

Again, he nodded.

Nell was blindsided by this information. It was one thing for her father to oppose Alec but to put his own money into a campaign against her husband was quite another. She had been betrayed by her own father. She could barely speak. She took a moment to muster all her strength and take a few tentative steps towards him. He was hunched over, looking up at the mountains.

'I … I can understand my brother …' She tried to make sense of what she had been told. 'He's never had any principles. But … Father?'

There was no response from Alec.

'Do you think he knew?' It was too terrible to contemplate.

Again silence.

'Would he have known that the money he donated would be used to switch votes?'

Alec couldn't help her. Nell was struggling to comprehend the enormity of it all.

'My father wouldn't have … couldn't have … surely whoever raised the money …' She couldn't finish the sentence.

She was shattered. Whatever the mechanics of it, her father had contributed to defeating Alec and, as a consequence, to sending them broke. And so had her brother. She was rocked to the core.

'My father …' Alec said quietly, through gritted teeth.

'What?'

He seemed to be battling to find the strength to spell it out.

'My father contributed to it too.'

Nell was stupefied. '*Your* father?'

'Yes. He was one of the donors. A major one.'

'Jesus!'

Nell was flabbergasted. Alec's own father put money into rigging his son's election? His own father! Just as she was trying to come to terms with this revelation, the flood waters broke and Alec started howling. All the pain he had been suppressing came gushing out of him. He stamped his feet and beat his fists against his forehead.

Nell was scared. She tried to comfort him but he was like a wild animal. She worried that he would do himself damage. She tried to get close to him, but it was impossible. He dragged himself to his feet and, clutching the railing, roared into the night.

Never had Nell felt so helpless. Alec was out of control and there was nothing she could do until the rage subsided. She watched him fearfully. He had given his heart and soul to a cause he believed in and had been brought to his knees by his own family.

The next few days were torture for Nell. Alec built a fortress around himself and receded into it, barely opening his mouth. He spent hour upon hour going over the books, searching for good news that Nell knew wouldn't be forthcoming. They had invested every last penny into the campaign and now the well was dry. They would be reliant on the understanding of the trustees to reboot the mortgage but they both knew they may well have used up all the goodwill they had been trading on.

She did her best to keep Kim amused. When he was having his afternoon sleep, she rode down to the letterbox to get the mail. At least a ride would make her feel better.

She leant down and flipped the letterbox open. She was praying that the wool firm had agreed to increase their credit. They had already extended their loan to get them through the campaign, but Alec had rolled the dice and asked for more. She pulled the mail out of the box. There was a letter from Douglas addressed in beautiful cursive writing. She tucked it under her arm and pulled out the rest of the mail. Her eyes lit on a letter typed formally with the distinctive coat of arms of the Australian House of Representatives.

The Parliament of the Commonwealth of Australia
Leader of the Opposition
Canberra, A.C.T.

If anything was going to cheer Alec up it would be a letter from Canberra. She dropped Doug's letter into her saddle bag and cantered home. 'Mail for you.'

Alec was poring over the books. He didn't respond.

'From Canberra.'

He swivelled in his chair and held his hand out.

'I thought that might bring you back to life!' She detected the slightest smile.

He got to his feet and took a few paces towards her.

'No …' Holding the letter like bait she backed into the doorway. 'Not until …'

He relented. 'I'm sorry.'

'Come and get it.'

He walked towards her and, searching for the letter, put his arms around her back. She raised her head. He closed his eyes for a moment before drawing her to him. They kissed.

A voice called out from the nursery.

'Someone's awake!' She handed him the letter. 'I'll get him.'

When she walked into the kitchen, soothing her little boy in her arms, Alec was sitting at the table.

He pointed to the postmark on the envelope. 'Fifth June 1951,' he said.

Nell worked out that date was six weeks after their world had fallen apart.

'What's the date today?' he asked.

She looked at the calendar on the wall. 'Thirteenth of June. Why?'

'The mail's slow.'

Nell put Kim down, filled the kettle and sat opposite him.

'Go on. Are you going to read it? We need something to cheer us up!'

He read quietly. She watched him while Kim amused himself with a piece of wood. As Alec perused the letter, his mood seemed to lift a little. He finished and was about to file it away when she raised her voice.

'I'm in this too!'

That snapped him out of it. He hesitated and then spoke deliberately, 'You sure are.'

She managed a smile. 'Read the best bit.'

He opened the letter and searched it before settling on a paragraph.

'*I heartily agree with your comment that it is better to go down fighting for principles than to pay homage to the god of expediency in the hope of gaining some temporary advantage. I always believe that courage and honesty pay in the long run.*'

Nell watched him. She wondered if Chifley knew that the Victorian Catholics had helped orchestrate his defeat. She got up from her chair, walked quietly towards him and, pushing his legs away from the table, sat in his lap. She hung her arm around his neck while he rested his head on her chest. The only sound was Kim banging his hunk of wood on the floor.

∗

In the early evening, just as the sun was setting, they rugged up and went for a walk to the creek. Alec gave Kim a ride on his shoulders. Nell walked alongside, a stick in hand. Mr Chips waddled behind, doing his best to keep up. They passed the cottage they had recently leased to Mary and Donny for a peppercorn rent. Donny was outside, shaking the dust out of a rug, and stopped to wave to them. Alec waved back.

They walked in silence. A flock of ducks took off from the creek. Alec held on to Kim's ankles while the little boy bounced along happily. Nell tapped her stick in the dirt, praying that they might be over the worst of it and that life might get back to normal. Whatever normal was.

'We'll get some money from somewhere.'

Alec laughed then said, 'We should ask your father. He's got plenty to throw about.'

She punched him in the arm. 'What about yours?'

They laughed. What else could they do?

That night, after they had put Kim to bed, they sat down with a drink to listen to a repeat of *The War of the Worlds* on the wireless. There was an announcement.

'We interrupt this program with the sad news that the Leader of the Opposition, The Honourable Ben Chifley, has had a heart attack in his hotel. He died on the way to hospital. The Prime Minister, Mr Menzies, made the announcement at a State Ball where both sides of Parliament are celebrating the fifty years of Federation.'

Alec froze as the voice of the Prime Minister crackled over the airwaves.

'Although we were political opponents, he was a friend of mine and yours, and a fine Australian. You will agree that in the circumstances the festivities should end. It doesn't matter about party politics on an occasion such as this. Oddly enough, in Parliament we get on very well. We sometimes we find we have the warmest friendships among people whose politics are not ours. Mr Chifley served this country magnificently for years.'

Alec swore that, whatever the cost, he was going to honour his hero's legacy.

74.

There was barely a blade of grass anywhere. They had sold all the stock. It was all he could do to scratch up some feed for Captain Midnight and the milking cows. The creek was as dry as a bone. Even the gum trees looked thirsty. Alec had no idea where he was going to find the money to restock when, and if, the drought broke.

He was treading water. Again. The trouble was, this time, he couldn't imagine where the rescue ship would come from. Worse, he was useless to Nell. He knew she was as devastated as he was, but he couldn't help her. Alec didn't know which way to turn.

He was rattling around in the study when he heard Nell call him. 'They're here.'

He walked onto the verandah. A car pulled into the front gate. Kim was playing in the dirt below. Nell joined him. They both watched as the car travelled up the road at a funereal pace. It was D Day.

Henry was on the way to deliver the resolution from the trustees. Alec didn't know what the answer would be, but he wasn't hopeful. He turned to Nell. She looked as anxious as he was feeling.

They were lost in their own thoughts while they waited. Eventually Alec heard the car door close and the gate open. Henry strode purposefully to the front yard followed by Daphne. Alec could barely bring himself to acknowledge his parents. He wondered what part his mother had played in his betrayal. While Henry mounted the steps,

Daphne paused and bent down to see what Kim was up to. The little boy stared up at his grandmother. Daphne called to Nell, 'Do you mind if I take him for a little explore?'

Nell managed a smile. 'Not at all.'

Alec watched his mother lead Kim around the banksias, bottlebrushes and kangaroo paws that Nell had planted. She had always avoided confrontation. He heard his father speak.

'The trustees have reached the end of their tether.'

Alec kept his eyes on Daphne and Kim. He realised that he was gripping the railing tightly. He released his hand.

'Is that so?'

Henry shoved his hands in pockets and started to rock backwards and forwards on his heels. Alec thought he looked like a parody of the prosecuting barrister Henry had wanted him to be.

He began his final summary. 'The fact is: you are bankrupt. You are mortgaged to the hilt ...'

Alec didn't need to hear any more. 'There is no need for you spell it out. I know exactly what the situation is. I also know why we're in the strife we're in. And so do you.'

He looked his father in the eyes, there was no way he was letting him off the hook.

'If you've got something to say, get on with it. Otherwise, you might as well go,' Alec said.

Henry jerked his head towards Nell as though he didn't want to have this conversation in front of her.

Alec was quick to dismiss the gesture. 'Nell and I share everything. This place is as much hers as it is mine. She has every right to hear what you have to say.'

Henry continued. 'The trustees have issued an ultimatum. If we are going to dig you out of this hole you've got yourself into you –'

'We?' Alec asked.

Henry coughed, then said, 'Your mother has asked me to deliver the news. You have a choice. Either give up this political nonsense or they are going to foreclose. They are not going to give financial backing for you to galivant all over the countryside while your property goes to rack and ruin.'

Alec bristled. 'I've got the place back on an even keel before. Look around you. It's been a terrible season. Everyone's struggling. Even Fred Hope has had to tighten his belt. All they need to do is extend the mortgage until I turn it around again. It's not as if there's going to be another election in the foreseeable –'

Henry warmed to his task. 'If you want to stay on this place there aren't going to be any elections, council or otherwise. We're sick of supporting you …'

Nell spoke up. 'Well, maybe you should have thought about that before you donated to pay crooks to rig the election.'

Alec could see that Henry was taken aback by this news.

'You didn't know?' Alec asked.

Clearly rattled by the directness of Nell's words, Henry faffed about before answering, 'Know what?

Nell took a step towards him. 'Know where your money was going?'

'No. They just said it was a fighting fund …'

There was fire in Nell's eyes as she attacked him. 'How could you? How could you betray your own son?'

She turned and walked inside, slamming the door behind her. Henry looked at Alec and shrugged helplessly.

Alec didn't let him speak. 'You can make all the threats you like. You can conspire against us, you can toss us off this place but I promise you one thing, Father, I will go to my grave fighting for the people who are trampled on by the likes of you. You can see yourself out.'

He walked inside. Nell was sobbing. He took her in her arms and held her tightly. He could hear his father's car start.

'I'd better get Kim,' Nell said, tears streaming down her face.

So, that was it. Alec knew he could never live with himself if he acceded to the trustees' demands and removed himself from public duty. Not even saving Toongowan was worth that.

75.

'It isn't a choice, is it?' Nell was left in no doubt that Alec was a stating a fact.

'We have to leave.'

She saw him clench his jaw as he uttered these words.

'I'll start organising ...' Alec said, then turned and walked to his office.

That's it? she thought.

They were going to walk off the property they'd built together to do ... what?

Nell had no idea and nor, she suspected, did Alec. His pride prevented him from being able to compromise and do some kind of a deal that would let them to stay on. Maybe he could have agreed to shelve his political ambitions while they restored Toongowan? But it wasn't an option he would entertain. Like his hero, Alec would go down fighting for his principles.

While that might have been all very well for Alec when he was a single man going off to war to defend his values, now he was part of a family. Nell wondered what effect packing up and moving to the city would have on her boys. Doug had been bullied at boarding school because of Alec's political leanings. Nell couldn't imagine what they would feel about having to say goodbye to their pets and the property they had been raised on. It was going to be a big adjustment for all of them.

She was distraught. The margin of the defeat might have been tiny, but she had learned that politics was a winner-takes-all game, so the margin was irrelevant. So was the fact that Nell had embraced being part of a movement whose stated goal was to improve the lot of people less well off than they were. All the well-meaning talk about creating better standards of living, making the people happier and giving them more security was just that: talk. They had lost and were walking off the property that Nell had poured her heart and soul into. Once again, she was upending everything and starting again. She wasn't at all sure how she was going to do it.

There was a time when Nell would have jumped at moving to the city. The trouble was, she was no longer a budding artist. She was no longer an artist. She felt as though she had burnt all those bridges and that, having tied herself to Toongowan and become the wife of a 'rebel from the backblocks', there was nothing left.

She was humiliated. Alec might have been able to dredge up the strength to carry on, but she wasn't at all sure she could. It was hard for her to put on a brave face. She was too deeply devastated. Toongowan may not have been her dream property but, with the help of others, she had made it hers. Theirs.

While Alec receded into himself and went about organising the sale with military precision, Nell was left trying to pick up the pieces of her own broken dreams.

As she closed the gate for one last time, she could see Kim and Mr Chips looking out the back window. The little boy was beaming at her. For him, this was a bright new adventure. She could see Alec's big, strong back ready as always to take on the world. He wasn't looking back.

Nell felt the presence of the Warrumbungles looking down on her. She met their gaze and was filled by their awe. She couldn't help but wonder how she'd paint them.

She carefully placed the latch on the bolt and walked back to the car.

She opened the door, climbed in, rested her head on the back of the seat and felt the car move onto the main road.

She fixed her eyes on the road and wondered what lay ahead.

Author's note

Painting the Light is a personal story on many levels. It is loosely based on the lives of my parents, Margot Body and Alan Manning, and has involved wide research into their lives as well as the events that surrounded and, eventually, overtook them.

It is based on fact. The major events in the book actually happened, although not necessarily in the way I have described them. The characters, some of whom are based on real people (others are invented), took on a life of their own as I began to write. This is a story about how those characters were affected by, and responded to, events that consumed them. They were thrust into a word of great upheaval, tectonic change and extraordinary challenges.

I used archival material in the form of letters, photographs, sketches, articles, war records and drawings as springboards to tell the story.

In essence it is a love story about two young Australians who, together, sacrificed their dreams to devote their lives to creating circumstances that would prevent an event as catastrophic as World War Two from ever happening again.

Both were committed to social change, to creating a truly egalitarian society, one in which every person, no matter what class or cultural background, would be afforded an equal opportunity in a new, outward looking and inclusive Australia.

I was particularly drawn to the fate of women during the war, whether they were left behind or travelled overseas to serve in the war effort. There is no question in my mind that many of these women suffered as much as the men, about whom so much has been written. Many found themselves married to men they hardly knew, bearing children they hadn't planned, and forced to abandon whatever dreams they may have harboured.

The ramifications of this were felt for generations to come.

Hence, *Painting the Light* charts the journeys of both the female and male characters, bringing them together and then charting their very different experiences from pre to post World War Two.

I would like to acknowledge the support and assistance I have received from Bernadette Foley and Broadcast Books, as well as all those who have encouraged me on this ten-year journey to publication.

Ned Manning is a writer, actor and teacher. His teaching memoir, *Playground Duty* (NewSouth Books), has become required reading for anyone interested in the real world of teaching. Ned is a committed advocate for both the teaching profession and for public education.

His large-cast play for young people, *Alice Dreaming* (Cambridge University Press), is widely produced in schools and youth theatre groups around Australia. Ned has written over twenty plays, including nine for the Bell Shakespeare Company's Actors at Work program and three in collections with 7ON. The success of his first play, *Us or Them*, led to the Griffin Theatre Company's transformation from a co-op to a professional theatre company. Other plays include *Milo*, *Close to the Bone* and *Kenny's Coming Home*.

Ned's acting credits in film include starring in the cult classic *Dead End Drive-In*, as well as appearing in *Looking for Alibrandi*. TV credits include *The Shiralee*, *Bodyline* and the recent FX hit, *Mr Inbetween*. Theatre credits include performances for STC, Griffin and the Q Theatre.

Painting the Light is his first novel.

www.nedmanning.com